LOVE
IS NOT THE
ANSWER

A NOVEL ABOUT AMERICA

LOVE
IS NOT THE
ANSWER

SCOTT MACKEY

The story, all names, characters, and incidents portrayed in this production are fictitious. No identification with actual persons (living or deceased) or organizations should be inferred.

Book Cover by Laura Duffy

Interior formatting by KUHN Design Group | kuhndesigngroup.com

First edition – January 2024

"A woman was sitting on a scarlet beast that was full of blasphemous names, and it had seven heads and ten horns. The woman was arrayed in purple and scarlet, and adorned with gold and jewels and pearls, holding in her hand a golden cup full of abominations and the impurities of her sexual immorality. And on her forehead was written a name of mystery: "Babylon the great, mother of prostitutes and of earth's abominations." And I saw the woman, drunk with the blood of the saints, the blood of the martyrs of Jesus."

REVELATION 17:3-6 ESV

CHAPTER 1

THE HEALING PATH

Julia Connor watched the darting bees, her silver-white curls bouncing in the breeze. Every few moments she caught the late-afternoon sun glinting off a bee's effervescent wing, a flash of light against the blue sky.

She looked at her bare, bee-covered hand and leaned closer to the open hive, feeling the same connective thrill she'd felt for decades whenever her uncovered skin vibrated at the frequency of ten thousand bees' beating wings. She saved such precautions as a bee suit for the rare occasions when she could sense her pleasant friends felt aggressive.

She'd almost worn a suit today, but not because the bees were off. No, she was unsettled, and she didn't want her energy to throw the bees into an uproar. Thankfully, the bees had preserved their workmanlike Zen.

"Hi, little ladies," she cooed, her face inches from the winged cacophony. "Your hive is healthy and gorgeous. No ants or beetles, and so much honey. Ciao for now." She gently shook her hand, knocking the bees off and back into their white bee box, replaced the lid, and slowly backed away.

When she turned her seventy-two-year-old frame towards her garden, a row of Swiss chard stretched before her. The green and red leafy shoots were almost six inches tall, yet the waist-high peas in the next row towered over them, casting thin shadows in the afternoon light.

Julia knelt to admire her horticultural handiwork, the fir-scented spring air making each breath a joy. She sampled the rich soil beneath her fingers and felt a wisp of gray hair blow into her mouth. Brushing the hair off her face, she again felt a twinge of anxiety and, with it, annoyance. The beehives and the garden were her escape, her refuge, the place she came to feel the presence of life, of God, but her new book was intruding.

This one, her twentieth, had been the hardest. While she had written on matters of the heart, the soul, and the psycho-emotional mind for almost fifty years, she'd avoided political pontification since the Vietnam War ended. But recently, as the world spun off its axis and the country she called home felt more broken than ever, she'd been compelled to act.

Love and Compassion: A Call for Political and Spiritual Revival was the result. With the book's official release only hours away, she was trapped in a purgatory of the unknown, ceaselessly wondering how her community of meditating moms and heart-centered environmentalists would react to her foray into matters that were, inescapably, less heart-and-healing and more realpolitik.

She checked the hands on her watch and sighed. It was time to shower and change. Her ride into Seattle would be there soon.

• • •

Weeks before, one of Mel P's Beeps had blasted across the digital ether, following the algorithmic trail straight onto the device screens of millions.

Her face filled the screen, black curls framing a brown face, her gold nose ring glinting beneath an overhead light. "My peeps," the clip began, "remember how oil company executives suppressed research showing the danger of climate change in the '80s? And how they've never faced consequences for their lies or their destruction?! That changes now."

With a funky beat playing in the background, the shot shifted to a crowd of yelling protestors surrounding the entrance to a hotel in downtown Seattle. A black car pulled to the curb. Mel P narrated the voiceover. "When American Petroleum's CEO Wesley Kinsey visited my city, I knew I had to act."

The chauffeur opened the back door, a suited man stepped out. Four people jumped the barricades. Security leapt to action, clotheslining protesters. Tackling them.

"I knew security would be tight, so four of my homies were decoys."

As her friends flailed on the ground, Mel P jumped the barricade, somehow not spilling a drop of the black liquid that filled the plastic pitcher in her hands. She raced at the CEO, paused to moonwalk before transitioning into a ballet leap and deking the last security guard, darting around him like an impala fleeing a lion. She launched her plastic vessel. The video slowed to trace the undulating black liquid on its journey toward the face of Big Oil.

"I delivered my message—fossil fuel in plastic, oil housed in oil—straight to Wesley Kinsley's evil, lying face."

The goopy used motor oil splashed through his cowering crossed arms, drenching his face and his suit. Before Mel P could run, security guards converged. One's fist drilled the side of her head. Another tackled her, his enormous frame crushing her on the sidewalk.

The video flashed back to Mel P's face, this time revealing the large bruise on her left temple. "You'd think the off-duty police officer that gave me a concussion would be in jail. But no, I'm the one who spent a day locked up and was called a domestic terrorist. But, my Beep-Beep peeps, it was worth it!" Mel P's grin shone as brightly as her red bruise. "It was only one small act of morality, but oily, evil Wesley Kinsey finally paid the price for the destruction he visits upon the environment every. Damn. Day. Now, fam, share this shit far and wide and let's put the fear of justice into those destroying our earth."

• • •

The afternoon sun felt familiar, the surprisingly hot spring heat a reminder of the harsh climates in which he used to ply his trade. The faded fatigues and tactical watch served the same purpose. They connected him to a past he couldn't quite forget.

Jonathan eyed his left hand supporting the AR-15's barrel, relaxed but ready, always alert. He put his finger on the trigger, oblivious to the sprawling green pastureland sitting between him and his target.

Pressure. Pull. Poof!! Glitter everywhere.

Pressure. Pull. Poof!! Glitter everywhere.

Jonathan took his eye off the iron optic and grinned at his buddy, Eli, who was on his knees in the dirt next to him. "Your daughter's glitter target idea was a good one."

Eli's eyes smiled back, binoculars grasped in his right hand. "Through the binocs, it's a sparkle show. Ten for ten. That's pretty good shootin from two hundred yards."

"For better or worse," Jonathan grunted, not at all impressed with himself, "I still got it."

The men settled into a pleased silence, communicating through the unspoken bond combat veterans often share, their thoughts drifting to the same place.

Eventually, Eli turned to Jonathan, grunting as he spun to sit on his butt. Ray, one of their clients, was on his mind. "Last night was nuts, wasn't it?"

"You know it," Jonathan said, picturing Ray's face, reliving the sound and feeling of a strong but shattered man's stoicism breaking behind a tidal wave of tears. "Ray said he saw them all. Made peace with each of them."

Eli slowly nodded. "All … How many do you think he meant?"

"He served for 15 years. Was a sniper. That's a lot of faces to see, conversations to have."

They grimly looked at each other and then broke into broad smiles, pain from what they used to do morphing into the joy of helping another man heal his wounded past. "He left feeling good?"

"Said it's the best he's ever felt."

Thirty minutes later Jonathan was in his truck, windows down, the now cooling afternoon air rushing through his bushy, black beard. Mount Ranier loomed in the distance, this valley's imposing, snow-covered sentinel.

Out of habit, he ran through the night's schedule. There wasn't much too it.
First up, grab Julia.
Drive her to the book launch in Seattle.
Then drive her back home from the book launch, probably stopping to grab a late dessert somewhere near the University.
Finally, he couldn't forget to grab another bag of Julia's mushrooms for a ceremony he was hosting the next weekend. Psychoactive elements did wonders for the PTSD veterans he worked with. Psilocybin was the key, or at least one of the keys, to facilitating subconscious exploration and emotional healing.

• • •

Hearing a vehicle pull up outside, Julia quickly applied her homemade lavender-rose spritz and walked out to the porch. A familiar, deep voice drifted from the truck in the driveway.

"Julia! Heloooooo."

Julia returned the smile and wave of the tall man, bearded and heavily tattooed, walking toward her. Army fatigues from his special forces days were accompanied—as ever, it seemed—by a tactical watch and a flannel shirt open at the chest.

She walked down the steps to meet her protégé's warm, bear-like embrace.

"I needed that hug." Julia sighed. "Thank you for coming, Jonathan."

Jonathan's black eyes glinted at her from behind his beard, his dark cheeks dimpling as he smiled at the subtle pleasure seeing his teacher always brought him.

"Feeling nervous about tonight?" he asked, sensing her unease.

"You have no idea!" Julia's eyes bugged out of her head. She laughed but then abruptly stopped. "I'm anxious, I'm anxious that I'm anxious, I'm laughing at myself for feeling anxious. I re-center and then get knocked off-center. This book, the book launch, the fact I'm voluntarily walking into the political firing line … I mean, this is a long way from poetry and heart connection!"

Jonathan looked deep into the eyes that had unlocked hidden pieces of himself and helped heal the broken ones. He put his hands on Julia's tiny shoulders, willing her to feel his confidence. "If the book leads even one person to ask why people so angry about our seemingly broken world have no interest in changing how they live, it will be a success beyond measure."

"That's the hope!" Julia brightened, releasing her tension. "I mean, if we're not able to see God in the earth and in other people, what are we even doing here!"

"When you phrase it like that, I'm less optimistic," Jonathan reached down to feel the fragile petals on a yet-to-bloom Rhododendron but didn't pause. "Empathy isn't exactly our collective calling card right now."

"Hrmph," Julia grunted, sounding exactly how she imagined a small hedgehog might sound. The point of her book was to offer hope and guidance to a nation that seemed to have lost its collective mind. She didn't mind whining, but once Jonathan humored her, she felt ridiculous.

Jonathan looked at her sideways, a sly smile stretching across his face. "We should go, but first, can I get a bag of medicine? I need more for the tea this weekend."

Julia clapped her hands in delight. "Shall we visit the shed?"

They walked toward the property line, reaching a structure that resembled a half-buried greenhouse. On the door a sign read, "The Universal Church of All." Upon walking down three stairs, they were bathed in sunlight filtered through translucent roof panels. Warm, humid air filled their lungs and their eyes settled on row after row of grow boxes, each containing mycelium in different stages of development. Boxes that contained yet-to-germinate spores appeared empty. Other boxes looked like an Alice in Wonderland fantasy, with purple streaked mushrooms of varying sizes darting out of the rich substrate at wild angles.

Jonathan whistled. "Will I be able to take any of these enormous P Cubensis off of you?"

"Ohhh yes. Absolutely! I have mushrooms coming out my ears. Do you want to pick a fresh batch or take a vacuum-pack of dried ones?"

CHAPTER 2

CLEARED HOT

Making her way through light drizzle, throwback Daft Punk blasting in her headphones, Melanie Pedreira was barely aware of the soft pitter-pat of raindrops on her hoodie or the silent figure walking beside her.

Passing beneath looming alder trees at the University of Washington, their spring-green leaves obscured by dusk and wet fog, Melanie ran scenarios through her mind. The outside world—even Jennifer—ceased to exist as she plotted her upcoming bit. She knew the magic was in the editing, that the story they wanted to tell could be told regardless of how she performed, but she was a perfectionist. That was why her content trended daily on Beep-Beep.

She ran her hand through the dark mess of hair beneath her hood. Her scalp tingled. Nervous energy twitched in every muscle. It was almost time, but she still wondered about the wisdom of switching up their target.

"Is this a mistake?" she asked, turning her head to speak to her friend.

"A mistake? Why?" Jennifer asked.

"I normally go after billionaires, executives, and racists. This is different."

Jennifer rolled her eyes beneath her hoodie. "Mel, please. Stupid shit is stupid shit. I read the synopsis for the book. 'Society won't heal until people take responsibility for their own healing'? Like we're somehow responsible for the world we live in? Like we invented capitalism, carbon emissions, and freon?"

"Yeah, but—"

"There's no buts. You'll crush it with the views. And the target, well, she's so easy. This thing will pop, I promise."

Melanie stopped at the foot of the steps to Gate's Hall and shrugged, flashing Jennifer an enormous grin that sparkled in the building's floodlight. "'Pop,' is what I do. Let's go make magic."

Pushing back their hoods, they entered the front doors, made their way to the lecture hall, walked down the steps, and took their seats on the middle aisle of the seventh row.

• • •

Julia Connor observed the packed University of Washington lecture hall.

On either side of her lectern, two identical banners trumpeted *Love and Compassion: A Call for Political and Spiritual Revival*. Behind her, a video showed clips from the ongoing Democratic and Republican primary campaigns for president. This election, like most in recent memory, had devolved into a circus. The Republican candidate, Senator Daniel Menendez, had floated, then retracted, then again mentioned that he "might be open to a Uganda-style law that treated homosexuals fairly." The Democratic candidate, Governor Kathleen O'Leary of Illinois, seemed intent on saying absolutely nothing of substance, staying above the Democratic primary fray while casually insulting those who didn't agree with her tech-centered approach to ensuring equality for all.

Julia, dressed in her traditional navy khaki slacks and loose-fitting short-sleeved blouse, looked over the audience of grandmas and soccer moms who had shown up to witness her initiation into the depressing world of politics.

A surprising number of men occupied the room as well; a surprise for someone whose readers had always been women. *Are they here to learn or to ostracize?* The thought made her laugh, and then cringe. She reminded herself there was nothing to be anxious about. This was a moment of enormous personal vulnerability, but—as she had counseled in her not quite a bestseller, *The Sharing Manifesto*—also an opportunity for growth.

Yes, that was her mission – to sit in her emotional center, allowing the truths she felt so strongly to pour out as a natural reflection of self, trusting they could help her readers live lives more focused on compassion, service, and empathy. And that, perhaps, would be enough to inspire the nation to do the same.

The lecture hall lights came back on. The rapid-fire video clips ended with Governor O'Leary's face frozen on the screen.

"Who hasn't seen these clips?" Julia asked her audience.

A few hands went up against a sprinkling of laughter.

"When we look at the immaturity and the bullying modeled by our politicians, the temptation for us all is to point fingers, claiming our national issues stem from bad political leadership. However, I disagree." Julia paused and looked around the auditorium, making eye contact with those who allowed her eyes to meet their own.

"Our politics reflect our society, and our society reflects the people within it. As a people and as a society, we've accepted anger, pain, numbness, and fear over emotional honesty, over healing, over love. This doesn't mean the anger or the pain that so many of us feel is wrong. Far from it, in fact, but in a society that invalidates people's feelings, ignores all people's need to heal, and is governed by abusive, profit-seeking systems, we're left with a destructive political reality that is unchecked by a population ill-equipped to deal with their personal or our collective pain."

Julia smiled as she registered the electric charge of being in her element with no disapproving glares from her audience. Maybe writing about politics wasn't as scary as she'd thought.

"So yes, it's a problem that our politicians and our political system model such abhorrent behavior, but if we're to address the enormous environmental and social problems that plague our country and our world, solutions will not come until the people in this nation have healed, grown and matured enough to begin holding our political system, and our politicians, accountable. How can we make this change? There is only one answer, and that answer is love."

No sooner had Julia paused for a breath than a young woman jumped to her feet, pirouetting into the aisle. A second followed close behind, her phone filming.

"Hi Julia. My name is Mel P I'm a social media influencer." She spoke fast.

"I'm sorry-not sorry to interrupt. But that's how I roll. How can you say that love will just, like, heal? Love won't bring back Muslim children killed by the American military. Compassion can't stop climate change and save the polar bears. Empathy isn't gonna pay my student loans!"

Julia—unprepared for Melanie's calculated interruption but strangely envious of her energy—froze for a moment, absorbing her inquisitor's gold nose ring, tattered jeans, and bright pink windbreaker over the top of a hooded sweatshirt. Was Melanie, she wondered, homeless or hip? What was it that the teen cart-pusher at the grocery store had called it, "drip"?

"Well, Mel P," she said, recovering, "I don't think love or compassion, on their own, can solve these problems. There are, after all, no silver bullets. But if we as a people embrace love and compassion and work to heal together, if we learn to align our lives with the highest, truest version of ourselves, if we choose to make policy based on principles of connectivity, perhaps we can imagine new solutions that will solve our current challenges and prevent future problems. The alternative, I'm afraid, is more of the same."

"Julia, look at this world." Melanie smirked. "We spend billions of dollars sending our soldiers off to kill yet we're unwilling to feed families or educate our young here at home. Deserts are expanding as rainforests shrink, yet we continue to do nothing on climate because brainless right-wingers and corporations of all types stand in our way. That's capitalism 101! Isn't the answer to fight until we win instead of focusing on meaningless emotional solutions to real-world problems?"

Julia felt her anxiety rise. Conflict! How could she reach this angry young woman?

"Oh, dear," she said. "I think—"

"Excuse me, Julia?" It was Jonathan, standing up in the first row. "Do you mind if I jump in here?"

"Oh, no!" cried Mel P in mock horror, playing to Jennifer's camera. "A mansplainer!"

"Yes, Jonathan, of course," said Julia. "Everybody, this is my friend Jonathan Robinson. He works with veterans healing from PTSD. And Mel P, he's usually more of a listener than an explainer. I'm excited to hear what he has to say."

Jonathan prepared to speak, looking at the girls and their camera.

"Hi Mel. I'm a student of Julia's. You don't think much of military veterans, do you?"

Melanie sneered for the camera before turning to Jonathan. "Uh, no, I don't support killers."

Jonathan was unperturbed. The reality of being a veteran meant putting up with the jingoistic language of freedom from supporters, being showered with scorn by urban liberals like this girl, and being used as a prop by politicians in both parties. He'd heard what Melanie had to say a million times.

"Do you know much about Julia's healing work?"

Melanie wrinkled her nose for the camera. "Healing through books, poetry, and meditation? Ha, nope, I don't know much about that."

"Julia is a lot more than writing. Yes, she's written twenty books and she went back to the land to farm twenty-five years before Brooklyn hipsters and Hollywood burnouts started doing the same. But her healing work with PTSD veterans like myself is less well known."

"Well, I bet you did some truly fucked-up shit. You'd need to heal."

Jonathan took several deep breaths to slow his heartbeat. "You're right, Mel, I did. Can I share a story?"

"It's Julia's show."

"Which you interrupted."

"Well—"

"Go on, Jonathan," Julia said. "In fact, come up here. You can use my mic. Thank you, everyone, for going with the flow."

Julia made room for Jonathan at the podium.

Closing his eyes, he dropped into himself. He accessed surface feelings of regret and despair before tracing those sensations back in time, back to a very specific moment in the Paktika Province in Eastern Afghanistan. He sunk into the pain of his memories and started his story.

"It was a clear, moonless night. Choppers inserted us two miles from our target, a group of Taliban that intel said were sheltering in a small mountain village. After an uneventful traverse we arrived around 0300 and identified the target—A small mud house. My team had years of experience in theater, from Kyber to Kabul. Getting pinned down in extended firefights was not the goal. Eliminating the enemy and returning to camp—*that* was the mission.

"We stood outside the house, surveying the building through night vision goggles. It didn't look like much. Two rooms? Three at the most. I looked at Reilly, our point man, and we both nodded. I kicked open the door, and he burst through, crouching low, his MK46 ready, shouting the phrases we'd been taught: "'*Harakat makawa, harakat makawa, harakat makawa!*' Don't move, don't move, don't move!' That was what we all said. And, *Taslim sha—* surrender!' As we burst in, one occupant jumped up." Jonathan averted his eyes from the room, then refocused. "We were cleared hot and cut him down immediately."

He paused to wipe a tear from his face.

"Over our yelling, I heard screams. Not the violent yelling of mujahadeen— the high shrill shriek of a little girl. We fanned through the small house, still yelling, kicking up sleeping mats, looking for stowaway Taliban, securing the interior, saving our asses. It took less than a minute. There were no Taliban.

"I moved toward the person we'd gunned down. It was a woman in a long robe with a bullet through her head. The screamer was a young girl, sobbing, moaning. I—I bent to my knees and picked her up. I can't even understand that action—did I want to comfort her or comfort myself for what I'd just done? She glowed green in my night vision goggles and screamed louder as I lifted her up. And then I realized she wasn't just screaming from heartbreak or fear. She'd been hit too. Blood poured through a gaping hole in her small, tattered abdomen."

Jonathan stopped, tears streamed down his face and through his thick beard. He heaved with the exertion of trying to control himself.

"Have some water, Jonathan," Julia said, a hand on his back.

"No, thank you." Jonathan wiped his eyes with his sleeve. "There were six of us there that night. Five years later, two of those men had committed suicide. I was going to be the third."

He paused again, gathering his thoughts. "I chose the military with all the best intentions. But years of concussions—the impact from explosions and automatic gunfire and slamming my steel helmet onto my head—and the shit I endured, well, they're not normal. They take their toll. They leave their scars. They turn into PTSD. When I came home, I was abandoned by this country to face my demons alone. Then I met Julia. She convinced me that healing was possible, and she helped me heal myself. What was my answer? It was love."

"Damn, this is some reverse-colonialism gaslighting right here!" Melanie shouted to the camera and the crowd, as if an increase in volume would make her point. "I mean that's a horrible story. But now this professional killer is sobbing and I feel like I did something wrong! WTF?!"

"Mel P," Julia said while rubbing Jonathan's shoulder, "the point Jonathan just made is that healing precedes grace. And only by healing can we learn to live in love and compassion for ourselves and others. Now, we all haven't been through what Jonathan has, but whether it is our reactions to the inevitable scars of childhood, an abusive relationship, or helplessness in the face of ecological catastrophe, we have all experienced trauma."

She slowed to make eye contact, continuing in her teacher's voice. "That trauma manifests itself in many ways, including the anxiety and the anger that so many of us in this country suffer from and surrender to. My goal with this book is to point out that if we are to solve any of the crises facing our nation, if we are to have any chance of course correcting away from environmental catastrophe, it will only happen if people heal from their pasts, connect with their true selves, and begin living from a place of love and compassion."

Melanie wanted to roll her eyes again, but she found herself strangely unable to summon her trademark scorn.

"Now, if you don't mind, Mel P, dear, I'd like to continue my presentation. Thank you for initiating this discussion. I hope your—what do you call them? Influencees?—enjoy it."

CHAPTER 3

BACKSLIDING

Watching from the side of the stage, Luke Lockwood shook his head, a grimace mixing with his smile. He wished he could set aside his misgivings and fully appreciate the joy of this moment, but winning a battle was of little consequence when the war still raged and one's primary weapon left so much to be desired. He looked toward the spot onstage where the cause of his elation and his frustration stood resplendent in a blue suit and a red tie.

Standing in front of the digital panels that read "2028 Republican Debate," beneath the soaring ceiling, and on top of the bright red debate stage carpet, his candidate, Senator Daniel Menendez, gloated to himself, a puffed up, suit-wearing form of ego and charisma. Luke remembered an interview Menendez had given in his pre-political years when he'd been a plastic manufacturing magnate on the rise. A reporter had asked why his appetite for growth was so insatiable. "Every hostile takeover, every time I expand my market share," Menendez had replied, "I know that I'm not only winning, but someone else is losing." Luke knew politics was no different.

"You're wrong," Luke often told him. "Winning isn't the purpose—governing is the goal. Only by wielding power can Jesus's values find fulfillment in the laws of this great nation."

Luke allowed himself a smile. Being the campaign manager for Senator Menendez was an imperfect role serving an imperfect man, but he had played his role to perfection. Going into primary season, Menendez had been one of three favorites to secure the Republican nomination for president, but with the final debate almost concluded and the delegate count in their favor, the nomination was theirs to lose.

Luke rehashed his masterstroke in the previous debate, three weeks earlier.

The last rivals standing—George Bush IV, the Governor of Wyoming, and Kathy Glockenspiel, the Governor of Florida—had gotten ahead of themselves. Assuming their anti-homosexual bona fides were secure after signing gay marriage bans in their respective states, both Bush IV and Glockenspiel began wooing independent voters.

The damaging exchange was seemingly straightforward. Responding to a question, Glockenspiel gathered her fit 5' 10" frame. "While I don't believe in gay rights or trans rights," Glockenspiel said, a sizable crucifix resting on her chest, "I do believe states have the right to decide if our sick brothers and sisters have the right to love."

"It's not just that, Kathy," said Bush IV, rushing to avoid being outflanked to the center. He adjusted his apple-red bowtie and elaborated in his perfect patrician's drawl. "While I am proud to have led the charge to protect God's people from the cultural vultures that live on our coasts, I do still believe that those vultures have the right to govern as they see fit. States' rights are a core constitutional value that I will protect as president."

Democrats with the stomach to sit through a Republican debate would certainly have written off both comments as empty posturing, which they were. Luke, however, anticipating that Bush IV and Glockenspiel might inadvertently commit political hara-kiri by tacking to the center too soon, had prepared Menendez for this exact moment.

"America," Menendez had said, glowering at Glockenspiel as he spoke, "what you just witnessed was backsliding. First, Governor Glockenspiel showed her true colors, making a mockery of the values-protecting governor she always claims to be. And then Bush the Cuatro showed that no matter how hard he tries to deny his heritage as a Bush, he's still a centrist shill without the backbone to persecute sinners! I'm not here to kowtow to both-way-ism. Ladies and gentlemen, you just heard them. *I* am the *true*

Republican and the only candidate with the courage to govern as Jesus Christ himself would."

It was the soundbite sequence of the night. The knockout blow. When the dust settled, when the social media stars' Flitters and Beeps had stopped flying, and when podcast hosts had completed their guttural descents into the fury and urgency of this magnificent political moment, Menendez boasted the backing of not only the mainstream and alternative right-wing media but also the most powerful pastors in the nation.

The irony, of course, was that Menendez was—or had been—the moderate in the race. He'd entered the election one year after securing what he expected would be his last six-year Senate term in the deeply purple state of New Mexico. That realization left him free to say and do whatever necessary to get elected. Menendez had traded in his Browning BLR Lightweight and reputation as a man of the ranchers and elk hunters for an AR-15, and he'd come up with a brilliant legislative play—his "God is on the Ballot Constitutional Amendment"—that gained the trust of Evangelicals and earned him the opportunity to work with Luke.

Menendez hadn't wanted to make the transition to die-hard cultural warrior, but his army of political consultants had convinced him that to win higher office, he had to ditch any hint of respect for his adversaries. "You've got to treat liberals as the human scum primary voters know them to be," was the advice that stuck with him.

Now, tonight, the last debate.

"Stay the course," Luke had told him. "Cocky confidence, righteous rage."

Damn straight, Menendez thought. He was pleased with what he saw on the monitor: Too much makeup on Glockenspiel but not enough to cover the wrinkles on her throat. Too little height on Bush IV, whose hair was thinning. As for Menendez, what was not to like?

He watched the moderator gather himself to ask the last question of the night.

A southern dandy with an angular, bearded face, Jed Abernathy was ROX News' go-to veteran anchor, a man whose ratings were unrivaled and whose values perfectly matched whatever the moment demanded. The latest in a long line of journalists-cum-entertainers who made their careers repeating poll-tested talking points designed to play to the worst, and therefore the most cherished, instincts of the American people, Jed was the debate's moderator.

As the on-air light glowed red, Jed scrunched his eyes, giving every appearance of being appropriately grave, while preparing to tee up Senator Menendez for the kill shot, just like Luke had arranged.

"The final closing statement goes to you, Senator Menendez."

Poised behind his podium, his broad chest puffed out to display his traditional red power tie, which was an exact replica of a tie Reagan wore on the campaign trail in 1980, Senator Menendez remembered his instructions: cocky confidence, righteous rage.

"Thank you, Jed. As we all know, I am going to be the Republican nominee for president. So, why did I even show up at this debate? I showed up because ideas matter even if these other candidates don't." Milking the moment, just as Luke had instructed him to do, he paused to flash his brilliant, broad-faced smile straight into the hearts of the voting public.

"Now, if you've listened to anything the Democratic candidates have been saying, it's clear I'm going to be running against a capitalism-hating, self-loathing, anti-American. As a God fearing, churchgoing man whose family emigrated to this country *legally*, I didn't want to use these words, but there are no other words to use."

Now he traded his smile for a scowl. The American people loved his scowl. Luke said it was Menendez's greatest weapon in this time of unrestrained American anger and advised him to use it sparingly. It was serious; it felt authentic; it carried major gravitas. The kind Dick Cheney once had.

"The Democratic candidate I'll be running against," Menendez continued, lifting his voice and his right hand like a preacher blessing his congregation, "whoever it is, will be a baby-killing, freedom-crushing, elitist tool of left-wing corporate corruption. The man or woman who becomes my opponent is a threat to all that makes America, America! As an Air Force veteran, the words I'm about to speak have real meaning: I vow to stop that threat or die for the country I love."

The debate crowd roared its approval.

Senator Menendez basked in the adoration.

Luke clapped slowly, thrilled with their success but distrustful of the candidate he managed. He understood the political game being played. But still, as a homeschooled preacher's kid who burned with the same righteous anger as his mentor, Pastor Josiah McMillan, he struggled with an uncomfortable truth: his candidate had no real appreciation for the word, or the power, of God.

CHAPTER 4

RULE #1 OF CAMPAIGNING

Dressed in a perfectly fitted wine-colored tweed coat and blue Burberry slacks, an outfit that cost three thousand dollars, Bradley Bishkoff watched what he hoped was the final Democratic primary presidential debate from a lounge chair in the spin room. He always watched debates from the spin room. "It's my patriotic duty," he told anyone who commented on his presence. "Letting journalists think for themselves is too great a risk to the democratic process."

He scanned the debate stage, marveling at a spectacularly diverse field of candidates. Seven in total. Four men and three women across a rainbow of skin tones.

They really did represent America. It was too bad he had spent the last nine months denigrating so many of them. It was all part of a strange process. He would tear them down at all costs to ensure his candidate, Illinois Governor Jacqueline O'Leary, became the Democratic nominee for president. But then, inevitably, Jacqi would have to prop them up, sing their praises, and unite them under the unhappy umbrella of Democratic party unity. And the one who made the strongest recovery? That's how you got a Vice Presidential nominee.

"It's called the Political Playground," he laughed to himself. "Insults for all!" Not a bad name for a book.

Of the contenders, the other six were currently far enough behind his candidate to render the whole process a waste of time. Still, there were more primaries to go, and you never knew. Obama and Trump had both come out of nowhere.

His mind drifting, Bradley failed to notice his candidate was also day-dreaming, meaning the pocket buzzer he used to shock her anytime her attention lapsed went unused.

Governor O'Leary was, in fact, thinking about the campaign donations that would roll in if she survived the next twenty minutes. While her rivals had foamed at the mouth about digital monopolies, she had deftly skirted the issue by stressing her commitment to digital infrastructure for all. She congratulated herself on having the foresight to hire a campaign manager with deep connections to big tech's endless well of campaign donations and visionary expertise. Who needed Wall Street anyway?

Her attention roamed to the monitors, where she checked the visage of her green and blue pantsuit. Stylish and form-fitting, it screamed for a cover of *Vogue*. She thought of Bradley pleading with her to wear a skirt. *Fuck that. I've got to show my boardroom and battlefield chops.*

It was in that moment of O'Leary's daydreamy self-congratulation that former Transportation Secretary Rajdeep Chandraksen—really, when had a former secretary ever won the presidency?—adjusted his turban and flagged the moderator, a liberal condescension machine named Heather Haliburton, by raising his hand.

Haliburton, bored by the debate, hoped Chandraksen would riff on his beloved proposal to solve urban congestion by scaling accessibility to electric-powered rickshaws. "Yes, Secretary?"

"While I've enjoyed the thrilling exchanges we've had about the environment and military industrial complex," Chandraksen said, "one of which must be saved and the other of which must be destroyed, I'd like to point out that despite the diversity here on stage, the Democratic Party, ultimately, has no interest in the voices of minority communities."

"Exactly right, Secretary Chandraksen!" It was Mary Hooks, now in her third decade as the congresswoman from Raleigh, North Carolina.

"Are you alluding to Governor O'Leary?" Haliburton asked Hooks.

"Draw your own conclusions. My issues with the governor are well documented. Just google mac and cheese."

The crowd hooted at this reference—the two women had previously battled over whether excluding fat and preservative-laden mac and cheese from school lunches was racist, or simply smart public health policy.

Congresswoman Hooks continued after the laughter died down. "Even more troubling is that when you follow the money, it still goes to white candidates, not black, brown, or sepia colored candidates."

"Fuck!" Bradley whispered, madly grasping for the pocket buzzer.

"For God's sake, Mary," Governor O'Leary said, ignoring the silent vibration in her pocket and taking the bait. "Who here is sepia colored?"

Congresswoman Hooks audibly gasped. She was not alone. In the spin room, a chorus of "Can you believe that?" and "Tone deaf!" filled the air.

Bradley winced. While most would describe the reactions as the sound of disbelief, he interpreted these expressions differently. He heard: "Pffffft!" The sound of the air going out of his perfectly orchestrated campaign. Governor O'Leary had broken rule number one of campaigning while white, which was to *never* mention skin tone except when showing sympathy or outrage.

Governor Ramon Martinez was quick to the mic. "Since my grandpa was farming goats deep in the dry heart of the Chihuahuan Desert," he said, his Ivy League elocution clashing with his bolo tie and cowboy boots, "and long before I became the humble governor of Texas, the Martinezes have been sepia-colored beneath the sunbaked brown of our hands and forearms."

Distracted by her envy of Ramon, whom Mary Hooks knew was only governor because Texas's last governor had been brought down by scandal after vetoing a self-incriminating anti-sodomy law, she failed to launch her zinger.

Stacey Chen, however, was ready. A famous farm-to-table-to-Congress rabble rouser who got into politics only after her favorite organic vineyard was destroyed to make way for a tofu processing plant, she'd split the vegan movement with her attacks on tofu while gaining unlikely support from cattle ranchers, the restaurant industry, and the annoyed significant others of tofu eaters everywhere.

With nothing to lose, because winning was never a realistic goal, she chose this moment to proudly carry the banner for all those who shared her heritage. "That's ridiculous, Ramon. Only individuals of East Asian descent such as myself can claim a gorgeous, pearly sepia hue."

Mary Hooks had gotten her bearings. "Stacey, please. Do you want to stand alongside the only white woman on stage and deny my brothers and sisters with African and Latinx ancestry their sepia inheritance?!" Glaring at the frontrunner, she went on. "Speaking of the white woman, Governor O'Leary, for the love of all that is appropriated in this world, what are you wearing? Have you—"

"I'll tell you what she's wearing!" chimed in Senator Jaden McClendon of New Jersey. He adjusted his tie, intent on creating his viral shining moment. "That, ladies and gentlemen and brothers and sisters, is a suburban white woman's attempt at a dashiki!"

Hooks glared at McClendon. She didn't believe in outing anyone, but she was prepared to make an exception in his case.

Bradley's panic turned to celebration. Jaden's outburst was the distraction they needed! He pressed his buzzer three times in quick succession, signaling the attack code that would get them out of this mess.

Governor O'Leary didn't hesitate. "This isn't a dashiki!" Her faux outrage felt real as her eyes flashed. "It's a green and blue pantsuit. I did not take this stage for a *man* to critique my choice of fashion!"

"No," Jaden McClendon said, speaking with the confidence of a veteran *Queer Eye* fan, "that's definitely a culturally appropriated dashiki-style pantsuit."

Mary Hooks's mind waged war on itself. Should she try to bury Jacqueline O'Leary for what very clearly was not but definitely could be construed as a dashiki-style-pantsuit, and risk sharing the glory with Jaden McClendon, or should she hope her identity points had already been scored and take Jaden down? She made the wrong decision.

"Oh, and there you go again, Jaden, just telling women how it is. Typical chauvinistic mansplaining."

"Boom!" shouted Bradley into the spin room.

Secretary Rajdeep Chandraksen, one of Bradley's favorites for VP, doubled down while gravely shaking his turbaned head. "I agree with Mary and Jacqueline. It's not any man's role to dictate stylistic definitions to a woman. I expect better, Jaden."

Martinez piled on. "I and my goat-farming abuelo agree with Rajdeep."

Having seen two men in a row try to steal Mary Hooks' thunder, and already upset that Hooks had stolen hers, Chen let it rip. "Gentlemen, please. If you believed in gender equality, you wouldn't even be on this stage!"

This was more than Larry Olafson, the self-proclaimed most moral senator in history, could take. As he stewed in his sweater vest, the righteous anger of a long-suffering public servant scorned boiled over. "Now Stacey," Larry droned in his slow, methodical way, "as the most senior and most progressive member of the Senate in this race, I think we can all agree that men have been and still are valuable allies to our female colleagues."

Hooks, Chen, and O'Leary's ire built to bursting as they withstood Olafson's snail's-pace response. When he'd crawled to the end of his last sentence, they erupted as one: "No!"

All three women and all four men on stage froze in surprise at this unintentional moment of unity, but Jacqueline O'Leary, who had been drilled by Bradley for the last week, was the first to pull a canned line out of her back pocket.

She pointed at Larry Olafson, raising her strong midwestern voice to dominate the airwaves. "You are wrong, Senator. We must hang on to the grievances of the past if only to ensure we don't repeat the same mistakes in the future. So no, Larry, your time is done, and your role is to follow me, Mary, and Stacey into the future!"

The audience detonated.

Hooks and Chen, fuming that O'Leary beat them to the punch, forced smiles onto their faces.

Bradley beamed. He could taste the nomination.

CHAPTER 5

CRYING VETERANS AND WHITE-HAIRED FORGIVENESS MACHINES

In the corner of a downtown Seattle apartment with floor to ceiling windows looking out over Puget Sound, Melanie and Jennifer huddled over a laptop, watching the edited video from Julia Connor's book launch.

"Mel," Jennifer said, "this is so off brand. You don't dance and there's no total burn. Like, the veteran comes off *looking good!*"

"Yeah, but it's a crying veteran! When does that ever happen? Can't I post a feel-good video that's not kittens?"

"I mean, of course you can, but you know the rules. Dancing, outrage, humiliation, and crazy laughs get clicks. Straightforward information gets ignored. This is *your* brand," Jennifer gestured around the gorgeous apartment, "and your business. I just don't want you to get sidetracked from what sells."

Melanie lapsed into silence, weighing this wisdom. "I can do what I want. But Jennifer, blast the soundtrack to make it feel more familiar and let's, like, use some bright purple text to make it fun and edgy."

Thirty minutes later, edits finished, Melanie typed out her Beep.

Beep Beep fam, Mel P here with a different type of post. Can killer, crying military veterans be believed? Do baby boomers have anything worthwhile to say? Is healing real? Watch the vid and let me know! I REALLY wanna hear from you!

She clicked upload and said, "Fingers crossed."

• • •

The book launch was a smashing success. For two hours, Julia signed books and chatted with her readers. Friends called from across the country to congratulate her.

The Seattle Times published a review calling her book "an interesting entry in the avalanche of voices capitalizing on the sorry state of American politics." In the *Austin American Statesmen*, a long-time local, overwhelmed by the city's growth, noted that "a gardening mystic from near Seattle has, somehow, captured the political whimsy of Austin's endless supply of New Age hipsters." Her editor said the book was exceeding expectations, with sales much stronger than expected among twenty-somethings. If the numbers and positive buzz kept climbing, her publisher might fund a book tour—a rarity.

The last time she'd gone out was with *Deep Roots, Soaring Branches*: her book of ecological poetry that had landed her on the *Tonight Show* with Jay Leno. On the show she'd read her poem "The Wealth of Soil," asking Jay and his viewers why no one seemed to care that our topsoil—home to fungus, bacteria, roots and animals—was slowly being killed by pesticides and irresponsible farming practices. She'd been overwhelmed with positive feedback; one congressman had even written her asking for more information. But then, as she had witnessed her entire life, nothing had changed.

Now, Julia sat at home in Tenino, Washington staring at the typewriter, contemplating her core belief—that for people and societies to change, individuals' hearts must change first. She thought back to the young woman at her book launch whose brash questions Jonathan had so expertly handled. She thought of her wonderful head of hair, the bright facial jewelry, and those ripped-up pants.

Julia held the image, and then went deeper, wondering about this girl's experience. She had read articles about how anxious, how angry, the youth were. How lost the young men seemed and how disillusioned the women were. She didn't blame them.

She felt it too. Had for years! Fury at the world's impotent response to environmental catastrophe. At the nation's unwillingness or inability to agree on a set of political and social rules to play by. At the selfish corporate interests that controlled both political parties. That's why she'd written the book! And yet that girl, Mel P, had attacked her.

Searching herself for anger, she found that all defensiveness had subsided. All she felt was curiosity and that ever-present instinct to serve and support those who needed a loving hand. How could she reach young people? How could she be a beacon of hope to a generation that spent more time on their phones than communing with nature, who all seemed to believe God didn't exist and to have no use for Jesus Christ, Buddha, or any other spiritual teacher?

Her fingers slowly moved on the typewriter's state-of-the-art circa 1973 keyboard.

Light fractures through crystal
Moving forward and back
Immune to time

Yet I am not so blessed
To have been absolved
Of life's linear march

So I, the time worn
Gaze into the past
Aware of regret

Bright opportunities missed
To heal and to act
To save and to love

Living in a world at war
With itself, Unaware of light's
propensity to transcend time

Has my time passed?
Or can opportunity
Again be found?

A humble seeker I am
As I ask with open heart
To serve the young

To teach them and to love them
Unveiling a path to the center
Of their hurting selves

And in doing so to prepare
For a world that may yet
Be reborn

• • •

Though elk and moose heads dotted the VFW hunting lodge's walls in abundance, the prize of the lodge was a Grizzly head and torso from a founding member's Alaskan hunting trip in 1923. As legend has it, the bear had proven too bulky to be flown home, but the happy hunter had been too proud of his trophy to see all but its head lost to history. So he had done the only logical thing and taxidermied half the bear, chartered a plane an Air Force buddy could fly, and had it brought back to Fort Leavenworth. Ever since, veterans from countless named and unnamed conflicts had sat beneath the bear on two armchairs upholstered with fur from the bear's bottom half.

Eli, who had a grizzly-like appearance himself, burst onto the deck, nearly causing Jonathan to topple off the rickety chair he sat on.

"Bro, you're a star! My daughter just sent me your video."

Jonathan looked up. "What do you mean, man? I haven't made a video in my life."

"Dude, you may not have made the video, but that's you in it. That was some deep shit." He handed the phone to Jonathan. "Watch it."

Jonathan pushed play.

The video had over 300,000 views! As Jonathan watched, the counter climbed and all sorts of weird heart and animal-shaped graphics and comments kept flashing on the screen.

The video ended with a close-up of Mel P's face, a driving electronic beat playing in the background. "So fam, what do you think? Do crying veterans and white-haired forgiveness machines deserve to be heard?"

Jonathan tried to scroll through the comments, but there were thousands of them. He looked at Eli. "What in the world?! This is wild. I mean, most of the comments are positive, but what if some people hate this? What if they come after me?"

"Come after you for what?"

"For anything! For admitting that I killed. For having ever been in the army. For not having a degree but having an opinion. You know how mean people are!"

Eli lovingly punched Jonathan's enormous shoulder. "Brother, I think the world is starting to see what's always been obvious to me. You're a star. And no matter what the response, our path of service has been clear since we started working with Julia. More attention can only increase our impact."

CHAPTER 6

PIVOTING TO
THE GENERAL

A week after the debate, Luke was back in D.C., sitting in Senator Menendez's Senate office. His eyes were closed, a bottle of sparkling water in hand. He was feeling good about trusting his instincts.

He could have joined Glockenspiel or Bush IV—both had approached him—but his gut told him Menendez was the guy. So, he'd gone to Pastor McMillan and told him the truth. He didn't want to work for the frontrunners. They were already playing by the rules. But Menendez, well, he was a loose cannon who seemed to have no respect for the power of God. He was just the type of candidate who needed Luke's expertise and spiritual leadership. Pastor Josiah agreed. He offered Menendez a deal: a promise that Salvation Megachurch would not oppose him if Luke was his campaign manager.

So here Luke was, taking the biggest swing of his life, managing the Republican nominee for president. Winning would not only mean that God's word and the church's values were safe for four more years but would also secure a lifetime's worth of access to the world's power structures. As Pastor McMillan sometimes asked him, "Why serve God as pauper and plebeian when you can be a disciple with power and wealth?"

Although he thought of the pastor like a father, Luke sometimes thought he was a bit too cynical. Yes, power was important, but so was service. What he most loved about Salvation Megachurch were the opportunities to give back. Between elections, when most political operatives disappeared to Caribbean resorts or Colorado ski slopes, he took off to volunteer at church projects in Uganda, Guatemala, or, most disturbing and rewarding of all, Appalachia.

Menendez walked into the office. "I know that look, Luke. You're getting satisfied. Dreaming of your consulting practice. Counting money from the oligarchs, executives, and idiot candidates that'll pay you to do jack shit for them once you've steered a president into the Oval Office."

Luke looked his candidate in the eye. "That's not who I am, Senator. I'm in this for the values, not the dollars. You know that."

"Whatever it is you're sitting there dreaming about, stop it. We haven't won a damn thing yet. We're months away from getting to hear the fat lady's sweet, victorious voice."

"You're right about that."

"Did you get the post-debate numbers?"

"Donations skyrocketed."

"I knew it! Any sector breakdowns?"

Luke winced. "Real-time debate donations spiked when you used the line I told you not to use."

"We have to protect America from the grasping poor!"

Goodness, Luke thought, staring at Menendez's shit-eating grin. *He's quoting himself.*

"Yes, sir. Jed Abernathy led with that line on ROX News' debate recap." He shook his head. "Talk about handing the opposition soundbites on a platter. Speaking of which—"

"Don't skip the most important part!" Menedez barked. "Has Wall Street delivered?"

"They also loved the grasping poor line." Luke smiled despite himself. "One of our bundlers actually hosted a dinner called 'Keep 'em in their place.' Jed reported on that too."

"And?"

"Ten thousand a plate. Sold out."

Menendez smiled. "Now that's what I'm talking about. If it comes down to me versus that she-snake O'Leary, a billion dollars raised won't cut it. Tech's gonna have her back, so we've gotta keep those Wall Street donors in our pocket."

"Again, the optics are not ideal."

"Since when did you care about optics, Luke? You're the one who's forced me to use all these lines about baby-killing this and un-American that. Do you know how poorly those lines poll with independents?"

"Those lines happen to be responsible for your Republican nomination." When Luke leaned forward, the florescent overheads reflected off his already-gleaming eyes. "And Senator, those lines are not just lines. They are God's truth. As long as illegals seek to take the promised land from God's American children, as long as the gays parade through our streets in their *disgusting* rainbow-colored short shorts, as long as Democrats persecute Christians for publicly professing their faith, our work is not done."

"Riigggghhhttttt." Menedez glanced at the ceiling to avoid Luke's intense eye contact. "Just don't get confused. We're here to win an election, not save souls."

· · ·

They breezed through the front doors of Rock Springs Elementary School in suburban Atlanta. An entourage on a mission. A campaign carrying the hopes and dreams of the Democratic party.

"You know how much I love children and public education, but, Bradley, please tell me we're not spending the entire day doing photo-ops with kids?"

Bradley looked at Governor O'Leary. Beautiful. A pro in every way. And while she was normally intense, she was especially locked in now that Georgia was the only thing standing between her and the candidacy.

She glanced at him. "How long are we here for?"

He caught the subtext while silently counting how many new notifications his phone registered. Thirty-nine since he'd last checked ten minutes before.

"Don't worry, Jaqui, you just need to hug some kids on camera, and then we're spending the rest of the day with executives and donors."

"Good. Every second has to be perfectly spent. We win Georgia, and I'm the candidate. Then we're on to the big time."

Bradley nodded, hiding his eye roll. She thought he didn't know this?

"Governor, don't sweat it. Like in Belshazzar's Babylon, the writings on the wall."

She spun to face him. "Is that another of the Old Testament stories left over from the bigoted homophobes that passed as your parents?"

Bradley was flattered. She remembered him sharing about his family and the Pentecostal church of his Kentucky youth. The fire and brimstone, the adultery and then God's punishment. In all the Old Testament, his pastor had most loved the story of Babylon. The Babylonians had destroyed God's temple and taken the Jewish people into captivity, only for God to smite them.

"It is. And you know the funny part?"

"What's that?" the governor asked as an aide handed her a Perrier.

"God delivered the Babylonians into the hands of the Persians. The Iranians! Ha, Iran, savior of Israel. Biblical history is great."

Every time O'Leary thought about Bradley's parents, her blood pressure spiked. But her job was to know stories. And look perfect. She checked herself in the mirror an aide held up and adjusted a hair.

"I'm set," she said to her aide. Then back to Bradley: "How'd you get outed anyways? Was it a teen lover?"

"Hardly. I told my pastor I was gay and he outed me. I'd wanted him to help me get conversion therapy, but instead he told my parents and the school."

"Your *pastor* outed you?!"

"Best thing that ever happened to me. My parents sent me to live with a black sheep aunt they refused to speak of," Bradley grinned, "a women's studies professor at Harvard."

"She's the one that set you on your path?"

"Exactly. I never knew I was particularly smart, but she saw it right away and paved my way. I was interning with Ted Kennedy by the time I was twenty and on Elizabeth Warren's staff two years later."

"I remember that," O'Leary said. Then she wondered: How did he go from staffing Warren to being the Big Tech guy? Oh well, questions for another day.

"By the way," Bradley said, "like me, your numbers are changing the same way a caterpillar turns into a butterfly. The polls after the debate were fantastic and they've just kept getting better."

"So, keep attacking male privilege and compliment black women at every turn?"

"Among primary voters, the 'fuck men' line polls off the charts. And the black women, well, they know none of the identity politics kooks or neo-socialist degenerates can beat Menendez. Speaking of which, are you ready?"

Governor O'Leary nodded, and then strode into the classroom, cameras rolling in each corner of the room. She exuded energy and charm, her scarf trailing behind her like a French diva. Before her sat twenty-eight fifth grad-ers, evenly split between boys and girls. Half the students were black, the rest an equal mixture of Latino, Asian, and white students, a perfect embodiment of America's rainbow nation.

"Hello, children! How are you all today?"

The class responded "Great!" in unison. Before the governor could ask her next question, a junior staffer whispered to Bradley.

He turned to the crew, exasperated. "Stop the cameras! Who was in charge of class optics?"

O'Leary raised her eyebrows as he whispered in her ear. She responded with a hiss. "And we're just figuring this out now? Jesus Christ. Then rear-range them!"

It was like someone pushed rewind on an old VHS tape.

Bradley and the governor left the room followed by their senior staff. The cameramen muttered to themselves, annoyed the shoot was already 30 minutes over time. The young staffers that hadn't left the room began bus-ily moving the children around in what seemed to be a disorganized game of musical chairs.

When everything was set, one of them stuck their head into the hallway, giving the all-clear.

This time, the shot was perfect. Governor O'Leary again swept into the room, her scarf trailing elegantly behind her, an idealized picture of leader-ship and nonchalant excellence. The class in front of her as seen from the cam-era was all black, Latino and Asian students. In the corner, unaware they'd been excluded from the shot, the white students cheered along with the rest.

This time a child immediately raised her hand.

"Yes, sweetie," Governor O'Leary said, "what would you like to know?"

"My mom says that carbon credits are a scam. That they just create a way for businesses to monetize their bad behavior."

"Economists, who are experts of market economics, suggest they can be very effective."

"She also said that carbon isn't the biggest issue," the girl continued, trying to remember the questions her mom had her memorize. "She said the point of our foreign policy should be to protect the world's oceans and forests and soil and animals, and that the only way for that to happen is for people to sacrifice our lifestyles."

O'Leary laughed despite herself. This child's mother had clearly never tried to win an election. "Your mom is right to be concerned. But I'm committed to making climate progress without disrupting our lives and our economy."

"My mom—"

"Why don't we take a question from someone else."

CHAPTER 7

ACTUAL BEES

Melanie's Nissan Sentra rolled down a rural, fir-tree-lined highway outside of Tenino, Washington. They passed a couple-acre spread with a crisscrossed wooden fence and a Pet Owl Preserve sign.

"Where are we?" said Jennifer hesitantly, eyeing the sign. They were only an hour south of Seattle, but it felt like a different world.

"The kind of place where people like Julia 'go back to the land,' I guess."

"We should just leave her *on* the land. I know the video crushed it, but we. Do. Not. Belong. Out. Here."

"Right? We belong in dance studios and record shops," Melanie said, scanning open farmland and small houses so foreign to her urban instincts. "But Jen, I'm curious. Everyone I talk to either wants a political war or is afraid of a civil war. I mean, my *job* is to channel that outrage, but what is it changing? Julia seems different."

"Different? What she is is nutty. Her generation did the peace and love thing, then turned into corporate psychopaths and built the suburbs. Why she thinks she gets to say anything now is beyond me."

"You're not wrong, but what if you're not right? You heard that veteran. She's been living on the land for twenty-five years. And I looked it up—she's been writing books about this kind of thing for decades. Maybe we can learn from her failures."

They pulled up to a double-story farmhouse sitting thirty yards off the road. Rows of blackberry bushes lined the front lawn and ran into a small orchard of apple trees. Inside, all the lights were off.

Melanie looked at Jennifer. "Do you think she's here?"

Jennifer examined the house from the passenger seat and opened the door. "I don't know, but we're here, so we might as well make this happen."

Jennifer got her phone out and played with the settings while Melanie stretched and did practice pirouettes. Sufficiently limbered, Mel nodded to Jennifer and they started up the porch to the front door.

At the top of the stairs, Jennifer split to the side and started filming as Melanie gathered herself, peeked at the camera out of the corner of her eyes, bent her knees, and knocked.

They froze. No one stirred inside. Melanie's knee started to hurt.

"Well," said Melanie, straightening and stretching her knee, "do you think she might be around back? I think she has a garden."

Jennifer scrunched her face and peeked through the window at the vintage furniture and collection of masks from around the world. "Or we could just leave? Those masks are creepy."

Melanie started toward the apple trees at the side of the house as Jennifer followed. Spying a figure hunched over a leafy row, they let themselves through the garden gate, walked past the rows of peas and Swiss chard and down a row of young kale.

Alerted by the clicking of the gate, Julia looked up, a smile spreading across her face.

"Melanie, you ready?" Jennifer said as she crouched and started to video, crushing a young kale plant in the process.

Rising to her tiptoes, Melanie looked over her shoulder at Jennifer, looked back at Julia, then jumped and spun 180, landing facing Jennifer and all her viewers. Not pausing, she threw her right arm into the air and then launched into a perfect rendition of Janet Jackson's dance from "Nasty"—which most of her followers were too young to have seen. Smooth like the '80s pop star as her arms and hips undulated, she blew through the first couple of moves, then froze facing the camera and rapped.

"I'm an activist, first of all."

She launched her left arm skyward, then spun, scattering dirt across Julia's perfect rows.

"I live to serve, justice is my call."

Melanie jumped, landing a perfect backflip and settling into a crouch, pointing at the camera as one foot turned another young kale to pulp.

"I'm here today, to see what Julia has to say."

Behind her, Julia's jaw was on the ground communing with her kale. She looked like a missionary forced to watch striptease—in shock and completely and totally at a loss as to why these kale-killing young women were dancing in her garden.

Before Julia could speak, Melanie nonchalantly answered her unspoken question. "Sorry about that Julia, we just had to shoot the opening to our video. This will be some killer new content."

"The video?" Julia asked.

It hadn't occurred to Melanie that Julia had seen zero Beep-Beep videos. "Yea! This interview for Beep-Beep we're about to do. Don't you remember me from Seattle?"

Julia thought of her poem. "Of course I remember! You were the sharp young lady with the questions."

"That was me! And this is my friend and comrade in arms Jennifer. She filmed our exchange the other night. Do you know how many views your video got?!"

"Views?" Julia remained lost.

"The video, Julia, got 3 million views and I was *flooded* with comments. Comments like"—Melanie paused and looked back at the still running camera, raising her eyebrows for the audience— "Comments like 'why have I never heard of Julia?' and 'OMG, I love her!' and 'If child killing veterans can heal, why can't we all?' But you know what was the most popular comment, the one that over one hundred and fifty thousand likes—and nobody gets that many likes for a comment— 'Why isn't Julia doing more to spread her message?'"

Julia looked at her dirt-covered hands and felt Melanie's energy and enthusiasm wash over her. "I'm thrilled your video got so many views. That's just … amazing. I also don't really understand how comments work, but maybe you could tell your viewers that I've been doing this work a long time. I've given hundreds of seminars—"

"Yet you're an unknown. Why might that be?"

Julia smiled. "I'm known to many, I even—"

Melanie turned away from Julia, now looking directly at Jennifer and into the camera. "What if that's not enough? Our country and our politics are broken. People are freaking the actual *fuck out*. Isn't it time someone like Julia Connor got off the bench and turn her little books into a political philosophy for future leaders like us?"

Melanie turned back to Julia. "Again, sorry about that, I just needed a hard frame for the video. But really, why don't you try to reach people like me and Jennifer and everyone on Beep-Beep? You do realize people my age pretty much only *watch* sweet content, right?"

Julia closed her eyes and took a deep breath, thinking of her poem, resting in the joy of an answered prayer. The feeling made her skin tingle and filled her with gratitude. Filled her as a vision fills the seeker, as an answer reaffirms trust between the beloved and her Creator.

Opening her eyes, she smiled, feet bouncing as her dry white hair bobbed. "Melanie, I've been asking myself the same question. Would the two of you like to come inside for some tea?"

Melanie and Jennifer sat on an overstuffed blue sofa that would have been considered vintage twenty years ago and took in Julia's living room while their host made tea. Plants hung in every window. Masks from who knows where—Africa? Asia? the Andes?—lined the walls. Next to them, one of Julia's feline friends curled up on a tabletop cat cushion.

Julia brought in a tray of teacups and sat across from them on a faded, forest-green divan. "Would you like some homegrown chamomile?"

Jennifer took a quick sip. "Julia, it's delicious. And so sweet!"

"I drizzled in some honey from my hives." Julia beamed. "I hope you don't mind."

"What?! You have, like, actual bees?"

"Jennifer, come on, girl. You heard about people freaking out about bees disappearing, right? No bees, then no honey," said Melanie.

"Actually, people were 'freaking out' about bees because bees pollinate fruit and vegetables. So, no bees, no food."

Jennifer's eyes narrowed and her lips pursed. She felt a familiar sense of dread rise in her gut. The same feeling she got whenever someone mentioned melting polar ice or gun sales. "Wait! You're telling me that if bees die, we starve?"

"It's a serious concern. Bees, birds, and butterflies do a lot of the work."

"I just had no idea. Literally no idea. Oh. My. God!"

"The encouraging news," Julia paused and smiled, placing a gentle hand on Jennifer's back, "is that bee populations have recovered. It turns out our little friends are resilient despite the pesticides we soak our fields and our food with."

Melanie rolled her eyes. She loved Jennifer, but sometimes she lived under a rock. "Julia, this is my whole point! Let us turn you and that veteran of yours into figures that can reach our generation."

Julia beamed, a thousand ideas running through her mind.

• • •

Jonathan stopped to gas up his truck on his way to Olympia. He was holding the nozzle when a silver Hyundai with a University of Washington sticker pulled up to the next pump. A young woman with a backward baseball cap got out of the car, nodded at him, and then did a double take.

"Hey, I know you."

"Really?" Jonathan tried to place the face. "I'm sorry, but I don't think we've met."

"No, I definitely know you." She stared at him. Then snapped her fingers. "You were the crying guy in Mel P's sick clip! No cap, I loved you."

"No cap?"

"It means 'no lie.' You've really never heard someone say that?"

"Oh, sorry."

"No, no, no. You were great! I mean, if someone like you can get past your trauma, maybe me and my friends can too."

Jonathan smiled broadly, his white teeth bursting through his black beard. "I think we all can."

"I hope you're right! That was crazy inspiring. And Julia, too. She's, like, the grandma me and all my friends wish we had."

"Well, thank you. I'm glad you didn't find it disturbing."

"Disturbing? I loved it! I can't wait to tell my friends I met you. They will freak out!"

That night Jonathan decided he was done pondering. Then he felt the release of tension he hadn't realized he'd been carrying. *Yes indeed,* he thought, *the body always knows.*

He picked up the phone to propose the craziest idea he'd ever had.

"Hello, this is Julia Connor's residence. How can I help you?"

Jonathan's smile stretched across his face. No matter how many times it happened, the fact Julia still had a landline caught him by surprise.

"It's Jonathan."

"Jonathan. I was just thinking about you!"

"Listen, Julia, this might sound nuts, but I've been thinking some strange thoughts—"

"About that young woman from the event?"

"How'd you know?"

"I knew," Julia said, the twinkle in her eyes practically audible across the phone line, "because Melanie was here and told me all about her video and the crying veteran that people loved. In fact, I invited her to your healing circle at the church next week. Do you think the participants will be OK if she observes?"

Jonathan sank into his couch, his enormous figure becoming one with the soft cushions. "So, she will be our messenger?"

"I've been praying for something just like this. When God acts, who are we to stand in the way?"

CHAPTER 8

DEEPENING

One and a half. Million. Dollars.

That's how much Bradley, dodging bustling pedestrian traffic on 14th Street NW in DC, had just leveraged the tech donors who powered O'Leary's campaign to raise for an organization called *All Types and Colors* that provided resources for the sort of children and teens he'd almost become. He was elated, buoyant, goosebumps spread across his arms and chest. If bastards like Menendez thought they were going to ride a regressive wave of hate to the White House, Bradley was going to do everything in his power to stem the tide. Not every teen had an aunt willing to take them in after their parents or pastor decided they were unworthy of love.

A scowl crossed his face as he sidestepped a fat man talking too loudly on his phone, a man whose very appearance reminded him of his parents' pastor and so many other conservative blowhards who automatically confused different with "dangerous."

Fuck them, Bradley thought. Impulsive rage pushed his satisfaction away.

Although he'd climbed the ladder until he was now sitting one rung away from summiting the political power structure, he'd come to recognize that a single election couldn't beat the bad guys. It would take a lifetime of effort and battle, and it would require him to leverage the mightiest systems in the world—politics *and* business. And that was no easy feat. He knew that to do so he had to channel his rage, the anger he felt watching self-righteous jerks inflict pain upon the poor and the vulnerable, the fury one feels when the world disrespects your right to exist.

His rage was what drove him to win, drove him to help, drove him in his pursuit of power.

At Jônt he breezed straight to his corner table, barely pausing to nod at Rene, the host with the diamond-studded plugs, his earlobes gauged to a degree both trendy and upscale; had he stretched them any wider, they may have crossed the line into decidedly un-Jônt-like territory. Though as it was, the view of Rene was reason enough to visit. His usual cocktail, a spicy tequila creation called the Sonoran Sunrise, arrived at the table unbidden and Bradley sighed with pleasure. They knew him here, and more importantly, they knew the fact that he routinely brought his contacts to dine was grist for the political rumor mill, adding to the eatery's see-or-be-seen stature, which kept denizens of the nation's most artificially wealthy city streaming through the restaurant's doors.

Bradley was studying the menu when a loud, familiar voice caught his ear. "I need a glass of Prosecco immediately." Looking up, he saw his former brunch buddy and recent debate moderator, Heather Haliburton, slide into the seat across from him. "Bradley, good fucking God, have you ever tried to have a substantive conversation with a Republican? It's like they're braindead."

Bradley raised his eyebrows. "This is not a breaking story, Heather."

Heather shook her head. "I read an interview yesterday where you said you don't date when on a campaign." She leaned in, making eye contact with her old friend. "That's a blatant lie. You were smiling when I came in. Level with me, I want the deets."

Bradley pursed his lips, unsuccessfully trying not to smile. "Not dating doesn't preclude an occasional classy Grindr connect."

"I knew it!"

"Why not? Anyways, hon, who are you to cast stones? You don't wear those tight sweaters just for the ratings."

Heather glanced at her chest. God, she loved gay men. So honest. So unthreatening. Straight men—well, *nice* straight men—were constantly trying to say the right thing and look at the right places so as not to offend. She appreciated the instinct to be respectful, but it was the curse of liberals to be overrun with respectful men. What she craved were men that respected her, wanted to fuck, AND weren't afraid to say it. #MeToo had been great, but some men learned the wrong lesson.

"Have you ever been hate-fucked by a musclehead marine in an admiral's office?"

Bradley's eyes widened. "Ohhh my God." His words were a moan.

"I'll take that as a no." Heather giggled and relaxed into the evening. "You ordered?"

Bradley let out a deep breath. "What I want to order is that marine you just mentioned, but I was thinking of the tasting menu for two? Thank one of my super PAC donors for their generosity."

"This is why I love democracy."

"And for the wine... Armand Rousseau Grand Cru from 2017." Bradley smirked. "I hear it's an especially affordable cabernet."

Heather acted out a pleasure shudder. "I'd be working for a nonprofit if I didn't want a grand worth of French red with dinner."

Bradley laughed. "That's how I started, remember? Street fundraising for the International Red Cross. Taught me the valuable lesson that you can be poor and work for a better world, or you can be rich working for a better world, and rich is better."

"Amen." Her wave caught the eye of their waiter, a fit twenty-something with a Republican haircut but a Democrat's ready-to-please smile. He didn't bat an eye at their order. Here, the price of everyone's meal rivaled a freshman's first semester at a community college.

"Speaking of rich"—Bradley never skipped a beat—"how's your book doing?"

"They sell themselves at speaking gigs," she said. "But really, why worry about the book or fight over my NATN salary when companies will pay me twenty-five grand to show up and talk to them for an hour?"

Their money conversations could go on for hours but this time consumed only a few minutes before Bradley grinned lasciviously and leaned forward. "Didn't you fuck General Electric's CEO at one of those executive retreats?"

Heather *almost* blushed. "He was no marine, but he had a different sort of power. Less in the arms and more in his—"

"Pocketbook?"

"I was going to say mind. Men with that much power actually believe they can do, or have, anything. It's sooo sexy." The seared, endangered bluefin tuna arrived. With the taste of its firm flesh lingering in her mouth, Heather said, "Bradley, is tonight all fun and gossip, or should we talk business?"

Staring at the three remaining bites of bluefin, Bradley shrugged. "Babe, we've been talking business since we were twenty-three-year-olds bouncing around house parties in Adams Morgan. What's left to talk about? O'Leary is the nominee and Menendez is the target. His voters are ... what was it that Hillary called them years ago?"

"Deplorables?"

"Ah yes, exactly."

"And one can assume his funders are still bastard Wall Street execs?" Heather rolled her eyes as she threw back a hearty sip of her French red.

"Right. Our voters are the union and minority base, well-educated community-minded citizens who believe in science and social justice. Our funders ..."

"Small-dollar donors and progressive tech execs. *Same it ever was.*"

"*Same as it ever was.*" Talking Heads. "Once in a Lifetime." A classic, and one they quoted often in their back-and-forth because in politics it was ... "The same fucking thing that's been true for twenty years. The country, the planet, and our future are fucked."

"And if we lose ..." Heather was only briefly distracted by the arrival of their Kobe beef tenderloin teased with a light pepper sauce. "... we'll all be musclehead-marine fucked."

She took another sip of the Grand Cru, nodded approvingly at her glass, but then pouted. "You've heard the latest? The senate is talking about rolling back cost-of-living increases in Medicare *and* Medicaid!"

"People like us are the only thing standing in the way of a true war on the poor!"

"Right?!" Heather refilled his glass with a generous pour.

"Just yesterday Menendez had the gall to suggest that Republicans who donate to charity are morally superior to Democrats supporting compassionate public policy. As if we can solve problems of inequality through token personal generosity!"

Now Heather refilled her own, more generously still, and took a slow, luxuriating sip.

"*I know*," she said, lifting her glass and shooting him a *so there* look. "To fucking suggest any one person is responsible for problems that are clearly systemic… I mean, the entire idea of personal responsibility is ridiculous."

"As is the notion that Republicans give a flying fuck about the poor just because some of them donate to their church."

Heather's phone buzzed. "The network president. I have to take this outside."

She stood up, her tall figure weaving among tables toward the door. Bradley asked the waiter for coffee and the bill. When they came, he peaked at the printout. Nineteen hundred bucks before tip. Not too bad.

• • •

The eight figures positioned around the large dining room table at the Antebellum-style McMansion in the DC suburb of Alexandria held hands, their heads bowed over the Bibles and devotionals sitting open in front of them, their pleas lofted skyward toward God's always-open ears, the sincerity of their hearts clear to any observer.

One skinny figure wearing a compatibly skinny tie breathed deeply, grateful to momentarily be in this safe space. Most days Luke found himself under attack, but on this night, surrounded by believers, he felt comfortable, certain in his mission and aware of the stakes in the battle he fought.

With every breath he relaxed more and more into the everlasting truths that shaped his life. Truths that had guided humanity closer to the Holy Trinity's plan for two thousand years.

"Father," the plaintive plea came from Rebecca, a LuluLemon wearing sister sitting next to him, "guide us as we seek to model your love to the world, as we live within the eternal, never-changing truth of your word."

"Yes, Lord," said Dale off to his right, who never met a golf polo he didn't want to buy, "help us to be righteous as you were righteous, and protect us from the evil that lurks around every corner in this world we call home."

It was Luke's turn. It was such a gift to pray with these good, God-fearing people—his Bible Study brothers and sisters.

"We're broken sinners, yet you have shown us your grace. Our bodies betray us and our instincts are to sin, yet your son Jesus Christ sacrificed his life so that we may have eternal life. Today, our nation faces the same threats the chosen have always faced. You are a God of Love, yet we, the community of believers, remain under attack from demonic secular forces."

His voice seemed to grow, not just in volume but in passion. He sensed the woman next to him stand up, and he felt his spirit lifting. He continued.

"Please, Lord, continue to guide us and show the way, so that we may free others with the glory of your love. You have shown us mercy so we could have everlasting life; you have given us your word and its wisdom so we can live righteously in this life. As I now stand in the gap, a soldier serving his savior, grant me the courage and the vision guaranteed by the sacrifice of your son Jesus Christ."

Luke poured out his soul to the Lord. Others stood up and moved toward him, laying hands on his back and shoulders. They knew the presidential burden he carried, the weight of responsibility that came with managing the campaign of a man like Menendez.

Lifting their voices and their eyes, they humbled themselves before the Lord, the deepest desires of their hearts pouring out in a wave of humility.

"Bless Luke!" Rebecca cried as a tear blotched her mascara, "He, like us all, is lost without you. Guide him and strengthen him in your word. The enemies are many, but with your love and the light of your word, we will persevere to victory!"

"Hold Luke in your peace, dear Lord," called a woman named Carol, who always arrived at Bible Study with muffins to share. "Bless him, keep him, and make your face to shine upon him as he works to defeat Democratic agents of evil."

"Yes, Lord, yes," cried an older man named John with a close-cropped gray beard, lifting his hands to the heavens. "Luke has chosen to be a soldier. He has chosen to serve. He has chosen to subsume himself in the truth of your love. Please fill him with your strength, bless him with Solomon's wisdom and King David's bravery that he may move us closer to the inevitable victory of your word over wokeness, equality, and socialism—the agents of ungodliness."

As the blessings were poured upon him, Luke began to cry.

This, he thought, *is God's Kingdom on earth.*

CHAPTER 9

PAIN IS POWER

Melanie's eyes were wild. Her hair a mess. She sat on the knife's edge between disgust and fascination as she rushed out of the high-ceilinged room, her bare feet gratefully gripping the warm green grass.

Jonathan followed her as she paced across the lawn, the midmorning sun beating down on both of them. "Are you okay?"

"Not really! What is going on in there?!"

"What do you mean?"

Bug-eyed disbelief met his innocent question. "I mean, there are men crying and other men cradling the crying men. And then there are still other men going out of their minds laughing uncontrollably. It's a psychotic circus. What is going on?!"

She had just walked out of the retreat center hosting Jonathan and Julia's Universal Church of All healing circle, and she was extremely confused.

Jonathan beamed a crescent moon through his night-colored beard. "This is what healing looks like."

"Sorry, but to me it looks like"—Melanie's mouth was open and her eyes wide—"a complete loss of control and a psychopathic level of tears."

"Exactly!" Jonathan's laugh was a roar. Mel P was a trip. "To heal we have to touch, acknowledge, accept, and *feel* the most painful, most raw pieces of ourselves. If there is anything we know, it's that feeling lives in the body and our subconscious. So yeah, men losing their shit while physically and emotionally processing their most heart-wrenching life experiences is what healing looks like."

"It's not normal!" *Normal* was this breeze blowing across the lawn, sweeping both stray fallen still-green leaves and strands of her hair along with it. Normal didn't belong anywhere close to this place.

"What we call normal, Melanie? It's avoiding the hard parts of life, never healing and always coping, prolonging our suffering."

"Therapy is *talk*. We heal by understanding. That's how we take control. Losing control on purpose is madness!"

Jonathan thought back several years, to a time when the word "feel" was scarier than "combat." How to explain to Melanie that healing didn't happen in the conscious mind but in the body and in the heart? That it was an emotional, not an intellectual, process? "As long as we're in our heads, we're easy victims for endless loops of negativity, fear and anxiety. Once we get out of our heads, into the depths of the subconscious and unconscious self, we can heal and calm our unregulated nervous systems."

Melanie stared at Jonathan, exasperated by this enormous, tattooed, freakishly emotionally in-tune man. "What are you even talking about?!"

Jonathan laughed again, then gave Melanie a warm hug, the type of hugs he saved for family members and lifelong friends. "Keep hanging out and you'll see. Your eyes, my friend, are just starting to open." He turned to leave. "I need to be inside, but stay out here. I'll see if I can send Julia out to work with you."

"Work with me?" Melanie watched Jonathan disappear back into the building. He must not have heard her. But work with her? What did that mean? Was Julia going to give her mushrooms?! That might have sounded good hours before, but the last thing she wanted was to end up on the ground with the psycho-crying middle-aged men inside.

She checked her phone and Beep-Beep stats, the distraction that kept on giving. Weekend traffic almost always dropped. Then Julia walked out the door.

"Whew! What a time," Julia said, beaming under her sweaty, wrinkled brow. "Healing energy can be exhausting."

"I guess so. Jonathan was just out here trying to explain. Something about feelings, not thoughts, and emotional energy being stored in the body." Mel looked intently at Julia, who was shielding her eyes from the bright sun. "To me, what's happening inside looks like madness. Like crazy people losing their minds. The mushrooms do this?"

"Not necessarily," replied Julia, "the mushrooms help people tap into their feelings by lowering the threshold between our conscious and subconscious. But the healing work can be done in all states of mind."

Melanie's eyes narrowed. There was that term again. "What's the work?"

"The work," Julia said as she nodded along with herself, repeating a short speech she'd been giving for forty years, "is to tap into our feelings, to leave the conscious mind and sit in our subconscious reality. It's by acknowledging our emotions and our painful memories, by giving them the outlet they were denied and the love they desperately needed, that we can free ourselves from the pain and trauma of our past." Julia paused, taking a deep breath of fir-scented air. "Do you want to try?"

Melanie was frozen. If a pastor had asked her if she wanted salvation, she'd have told him to beat it. That was easy. And if some New Age cult type had asked her if she wanted to be enlightened, she'd have told them to take a hike also. The last thing she needed was to meditate with some Hollywood freak selling spirituality and overpriced supplements. But being freed from her trauma, right here? Right now? By an elderly woman with a kind of sweaty face, who she was secretly becoming super obsessed with?

"I guess we could try." Melanie tucked her hair behind her ears; it kept blowing in her face. "What ... exactly would we be doing?"

Julia laughed happily, then turned serious. "Melanie, will you sit across from me on the ground? What you'll be doing is beginning to explore your subconscious and your past. What I'll be doing is guiding you in the process. That's it."

They made their way to the shade under a sprawling tree and settled into the thick grass. Julia stared at Melanie, again taking stock of this young woman who had stumbled into her life. Melanie was so inquisitive, but she had such thick armor and so much anger to accompany her curiosity and kindness.

Even though she smiled and laughed almost all the time, Julia could see a wounded young woman hurt by the world. She knew this session wouldn't go badly, but she wondered if they would be able to break through on the first try. It was hard work when one first began to seek self, dropping beneath conscious thought.

She took Melanie's hands in her own and they matched breaths and heartbeats, breathing together for several minutes and maintaining eye contact.

"Melanie," Julia began, "close your eyes. Start by imagining the place or the person or the space that makes you feel the safest, the most at peace, the place where you love who you are. Can you see it, can you feel it?"

Her eyes clenched, Melanie took a few moments then replied. "Yes. I'm sitting next to Green Lake, just north of downtown Seattle. The sun's shining on me, ducks are quacking in the water, children are playing nearby. I feel wonderful, warm, safe. This is the world as it's supposed to be."

"OK, great. Now focus on that feeling. That feeling of peace, of safety. Hold that in your mind. We're going to use that for the rest of our session. Do you have it?"

Melanie felt her heart rate slow. She seemed to sink into the ground. She felt the glow she imagined she would see if she opened her eyes. "I do."

"Perfect. Now, Melanie. I don't know you that well yet, but I know you are a woman of great purpose and passion, and also a woman who carries a great deal of anger. Is that accurate?"

"It is."

"OK then," Julia spoke in her most comforting voice, a voice that had brought thousands to a place of loving self-acceptance over the decades, "focus on a piece of the pain or anger or anxiety that is alive in you right now. Feel that feeling, and tell me about it."

"Wait." Melanie's eyelids fluttered, but she managed to stop herself from opening them. "You want me to feel the pain on purpose?"

"Of course."

"But it will hurt!"

"Well, Melanie. This is one of the choices we all have. We either choose to confront our pain and heal our wounds, or we cope. When we hide from our pain or when we avoid confronting it, it doesn't make the pain go away, it just means the emotional wound is there in the background, festering and controlling us, causing suffering. Do you want to confront your pain?"

Melanie took a deep breath. She was used to her trauma, familiar with her triggers, aware she was always fighting to do what was right—instead of what her instincts told her was necessary. A battle for sanity was how she viewed it.

"OK, Julia, I'll try. But honestly, I'm scared. There's so much."

"Thank you for being so courageous, Melanie. Now, can you still find that feeling of peace and love next to the lake?"

"I can."

"Good. Now, tell me about a challenging feeling or emotion that is alive in you right now?"

"Whew!" Melanie grinned to cut the tension she felt inside, her eyes still closed. "OK, I'll try. This morning I got triggered and insanely pissed at this old woman. It was, like, totally irrational, yet it happened. I was at a coffee shop, buying a coffee, telling the guy working about one of my content projects when the woman behind said 'Honey, no one cares. Pay for your coffee so I can buy mine.'"

"And—?"

Melanie breathed deeply. "I wanted to light her up! Call her a bitch. I was *SO MAD*."

"Did you yell at her?"

"No. But I did spend like the next three hours in a foul mood, fighting this terrible sense of fury that was almost bursting out of my chest."

"Melanie, you are so strong to have controlled yourself enough not to yell. Congratulations for being so strong. Now, will you keep feeling that terrible sense of fury and tell me about it?

Melanie breathed deeply. Willing herself to feel, fighting her every instinct, which told her to clam up, to make a joke, to do anything but feel. She plowed ahead.

"It felt like I'd been possessed by a demon. I felt a black fury in my chest. I wanted to find that woman and scream at her. I wanted to find some rich white gentrifier and tell him he was a selfish prick destroying my city. It felt terrible, and I felt out of control, which made me feel shame, and made me start judging myself, which made me feel just really shitty."

Julia looked at Melanie. Her face was screwed up, veins popping on her forehead, the energy of her emotions leaking out of every pore as her hands tightly gripped Julia's.

"Melanie, stay in the pain, but also make space for the peace you felt at the lake. Can you do that?"

"I can," Melanie said, feeling her happy glow clash with the darkness she felt inside of her.

"I want to affirm this in you, Melanie. You are loved. You love yourself. I love you. I see your immense value and innate brilliance. Can you feel it deeply, Melanie, the love, the safety you have with yourself?"

"I can," she said, slightly releasing her grip on Julia's hands, a gentle tear pooling on her right eye.

"Good, now we get to the fun part. I want you to stay in the pain, feeling every ounce of the anger and the hurt and the shame. Try to visualize your feelings as a track within your soul. You're at the beginning of the track, feeling the pain of this moment, but now let that track take you back in time, do this without thinking, just by sitting in your emotions."

"Okay, I'm doing it."

"You're doing so great. Now remember, feel but don't think as you follow that track, allowing it to take you wherever it wishes."

Julia stayed silent for several minutes, intently watching Melanie's face. Julia saw focus and concentration turn to the surprise of arrival.

"Melanie, where are you now?"

"I'm back at home. With my mom. I'm seven. I'd just come home from school so sad. I'd gotten in trouble because I got in a fight with a boy who called me stupid. They took away my recess! I told my mom and she told me I deserved it. She told me I needed to learn to shut up, that I couldn't afford to get in trouble if I was to succeed. Then she unplugged the TV!"

"How did that feel?"

"Oh my gosh, Julia, it felt so terrible. I'd been wronged! I wanted to be comforted, affirmed, but she got mad at me. I understand why: she'd had the same experiences, she was trying to prepare me to be a brown woman in a white world, she—"

"Melanie, stay out of your head, ignore the 'why's.' This is your experience. We can think about your mom's rationale later. So, how did little you feel when your mom failed to acknowledge your feelings?"

"Little me felt terrible, betrayed! I felt like shit. I felt so small, so worthless."

"OK, now sit in that feeling. The feeling of being made to feel worthless by your mom."

Behind Melanie's closed eyes tears began to flow. She'd felt so bad. She was voiceless. Unsupported. Not allowed to say or feel anything she was thinking. It felt like death! Like oppression at the hands of the one she loved the most. She remembered lying on her bed bawling, desperately wanting to be held, but sure her mom wasn't coming.

"Julia, it was so dumb! It was just a little thing, but I was crushed. I mean, I feel dumb now too! I have friends that have been raped and molested, harmed in so many ways. All I had to do was deal with a mean mom."

"It wasn't dumb, you needed love and you received punishment. And you're not dumb now. Your friends have had horrible experiences, but the extent of their pain doesn't minimize your own. Now Melanie, can you still feel the peace of the lake, a deep love for yourself?"

Melanie felt inside herself. She was surprised to find the feeling from the lake existing alongside the living mass of darkness that was her memory. She told Julia.

"Okay, great. I want adult you to sit with child you and give her a hug. Hold yourself, tell that child how valued it is, and show that child the love, the support and the words you didn't receive."

Melanie shook, her arms involuntarily around herself, a picture of little-her pasted behind closed eyes.

She felt the pain from the past, it was as alive now as it had been then. It sat in her chest, creating physical pressure. She felt the pressure, and through her embrace she entered it. Once inside her pain, she could see the child's hurt growing. It grew, it turned black, and as childhood turned to adulthood, the old pain became an ever-present wound she didn't even know she had.

Mel couldn't remember the exact words, the words she wished her mom had said, but she knew the feeling she wanted. "I love you. I love you. I love." She told the child version of herself that was still, somehow, alive in both her present and her past.

Then, slowly, she witnessed the wound dissolve in the light of the loving words she was repeating. The pressure in her chest subsided. She gasped for air. She didn't know she hadn't been able to breath, but now, sweet breath!

Tears poured, a salty rivulet of purification cascading past her nose and into her mouth. Her tears tasted of healing, they tasted of the joy found when free from the effects of a decades old wound. After ten minutes she opened her eyes.

"How are you feeling?"

"What just happened?!" Melanie's face was aflame with the delight of discovery. "I feel amazing!"

Julia radiated pleasure. Her eyes gleamed. She resisted the urge to start singing.

"That's the power of love, the power we each have to heal ourselves! Big progress doesn't always happen this fast, but you just released some of your trauma." Julia leaned over and gave Melanie a hug. "You've started the work of aligning with your true self."

CHAPTER 10

MOVING TO THE FARM

Melanie had supplemented the typical opener of electronic music throbbing while she danced with an introduction of "the AmAAAAAAZING footage" she was about to share. "Beep-Beep peeps, see if I'm exaggerating and set me straight if you've seen better content. But this is like digitized, physicalized cosmic LOVE, y'all!" From Mel's face, the Beep cut back to the retreat center.

"You'll soon feel the medicine," Julia said softly to a lean man named Michael whose haircut shaped his head into a nearly perfect square. "When you do, surrender to self and to the experience. Allow all thoughts to emerge, judging none of them. If you feel unsafe, remember your mantra and repeat it. Can you say it to me now?"

He sat cross-legged in front of her on the floor, the room's high ceilings arching behind him. A look of uncertainty flashed across his face, not as though he'd forgotten but as though, in a moment of emotional intimidation, he was rethinking everything about this. He breathed in deeply, lifting his shoulders. "I am love. I am loved. I am safe here with my family."

Julie offered him a kind smile. "Now will you repeat your intention back to me?"

Michael nodded, his hesitation having given way to inner strength. "I am overwhelmed by shame. Overcome by guilt. I have been since I left active service and moved home. I'm trapped in this cycle and I can't escape. I want to lead my family, love my wife and kids, and I try! But instead of leading, I yell and belittle, then I apologize. Then I do it again. I want these behaviors to stop, so today, I seek freedom."

Now the camera spun to slowly reveal six groups of two, forming a wide circle, all having versions of the same conversation as Julia and Michael. Men in jeans, Bass Pro shirts, and Carhart jackets unleashing their hearts to serene-faced facilitators, all of whom but Julia were veterans.

Then the music swelled to a quick-cutting montage of scenes. It was chaos!

Julia wrapping her arms around the bawling, convulsing Michael, soothing him.

A wiry veteran with a scar across his face spooning an obese man who couldn't stop repeating, "I love myself, I love myself."

A man dressed in camo with his legs crossed, smiling uncontrollably and laughing intermittently, a cross between a cockatoo and a howler monkey.

In the middle of the room, a crying man with a graying Elvis cut made snow angels on the wooden floor. His unblinking eyes locked on a vision only he could see.

Melanie's face reappeared on screen. "Then, at the end of the event, Julia sat with me and did an exercise. I don't understand what happened, but she helped me heal! It was like drugs, but unlike the vets, I didn't take ANY mushrooms. Somehow, I got high on processing my past!"

Across the screen, the bright green words flashed: "High on Healing!"

"Julia tells me that trauma is a prison with an escape hatch, treasure that can become our greatest power once healed. That if we're willing to go through our pain; freedom, joy, and love lie on the other side. I'm starting to get it. Peeps, what do you think?"

Across America, endorphin-driven eyes ate it up. Melanie's videos of the healing ceremony were breaking Beep-Beep.

• • •

Melanie paused, her heart racing, the fear real. Her followers had become her entire life. What had started as a whim, a fun way to dance while attacking those destroying the environment, had evolved. Beep-Beep peeps were the only thing that made her feel important. The lines had blurred; they were her source of income, and they were her family too.

"Fam," Melanie continued, her heart pounding in her ears, her eyes serious, her nose ring glinting beneath the bouncy tangle of her hair, "the videos of Mel P chaining myself to billionaires' yachts or defacing climate killers' art are done for now. I'm moving to Julia's farm. I'm moving to learn, and I'm going to take all of you on the ride with me. I believe Julia when she says that we too often become what we fight. I believe Jonathan when he says that to change the world, we must first change ourselves. I might be wrong. But I don't think so."

The urge was overwhelming. She tried to hide them, to stop them, but it was no use. The tears dripped down her face.

She was bawling. Live on Beep-Beep. Her too-cool, tough-girl image melting down her face.

"Guys!" she said, wiping her face. "Y'all have probably never seen me cry. I mean, shit, I've hardly ever seen myself cry. But this is me, twice this week now."

She looked at the camera, propped against a book on the table in front of her, and finished. "I hope you'll come along on this new journey with me."

As she stopped the video, she looked around her empty apartment. Who knew how her followers would react? But she'd already paid a price—just an hour earlier, Jennifer had looked her in the eye, sighed, and shook her head. "Mel, you're nuts. There's no way I'm moving to that farm with you. Good luck."

• • •

In Los Angeles, Lillie Rift, the pop-star master of America's tweens and twenty-somethings, smiled through her tears. She clicked the heart icon, and then she shared the video with her three hundred million followers.

• • •

Governor O'Leary hoped the fact that Bradley was gawking slack-jawed at his screen meant good news for her.

"Governor, you won't believe this."

"What's that?"

"That dancing Beep-Beep girl we love so much, Mel P, the one that pulls all those crazy environmentalist stunts? She's moving to a farm to live with some old lady that's really into God."

Governor O'Leary's eyes narrowed. "God?"

"Yeah. God." Bradley shook his head. "What a waste."

CHAPTER 11

INNOCENT, BEEP-BEEPING YOUTH

Julia stroked Gaia, the cat on her lap, the wafting scent of her lavender tea providing a pleasant olfactory backdrop. Her feet ached slightly, the result of a long morning hike she'd shared with Melanie, who sat beside her on the faded blue living room couch while they watched their most recent Beep on Melanie's phone.

A dragonfly darted around Julia's head as on the screen, she said, "Melanie, the journey toward a healthy, whole self and away from the pain of our pasts starts with the simple act of beginning to walk the healing path. The more we heal, the closer we come to knowing self, and the closer we come to knowing self, the more we're able to authentically live, no longer controlled by the pain, anxiety and expectations that life places upon us."

"I guess," Melanie said, glancing at the camera as she spoke, "this should be obvious, but for those of us who are wondering, what exactly are we healing from?"

"Life!" Julia said with a grin, before turning serious. "When a need is unmet as a child, when we internalize outside expectations, when we're exposed to pain, heartbreak, poverty, or catastrophe—we react, taking the steps necessary to ensure we survive. But Melanie, the subconscious decisions we make as six-year-olds to deal with the fact that our parents sometimes yell at us serve our six-year-old self, but do they serve us as adults? By healing our emotional wounds, we free ourselves from coping mechanisms that served us in the past but no longer serve us now."

"So you're saying we're like computers? We have old code that is bugging up the system, and we all gotta figure out how to re-code ourselves?"

"Well," Julia sighed, more amused than exasperated, was there no way to escape computers or computer analogies? "That's certainly one way of putting it."

The clip ended with flashing letters across the screen: "My Peeps, let's recode ourselves!"

Julia, increasingly used to the Beep-Beep theatrics, sipped her tea and then turned to look at Melanie, who was curled up on the other end of the couch. "So how did people respond?"

Melanie smiled broadly. "Not so good as when veterans cry, and not quite as good as when you asked the sky for butterflies and ten landed on your arm, but we got over a million views!"

Soon other influencers caught on to the fact that Melanie had caught sweet-old-lady-lightning in a Beep-Beep bottle. No longer was it just Melanie sitting on Julia's couch.

Mohawked influencers from L.A. joined leather-clad curators from New York in the pilgrimage to Julia's farm. Their videos begot videos and the content created more content.

In another video, Julia sat in front of a row of blackberry brambles heavy with red, not yet ripened fruit facing Melanie and @Alicia_Jets_In_Style, a blonde travel influencer from Miami who specialized in luxury safaris and wore jungle feathers in her hair.

"Melanie and Alicia-Jets," she began, "are your cameras on. Yes? OK, good. I want to share two lessons that have shaped my life." She took a breath. These were the teachings that upset the most people. They removed excuses, even valid excuses. Especially valid excuses. "The first thing we all must know is that everything we need, including all the love we crave, is already inside of us. The second is that we are in control. This doesn't mean we can automatically meet our own need for love, and it doesn't mean we control life's events, but it does mean we can control how we respond to life and ourselves."

"That sounds nice," Melanie said, "but give us more detail. How do we generate love and control our lives?"

"Well," Julia paused with furrowed brow and a broad smile. "I could tell you the answer is to know self, to know God, to know the quiet voice within that *is* both self and God, and to learn to live in love at all times. But I'll try to be more practical ..."

Looking into the camera, trying to imagine the faces of her audience, aware that words spoken were a poor substitute for daily work done over years, she narrowed a life and a world's worth of practical wisdom into a few sentences.

"Melanie, we are the beloved. There is nothing you need to do and no one you need to be, to be worthy of God's unconditional love. If you come to believe this, it will change your life." As Julia spoke, she felt what she was saying, her heart filled to bursting, and her eyes got misty. Millions of young eyes stared back at the screen, wondering if what she said could be true, their eyes misting too. "And if you spend the time to find the core of yourself sitting beneath all the stories and beliefs society has gifted you, you will discover that everything you need is already within, and everything external you think you need from a lover or a boss or a child or your friends, is the distracting voice of a world that wishes to diminish your innate value."

Melanie and @Alicia_Jets_In_Style sniffled simultaneously, the warm kernel of love catching fire within.

"The second lesson is that no one will rescue us. Either we choose to take control of our emotional and spiritual existence; we figure out how to heal, to find the unconditional love that lives within us all, and to take responsibility for all our actions and beliefs; or we live at the mercy of life circumstances we didn't choose. There is nothing more unfair, and nothing truer about life."

Days later, Julia responded directly to one of the thousands of messages Melanie received. "Where does my wisdom come from? That's just a lovely question @purpleprancer837, thank you for asking."

Julia closed her eyes and breathed deeply, tracing a lifetime of books, prayers and travels across the topography of her mind and soul. "My wisdom, if that is what you wish to call it, comes from the unity of truth found across spiritual traditions. Whether we're talking Buddhists or Hindus, Muslims or Jews,

Catholics or Protestants, Toltecs or Ayahuasceros, psychologists or therapists, this truth and this wisdom is not found through religious or academic dogma and doctrine—which reflect man's desire to explain the unexplainable—but at the heart of spiritual and emotional experience, which reflects God's mysterious and magnificent presence within each of us. These are the paths I've followed, and this is the source of my knowing."

In bedrooms and on playgrounds, at work and at the bar, what had been a hundred thousand views became a million, and then ten million. Rumi, Hafiz, Richard Rohr, Mirabai Starr, and the Bhagavad Gita began to trend on Beep-Beep. Young readers discovered old authors Anne Lamott and Starhawk. Bewildered algorithms adjusted to a new advertising reality.

The likes stacked up and the messages flowed. Melanie hired three outsourced assistants just to track comments and routinely asked questions. Out of all the comments and questions and stories and testimonials, one question came up more than the rest: "What is the single core truth that can unite us all?"

When Melanie relayed this question, Julia didn't hesitate. "Beep-Beep fam—if you don't mind me saying that—we are all one. One with ourselves, one with each other, one with the earth, one with God. If we live and we act from this single point of knowledge, we cannot help but live from a place of love and compassion."

"But what does that mean?" Melanie asked as @Alicia_Jets and several other influencers filmed next to her.

Julia thought of a favorite ritual. A heartbreaking, life-affirming act she practiced whenever another's broken body and her living spirit presented the opportunity.

"Can we go for a ride?" A moment later they were all in Julia's Prius.

"A neighbor called me earlier," Julia said as she drove down the single-lane country road, glancing at the array of cameras influencers aimed at her, "and alerted me to something I want to show you all."

A few minutes later, where the road cut through a meadow, they pulled over beside a roadkill coyote nestled amidst the tall roadside grass. While the influencers filmed, Julia gathered branches and wildflowers. She gently carried the dead coyote farther from the side of the road and began to work.

Through her lens, Melanie observed the coyote lying in the green grass surrounded by fir boughs. It looked alive, its gray and brown fur gleaming with dew. A garland of wild blue and orange flowers ringed its head. Small white flowers were sprinkled on its abdomen and the fir boughs. When she'd finished honoring the animal, Julia sunk to her knees and wept, evergreen colored Central Washington hillsides rising in the background.

"Julia, what is this?"

"This," Julia said, her wet eyes shining while staring at the gawking cameras, "is the opposite of separation. All people are part of the natural world, but our lives leave us disconnected from natural rhythms. We poison the earth to grow food and manufacture products, we kill animals without a thought, and we have an endless number of reasons to justify any war we wish to fight.

"We accept it all." Julia's eyes glazed with tears that turned the coyote into a blur of color. "We accept this reality like we have no other option because we have all surrendered to the world as it is."

Melanie zoomed in on the coyote. In death, surrounded by flowers and embraced by the meadow, it was dignified, beautiful.

"I'm showing you this noble creature," Julia continued, "to illustrate that when we heal and align with ourselves, we can also renew our connection to all life. You want to solve environmental crises? You want to build a world where we treat other people with compassion and respect? Heal your emotional wounds and grow in alignment with self, work to facilitate the same in your community, experience and come to know God or source or Earth Mother or whatever you wish to call it, and then watch as all our beliefs and actions begin to change."

• • •

"Why," Heather Haliburton asked with her polished and professional scowl, "do half-baked truths borrowed from gurus' seminars and life coaches' Fastagram feeds suddenly leap from the anonymity of a naïve cultural niche to become a popular tidal wave that has turned an aged author into a Beep-Beep phenomenon?"

"How," Jed Abernathy asked during a ROX News segment called The Dumb Getting Dumber, "can we protect the innocent, Beep-Beeping youth

of this nation from those who seek to prey upon their vulnerability by leading them away from our nation's fundamental Christian values with their
dangerous, heretical ideas?"

CHAPTER 12

TWO BILLION DOLLARS

Jacqueline O'Leary, Bradley Bishkoff mused to himself, overcame her fear of failure by addictively pursuing—and achieving—ever larger goals, therefore proving to herself that she *had* overcome her fear of failure and therefore had nothing to fear. This was a useful character flaw in a politician, especially when she and the campaign needed to raise two billion dollars to do battle with Menendez.

Bradley, on the other hand, was completely unafraid of failure; the worst rejection life can offer—rejection by one's parents—stuck with him for worse and, occasionally, for better. The prospect of raising such a large sum of money under the crippling pressure of the national spotlight made him feel no more nervous than he had last month when picking out new wrinkle-free dress shirts. His previous brand had failed the suitcase test.

Raising two billion dollars would give him and O'Leary the best chance of winning the election, but there was more to it than that.

If they lost after raising two billion dollars, there was no way anyone could blame them. "Look at the prevailing political winds," Bradley would say. "Victory was impossible despite the fact we ran the best-funded campaign in US history."

Most importantly, raising and spending two billion dollars would guarantee his post-campaign payday would measure in many, many millions.

Everyone would want to associate with the man that orchestrated the two-billion-dollar campaign.

All he had to do was keep the governor from politically imploding in the face of Menendez's blustering broadsides, use his Big Tech billionaire contacts to raise the money, and ensure he had enough gentlemen's agreements in place with lobbyists, donors, and PACs to flood him with contracts after election day.

Piece of cake, he thought, glancing at his shirt. Not a wrinkle on it.

Bradley was huddled with O'Leary at her husband's estate in northern Wisconsin, where they awaited the arrival of the campaign's finance chairs. The deck offered such a clear view of the property's lake that Bradley could make out pine needles in the forest trees' reflection on the smooth surface of the water.

"Listen, Governor," he said, "tonight we build the financial foundation for the campaign. Half of our finance chairs supported other candidates in the primaries. In the primaries, we had to cast a vision that donors bought into. Now, tactics shift."

She side-eyed him. "Shift how?"

"These folks only have one option: you. So let's not get ideological on them. We're a blank slate for them to cast their ambitions and their ideals upon. So we say nothing that might dissuade them from supporting us. The only thing they need to hear is that Menendez is a tool of Big Oil—"

"Which he is."

"That Menendez is a tool of fascists—"

"Obviously."

"And that Menendez is a tool of that hatemonger Pastor Josiah McMillan."

"Jesus, Bradley! That's plain as day. Do you have anything to tell me I don't already know?"

Bradley controlled his annoyance. He wanted to remind her that his prep got her through the debates and his fundraisers funded her commercials. But that would be petty. He surrendered.

"That's it, Governor. Just don't forget, it's easier for people to be against things than for things. So, let's make sure these walking, talking checkbooks know being against Menendez means being for us, OK?"

Several hours later, the governor was holding court with drunk, belly-laughing donors while Bradley was deep in conversation with Troojle's CEO, Ben Blankenship.

"Bradley," Ben was saying, "what you can't do is get distracted by the shrill nutcases. Some of the shit Republicans always say is correct. The poor will always be among us. So will war and climate catastrophe. I promise, if you spend too much time focusing on all the things we can't control, it will hurt you. The world is as it is. What's important is that companies like mine continue to stabilize global information and digital commerce while people like you and Governor O'Leary sit in elected office, ensuring the foundational elements of modern capitalism are safe. So as long as these core tenants of modern prosperity remain in place, we can keep doing the work to create a more equitable world."

Bradley nodded hard, signaling agreement while wondering if Blankenship actually believed a word he was saying.

On the other side of the room, Governor O'Leary was getting rhetorically reamed by Rain Reynolds. The fourth wealthiest woman in America, Rain was the only child of September Reynolds, who had become the hippie trophy wife of the founder of the world's largest microchip producer during his late-life identity crisis. "Jacqueline, I know what all your sell-out political consultants are telling you. It's probably the same thing your instincts are saying. You *have* to ignore them."

Rain leaned in closer, the pink pepper, cardamom, and grapefruit top notes of her Parisian parfum overtaking the leather perfume that had set the governor back a grand. Rain, she figured, must have spent quadruple that. O'Leary tried to step back subtly.

"I'm not going to pour a hundred million into this race just to see you appease middle America. No issue matters except climate. Forget people, forget communities, forget anti-racist justice or whatever the fuck. We have to stop shitting carbon into the air and start removing it. We have to save the oceans and rainforests. Otherwise, there will *be* no people and no communities. Understand?!"

"Absolutely. I see your point. I assure you, Menendez and his buddies consider carbon an aphrodisiac."

"Excuse me, Governor, it's an urgent matter." Bradley to the rescue. He could pinpoint every aggressive single-issue voter in the room, and none held a candle to Rain Reynolds. He steered the governor away by her elbow.

"How'd *that* go?"

Governor O'Leary smiled. "I asked her what she thought. I nodded. I said I thought Menendez considers carbon an aphrodisiac."

Bradley inhaled the pleasure of a perfect political response.

"Just think," he said. "We get a check the size she'll cut to save the whales and we get right to work building the largest field operation this country has ever seen. A world-class data operation. I guarantee you, we're leaving here with the fortune it's going to take to integrate all of Troojle's data into our voter files."

"Then it's worth choking on her hippie highness's perfume."

"And we'll be able to match Menendez's ad buys dollar for dollar." Bradley's eyes gleamed at the thought.

"Speaking of ad buys," O'Leary said, "today I got separate calls from my former chief of staff, my cousin, and Senator Campbell's son asking how many millions worth of contracts their advertising firms should expect from the campaign. I told them our budget would be over a billion and we'd make sure they did alright. You're taking care of onboarding them, right?"

Bradley scowled. He wanted to use the advertising firms owned by his former boss, his old roommate, and Senator Cunningham's wife. But then again, with a billion-plus budget, he could share the wealth with his preferred consultants and O'Leary's contacts.

"Of course, I'll take care of them. This is why we hired a ten-person team to manage our media consultants! We're perfectly situated for— What? What's wrong?" He could read her expressions from a mile away, and right now he was standing close enough to smell the remnants of Rain's perfume.

"I just realized none of my Big Ag donors came. I mean, I'm midwestern. Should I be concerned?"

"Of course not," Bradley said, giving her a reassuring stare. "They'll write checks, but I won't let them show up in person. That would be terrible optics."

CHAPTER 13

PRAYER BREAKFAST

W hy," Menendez roared, his hair a vulture's nest, "in the unholy name of goddamn whiskey is this event starting so early in the morning?"

Luke winced at his boss's misuse of the Lord's name—and his red-rimmed glare.

Luke hated having to put up with CINOs—Christians in name only—but if the price of power was dealing with Menendez's unapologetic unbelief, that was a small price to pay to be God's man in the camp of the candidate who would soon be president.

"Well, Senator, the way I see it, God created whiskey and God created the church. So, there's no reason they can't go hand in glove for you today. Why don't you gulp down that coffee and then we'll go wow Pastor McMillan and the Salvation Summit?"

• • •

Pastor Josiah McMillan read the text from Luke.

> *The Senator is running late. A call with his national security advisor ran long. We'll be there soon.*

The pastor rolled his eyes. Every time a hung-over politician was running late for a morning meeting, it was national security concern this and strategy session that.

Goodness, he thought, *this would have been so much easier if Glockenspiel or even Bush IV were the nominee.* They had been marching to his drumbeat for years. They were trained.

They had been part of his Salvation Megachurch Network since he'd burst onto the national scene, arriving in Northern Virginia as the golden boy from rural Kentucky. He had taken the baton from the televangelists of old, bringing God's word to the thirsty masses through his Salvation Streaming Platform. If Obama was the first digital president and Trump was the first social media president, he was the first digital platform preacher—videogenic, Bee-Beep-literate, and congregation-response-marketing savvy.

He leveraged his network and streaming platform into regular appearances on ROX News. By the age of thirty-five, he had become the most sought-after pastor in Republican politics. Now forty-five, he intended to leverage his power to steer America's march toward the promised land.

When a new Republican decided to run for office, the first thing many of them did was join the Salvation Megachurch Network. The pastor cashed their checks to Salvation PAC, led bible studies in the Capitol, and distributed his tailored talking points to every member of Congress.

A notable exception had been that wayward oaf Menendez. In his first six years as a senator, Menendez had never set foot in Salvation Megachurch. He'd hadn't so much as asked the pastor to come by his office and pray for him!

At least not until he decided to run for president.

Even then, Menendez hadn't become a regular at church or bible study. No, he had invited the pastor out to his ranch in Chama Valley, New Mexico, for a weekend of hunting, drinking, and, as the remote third activity, prayer.

Pastor McMillan had accepted the invitation because as powerful as he was, he knew there was no guarantee his chosen Republican candidate would prevail in the primary. If that sad eventuality did come to pass, he knew Menendez could be the guy. And he needed to have him on the hook.

So he went to the Senator's ranch and left only after securing a senior campaign position for his eager young protégé, Luke.

It was a great move because the worst *had* happened, but the pastor's wisdom and patience paid off. Luke was running Menendez's campaign and the pastor, based on Luke's reports, felt he had the senator dancing to his tune.

He laughed to himself. A 7 a.m. prayer breakfast! Of course that high-functioning alcoholic was going to be late.

The prayer breakfast was over by the time Menendez finally arrived. A few last pastors lingered in the dining hall, hoping for face time with the great Josiah McMillan, but most had already left to secure a good seat at the upcoming Salvation Voters Plenary session.

"What the hell, Luke?" Menendez looked around the gutted dining hall. "I didn't drag myself out of bed to be stood up by your pastor friend for an audience of congealed syrup and pasty pancakes."

Makeup is a miracle, Luke thought. The bags under Menendez's eyes had disappeared under lightly applied face paint, leaving the senator looking normal ... more or less.

"Senator," Luke replied, "we're ninety minutes late. You're just going to have to get your face time when you take the stage for the Q&A."

"No trick questions, right? Just what we reviewed yesterday?"

"Verbatim. Want another practice round?"

"Hell no. I just don't want to get caught off guard by some theological bullshit or an inane question about signing an anti-sodomy law. I can't have the pastor forgetting I have to win an election that includes every voter in this great nation, not just your happy-clappy congregation members."

Luke grabbed his boss's arm and leaned in close. "Senator, this crowd thinks in terms of eternity. They won't turn on you if you piss them off now, because they need you, but their memory is long. If you piss on them, they'll find a way to piss on you later. Dance to their tune, and then we can get out of here."

Menendez sighed. Luke was right. But damnit, he couldn't stand the self-righteous superiority. And in this crowd, he couldn't help feeling like every man he spoke with was judging him and his immigrant-and-Catholic-sounding last name.

But it was no use fighting forces that were beyond his control. "Ok, Luke. Let's do this. We spend ten minutes shaking hands and then make our way to the plenary session?"

Ten minutes later, having told seven different groups of pastors that he prayed he'd someday get to visit their congregation, Senator Menendez took the stage in an opulent, convention center-sized sanctuary that held forty thousand true believers.

Pastor Josiah finished his introduction: "Now, please welcome a true champion of God's word, and the next president of these United States, Senator Daniel Menendez." The senator bounded on stage with surprising grace for a large man with a hangover. The adrenaline rush of being on the stump transformed him; he was sharp, oozing charisma, ready to perform.

He waved to the clapping crowd, flashing his patented smile, and took a perfectly angled seat with a view of the pastor and the audience. "Pastor Josiah, it is such an honor to be here today," he gushed. "I can feel the holy spirit moving through this room, and I can feel the power of God emanating from your person. I am truly humbled. I have been looking forward to our conversation all week."

CHAPTER 14

INDISTINGUISHABLE

Tight old-skool B-girl moves from the '90s and those classic '80s pop routines. That had been Mel P's jam.

She'd also cribbed hand moves from Kathakali dance. Those Indians, man, they were good. She'd borrowed the eye-dancing moves too. Everyone went nuts for that! She'd had to close her DMs when every Desi boy in the world started coming on to her. And non-Desi boys too. Those DMs were a portal into a dark world, into the minds of men who thought no one was watching.

The political stunts had faded as well. It had been a month since she'd trapped a salmon fisherman in a net or shut a car business down for a week with one of her patented scream-ins. When she'd combined the dances with in-their-face activist assaults, she had been unstoppable. But that was all before Julia and Jonathan. Their beeps didn't need moves or stunts.

The lady was seventy-two years old and killing it just by being her.

Julia's videos about emotional mastery and spiritual awakening turned into memes of Julia soaring like Superman, sitting in space shuttles, and raising the hilltop flag at Iwo Jima.

Melanie wasn't the only one amazed. The fact was, as one columnist wrote, Julia's content was more popular than cats. Soccer moms shared videos of emotional healings instead of recipes. Snarky political content was partially replaced by optimistic yearnings for a world in which people respected one another and understood the psycho-emotional roots of their least attractive behaviors.

Jonathan fared almost as well. If there was anything Melanie had learned, it was that Jonathan's veterans and her Beep-Beepers had more in common than she ever could have imagined. She started pulling double duty, working with Julia on the farm in the morning and then traveling with Jonathan in the afternoons and evenings.

Some days he talked about all he'd learned while working with veterans who weren't yet on the healing path. Other days he carried stacks of Julia's books to his increasingly frequent meetings with veteran groups all over the Pacific Northwest.

It was almost always the same. Jonathan would tell his story, men and women would ask questions, Jonathan would guide a group mediation and direct the conversation towards feelings until finally someone would stand up and break down. "I thought I had to live in silence. That my burden was unique to me and mine alone to bear. But I've learned," and here they would start crying, "that there is a way out of this. That I can heal. That I can be the man I want to be and my family needs me to be."

The more Melanie watched this happen, the more she realized that she and these men were the same. They were wounded creatures, suffering in their own ways.

Since her first breakthrough with Julia, she'd had dozens more. She'd learned that she was worthy of unconditional love and she'd accepted that she was a complete mess with a lifetimes worth of life to heal, update and reprogram. She'd even had Julia start hosting live sessions on Beep-Beep, where people began to acknowledge their pain and heal a small piece of themselves.

Melanie's followers, the anxious victims of the world, were learning to take control. Just like the veterans. Their pain was different. Their politics clashed. But in their hearts, they were indistinguishable; they were humans trying to make their way in a very hard world.

. . .

Julia hardly knew what it meant when Melanie told her she'd become a "viral sensation." Her typewriter didn't have a wireless signal. She used the computer at the public library to check her email twice a week and conduct research, but she never watched social media. Sure, she made a lot of videos with Melanie that apparently got great responses, but the digital enthusiasm didn't translate.

The only big difference in her life involved teenagers at the local Market Fresh Grocer. The checkout girls who once had barely responded to her hellos now squealed when she put her produce and bags of buckwheat flour on the counter. The kids who loitered outside with their vapes and skateboards asked if she would teach them to free themselves from themselves by helping them to meet themselves. Some of them even started coming out to her farm, learning about fungal networks and emotional coding.

With each interaction and each visit to her farm, she found a new hope growing inside of her. A hope born of seedlings planted in the previous decades finding germination in the unlikely soil of a brash Beep-Beeper's followers. The hope warmed her. It made her forget the misgivings she'd had about her book. It gave extra meaning to a life that was, she thought, already overflowing with meaning and satisfaction. She still worked with veterans, but her work with Melanie and all those internet kids was having an effect.

Yet slowly, over time, the idyllic ignorance of America's favorite unknowing influencer began to fade in the face of her book's undeniable success. By early July *Love and Compassion: A Call for Political and Spiritual Revival* had surged onto the NYTimes best sellers list. Her agent, Doris Lederman, called with an offer. "This is an opportunity that simply cannot be missed. Your VP of marketing, Alegra Torro, wants to send you out on a national book tour. I know you haven't been in the business of leaving your garden, but will you go?"

"Oh! Of course, I'm thrilled, a book tour is the obvious next step," Julia said, while sitting with her fingers softly resting on her typewriter's aged keys, fantasizing about all the teenagers that might show up to meet her. Then she thought of her most trusted friend. "I'm in so long as Jonathan comes with me."

"Absolutely, on our dime. He's become quite the phenomenon himself. And why not invite Melanie too?"

"You know about Melanie?"

"Julia! Everyone in the Western Hemisphere knows about you and Mel P."

"Really?"

"You have the number-one nonfiction book in the country and your name is trending on Flitter and Beep-Beep daily! Why do you think we are rushing to plan the tour?"

"Right," Julia said, feeling naïve. "Yes, I'll ask, Melanie. And can we call it the Love Heals Book Tour?"

"I love it, love it, love it. We are going to pull out all the stops. Any particular cities you really want to visit?"

Julia mentally cataloged the places that had always made her so welcome. "Well, I can't not go to Boston and Asheville and Santa Fe and Sedona. The rest, well, you're the expert and you know what is selling where."

Melanie revived her dance moves for a few minutes when Julia told her the news. "This is amazing! You have no idea what we can make happen once we get out there. I think we can start putting your people, Jonathan's people, and my people in the same room. It could be just what America needs!"

CHAPTER 15

THE LOVE HEALS MOVEMENT

The first book tour stop was set for St. Andrew's United Methodist Church in Boston, Massachusetts.

Sitting in the back of the church in a small room, light filtering through the closed drapes as humid summer air filled her lungs, Julia had difficulty focusing. Whatever Melanie and Jonathan were doing was working, but she didn't understand what it all meant for her.

In Julia's mind, she was what she had always been—the young girl who loved the sense of awe and peace she felt sitting in church; the earnest teen who loved poetry and nature; the angry college student who had opposed the Vietnam war with every ounce of her energy; the distraught and disillusioned twenty-something who'd watched her ideals and her faith turn to dust as cars and gasoline had proven more important than human or environmental health; the seeking thirty-something who had traveled, witnessing daily miracles—sunrises, births, toddlers waddling and dawdling on the playground—and studied under elderly nuns in Spain; young, saffron-robed monks in Dham; and wizened medicine-men in Peru.

And finally, the woman who'd learned to harness God's love and sought to communicate that love to others in every act of her life, a woman who had opted out of the "real world," choosing to live where she was most at home—on her farm, communing with her neighbors and the bees and the spirit of the land.

Yet here she was, sitting in a small church about to speak on love and politics to a crowd spilling into the aisles, sitting and standing in every available space.

That night, to the few hundred attendees at St. Andrews United Methodist Church, Julia said, "We launched the Love Heals movement when a twenty-four-year-old Beep-Beeper challenged me to think bigger. The truth is people in this country are in pain—we're suffering and we live in fear. We sense something is wrong, that our lives and the lives of those we love are out of sync with the natural world and with our true selves, yet most of us feel we have no recourse except to survive in the world as it exists."

From the attendees' phones, Beep-Beeps, Flitters, Fastagrams and texts shot around the nation as Julia's unlikely fame grew on the wings of Melanie's digital mastery and their fan's grassroots efforts.

To five hundred attendees in Washington, DC, Julia continued her speech.

"What are the features of the world as it exists? A political system that is built to destroy the enemy while encouraging us to identify the enemy as each other. Collective values that celebrate resource hoarding by the wealthiest, best-connected, and most ambitious citizens while turning a blind eye to our neighbors' suffering and the earth's destruction. Unbelievable levels of corruption by leaders who've been empowered by our laws to treat public service like a business. So yes, of course people live in fear of the damage our political and economic systems can do to them. And the symptoms? Well, we see the symptoms of anxiety and fear and depression and unhealth in so many of our lives."

Americans on the political right and left nodded to their screens, certain Julia saw the world just as they did.

After she had spoken to over two thousand attendees crammed into a small high school gym in St. Louis, Missouri, Julia's popularity began to cause problems. Books signings—the fundamental point of any author tour—had grown chaotic and unwieldy. With her previous books, Julia had loved these quick, joyful bonding sessions. She would listen with her eyes and ears, then sign her name. And in that brief moment, she would connect with a stranger—turning an unknown into a known. Now though, it was impossible to sign every book. She lacked the time and her hands lacked the strength.

At her event in Denver nine days later, the Spiritualism Book Center and Yoga Studio shifted her reading to Cheesman Park because the venue was too small to accommodate the thousands who had RSVP'd.

"This is more a rally than a signing," Melanie commented to Jonathan.

"I know. But I'm wondering if Julia knows."

"She must! People are showing up with signs! 'We Can Heal!'"

"I saw a Julia for President sign."

"No? Really? And you didn't take a picture? I need that photo!"

The rapt Denver audience hung on to her words, absorbing her message in the waning light of a gorgeous August afternoon.

"There are ways to fix our angry and broken nation, but to fix our politics, to hold abusive systems accountable, we first must heal people and communities. To heal, we must focus on the world's most powerful force. The force that sits at the center of every major faith and spiritual tradition. The force that electrifies the promise found in knowing God and self. Yes, I'm speaking of *love*, and I am also speaking of love's companion, compassion. So how can we bring love and compassion into our political calculus?

"The answer is two-fold. First, the people of this country must choose to heal and to grow, to take control. Until we as individuals are committed to healing ourselves, we cannot look upon our fellow citizens with the compassion and the grace necessary to find common ground in a world determined to separate us."

Even though Julia was breaking rule number-one of American politics—always tell citizens their problems can be blamed on someone else—the people kept coming. Two weeks after Denver, five thousand people listened to Julia speak at Seattle's Washington Park.

"And yet, those of us who see that a new reality is necessary must demand that we begin to fix political and economic systems designed to prey upon us all!" Julia told her flannel and light-layers-wearing crowd. "Is it any wonder people in this country are lashing out when we are overwhelmingly saddled with debt, unable to earn a living that ensures access to healthcare, education, and retirement? Are we shocked people are overcome by fear and anxiety when we're not taught the emotional skills to understand ourselves or others? In such a world, how can our politics be anything but broken?"

Sitting together in a friend's home on a warm September evening the night before the last scheduled stop of the book tour, Julia's face softened under Melanie and Jonathan's intent stares and intensely ambitious ideas.

"I feel the world bending," Jonathan said as Melanie nodded beside him.

His words echoed in her mind.

She could feel herself bending.

Bending towards the feeling of power yielded on behalf of a just cause. It was an amazing, empowering feeling. The high and joy of healing and being healed all at once. It was unlike any feeling any of them had known. It filled them with purpose. It filled them with hope.

Julia looked up and nodded. "OK, you're right. We have to keep going. Tomorrow night I'll make the ask."

At the Hollywood Bowl in LA, Julia ended her speech the way she had twenty-one times before. This time, though, she wasn't just inspiring; she was asking for action.

"My friends, now I need your help. In just three days, I am taking the stage in Sedona, Arizona, for a special event. I have invited Senator Menendez and Governor O'Leary to the event to sign the Love in Politics Pledge. What is love, what is compassion, when applied to our lives? I will tell you, it is *connection*. The Love in Politics Pledge commits them to applying my Love, Compassion and Connection Rubric to every piece of legislation and executive order they sign by publicly explaining how that law or regulation will balance the well-being of individual people, communities, and the environment." Julia stopped, her eyes imploring her audience. "If O'Leary and Menendez are to show up at the event, if they are to sign the pledge, if they are to commit to making love a governing principle, they will do so only because people like you demand that our political parties prioritize healing over division by choosing love over fear!"

News of the Love in Politics Pledge spread like wildfire as videos and memes Flitted, Fastagramed, and Beep-Beeped their way across the digital commons. But this time, there was new gasoline for the flames: Julia made the ten o'clock news.

CHAPTER 16

BUTTER OF THE TREES

hat fucking white-haired mouse of a woman. That goddamned beekeeping grandma.

The news had been delivered via one of those stupid Beep-Beep videos only an hour before: Julia Connor had invited her and Senator Menendez to a rally to sign that *pledge* in just three days.

As the Boeing 737 lifted off the tarmac at Chicago O'Hare, Governor O'Leary silently scowled. It was one thing for a donor or a company or another politician to strongarm her. That was just life. But a God-loving gardener with a couple generic peace-love-and-happiness books published? Didn't Julia know that she did not fucking matter? Didn't she know they had a schedule to keep? Did she not realize how much stress a governor running for president was under when a campaign kicked into high gear?

How was O'Leary supposed to keep the feuding elements of her party at bay when she also had to cater to the whims of a naïve shroomhead who seemed to think yoga and nirvana were a constitutional right?

"Did you know the French used to call avocados 'butter of the trees?'"

Across the walnut table, Bradley was surrounded by his laptop and stacks of printed spreadsheets, a small plate with a slice of avocado toast sitting in front of him. Noting O'Leary's scowl, and understanding the fury driven loops her mind created, he was trying to lighten the mood.

"What?" O'Leary snapped, shifting her look of disgust from nowhere in particular to him.

"Yeah. You know how the French love fat and adjectives. Back before the miracle of supply chains, they called this mysterious tropical fruit 'tree butter.' And you know the funny thing?"

O'Leary's expression indicated she would not find *anything* funny about avocados.

"Now, a few hundred years later, brunch quaffing millennials and yours truly have made that name a reality, spreading avocado on any and every toastable bread."

Her face had to unfreeze from its rictus of disbelief. "Christ, Bradley, we're tied in the polls with a Mexican-American Mussolini while a beekeeper holds a political gun to our head, and you're talking about avocados?!"

Bradley smiled. "Relaaaaax. That's not a gun Julia is holding. It's a hug. So we take her hug and give it right back to her."

"You mean we sign her pledge?"

"You think we shouldn't?"

The governor paused, her analytical gears beginning to churn. "I don't *want* to. It sets a terrible precedent."

Bradley stayed silent.

"But"—she leaned back a little, keeping her spine straight—"we kind of have to sign it, don't we?"

"You're exactly right, Governor. If we don't and Menendez does, we're compassionless hacks who hate love and God."

"If we do sign it and he doesn't, he probably calls us pussy liberals." Now her spine went limp. It felt good: the firm-soft buttery airplane-couch leather accepting her posture of defeat.

"But in doing so," Bradley picked up the sheets of polling data and waved them in front of her face, "he'd risk alienating the 27.3 percent of likely voters that view her more favorably than either him or you."

"So we get all up in her patchouli-scented ass?"

Bradley, who liked having his nose in patchouli-scented asses, nodded. "And we win over that 27.3 percent of the voting population that buys her love-as-the-solution snake oil."

The leathery chair made a faint unsticking sound as O'Leary leaned forward. "You know, outside of the whole God thing, I have so much in common with her. She's an environmentalist, I'm sure she wants to rein in Wall Street, and I haven't heard a single Big Tech person say anything bad about her. I mean, she's a social media phenomenon. Maybe she will actually support our Data Rights Are Human Rights Act."

Bradley's eyes lit up. He leaned forward in the spirit of conspiratorial juiciness that defined his lunches with Heather, ready to give O'Leary credit for his idea. "I hadn't thought of that! Who better to convince the American people that Big Tech's right to their data is a human right than a Beep-Beep phenomenon?"

Moments later, he heard his friend's "hello" through his secure satellite connection. "Listen Heather," he said, "we're going to sign Julia Connor's pledge. We're—"

"*Go for it.*" Heather was walking through the halls of Congress, or maybe a subway station; Bradley guessed as much from the echo in her voice. "And then, why don't you sign a pledge from some crazy African witch doctor or an anti-vaxx survivalist canning vegetables in Idaho? Either way, none of those will help you win—but maybe you'll get to pick your absolute *faves* from the organic cucumber harvest, or have an evil spirit cleared by some potion-peddling Congolese healer."

"You sound like you're revving up to a marathon." Bradley listened to the sound of her heels on a marble floor. "Why can't you walk at a normal human pace?" Bradley rolled his eyes. "And, look, a lot of our bleeding-heart voters are obsessed with her. So, we're going to make her ideas our own."

The clacking of Heather's heels stopped, Bradley heard a male voice. "When can I be a guest on NATN? Did you see my floor speech yesterday? My take on Menendez's racist self-loathing is hot."

"Congressman, no. You've been in office a year and you're about to lose. Bye." The heels resumed their pitter-patter.

"Bradley, OMG." Heather was back. "I get propositioned for airtime everytime I visit the Capitol. Why would I put a doomed junior Congressman on my show? I mean, he's white and he's from Oregon. There couldn't be a less interesting interview." She still hadn't paused for a breath. "Anyways, do what you want. It's your funeral. If you want to tie your financial and polit- ical future to Julia Connor's half-witted ramblings..."

"Are you almost done?"

"I'm just starting. But for you, I'll stop."

"Thank God. Jokes aside, Heather, what I want to do is win, and if that means bending the knee so Julia can place her crown upon our head, I'm going to do it. What we need from you is full coverage of us signing the pledge that sticks to the talking points I'll send you. Bring Jamal—and here's the important part. Don't say a word about it until you launch coverage an hour before the event."

"Going to surprise Menendez?"

"Going to knock him on his ass."

• • •

Alongside her colleague Jamal Johnston, Heather sat on the NATN plat- form stage, the Sedona Center for Energy and Flow's bright lawn stretched out behind her.

Below her, workers in black polos scurried about building a stage and assembling fencing. O'Leary's campaign staff were setting up tables to reg- ister voters and sign up volunteers. The enormous banner draped over the stage read, "The Love in Politics Pledge."

Outside the newly installed fencing, lines formed. Heather shook her head at the sight of Julia's fans queuing up. "This is the stupidest thing I've ever seen," she said. "These morons are bobbleheads just like Menendez's voters."

Jamal, who had a husky, made-for-TV-news voice that Heather loved, didn't look convinced. "Maybe... but if O'Leary can harness this love thing and make it her own, it could neutralize the stench of all those 'no-gover- nance, anarchy for all, let the homeless and Antifa rule our streets' West Coast mayors and governors."

A group wearing harem pants walked by, carrying what Heather took to be broomsticks. She couldn't help herself. "Hey guys! Yeah, you. Off to play quidditch?"

"Broomsticks? More like matchsticks," called the one carrying a five-gallon gasoline container. "Guess you've never seen a spirit channeling fire spinner before!"

The segment producer's voice appeared in Heather's ear before she could respond. "OK guys, one minute then we're on!"

Heather turned around and settled her hands on the table, preparing to guide the American people. This was a big moment, and she was determined to do all she could to make this work for O'Leary, who deserved to finally make history and become president, offering a symbolic statement against the misogyny that had plagued America for centuries.

The camera light clicked on and the producer behind the camera operator pointed to her. "Thank you to the American Sugar Association, which has been bringing joy to American's lives for over two hundred years."

Her commercial duty completed, Heather cleared her throat and let her voice—low, powerful, sexy—do the work. "America, Heather Haliburton here with Jamal Johnston, coming to you live from Sedona, Arizona, where Julia Connor and her movement for Love in Politics is holding an event with Governor O'Leary. Jamal, this is unusual, to say the least! A woo-woo crusader at the head of a non-political political movement partnering with the major political parties?"

"Absolutely, Heather. I was walking through the crowd when a woman told me she could 'read my aura.' Then someone asked me if my central nervous system was regulated and someone else asked me what my gene keys were."

"Those confusing encounters speak volumes. This is not politics as usual. Julia Connor has stated she believes in harnessing love and healing to make America a better place. And her message, judging by the massive crowds she attracts, is resonating with a significant segment of the population." Heather glanced down at the talking points Bradley had given her. "While Governor Jacqueline O'Leary is enthusiastically embracing the love vote, Senator Menendez has shown no interest in Connor's call to build better, more just communities. This illustrates just how much the love movement has in common with the Democratic party and foreshadows the significant new support we expect Governor O'Leary to receive after the event tonight."

"Correct, Heather" Jamal said. "The question is, how much will Senator Menendez suffer from ignoring Julia Connor's call to love and ignoring voters who like her more than him."

Melanie had her phone out, filming the broadcast just because, well, that's what she did. She felt a tap on her shoulder, hit pause and turned around to see Jonathan's unsmiling face.

"You okay?" she asked.

"No." His gentleness didn't vanish, even when he was upset. But Melanie could see the distress in his eyes and his scrunched forehead. "No, I'm not okay. We've built a national movement focused on compassion and healing, inspiring people to know and love themselves and their neighbors, and these media clowns are talking like O'Leary owns the movement now?"

"What do you expect? Heather Haliburton is part of the system. She's in with the Democratic machine and her network attracts Democratic voters. It's, like, their entire business model."

Jonathan grunted. "Total bullshit."

"That, my dear man, is why we make our videos and why my Beeper team is so important."

"Your Beeper Team?"

"Yeah. We have a whole gang to replicate, target and disseminate. They build on my message and film their own, hyping our message. But I don't want to just leave it to the algorithm. They're hitting niche audiences."

"Like who?"

"Like fitness freaks, hip hop dancers, cheerleaders, music fans, gamers, jocks, librarians, Dungeon and Dragons scrum masters. You name it."

"Wow."

"Exactly! Hold this?" Handing the camera to Jonathan, Melanie embodied Mel P and smiled slyly. "OK, push play."

Jonathan pushed play and Melanie spoke, leaning into the camera. "My peeps, Mel P here. What you just saw is the pay-to-play banter that passes as political news. Never forget media and politics are symbiotic businesses that exist to win elections and rating wars, not to solve problems. That's why we're in Sedona asking both presidential candidates to sign our Love in

Politics pledge. Make sure to Beep and Flitter both candidates to make sure they get the message."

Not for the first time, Jonathan thought that he could understand how Mel P was able to engage people across the world with the ease of striking a pirouette. She always sounded like she was talking directly to you—and only you. Hell, watching her lean toward the camera, he still felt that she was making eye contact with him. That her words were specially directed at him.

"This won't change," Mel P was saying, "unless we accept responsibility to make it change."

CHAPTER 17

STRATEGY RETREAT

"H er plane's going where?!" Jed Abernathy's mouth hung open, his arm resting on one of ROX News' finest conference tables. "You're certain?"

A surprisingly gentle figure in the cutthroat world of political media, his producer, Nancy, stood in the doorway. She wore her gentle like a shield— soft copper curls, an inclination toward denim, rotating earrings typically designed to look like animals. She was looking at Flighttracker.com open on her screen. "I'm certain."

"That is absolutely nuts." Jed shook his head, thinking about his conversation the day before. "Oh, shit! They may not know."

He swiveled away from his producer and punched in a number.

"Hello, this is Luke Lockwood. I'm not available right now. Leave a message and I'll do my best to respond. God bless you."

"Damnit!" Jed squealed.

He dialed again. Voicemail. Again. Voicemail.

He punched a different name into his contacts and pressed "call." He hated going over Luke's head, but this just couldn't wait.

• • •

"Goodness," Luke said, "Can he not stop? That's three from Jed."

Menendez eyed him languidly, more interested in the mountainous northern New Mexico landscape than Luke's annoyance. To him, two days of off-site strategy meetings at his ranch meant a working vacation. A weeklong hunting trip would be even better, but if the price of being president was missing the elk hunt, he could make the sacrifice for a year. "You sure we shouldn't be taking those calls? Jed's my guy, you know."

Luke grimaced. He'd fought Jed Abernathy to the death the night before, and he'd won. He did not need to speak with that grasping twit again; even though Jed and the senator had disagreed last night, Jed shared too many of Menendez's amoral instincts to be trusted.

"Senator, let's just get back to the list."

Menendez eyed the document while fondling a .30-06 elk cartridge in his right hand. "This looks like *your* list. I don't care who your friends and enemies are. I need a list of *my* friends and enemies. I mean, why in God's name are the Rook brothers on the enemies list? They've raised half a billion!"

"But Senator, they called Pastor McMillan an unholy distraction! We can't let that sort of talk slide."

"They can call your pastor whatever they want if they write checks! Don't forget, Luke, you work for me."

Luke was about to remind Menendez that they all worked for their Lord and Savior, Jesus Christ, when the senator's private phone buzzed. He answered.

"Hey Jed," Menendez said, grinning at Luke as he spoke, "Luke's sitting here ignoring your calls, but I always have time for my favorite journalist."

He listened, brow wrinkled. "Sure thing."

He set the phone on the table, putting it on speaker.

"Hey Luke," Jed's voice rang out, "you remember what the senator called me last night."

Luke didn't want those words in his mouth.

Menendez's eyes lit up. "'Ass-sniffing queer bait,' wasn't it?"

"And you remember *why*?"

Menendez felt his blood pressure tick up just remembering the exchange. "Because you wanted me to sign that frumpy little bird's love pledge! I'll tell you again what Luke and I said last night. 'It's a fucking trap!'"

Luke fought the urge to assure Jed those weren't the words *he* had used. The last thing he needed was a rumor that he'd started cursing.

"There's no way Governor O'Leary will sign," Menendez blustered on, "and there is no way I will sign. I don't care what the polling says, I will not be dictated to by that woman!"

"Cut to the chase Jed," Luke said, "we're busy here. Going to Julia Connor's rally is bad politics and bad theology. I don't know why we're rehashing this."

"Well," said Jed, the swagger audible in his voice, "what if I told you the information from flighttracker.com says Jacqueline O'Leary's plane just landed in Sedona, and that Heather Haliburton and the entire NATN team are on the ground reporting live as we speak."

Menendez's face turned redder than a New Mexico sunset beneath his Mexican-American tan. "You better be goddamn dryhumping me!" He turned to Luke. "What in fuck's fucking sake do I even pay dipshits like you for?"

Luke had no answer.

"Well, then ask the Lord for some timely advice, because I need an idea here—calling in bomb threats, whatever!"

"I've got an idea," Jed said, "It's made for TV and will put your Air Force training to good use."

Menedez looked across at Luke once more and shook his head in disgust. "Ok Jed, let's hear it."

· · ·

Jed turned back to Nancy. "What does that minx Haliburton have to say?"

She picked up the TV remote labeled "libtard" and pressed the volume up button.

"This just in, a Flitter from Senator Menendez." Heather Haliburton's voice filled the room as a graphic flashed on screen:

"Big Surprise tonight. LOVE IS FREEDOM. Let it FLY."

Nancy's macaw earrings swung as she cocked her head sideways. "I'm truly disappointed we'll miss this."

"Miss it? I'm not missing this! This will be fucking awesome!" Jed replied. "If we hop a plane now, we can make it there in time!"

Jed bounded from the room, dialing a real estate tycoon who owned a private plane and owed him a favor.

CHAPTER 18

LOVE GURU

This is really not a great time," Julia told Doris as she cradled her flip phone, the enormous crowd's pulsing energy making her hair stand on end, "You know I always take my agents calls, but goodness Doris, this couldn't wait until tomorrow?"

"I'm sorry, but it just couldn't," Doris Lederman huffed, NATN broadcasting in the background. "You are on the cover of *People*!"

"*People* magazine?!" Julia squealed, her eyebrows attempting to exit the top of her head, momentarily forgetting she would soon be taking the stage in front of ten thousand adoring fans.

"Apparently they've been following your book tour, talked to some neighbors, and interviewed a ton of teen girls. But Julia, there's something you may not love."

"Oh dear." Julia sensed where this was going. "What does the cover say?"

"Well, don't take this the wrong way. But ... 'Love Guru: America's number-one influencer is old enough to be your granny!'"

"That's outrageous! And humiliating. The last thing I need is for people to start calling me a guru!" Julia's face fell. Her stomach lurched. An unusual feeling of shame swept over her. And then she giggled, the image of her poem morphing into a magazine cover filling her vision.

Julia paused to feel into herself. Exasperated. Amused. Distracted when she needed to be focused.

"I have to run, Doris, but thank you for the heads up."

She thought how misleading the *People* title was. It was mostly about celebrities. Beekeepers and writers, particularly spiritual writers, weren't exactly on par with movie stars. But maybe that was changing.

Maybe a lot was changing. She'd always known God worked in mysterious ways, but nothing had prepared her for this!

As day faded to dusk, she peaked around Jonathan's broad shoulders, gazing out at the crowd as Martha Lobel, Yale Divinity School's dean, spoke of God's universal call to compassion. There were thousands of people stretched as far as she could see. They had signs. The old and young. Hip and plain. White and Black and Brown. All here for love. For *her*.

Julia felt the rhythmic beat in her chest and marveled that this heart of hers—a seventy-two-year-old muscle, symbol, and force—contained love enough to help inspire and launch the day's event.

Melanie grabbed her hand and squeezed it. "It's time!"

"And now," Dean Lobel said, her voice growing louder, "please welcome the woman who's helped to wake America. The woman who spent her life humbly answering God's call. A woman we all call our friend, Julia Connor!"

The crowd went wild, uncoiling a high-pitched squeal of approval, as Julia stepped onto stage, beaming and waving. A group of women in their fifties waved signs reading Therapists for Julia and Love & Heal. A leather-clad group of men, whose tattoos' once-black outlines had started going green with age, waved signs reading, I Healed My Inner Child and Just Say No to PTSD! Bikers, veterans, maybe an escaped convict or two—Julia giggled at her wit— they must have been friends with Jonathan. But most of the audience were young people. Or more accurately, young women who jumped and screamed.

In the middle of the crowd, a wide berth was given to a group of fire spinners who launched their burning staffs into the air.

Taking the mic, Julia closed her eyes and sought the divine spark within. She felt the peace of God flow through her, bringing calm to a mind startled to be standing in front of so many people. She gave thanks for the moment, the lives that were being touched, and the presence of spirit.

The crowd finally quieted and Julia found her voice. "I've built my life on dreams. But never did I dream I would be on stage, standing before ten thousand beautiful humans who understand that to heal our nation, we all must first heal ourselves. Yet here I am, floating on a sea of your positive energy, buoyed by each of you and your commitment to yourselves and to each other and to God's love!"

The crowd cheered. A rhythmic chant of "Ju-Lee-Aa! Ju-Lee-Aa! Ju-Lee-Aa" echoed in her ears.

"I look out," Julia continued, "and I see fire flying in the air—be careful, please—and neon glowsticks. And I think about us unleashing that energy, that electricity, to focus on our scars and on the opportunity our future holds. To open up and allow ourselves to glow and heal so we can, together, meet the challenges that stand between us and our more perfect future! This, of course, is why we are here—coming together to bring love and compassion to the forefront of policymaking in America."

Julia looked stage right. Governor Jacqueline O'Leary waited in the wings. Melanie had told her it could happen, but never in her wildest dreams had she thought establishment politicians would care about her book. She knew the governor was probably just here because she thought it was good politics, but Julia hoped something bigger was afoot. *What if*, Julia thought, *O'Leary is transformed by this experience? What if she doesn't just sign the pledge but decides to enact a policy platform of love? What if she becomes a president who prioritizes people's healing and well-being above profit and exploitation?*

"My friends! Please join me in welcoming Illinois Governor Jacqueline O'Leary, who is here to speak about the power of love, and to sign the Love in Politics Pledge!!"

O'Leary had so many conflicting emotions. Part of her was irate, sure she'd never get over having to yield to the whims of this gardening, granny nut bag. How was it she'd wrangled ten thousand followers here? Was she raffling off crystals? But she was amazed too. Like Julia, she'd once marched in antiwar rallies. She'd even gone through a hippie stage in college. Maybe Julia's movement was what she needed to ensure victory!

She went into full candidate mode as she strode across the stage, waving both arms and briefly pushing back the Jennifer Aniston-esque $1,000 haircut and color job from Jaques Frerrer-Pierre that framed her face. The crowd roared, but not as loudly as when Julia had entered. O'Leary needed to up the drama. She cut short the stage parade and homed in on Julia, clapping for her, and then delivering a one-hundred-watt smile, hug, and air kiss.

Now the crowd whooped. That was better. She locked arms with the older woman and waved, projecting a vitality—a *youth*—that she hoped dwarfed Julia.

Finally, they circled back to the podium. "Hello America!" O'Leary greeted the crowd. "Julia, I think you're a genius for reminding us all that to solve matters of injustice, to ensure freedom and opportunity for all, we can't just lead with policy. We have to lead with love."

She paused to let the crowd cheer and geared up to claim the mantle of love for herself.

But just as she was about to launch her perfectly crafted speech, Julia gasped and pointed to the sky.

Turning to look into the darkening night, Governor O'Leary saw a spotlighted American-flag parachute descending toward the crowd. Her first thought was that she was under attack. She looked to the side of the stage for her bodyman, Nelson Rivera, the Secret Service agent assigned to stay at or near her side and protect her at all costs. He was listening intently to his earpiece.

What the fuck was he waiting for? O'Leary gave him a look and pointed upward. The guy should be racing to sweep her up in his arms or tackle and roll over on her.

Instead, he took his hand away from his earpiece, smiled, and gave her a thumbs-up sign. A few more agents in their dark suits came up behind Rivera and patted him on the back.

Look at all of them. Why weren't they doing anything? It's like there was a second detail . . .

She looked back at the sky.

Fuck! That was Menendez in the parachute. The attention-obsessed motherfucker was stealing her moment of love!

CHAPTER 19

BURNING MAN, DESERT DELIGHT

resident Menendez took one last look around the luxurious Bombardier Global 7500. His jet was smaller than most politicians' planes—it
was built for eight passengers, max—but what he gave up in size he gained
in speed, luxury, and a ready-made excuse that he just didn't have space for
staff or annoying lobbyists to make the trip with him.

He knew he'd get a bigger plane once he was president, but until Air Force
One was his, the Bombardier was perfect. There was no way a larger, slower
plane would have allowed him to pull off what he was about to do.

"You have the Kevlar on?" It was Williams, his bodyman. The guy had tried
to insist on joining him, but that would have ruined everything. So Menendez had offered to wear body armor. It was a pain in the ass, but what could
he do? The whole point was to go solo.

"Target in sixty seconds!" yelled the pilot.

The door opened and wind roared into the cabin. Menendez took one last
sip of his Pappy Van Winkle 20-year Family Reserve liquid courage, strapped
on his Go-Pro, buckled the last strap on his harness, and ran through the
safety checks he'd learned in the Air Force.

Turning around to face Luke, he smiled and yelled, "If you'd given me
halfway decent advice about this event, I'd be on the ground kissing babies

and shaking hands. As it is … well, I've never been more excited about any-thing in my life!"

"Drop zone, sir!" called the pilot.

"Roger that," Menendez responded. He smiled at Luke. "Thanks for being shit at your joooobbbbb!!!"

Menendez fell backward out of the jet, flipping before regaining equi-librium and settling into a controlled skydive. The wind whipped across his face as he blasted past the few high clouds visible in the fading desert light.

"I'm the KING OF THE WORLD!" he yelled. "I'M GOING TO BE PRESIDENT OF THE UNITED STATES OF AMERICAAAA!"

This was living! He couldn't believe he had to spend so much time talk-ing to those pansy pastors and mindless voters. He wasn't an ass-kisser—he was the type of guy that jumped out of planes!

Then again, if ass-kissing is what it took to win the election and have pow-erful men come to him on bended knee … Because, well, yeah, skydiving was incredible. But telling some Arabian head of state to lower gas prices or to bomb a neighboring tribal minority would be better.

At 2,000 feet, he pulled the cord and his parachute burst behind him, slowing his fall, allowing him to focus on the spectacle of lights and people that blazed from the black desert night. He could hear now too. The giant "Ooooooh!" as they watched the chute—Old Glory!—unfurl like a patriotic miracle.

A huge cheer went up.

Did they know it was him?

He began pulling on the steering lines, aiming for the stage. This was tricky and he was out of practice. He tugged the left rope too hard. He countered with the opposite line as two realizations dawned simultaneously.

The first, he was coming in too fast.

The second, unexpected crosswinds were knocking him off course.

Menendez glanced at the rapidly approaching ground. Where was he supposed to land?! He'd been planning to land on stage, but he was drifting.

He remembered Willams, his body man. He'd said there would be a bat-talion of Secret Service on the ground, ready to secure the area. Okay! He Thought. *Doesn't matter where I land. I'm just going to go for it.*

The wind came up, carrying the screams of the crowd and pitching him farther from the stage. He spotted a circular opening in the throng and made for it.

The fire spinners, lost in their flow, hadn't noticed the speakers stop speaking, or the crowd scream and point skyward. They were high on life and love and gas fumes, channeling their hope for a better future into the blazing balls of kerosene-soaked flame that sat on either end of their fire staffs.

They normally spun at EDM shows and forest parties. None of them had ever even voted, much less brought fire to a political event. But they'd heard this was a gathering for love with some Washington geezers. The one who owned a bong embedded with rose quartz had cried, "Love wins!" It was all the argument they'd needed.

They spun their staffs and they spun themselves, focused on the flames and energy that directed their every move. Smiles huge and minds unaware, they were taken completely off guard when, out of nowhere, an old dude connected to a parachute burst through their midst and somersaulted forward into a group of man-bunned, muscular, tank-topped guys in short shorts.

Menendez jumped to his feet and released his harness, oblivious to the entangled fire spinners desperately fighting to free themselves from the cords and melting nylon of his now flaming parachute.

Menendez straightened his suit, shrugged out of the Kevlar, and looked at the tank-topped guys around him. One of them spoke. "Bro, you missed the breathwork. It was epically centering."

"Breathwork?" Menendez had no idea what this person was talking about. "I'm not here for breathwork. I'm here to rock the love, baby!"

He looked toward the stage. What a nightmare. A sea of people, shoulder to shoulder, between him and his goal. But then the crowd parted before him like the Red Sea before Moses. He felt like an action star! A god!

"Secret Service! Coming through! Move, please. Move! Secret Service."

About a dozen strapping men in suits, sunglasses, crewcuts, and headsets zipped toward him. The man in front of the pack, a huge specimen whose biceps threatened the seams of his jacket, pulled out an ID card from inside his shirt and waved it in Menendez's direction.

"Special Agent August Davenport, Senator!" he barked, grabbing the candidate's elbow. "I'm lead agent for the event. We will now proceed to the stage, sir."

"Great. Fantastic! Lead on."

"Assume formation!" Davenport yelled, and his team surrounded them. "Let's move!"

In a matter of minutes, the phalanx had him at the portable stairs on the side of the stage, behind the safety of crowd-control barriers.

Menendez launched himself up the stairs, grabbed a mic from an assistant, and sprinted onstage with his hands raised in triumph, ready to interrupt the crowd's roar with his opening line—"Hi, I just dropped in to share the love."

He heard a roar from the crowd, but something was off. It wasn't the full-throated blast he had grown accustomed to at Republican rallies. Had they not seen him plunge into a burning ring of actual fire?

He moved toward his stage mates—his partners in the Love Pledge—but they didn't even notice him.

Julia was focused only on the fireball in the center of her people. "Everyone, please stay calm! Medics and EMTs are on their way. Please give them room to reach the burning men!"

The event DJs, Sophie and Tukker, spent ten days every summer blasting beats into the desert night at the world's biggest party. Sophie, in fact, loved dancing on the desert playa more than anything else on earth, which is why she'd written their hit dance track "Burning Man, A Desert Delight."

Now they turned to each other, confused. They'd been in a trance, a glorious bubble of love formed by this event and the half a tab of LSD coursing through their veins.

"Did she just say Burning Man?" Tukker asked.

"I heard that too! That's our cue!"

"Let's hit it!"

Tukker rapidly adjusted the dials on the DJ deck. In a split second, Julia's entreaties for safety were overlaid by a dance track that exploded over the crowd in a tidal wave of sonic bliss.

Back on stage, Menendez was annoyed, so he smiled and spread his arms wide, yelling into his mic to be heard over the music. "Julia and Jacqueline, what's this, no hello? Now that's not very loving, is it?"

This was far more than O'Leary could handle. She'd been upstaged, she'd been diminished, and now that prick Menendez was standing in front of her, beaming like a potty-training toddler who'd just hit the target for the first time—no doubt aware his fucking parachute stunt was already being broadcast across the world.

She yelled, her voice echoing across the event, mixing with the beats in a musical moment that was soon to be remixed into dance tracks across the world. "I'll tell you what love is to me, Menendez. Love is having the decency to announce ahead of time when you'll be showing up at someone else's event in a parachute of flaming destruction!"

Menendez was having none of it. "Oh can it, Jacqueline. Don't talk to me about love! You support pulling viable fetuses out of their mother's wombs!"

"How dare you! You're running on a race-baiting, trans-hating, gay-bashing platform, and you dare to question me?!"

"Trans hating? I don't hate the *they*s. I just looovvveee the *he*s and *she*s!"

Melanie raced over to Tukker and Sophie.

"What are you doing?! Cut the music!"

"Julia said 'Burning Man,'" Sophie objected. "And the crowd loves it!"

"Oh my God!" said Melanie. "She said *burning—men*! There are *men—on—fire* in the audience!"

"Ohhhh!" Tukker squeaked, cutting the music.

Silence descended. The crowd stilled. Sirens whirled in the distance. The fire spinners smoldered, wrapped in flame-smothering blankets delivered by paramedics.

The Love in Politics Pledge remained unsigned.

In the quiet, only Julia's sobs could be heard.

• • •

Jed marveled at his luck. He'd jetted in just in time to see the senator plow into the crowd of wacko-pyromaniac freaks. He'd witnessed the carnage and the argument on stage, he felt a surge of journalistic schadenfreude: this was going to be the campaign season in which he went from star to superstar within the ROX News orbit!

Now, standing amid the wreckage of the Love Pledge jamboree at the almost-empty Sedona Center for Energy and Flow, Jed heard ROX News anchor Jerry Sparks in his earpiece. "Earlier this evening, Senator Menendez made a dynamic, dramatic surprise entrance by parachuting into Julia Connor's Love in Politics Pledge event. Jed, can you tell us what you saw?"

Looking directly into the mobile broadcasting video unit, Jed replied, "The footage of Menendez's triumphant, unexpected airdrop speaks for itself. But as an observer on the ground, I can tell you it left the crowd in shock and awe. Especially the terrifying moment when it became apparent Menendez was landing amid a dangerous group of fire-worshipers. But in keeping with the spirit of the event, Menendez reached out to one of the men who had put him and so many others in danger, instructing him to stop, drop, and roll to quench the flames."

"What leadership, what courage. What commitment to love," Jerry said. "Jed, I'm going to read you a quote from Senator Menendez's press release. 'While I may not agree with Julia Connor's theology, I believe Julia is anointed by God to lead us out of darkness and into love's light.'"

"Wow, what powerful words. That speaks volumes about Senator Menendez's commitment to love," Jed replied. "This is also a clear sign that Julia Connor has, improbably, become an influential force in this campaign, a force that is sure to benefit Senator Menendez and all God-and-love-fearing Republican candidates in the coming months."

"I'm glad you brought this up, Jed. ROX has been tracking public figures' popularity over the last several months. We conducted a flash poll following the event and found that Julia's popularity has skyrocketed." A graphic flashed onto the screen titled "America 2028: Head-to-Head Popularity."

Julia Connor: 27.3% to 45.9%

Governor O'Leary: 31.4% to 27.1%

Senator Menendez: 29.5% to 27.1%

Looking at the graphic on the monitor, Jed struggled to maintain his poker face. Thank God this Julia woman wasn't actually running for president.

"Those are astounding numbers. But they come with questions. Is that a one-off based on today's event, her book, or her hyperactive fans on social media? And more importantly, if it's not a flash-in-the-pan result, can either political party afford to ignore her, or"—Jed lowered his chin, looking deep into the camera lens—"is Julia Connor now the kingmaker in this presidential race?"

CHAPTER 20

WHAT ARE PEOPLE FOR?

I n the early morning sunlight, Julia Connor sat on a rock at the Sedona Meditation Station holding a small book with a title in giant font, Wendell Berry's *What Are People For?*

She was there to ask for peace and guidance. Was last night the fiery end? Throughout her book tour, she had been grateful for the crowds and the support she felt. She was having impact beyond her wildest dreams, but even on a *normal basis*, it was so tiring—thousands of autographs, infinite smiles and words of praise, and just as many questions from seekers.

Then, last night. What should have been the crowning moment of the tour. Thank God only two of the fire spinners suffered serious burns... part of her wanted to believe it was a sign things were over. Still, the optics of the whole thing—Menendez's look-at-me stunt, the fire, the screaming match on stage—seemed to underscore the fact that her work—her message—was needed more than ever.

She was exhausted. The work was exhausting. No wonder all she wanted to do right now was tend to the late summer harvest she was missing in her garden and go home to her bees.

Instead, she focused on Melanie, who impressed her so much. This was a powerful, charismatic young woman. Julia wished she had Melanie's energy and capacity to learn and grow. She was just the person to lead her generation to a clear understanding of the spirit that lived within. Jonathan—older, quieter, more at peace—already her favorite, he had blossomed over the last months. Authoritative and compassionate, he was a leader, admired by other veterans. What an ideal combination to reach so many of America's wounded citizens. She was proud of them both. Joyful even.

As her equilibrium shifted into place, she was reminded that the movement didn't depend on her or on that silly event. The movement was its own thing, a result of people's desperate need to heal and to live in a country that put people first.

She shivered in the morning cool, a dart of energy down her spine, reminding her she lived within her dharma. She lifted her head, watching the morning's rays light the mountainside across the valley. *How blessed I am to be a servant in God's larger plan.*

"Excuse us, Julia?" Melanie walked up, flashing an apologetic smile. Alongside her, Jonathan stood gray and grim. A man of worn steel.

Julia motioned for them to sit. "Last night didn't go exactly as planned, did it?"

"It was a disaster," Jonathan said. "All the news coverage is about the parachute, irresponsible arsonists, and Menendez's so-called heroism. And the pledge—it never got signed! What a joke!"

"It's not all bad news," said Melanie, who was in a much better mood. "Beep-Beep has gone nuts! If thirteen-year-old girls were in charge, they'd follow Lillie Rift straight into the fray!"

Julia perked up. "Lillie Rift?!"

"Yeah, she thinks you're the shit! She posted a video supporting us." Then Melanie paused. "You know who Lillie Rift is?"

"I *love* Lillie Rift!" Julia squealed. "A friend's granddaughter showed me a clip of her talking about mental health and how seeking help can be a sign of strength, not weakness. I think she's brilliant and is the exact type of pop star this country needs."

"Wonders never cease," Jonathan grunted.

"Listen, you two," Julia said, bemused they thought she was so out of it to be unfamiliar with the world's most popular singer, "don't panic after last night. I know that was hard. I was horrified too. But it's all as it should be. We'll allow reality to unfold, trusting God to guide us."

"Well," Melanie said, "before you settle into stoic acceptance of all that is terrible, watch this one video? This guy has thirty-five million followers!"

Melanie pulled out an iPad and showed them the Beep-Beep account of Noah Glasnapp, a beautiful bald man with perfect teeth and a thing for white linen clothes. As promised, he had over thirty-five million followers. His bio read, "Truth Seeker. Truth Teller. Austin, TX based."

The top video on his feed was titled *The Future We Must Demand*. Melanie clicked it, and Noah's wide eyes and perfect skin filled the screen, candles burning behind him.

"You all know I hate politicians, but Julia Connor is bringing the hope of love into politics. Last night she tried to bring both political parties in line. It fucking failed! Senator Menendez parachuted in, seriously wounding two fire-spinning brothers. Then he and Governor O'Leary started yelling at each other. Politicians in America want to fight but are unwilling to heal. For the rest of this year, I have only one goal. I am going to get Julia Connor elected president. To join the movement as a founding member, buy my new course. Link in bio."

As Noah talked, his comments floated at the top of the screen: "Love into politics," "fucking failed," "fight," and "heal." As the video ended, "Join us— Link in Bio" filled the entire screen.

Julia started laughing. Elected president?! Now she threw her head back, chortling. This was too much. She could not. Stop. Laughing. It was so silly.

"Julia, it's not that—"

"I'm ... I'm sorry. Let me catch my breath. Oh, my! I can't believe that! That is just so kind, Melanie. But really, what a lark."

"Maybe. But the internet doesn't agree. That video has over nine million views just this morning. It's being cross-posted everywhere."

"I didn't take it seriously either," Jonathan said. "But I've had ten different veterans groups call to ask if they should post the video."

"These internet folk are just silly," Julia managed through her giggles. "Like dragonflies playing on a sunny afternoon. Just adorable and silly."

Melanie's phone pinged. She checked it, then bolted to her feet.

"Oh my God! Guys, you won't believe this." She read from her phone:

> "Melanie, I think you'll know how to get this message to Julia.
> Will you ask her if she would be willing to appear at a small event
> I and a few friends are organizing in Austin on Tuesday? Think
> of it as a thank you for all the amazing work over the last several
> months. Love, Lillie Rift."

Jonathan blinked heavily, his mouth hanging open, and shook his head. "Speak of the devil."

"You mean saint!"

"Julia?"

"To be honest? I wanted to go home to my garden. I've been away for months."

"Neighbors are taking care of your garden," Melanie said, her eyes pleading. "And I'd imagine your bees are fine. But this is Lillie Rift. We can't say no to Lillie!"

Julia tried to puzzle it out. Why had this message come now? Was it because she was on the cover of *People*? Because Mercury was in retrograde? Because God worked in mysterious ways?

But the why didn't matter, did it? She'd given herself to her dharma, to her purpose, and in this moment, her purpose was the movement. If one of the biggest pop stars in the world wanted to help spread love, who was she to say no?

"What do you think, Julia?" Jonathan asked, concerned for her energy and her health. "A few more days away?"

"I think I'd be crazy to say no." Julia smiled.

"Awesome!" Melanie crowed, visions of grandeur sprouting in her mind.

They started downhill to plan and pack for Austin. Walking beside Julia, a thought nagged at Melanie's mind. Lillie had invited them to Austin, and that guy Noah, the one who made the video, lived there. Was that a coincidence?

• • •

"Well, Luke! I hate to say I told you so," crowed the senator as soon as he stepped into the limousine, sounding like he didn't hate it at all. "But that went pretty damn well yesterday! Have you watched the footage from my Go-Pro? The look on those fire freaks' faces right before I plowed into them was priceless!"

Luke shook his head, his lips pursed in a scowl he hadn't stopped wearing since he'd seen Menendez's edits on the campaign's statement. He certainly wasn't in the mood to attend a donor breakfast with construction industry CEOs whose firms were intermittently tasked with building and then removing segments of Arizona's border wall per the whims of leaders and lawsuits.

"I disagree, Senator. You called Julia anointed by God in the press release. Do you even know what that means? That woman is dangerous. She's not a Christian. Do not mock the Lord."

"Come off of it, Luke. We had to go big after the guy caught on fire. And you've seen the polling, a lot of Evangelicals like her message! We need to reassure them."

"We risk splitting our base if we pander to her. She is a Jezebel. Love is a false prophet. It embraces everything and nothing."

"I don't know what that means, Luke," Menendez said scowling, "but my gut instinct says she's gonna split O'Leary's vote, not ours."

• • •

Driving to breakfast at the Amalgamated Fence Builder and Demolition Union, Jaqueline O'Leary was in the middle of a red-faced tantrum. "What the actual fuck, Bradley? How could you let that happen?!"

"How could I have known he was going to jump out of a plane and set the fire spinners on fire!"

"Your job is to have me prepared and I wasn't," she hissed.

"I didn't realize clairvoyance was part of my job description."

"Well, it fucking is." Had O'Leary possessed a sense of humor about her work, or herself, this is where she would've laughed at herself. She scowled. "So, now what?"

Bradley paused, calming his temper and preparing to launch the salvo he'd been thinking about all night. "After the post-event polls, we have two options. We can continue to adopt Julia's talking points and try to capitalize on the love vote's power. Or we can surprise the world and guarantee we win the election right now."

"Guarantee victory?" Jacqueline raised her eyebrows. "How?"

"You," Bradley said, letting the anticipation hang in the air, "ask her to be your vice president."

Jacqueline froze.

Bradley could see her mind working and he knew every question she was asking herself.

"I'd have to see the polling breakdown."

"I'll have it to you by lunch. And I'll tell you this," he said, launching a white lie and wishing he'd had the foresight to poll Julia's popularity with O'Leary's voters. "The numbers say it's a no-brainer."

"I guess it wouldn't be such a bad thing to have her on the ticket. I mean, we don't disagree with much of anything she says on principle."

"How could we? She doesn't say anything of substance except 'love is the answer.' The only issue is that she's not a Democrat."

"She's a Republican?!"

"Worse. An independent."

"*Unbelievable*. Well, at least she's not a libertarian, refusing to take a real stance on anything, babbling on about limited government. As if government can be limited in a chaotic democracy of three hundred million people."

"*Last night* was limited government."

"Last night," she smiled, "was a libertarian wet dream."

"Exactly," Bradley said, grateful to seemingly be in her good graces after the whole lacking-psychic-powers thing, "I'm sure our base will be able to get over her being an independent once they understand we have the most popular woman in America running on our ticket."

"Excuse me?"

And on the shit list again *so* fast.

"Sorry. I mean second most popular woman." Another lie. He did have the polling for this. Jacqueline was nowhere close to being the most popular woman in America.

"I heard you the first time."

"Apologies. So, should I call her people?"

Governor O'Leary frowned. "We have a vice president. Won't it look weak if we kick Ramon off the ticket?"

"Ramon is the epitome of weak! He was supposed to help us in Texas, but Menendez is smoking us there. I say we tell him to step aside for 'family reasons.' Maybe he needs to help that goat farming grandpa of his milk goats. Once he's gone, we can secure Julia's fruitcake vote."

Bradley knew she was tempted, but he also knew that being a Democrat was the most important thing in the world to her because, in fact, party affiliation was the most important thing to most of their voters. He had no idea if putting Julia on the ticket was supported by the numbers. But her momentum was palpable, and the strategist in him knew it was the right thing to do.

"I'll think about it," Governor O'Leary finally said, "but that's a hell of a gamble, Bradley. You'd better be right."

CHAPTER 21

HUGS AND
HEART CHAKRAS

Noah's message said he would be at an "ecstatic dance and manifestation meetup" and invited them to meet "the most heart-centered community in Austin."

"The weirdness of some of Julia's supporters never ceases to amaze me," Melanie said to Jonathan as he hunched over the wheel in their rented MINI coupe, his muscled figure wedged between the seat and the ceiling. "I mean, why were there even fire spinners at the event? And *what* is an ecstatic dance?"

"Julia looks like the world's most innocent lady, but she had a wild side." Jonathan chuckled to himself, thinking of the memory. "A few years back she took me to what she called a 'burner' party outside of Seattle. The dress code, for those who decided to wear much of anything, was tight purple pants and sparkles. I felt like I was visiting Mars—"

"I don't think Martians wear flannel."

"—but Julia fit right in. Those types love her and her books. There's this entire spiritual counterculture that reveres her. Kind of like the hippies in the sixties, except many of them work and a lot are life coaches."

"Life coaches—like all the celebrities have?" Melanie asked.

"Yeah, and like all those friends of Julia's in Seattle. But they're not just for celebrities. I think a lot of folks use them like they're a therapist, or their pastor."

Melanie looked dubious. "I'm not into sparkles," she laughed. "Or getting coached by naked strangers. Or even casual acquaintances. Sorry."

They pulled up to a modern mansion made of glass and steel beside an urban forest. Thumping jungle beats boomed from the backyard, jarring the otherwise quiet, peaceful neighborhood.

They followed a pebble path and the beats to a gate at the side of the house.

Opening the gate, they saw a DJ booth suspended high between two trees. On the lawn below, a hundred-odd dancers clad in various combinations of robes, fur, and tights jumped and spun. Or writhed on the ground making animal noises. Or swung their arms and bodies in ribbon-like flow. It was a complete dance release.

A woman wearing skintight, blush-colored velvet shorts and one-third of a baggy T-shirt spotted them and beelined over. "Hi! Welcome! You can leave your shoes there." She pointed to a pile of shoes. "Do y'all hug?"

"Hug?" Melanie looked at Jonathan, trying to make sure he'd heard what she had.

"Yeah, do you hug?"

"Uhm, no. Not with strangers." The woman appeared so disappointed Mel was worried for a moment they'd already blown it with this crowd. She made an expression she hoped came off as more smile than grimace. "So, some of you are life coaches? Are *you?*"

"Oh yeah! Not everyone, but a lot of us are."

"Hmm, interesting," Melanie said, sounding as awkward as she felt. Jonathan had been right. But who wanted to be coached by a barefoot woman with pink hair? Or a dude wearing fur who rolled on the ground and grunted? No thank you. "So, who do you coach?"

"Well, we mostly coach other coaches," the woman responded enthusiastically.

"Then … who do the new coaches coach?"

"They coach other coaches too!"

"So when do the coaches stop coaching coaches?"

The woman paused, struggling to grasp the implications of this logic. "I think a lot of the coaches do coach folks that aren't coaches, but most come back to coaching coaches. It's a better business model."

Mel's economics professor used to rant about a conman named Bernie Madoff, working himself in a fury over not only Madoff's corruption but the fact that everyone around him—his staff, his victims, everyone—had been so greedy. But this woman in crushed velvet short shorts seemed like a true believer. And she definitely wasn't rich. Plus, Julia was kind of like a life coach to all her followers on Beep-Beep. Maybe they weren't so bad?

She heard someone yell, "Brother!"

A bald man whose white tank top exhibited his lean muscle, who wore layers of beads and bangles along with slouchy harem pants, was jogging toward them. Melanie stepped back and watched as Noah put one hand on Jonathan's heart and then corralled him in an all-encompassing embrace that lasted . . .

And lasted.

And lasted.

Jonathan, no stranger to post-treatment embraces, fought the urge to recoil. Instead, he squinched his nose to cope with the unholy scent of his assailant.

The man placed his forehead against Jonathan's and stared into his eyes for an eternity. Then he stepped back and turned to Melanie.

"Sister!!!" he exclaimed, going in for a hug.

Melanie put her palm into Noah's chest. "Stop! Don't even think of it."

Noah blinked. Then looked at her as though *she* were visiting from Mars. "But our heart chakras—"

"Will have to wait. Maybe try a shower and a verbal introduction first. I'll start. Hello, Noah. I'm Mel P or Mel, or Melanie."

"OK, I'm cool with that, Mel." Noah dropped his hands to his side. "But I hope you understand, I can't risk destroying my microbiome with soap. That's why I swim in freshwater a few times a day."

"Oooookkkkk." Melanie's face said it all. "Jonathan, I think we should leave."

Jonathan burst out laughing. For such a badass, Melanie could be a bit uptight.

"Come on Mel," he said, "we just got here. Remember our counterculture convo? This was bound to be weird, let's just go with the flow."

Melanie wished she were filming. She could roast the fuck out of these jokers on Beep-Beep. "Fine. But can we go inside? I can't hear another person make monkey noises."

"Sure thing!" said Noah. "But let me sage y'all first. We don't want to bring any bad energies into the sacred space. Come on."

Noah walked them over to the deck, grabbed a Tibetan singing bowl that held burning sage, and waved it around his guests' bodies, its fragrant whisps dissipating in the breeze. Then he led them through the doors into a large room with a different Hindu deity painted in spectacularly garish colors on each wall. The ground was scattered with pillows and large blankets.

"This is the cuddle room," Noah said the way a normal person, who bathed and didn't wear bangles, might have introduced the dining room. "Lots of love in here! It'll be the perfect place for us to talk."

Melanie looked at him in alarm.

"Don't worry, Melanie, this'll all be business." His tone shifted into business mode, the voice of a man with a business empire. "We have a lot to do if we're going to get Julia elected president. So, here's what I'm going to do—"

"Noah!" A breathless strawberry blonde burst into the room, looking like she'd just arrived from Bali. "Are these Julia Connor's people?!"

"Nicole, please."

"I love your love thing!" she said, clapping her hands and turning to Jonathan. "I just had to tell you!" She rushed from the room.

"So, as I was saying," Noah continued, "I already coordinated with Lillie Rift. I think I can activate Austin to get one hundred thousand—"

The glass door flung open again. The orgiastic dance crowd from outside entered the room in a swarm of sweat, smiles, undulating arms, and monkey howls.

Nicole was back, and she'd brought the crowd. She rushed over to Jonathan and Melanie and dropped to her knees, touching both of their legs and speaking with complete sincerity. "Friends, we are so, so, so honored you are here. We love Julia Connor! We think she's changing the world. And we all want to be part of God's plan for her and for this country. Can we give you a hug to express our gratitude for the work you're doing?"

Melanie looked Nicole over. She was dressed well, and her olfactory senses indicated Nicole favored lavender and rose water. Not wanting to seem rude in the face of so much adoration she said, "Sure, I'll accept a hug."

"Cuddle puddle!" someone yelled.

Immediately, all the dancers followed Nicole, enveloping Melanie and Jonathan in an enormous, exuberant, human-scented group hug.

Crushed beneath the pile of bodies, Melanie wanted to explode. Fucking idiots! But Nicole was giggling, their cheeks pressed together, and she heard someone say, "Don't crush the love ambassadors!" And then there was more laughing. Someone kneaded her left calf. Someone else gently rubbed her head. "Ooooh, cuddle puddle!" cooed a high voice. Everyone was laughing.

"You OK, Mel?" Jonathan called, his head sticking out from under the fur-clad guy.

Her fury lessened. Could such happy people be all that bad? "I'm fine," she heard herself say. Still, it wasn't long before Noah called the puddle to an end, saying, "OK, everyone. Let's give them some space. We've got a guru to elect."

CHAPTER 22

HOW DID THIS HAPPEN?

Not even two full days later, Jonathan stood beside Noah on the event stage as downtown Austin glowed red in the setting sun, a look of profound befuddlement upon his face. "Where did all these people come from?!"

It was a rhetorical question. He kind of knew the answer. The morning before, Jonathan and Melanie had spent an hour talking to Oscar De La Cruz, a business reporter at *The Austin Statesman* and the brother of Nelson De La Cruz, who had his life and leg blown apart by an IED outside Baghdad. Jonathan had helped Nelson patch up his heart and his mind. The leg was another story.

"Noah Glasnapp? He's the real deal. I mean, the huggy-crunchy coaching network has critics, but it's not like typical MLM because none of those funds get kicked upstairs. He's just a super tech-savvy organizer, a shrewd start-up investor, and, if you can overlook the whole energy-suck reality of the digital revolution, a guy who is committed to saving the environment on a massive scale. Like, he thinks the US Navy should be a global anti-poaching unit to protect endangered fish stocks."

"What does he invest in?" Melanie asked. "Is he another pharma bro?"

Oscar De La Cruz didn't have to pause. "He owns a national network of gyms and yoga studios, he invests in a variety of psilocybin optimization and regenerative agriculture startups, his podcast reaches tens of millions—which is a cash cow right there—he owns ConsciousAds, his own digital marketing arm, and he's a self-styled CEO shaman. His retreats attract nouveau bigwigs from the highest echelons of the American power structure."

It was a sobering meeting. The guy was loaded and connected in ways that left Jonathan and Melanie impressed but skeptical.

Then Noah had shown up, laptop, PowerPoint, and hummus-guacamole sandwiches on seven-grain, gluten-free bread in tow—no monkey dancers to be seen. He talked for an hour straight about making connections along the righteous path to power.

"I know it's a radical idea. But it's also not. You've heard of surveillance capitalism, right? That's what Troojle and the digiverse are obsessed with—that's why they love O'Leary so much. Her Data Rights are Human Rights Act is just looking to legislate what Troojle's done from the start. What I do is a twist on that. I call it Inverse-Surveillance Cultural Capitalism to play on the dominant concept and turn it upside down. It's zeitgeist surfing, but it's giving. It's aspirational networking, but it's about elevating everyone."

When he showed them his Pyramid of Dreams, Melanie shot Jonathan a glance. It was *literally* a pyramid, the official shape of scams. But then Noah turned the visual aid on its head.

"Pyramid schemes are bottom-up enterprises. Build a huge base and loot it. A Pyramid of Dreams, in our stressed-out society, requires inspiration and idealism at the top that is filtered down. Is that cynical? Maybe." Whether it was or not, they had to agree that cynicism wasn't out of place in a society narcoticized, drugged, Setflixed, Beep-Beeped, and paralyzed by phone and feed addictions. "So my vision was to build a pyramid made of pyramids. Remember: a triangle is the strongest, most stable shape in geometry, so I thought that made sense. And to be honest, I used some of Julia's work to identify the pyramids at the top." He jiggled his finger on the mousepad to jumpstart his screen, already open to PowerPoint. "The big one: Self, which consists of four smaller triangles—Spiritual Alignment, Community Consciousness, Ecology of Oneness, Physical Health. See how they all fit together?"

That slide gave way to another, and another. Triangles within triangles. Each with advocates and networks. From Fastagram to Flitter, from EcoBeeps to RightsBeeps to FitnessBeeps. And Fleets, and Heddit and Wetube channels. And collectives and groups and email lists.

Melanie was in awe. The guy had mapped it out! The cartography he navigated as the influencer behind the influencers to become the influencer above the influencers. *Where we push love*, she thought, *he pushes the fulfillment of self.* The difference made her contemplate how complicated love could be. Simple, but complicated in action. Self, though, was something everyone understood, something you could segment, because every individual was different in a predictable sort of way.

The next screenshot—hundreds of tiny triangles massing into one giant three-sided beast superimposed over a map of America—said it all. "This," Noah summarized, "is why I was able to have Lillie send you that message the morning after the event. And it's why, by tomorrow night, I will have a festival-sized crowd gathered for Julia."

Now, looking over the crowd of one hundred thousand people that filled the vast expanse of Zilker Park, Noah grinned at Jonathan. "See bro? Triangles! And trust! Melanie isn't the only one who can leverage social media. I don't mess around when it comes to channeling spirit. When I receive a download, I act."

And act Noah had. He knew Melanie was a great boot-strap influencer, but Julia didn't have any top-notch organizational minds running the show. So he had put his triangles and ConsciousAds to work, activating his network of influencers to go wild on social media, digital media, and every other type of media imaginable. It was marketing in overdrive: Beep-Beep videos dashed across digital space. Flitters were fleeted with unimaginable speed. Podcasts poured forth. In every piece of content from thousands of different creators, the same message was heard—"Come to Zilker Park. Come to play, come to pray, and come to convince Julia Connor to run for president."

Now, despite the fact he still hadn't met Julia Connor, it was all coming together. The people were here, the plan was set, and Lillie Rift was waiting in the wings.

• • •

Standing on the other side of the stage with Melanie, Julia was befuddled. "Melanie," she asked, how did this happen? I thought we were done for after Sedona, but this crowd is ten times as big!"

"Do you want the long or the short answer?" Melanie asked, wondering if they were right to leave Noah's surprise to be revealed on stage.

"I want the real answer."

"People have been learning about you. They saw what happened in Sedona, they were outraged, and now they're here to show their support and make a statement."

"Sedona was a one-time fiasco! And the news picks up a new fiasco every day."

"But you've gone totally, explosively viral. Like the most infectious hit song ever. Corporations pay fortunes trying to engineer such moments. But what you've done—"

"I just wrote a book!"

"Yes, but then you appeared in like two hundred Beep-Beeps with me and Jonathan. America lost its mind for you. The *People Magazine* cover is the least of it."

"OK. A book plus Beep-Beep. So—"

"So unlike corporate viral content, what we have done hasn't been engineered. It's been organic. Free. Unpaid. At least until now."

Julia thought of her garden and of the enormous blackberry brambles that grew along the river near her home. "That's a funny use of 'organic.' I guess it fits too. But what do you mean 'until now'?"

"Before now my Beeps blew up. Others shared them. They multiplied. And they didn't cost us a penny. But that Noah guy—you laughed at his video in Sedona? Well, he's a tech-savvy multi-millionaire with an influencer empire. You'll meet him later tonight. He and Lillie Rift organized this. For you."

"I still can't believe *Lillie Rift*—"

"Is going to help us capitalize on an entire nation's worth of frustration, fury, and budding optimism?"

"Mel, I know so much more about bees than Beeps or … algor …"

"Algorithms. And you don't have to—that's the point. Noah has networks and know-how that you don't, that *I* don't. And where the growth has been completely organic so far, now it's going to be a little more … triangular."

Julia shook her head and sighed. "I can't believe they are doing this all just to say thank you to me."

"They appreciate you and what you're doing that much." Melanie held her tongue. Julia would soon know the night's real purpose.

"But 'me.'" Julia looked into the distance, the image of her garden flooding her memory once more, in greater detail now. She stopped to savor the image of her own hands massaging the rich topsoil before helping new seeds burrow in. That work made so much sense to her. That type of "getting her hands dirty." She was still looking away when she said to Mel, "Me was just never the point, you know?"

CHAPTER 23

BREACHING REALITY

Against the backdrop of a pink and orange sky, the program kicked off. The Monkey Tree drum circle, joined by local Hollywood legend Mathias Hustusay, bongoed and danced their hearts out in the center of the stage, whipping up the crowd in the day's dying light.

Jeremiah Salpray, a famous bio-hacker and fitness coach, spoke about the power of self-discipline, the freedom found in focus, and the inspiration he found in this movement of love.

A veteran spoke about the power of healing, thanking Julia and Jonathan for teaching America that trauma, if acknowledged and healed with love, was a source of power and freedom for every person.

The crowd's enthusiasm built as the sun's last rays blasted vertically above the horizon.

A Methodist Minister wrapped up his call for understanding and acceptance. "Friends, I was supposed to introduce Julia Connor to you. But I've been told a special guest will have that honor. So instead, please join me in welcoming Lillie Rift!"

Roars! Cheers! Screams! Clapping! Ululations! Jonathan, who had endured more than his fair share of sonic concussions, pinned his hands over his ears. Melanie had warned him. Lillie Rift was this crowd's moral north star. Their informal therapist. Their God by another name. Like them, she was flawed but, you know, perfect too.

Lillie walked onto stage, sporting her traditional oversized T-shirt and black leather pants. This was her crowd, her world. There had been nights when a hundred thousand fans stood in this very spot as she headlined Austin City Limits Music Festival, cheering her every song, every word, every gesture.

She'd always tried to lead these fans she thought of as her flock as honestly as possible. Now, according to her politely critical manager, she was taking the biggest risk of her career. "Pop and independent politics don't mix," she'd been warned.

Lillie didn't care. She had to do it. She believed.

"Helloooooooo, Austin!" She paused as the crowd roared its approval and then continued. "I'll be back in a bit, so I'll keep this short. I'm here because this night is not about me. This is about us. I believe we need a new focus as a nation. Solutions for the problems that have broken the world we were born into will not come from the political parties that have caused and allowed the problems to occur. Solutions will not appear if we all continue to live as we always have, believing the things we've always believed!"

The crowd erupted with Amens, whistles, and cheers.

"One woman, in particular," Lillie continued, "has given voice to a beautiful, logical, compassionate ideal: if people heal, politics will heal! And if politics heals, we can address the environmental and social problems plaguing our broken world. That's beautiful, right?"

Shrieks! Thirty seconds of cheers, screams and cries, with Lillie using her hands to raise the volume of the adoring crowd.

"Thank you! You agree! Yay us! So without further ado, we—all of us!—are honored to welcome Julia Connor to the stage!"

Julia walked onto stage, beaming and waving every step of the way, letting the roar of the crowd wash over her as Lillie, cheerleader in chief, urged the crowd on, conducting them with waves, claps, and an almost deafening finger-in-mouth whistle. These, Julia thought, were the vibrations of love she had written about in *The Sound of Our Souls*. She wanted to close her eyes, bathe in the decibel waves, and thank the world for this moment. But she knew this wasn't the time to pause. She would give thanks later, in a quiet moment she would carve out for herself.

Gathering her thoughts after a long, tearful hug with Lillie, Julia looked over the crowd and tried to keep it together. This audience seemed a thousand times larger than Sedona's. She was again overcome with gratitude. These supporters were embodying grace by showing up after O'Leary and Menendez had ruined the last event. She felt their grace seeping through every part of her body. It was warm and it was comforting. She breathed through the sensation and prepared to speak.

"Hello, everyone," Julia began, sounding almost hesitant. "I am blown away to see so many of you here. From this stage, I see people stretched as far as I can look in any direction. I hope you understand this event has taken me a bit by surprise. I wasn't prepared for this. My last appearance had some unexpected 'problems,' which you may all recall."

"We love you!" a chorus of girls in the front screamed as many in the crowd laughed along with Julia.

"Oh, I love you too. I certainly do. All of you! Love is at the heart of the ideas I've been exploring. And if you don't mind, I'd like to talk about some of those concepts and then tie them to our current election. I won't prattle on too long."

Julia launched into an abbreviated version of her book tour speech. About the dangers of politics without empathy, of promoting wealth without social responsibility and without understanding our impact upon the environment, of denying the fundamental emotional and spiritual needs all people share. She reached her crescendo while reliving the horror from Sedona. "Even after all we've done, even after both candidates made a mockery of themselves at our event, the media still treats the ideas I've touched on—and the people who embrace those ideas—as a joke. But look at us. Look at your neighbors, your friends, complete strangers. Look them in the eye! None of us are a joke. All of us matter. *All* of us. That's why we must keep going, demanding a world that respects us for who we are and honors the natural world we are all part of! We can do this, together. Thank you for coming tonight, for uniting with each other, and showering the world with your love!"

Fireworks erupted in the sky all around Zilker Park. Brilliant reds, greens, and yellows lit the night. Some in the audience cheered while others, planted by Noah and holding bullhorns, began to chant.

The chant began slowly but soon spread like wildfire through the crowd. As it grew, the chant became audible to Julia, who was walking off stage. Her heart plunged to her belly. She couldn't believe her ears at first, but there was no denying it.

"Julia for president! Julia for president! Julia for president!"

"Boss," Melanie said. "I think this demands an encore."

As the chant swelled to fill the Texas night sky, Julia felt her smallness, there on the side of the stage, as an observer of a thing far larger than herself.

Melanie grabbed Julia by the hand and led her back on stage, depositing her beside Noah, who'd claimed the stage as his own, and who now made bowing, I'm-not-worthy hand motions.

When it seemed the chant might grow no louder, Julia touched her heart. She did it again. She clasped her hands together and lifted them up to the crowd.

Noah handed her the microphone.

"Thank you," she said into the swirl of noise.

No one could hear her, but she said it again. "Thank you, that's so kind. But really, there's no need—"

"OH YES THERE IS!" a soaring voice boomed on the PA.

Lillie Rift bolted out. "There is a need!" she said. "And you can hear it! Come on people!!" She pointed her microphone at the crowd for the answer.

"Julia for president! JULIA FOR PRESIDENT! JULIA FOR PRESIDENT!"

The fleeting nature of the moment took nothing away from its transcendent power. The crowd's collective energy surged on, powered by three words that pleaded for a better world—demanded one. "JULIA FOR PRESIDENT!"

Reality had been breached.

The energy of the moment rose as a wave and then crashed down upon the stage, carrying Julia with it high into the sky.

Fully out of body, she looked down upon the crowd and upon the slight white-haired woman at the center of a celestial shockwave. She floated in this moment until the cord seemed to snap and she was sucked back into her minute physical form.

Tears ran down Julia's cheeks. Jonathan and Melanie stood next to her, holding both her hands, feeling the rapid beat of her heart through the veins in her palms.

"OK, peeps," Melanie said into the mic. "We aren't done yet. Let's bring it down a bit."

The crowd began to quiet.

"The community has spoken," Noah said, "Julia. Will you answer?"

"But I don't know anything about politics," Julia replied, her voice sounding as small as her frame.

"But Julia!" It was Lillie Rift. "You know people. And you know the force of creation, God, in all its forms. The people are calling you, Julia. Just say yes. For us. And for love."

The crowd of one hundred thousand looked on, watching, holding its collective breath. Julia returned their gaze. She thought of her beloved bees. Someone would take care of them. She thought about what it meant to be a servant to something far, far bigger than self. Something that seemed to strain even the limits of God, and far surpassed any ability she ever thought she'd had.

She gave a microscopic nod, then realized she needed to do more. She took a lung-filling deep breath and exhaled. "Yes. Yes, of course I will!"

• • •

"BREAKING NEWS" flashed across the screen in a panic-red font. Jamal Johnston and Heather Haliburton came into focus, sitting next to each other in NATN's New York Studio.

"Just an hour ago," Jamal began, "America's favorite spiritual gangster declared for president during a mammoth rally in Austin, Texas, that included controversial free-thought activist Noah Glasnapp and Lillie Rift, who was, until last night, the favorite mega-pop star of Democrats everywhere."

"That's right," said Heather, shooting for eye contact with every viewer in the nation. "In news that will shake pundits to their core, the flash polling numbers are in. Let's take a look."

A graphic appeared on screen as Jamal read:

Julia Connor 30%
Senator Menendez 30%

Governor O'Leary 30%

Undecided 10%

"There you have it: newcomer Julia Connor, with her nascent campaign of love, appears tied for the lead with the presidential candidates from both major political parties. This is history in the making, Heather."

"The question, Jamal, is this—can Julia Connor, an untested candidate seemingly obsessed with the imaginary power of what she calls God, maintain these numbers when we, I mean, when ROX News and rival candidates, begin to attack her?"

"Great questions, Heather. We'll know more in a few days. For now, the best we can say is the election is as fluid as it's ever been."

As soon as the recording stopped, Heather detached her mic and shook her head in disbelief.

"Can you believe this? This is a goldmine, Jamal! A fucking goldmine."

"Right? The clicks and the views for Julia content are already off the charts. It's better than a sex scandal! Or Trump!"

"Our numbers are going to go through the roof."

"But do we actually worry about her as a candidate?"

"Jamal. Please." With the pad of her ring finger, Heather rubbed in her eyeshadow to prevent it from caking in the crease of her eyelid. "Once people see past her friendly little facade she'll crumble. There's nothing there. You can't eat love! Or drive it to work! I mean, just wait until she gets in front of reporters." She checked herself in a compact mirror. *God*, did she know how to accentuate her eyes. "Mark my words. Julia O'Connor is built to fail."

CHAPTER 24

BARTON SPRINGS

Julia was soaking wet and covered in goosebumps, sitting wrapped in a towel on the grassy lawn at one of her favorite places in the entire country. This was the next best thing to being at home tending her garden. In fact, in small doses, it was better than home. A pecan tree stretched above her, framing the robin's-egg blue morning sky beyond. She glanced down the sloping grass hill toward the perfectly clear, cold, spring-fed pool she had just exited.

She loved Barton Springs's healing waters and was grateful to be grounded in nature after last night.

President? Me? A campaign? The whole thing felt ridiculous. More than ridiculous. Last night's hope had morphed as each hour ticked by. Fears and what-ifs fed her imagination. Defeat. Humiliation. And something much worse: failing to serve the principles that were the foundation of her life. Politics was about winning, about destroying the enemy. It assumed self-compromise as the price of doing business.

The book was now more than a book. The book tour more than a book tour. Everything was growing beyond all comprehension. One hundred thousand people had gathered to convince HER to run for president!

She closed her eyes.

A deep, deep breath in, to fill her lungs. She held it. Held it. And then released. S-l-o-w-l-y. Then did it again and again, allowing her wild fears to churn through her mind. She noticed each thought, accepted it, and then released it along with her breath.

She felt her heartbeat slow. She focused on God, on the energy that coursed through the world and herself, part of the soil and trees and every person on earth. The energy of creation, and of life. She'd felt it last night. She felt it now.

The chants had power. The power of emotion, the language of God expressed in humanity. Physicists couldn't yet measure the energetic force of hope and love, but it was there. And that energy, once created, could not be destroyed. Should not be destroyed. It was transmuting, becoming part of God's universal truth existing inside of her and all creation.

Her feelings turned to thought. Politics wasn't bad. Politics was little more than people's collective decision-making, a process that allowed conflict to be resolved without resorting to physical violence. What felt so wrong was how politics worked in this place and time. She didn't have to become a politician of the sort she saw around her; she only had to do what she had always done. She had only to serve. To act in love and compassion and humility, allowing God to move in her and through her.

Winning didn't matter. Losing didn't matter. *I am but a vessel*, she thought. "A vessel in the springs," she said out loud as she laughed.

Julia left her towel on the grass and walked back to the spring-fed pool, diving into the clear water, feeling the shock of the cold turn into an invigorating rush. She swam and scissor-kicked and flipped onto her back to admire the clear morning sky.

• • •

Melanie and Jonathan were riding the highest high of their lives.

For Jonathan, there was a familiar sense of heightened alert, not unlike the singular focus he'd felt in combat. The world slowed, every sense was on edge and on alert. But this, thankfully, was much different. He was motivated by hope, not fear. He was crusading for a world where broken people healed alongside the person he respected most in the world.

For Melanie, it was destiny. She'd never admit it to her followers, or anyone, but she'd always imagined moments like this—where she was with the people who mattered. Where she mattered. Ever since she was twelve, when she first discovered that social media wasn't just a way to escape her mom, but a way to bring justice to those who deserved it, she'd known she was going to yield her phone like a weapon. She knew Beep-Beep was the start—but this? This was crazy! She got stopped on the street all the time. She was a top-ten Beeper. Number one in the PoliBeep segment! Bigger than that hatemonger, dog-whistling racist Frederick Borgese and his whole IntelBattle webcast.

And she was changing the world. For the better.

In their shared elation, they approached the towel where Julia lay with her eyes closed.

"Hey Julia," Jonathan began, "quite a night, huh?"

"A night to end all nights, I think." Julia opened her eyes and smiled. "And a beginning, from what I can tell."

Jonathan grinned. "Not to wreck your moment of zen, but your to-do list for the day is already enormous."

"Enormous is an understatement," Melanie said. "I've received over five hundred requests for interviews. And Noah has a team of political consultants he says urgently need to meet with you."

"There's also the Secret Service. Noah's request for protection has already been turned down. So we have to figure out security."

"Jonathan!" Julia was startled. "What on earth would I need security for?"

"I can think of a million reasons." Jonathan replied, thinking of the intelligence briefings that had preceded all his missions, concern showing on his face.

"Well, I can't. I'm happy to stick to my security-free way of life." Julia shuddered at the image of a phalanx of armed agents in monochrome suits breathing down her neck.

"I'll keep that in mind," Jonathan said, unsurprised despite his misgivings. "We've also received funding offers from what feels like every corporation, association, and billionaire in the country. I'm guessing that may be a problem for us."

"I only see opportunity," Julia said, grinning like a fox. She could immediately see that Mel and Jonathan misunderstood her. "Think back to chapter six of my book. One of the few things the far left and right agree on is that big money corrupts politics. This is just a chance to live our values."

"We'll say no to all of them?" Melanie's face was ashen. "Even the Motion Picture Association of America?"

"From what I've read about campaigns, they employ enormous compliance staff to vet their donations. I don't want an enormous compliance staff. So no, we won't say no, but let's make a donations policy. We will accept donations from anyone, but we will limit all donations to an innocuous sum. Say, two hundred dollars maximum?"

Melanie's eyes bugged. "But Julia, how are we going to staff up?! Hire our teams? Menendez and O'Leary are spending billions and employ over five thousand people each!" Her arms moved like a distressed bird's wings. "They have entire Beep-Beep teams!"

Julia was up, sitting cross-legged, a glint in her eye. "There won't be much staffing up at all. I'm sure we can get a basic team hired, but I don't want anything to change. This movement is about people acting in integrity with themselves, and that can't change. So anyone or any group can campaign for me as they see fit, but we won't be directing it at all."

"But what about my team?" Melanie said. "I have so many ideas!"

"Melanie, you already have a team. Why would we change anything when everything's worked so well?"

"Mel," Jonathan said, "I agree with Julia. We have to accept help, but we can't let the heart of what we're doing be polluted. The best way to resist the system is to reject that system altogether. If we become the system in an effort to win, then we've lost."

Melanie's eyes brightened. "So we're creating an alternative?"

"Exactly!" Julia beamed.

"Well," said Melanie, "that's all well and good, but Noah isn't going to like it. He showed us his one-hundred-and-fifty-page campaign plan. The consultants are collecting resumes right now."

Julia paused to consider her words as a fear resurfaced in her mind. "I'm not certain I trust Noah."

"Maybe," said Jonathan, "though man does he ever have connections. And I have to admit, he's incredibly savvy."

"But he SELLS spirituality," Julia stressed. "Spiritual and emotional growth is a process. It's the work of a lifetime, not a product."

"Now it's my turn to say, 'I only see opportunity,'" Melanie said. "He brought a hundred thousand people out last night. He got Lillie Rift to show up! Now that you're running for president, we need people like him."

"My loves. Every movement, every ideology, every system, every person has a shadow. Nothing is perfect, no one is always right. I'm just worried Noah is our shadow."

Melanie pursed her lips. "Worry later, Julia. Now we have to win."

CHAPTER 25

GOD IS ON THE BALLOT

Menedez's nostrils flared like a bull's snorting a rodeo clown. "How in the ever-loving name of God did Julia Connor get on the ballot in all fifty states? I thought our entire system of governance was designed to prevent this type of undemocratic shit from happening."

Luke Lockwood sat in silence. He glanced woefully at the open chair saved for Paster McMillan who was running late. But Jed Abernathy, who'd come to represent ROX News along with his producer Nancy, smirked. "Do you want to know what my sources are saying?"

"Hell yeah, I want to know! It can't be worse than the goddamn nothing everyone that works for me seems to know." Menendez glared at Luke. Everyone in the room registered the slap-like sting of his words.

"Word on the street," Jed said, relishing the moment, "is that Noah Glasnapp, the digi-guru that put together her rally in Austin, met a lawyer who spent a lot of time in Peru drinking a hallucinogenic tea of some sort. Now get this: the lawyer told Noah that the spirit of the tea told him that the constitutional amendment you sponsored last year—"

"How," Menendez roared, "can this have anything to do with my 'God is on the Ballot' constitutional amendment?"

"That's the kicker." Jed checked the notes in front of him. "A line in the amendment read, 'God, and those that believe in God, will from this day forth be assumed to be on the ballot at all times in order to reflect God's everlasting blessing of these United States of America.'"

"That was a horse-shit line in a horse-shit constitutional amendment. It wasn't literal. It's symbolic. What does that have to do with this?"

"Well, last week after your parachute incident, Noah's network ran a simultaneous shadow effort and took that legislative line to election officials in all fifty states, explained to them that because Julia believed in God she was, effectively, already on the ballot, and the election officials agreed." Jed leaned back in his chair and shrugged. "Between that line in the amendment and the fifty thousand signatures he gathered in each state using a strategy he calls 'triangles,' she got on the ballot. There you go, simple as that."

Menendez was stunned. Silent for once. Unable to summon a response to the most ridiculous—yet plausible—rumor he'd ever heard.

Luke's tight-faced scowl was locked on Senator Menendez. As Jed's story slowly settled into the room, he exploded. "This whole frickin' thing, this theological catastrophe, this act of political malpractice—it's all your fault!"

"Listen you little shit," Menendez thundered, his finger jabbing the air, "my job is to raise money and do what you tell me to do, say what you tell me to say. The fact that our state election operations teams got caught with their pants down is not my fault. It's your fault! I oughta fire you right now! Shouldn't we be suing, isn't the Supreme Court on our side?"

"Oh, we'll sue them," Luke said, "sue them all. But the fact that she's on the ballot isn't the worst of it. You went out and said all these nice things about Julia. You let her dictate the gosh-darn terms with her all love is God's love doctrinal heresy, and now we have to backtrack, attacking someone you just called 'anointed by God.' I mean, have you seen her commercial?!"

"Commercial? What commercial?!"

"What," Luke seethed, "have you been doing the last two hours? I sent you the link first thing this morning. It's the only thing playing on the news. It—"

Pastor Josiah McMillan burst into the room, veins bulging in his neck, face red as the assumed skin tone of Satan himself.

"Menendez, you degenerate! You've gone off and opened the door for the Devil."

"Pastor Josiah, come on. The Devil? This isn't Sunday school. Why don't you channel some of that love Julia Connor keeps saying comes from your God?"

"Don't talk to me about love," Pastor McMillan snarled. "I'm here to talk about power. Power I've earned, power that is going to help you become president—as long as you get your act together."

Menedez threw his head back and laughed. *This prick thinks he can tell me what to do?*

He leaned close to Pastor McMillan's pulsating face and lowered his voice: "Listen, Pastor. I have never lost an election. I maintained a wonderful relationship with Christians across this fine country long before I let you into my orbit. Now, I need you and Luke to keep doing whatever it is you do to keep your flock riled up, and I'll keep doing what I have to do to win this election. Why don't you go back to your church to cool down? Maybe read some scripture while we talk strategy?"

"You want to talk strategy? Great, talk strategy. But I don't want to hear a word from Luke about you thinking for yourself. You got yourself into this mess, now let the professionals get you out." He turned and stormed out of the room.

In the silence that followed, Micah, Senator Menedez's new chief strategist and Luke's deputy, decided to flex his campaign muscles. "Exactly right, Senator. Exactly right. You've never lost—why would you now?" Encouraged by the damn-right nod he received from Menendez, Micah powered on. "So why don't we pull up that new ad of Julia's and see what we're dealing with? Then let's figure out how we're going to chop the legs out from under the love movement."

The commercial for Julia Connor, released by Noah's Sovereign Love Super PAC, used footage of Julia's Love and Compassion book tour and excerpts from Melanie's Beeps.

The spot opened with a shot of Julia walking in her garden and then segued to her standing at the pulpit of St. Andrews United Methodist Church at the book tour launch in Boston.

"Julia Connor is running for president to bring the universal love of God to the center of American life," rumbled the deep-voiced narrator. "Senator Menendez called Julia 'a prophet anointed by God.' Governor O'Leary said Julia is—"

Here it cut to O'Leary on stage in Sedona, "Julia is a genius for reminding us all that to solve matters of injustice, we can't just lead with policy, we have to lead with love."

"Who paid for this shit," Jed interrupted, his eyes switching from the TV monitor to his phone. "There's a ten million dollar buy on it."

The narrator continued over a montage of Julia sitting with a group of mothers and their children, then college students, and finally a room full of veterans. "Our economic system has crushed the American people. Our political system excludes voices proposing new solutions. Only by learning to love each other and ourselves can we fulfill the promise of America."

A final graphic appeared on screen. "Vote Julia. Vote Yes for Love. Paid for by the Sovereign Love Super PAC."

The screen went dark. The men in the room avoided making sound or eye contact.

Finally Menendez spoke. "Well, Luke, I guess your pastor had a point this once. Will you set up a call so I can eat some crow?"

Luke sighed. "I sure will, Senator. But first, we have to start taking care of Julia." Turning to look at Jed, he said, "You know the playbook. I think it's time you had a little sit-down interview with the candidate."

• • •

On the other side of the country, in the O'Leary for President campaign office in Portland, Oregon, Bradley Bishkoff and Governor Jacqueline O'Leary sat with their newest team member, political strategist Alison Ignatius.

Alison Ignatius had spent recent weeks moping and castigating herself for having signed on with the wrong primary candidate—Mary Hooks. What a waste. She'd been so torn up about it she had almost given in to the temptation to toss a pint of ice cream in with her kale smoothie mix, riced cauliflower, and freshly frozen berries. But distressed or not, Alison had the figure of a twenty-two-year-old track star to maintain. And now was she ever glad she hadn't scraped the bottom of the barrel for a spoonful of unpronounceable-ingredient-laden refined sugar.

Here she was, back in the big time, called in by Bradley to lend a much-needed hand. She looked at Bradley and Governor O'Leary, both of whom looked great considering they'd just been blindsided by the most confusing campaign development in the United States' history.

They studied the Julia Connor campaign ad, watching it three times in a row without saying a word.

Alison spoke first. "I did not see this coming. None of it. The commercial. Her entering the race. The operation to get her on the ballot in all fifty states. It's amazing, really, and a total surprise!"

Bradley, who'd spent his life escaping the judgment of those who followed God, couldn't contain himself.

"What. A. Fucking. Nightmare. We're in a theological election all of a sudden, tied in the polls with an Evangelical-pandering, gay-bashing, immigrant-hating son of an immigrant and a woo-woo kook who can't stop talking about love and God. Are we going to join this God-worshiping circle jerk?"

Governor O'Leary could see it both ways. "Bringing God into politics isn't always bad. A lot of Democrats are Christians. Clinton was. He played saxophone in a black church!"

Bradley wrinkled his face. "Oh my gawd, please. Clinton got blown by a child in the Oval Office."

Alison, who made it a priority not to put candidates on the defensive, tried again. "Obama was a Christian too."

"Maybe," Bradley replied, remembering childhood Sunday school lessons, "but the first thing he did after leaving office was jet ski on Richard Branson's private island, not minister to the poor."

"Bradley," O'Leary scowled, "billionaires are your forte."

"Their contributions are my forte. I tell them to their face all the time, 'In a sane world, you'd meet the guillotine.' But as it is, I like to win."

"Well"—Alison risked stating the obvious—"we have to do something. And that's why I'm here. If we don't drive up the negatives on Julia, she'll steal all our white women!"

"White women?" O'Leary said. "I thought I needed black women?"

"That was in the primaries, Governor," Bradley said. "To win the general election, we need white women."

"Exactly!" Alison said. "We have to destroy Julia's popularity with white women ASAP."

Bradly rolled his eyes. "So spread the rumor she owns just *one* pair of shoes and doesn't like pumpkin spice lattes."

"Enough," O'Leary said. "I still can't help feeling she's some flavor-of-the-minute fad. I can't see how this geriatric, who has no experience in the crucible of public service, is as big an obstacle as Menendez."

"If you look at the polling, Governor, and if you spend any time on Beep-Beep, or watch the videos of her events," Alison continued, "it's clear Julia Connor is an enormous threat to both campaigns. But since she's a woman and so are you, she's more of a threat to us."

"But," Bradley said, "we have to be careful. We share a lot of the same values. So we're going to bifurcate our efforts. We'll turn NATN News and our surrogates loose to denigrate her at every turn, but you need to stay respectful—and figure out how to walk back calling her a genius a week ago."

"Einstein was a genius, too. That doesn't mean I want him playing violin naked in the Oval Office."

"Bingo!" said Alison. "Maybe that's the exact point we need to make to neutralize the soundbite."

"You're exactly right," Bradley told Alison, thinking, *And you're a better ass-kisser than me.* "I mean, she has no media training whatsoever, right? We'll get our reporter pals to trip her up. Should be a piece of cake."

CHAPTER 26

GONGS

CBS, ABC, NBC, CSPAN, ROX News' Jed Abernathy and NATN's Heather Haliburton—all the usual suspects—were on deck for Julia's first press conference. The *New York Times* had dispatched two reporters to play catch-up. Ditto the *Washington Post*. *USA Today*, *Time*, the AP, Reuters, and Bloomberg sent correspondents. *Christianity Today*, *The Buddhist Quarterly*, the *Islamic Advocate*, and *Crystal Energy Now* sent reporters too.

These reporters, along with cameramen and photographers, crammed into the enormous yoga room at Austin's Consciousness Hub, the Noah-owned and self-declared "heartbeat of Austin's spiritual community," which now served as the Connor campaign headquarters.

Noah couldn't have been more pleased with himself. He had seen an opportunity and pounced. He had researched legal loopholes to get Julia on the ballot nationwide, launched Sovereign Love Super PAC before she even agreed to run, and hired two of the top independent political consultants in the country.

The consultants brought the know-how, the experience, and the connections needed to win. They had relationships with the AFL-CIO, the Chamber of Commerce, the American Healthcare Association, the American Data Freedom Association, the Social Networks for Peace and Justice Coalition, and dozens of other associations, coalitions and trade groups with checkbooks and bodies to lend campaign support.

And yet, Julia hadn't seemed inclined to let him take over her campaign.

"That's very nice, Noah," Julia had said, in the tone of a busy but kind grandmother praising her child's art project, when Melanie and Jonathan had brought him in for a breakfast meeting along with both consultants. "You're doing truly wonderful work."

"I want to do even more. I want to turn your vision into the most optimized grassroots movement the world has ever seen. I want to put triangles—triangles!—to work to turn this country upside down!"

"Triangles?"

"Melanie and Jonathan didn't tell you about the triangles? Let me give you the five-minute demo!" He pulled out an iPad and shared his "triangles of power" theory.

"What you're saying," Julia asked, "is that our broad-based, decentralized movement to bring love and compassion into politics is changing the political conversation and elevating the energy, vibes, and level of consciousness of people across the country?"

"Yes, exactly! And we can—"

"Not change a thing," Julia finished for him. "If it's working so well already, why mix things up? Anyways, I prefer mycelial analogies."

"But Julia," one of the consultants had said, "There's so much to change. The American people expect a president that looks and acts and talks a certain way. You need"—he paused, looking for inspiration—"you need pantsuits! And generals! And a grassroots operation to knock on doors and win votes. You need a symbolic first appearance as a candidate, maybe the Texas state capitol or the Lincoln Memorial? Or—given your passion for climate issues—the Hoover Dam or a wind farm?"

"No," Julia had said. She had never been a shrinking violet when it came to her principles, but this campaign experience was making her all the more confident and firm about standing up for them. "No, I want to hold my first press conference in the Yoga studio at the Consciousness Hub that Noah so generously donated to the campaign. I want my campaign to reflect my values."

While Noah was thrilled for all the free PR, he would have much preferred for Julia to start acting like someone who wanted to win, instead of doing whatever it was she thought she was doing by hosting the press conference in his yoga studio.

Julia was unconcerned. She knew he wanted control, and she was equally certain she wasn't going to give it to Noah. She'd gotten this far relying on Melanie, Jonathan, and her army of supporters; while she was open to people like Noah helping get her elected, she wasn't going to stop doing things her way.

"Melanie, how does it look in there?" Julia asked.

Melanie peaked into Yoga Studio #1 through a window in the door.

"Very crowded." She grinned. "Think they're comfortable?"

• • •

Sitting on a yoga mat, legs bent beneath, her pencil skirt bursting at the seams, Heather Haliburton hissed, "Is this a fucking joke? I've never seen anything less professional in my life."

Sally Carlson from *USA Today* nodded. "No joke. If I hadn't worn panties, I'd be flashing the whole room!"

"OMG, same!" Heather burst out laughing. "What a shit show."

"Gooooonnnnngggggggg."

A murmur of disbelief filled the room.

"Gooooonnnnngggggggg."

Heather's, Sally's, and their colleagues' quantum centers quivered under the sustained assault of a gonging gong's gonging reverberations.

"Goooooooooooonnnnnnggggggggggg."

Julia Connor entered wearing a simple blouse; the same faded, navy-blue khakis she wore at every event; and a blissed-out, smooth-faced smile framed by her lustrous silver-white hair, the kind of hair that refuted the age it was supposed to telegraph.

"She looks so normal," Sally Carlson whispered to Heather.

Heather side-eyed Sally. "What normal person enters a room to gongs? And look at her fucking smile. How can she look so happy, so cheerful? She's mocking us."

Heather was right.

Julia had decided to make covering her campaign as edifying as possible for traditional media, the spewers of instantly profitable opinion, venom, and contrived controversy. It's not that they were bad people, but the system they worked within and the people they performed for demanded consistently bad behavior.

A few moments of enforced silent contemplation seemed the most appropriate, if not the most painful, practice to inflict upon them.

Sitting on a cushioned rattan bench in the front of the room, Julia beamed. "Well, hello, everyone! We'll start this press conference like we'll start every Julia Connor for President press conference, with centering prayer."

Her proclamation was met with silent confusion until Sally called out, "Julia, what's that?"

"Oh, dear. I didn't mean to catch you off guard! Silly me. Centering prayer is a spiritual innovation pioneered by the Desert Fathers. It's similar to Lectio Divina or a Buddhist mindfulness practice. If you need assistance, we have some local yogis on hand to offer support."

The room fell back into silence.

"Who is this person?" Heather stage whispered.

Julia sat back, straightened her frame, and spread her hands, opening herself to the room and the universe beyond.

"I invite each of you," Julia said in her most gentle voice, "to choose a word signifying one of your values. Perhaps compassion or forgiveness will do. Now close your eyes and focus on that word. Let it settle into your mind."

The press tried to comply. People unused to silence squirmed awkwardly in their made-for-TV work wear, doing their best to find physical comfort on the yoga mats and mental comfort in the room's resounding quiet.

Then the local yogis Julia had asked to help began circulating through the room, guiding reporters toward the correct posture, asking them to respect the silence when they grunted, groaned, and swore.

Julia continued. "Open yourself to God and to yourself as you focus on your word, making yourself available to the divine source of wisdom and love. Rest here, in this moment of inner availability, and listen."

"Is she trolling us?" Heather whisper-squealed to Sally.

"This is the most useless thing I've ever seen. What is she hoping for, that we'll somehow experience this 'healing' she keeps talking about?"

Jed Abernathy had wisely positioned himself by the door. Sensing a press conference disaster in the making, he stepped outside, lit a cigarette, and watched his colleagues through a large picture window.

He observed as one of the serene yogis approached Heather, her face still snarled with angry whispering despite repeated requests for everyone to "find their centers and rest there."

Getting on her knees next to Heather, a young woman gently murmured, "Friend, please respect yourself and the other seekers. We are listening in silence, together."

"You listen to me," Heather hissed in the yogi's face. "I don't think it's very respectful to make a group of professionals sit with our hoohas on display on fucking kindergarten mats when we came here for a *press conference*."

Placing a hand on this hurting soul's shoulder, the yogi looked deep into Heather's admittedly gorgeous blue eyes and replied, "Can I channel peace for you?"

Heather slapped the gentle hand off her shoulder, making sure to leave a mark. "You can keep your hands to yourself is what you can do!"

Julia opened her eyes to join everyone else in staring at Heather. And at the yogi, who wore a look of such hurt that Heather, in any circumstance where her inner calm was not being attacked by centering prayer, would have felt bad for her.

"Well, friends, perhaps this is our stopping place," Julia said, her smile still in place. "Would my friend who does not want to be touched—which is totally understandable—like to ask the first question? I'm sorry I don't know your name."

"My name?" It had been years since someone hadn't recognized her.

"Yes, your name," said Julia, who'd hadn't watched NATN since 2006. "I'd love to know who I'm speaking with."

"I'm Heather Haliburton with NATN." She paused to make sure she got the question Bradley had fed her just right. "Julia, what do you say to women who think you're cheapening their fight for equality by focusing on love and healing instead of real-world issues?"

Julia smiled. She was impressed—not with the question but with the fact that one of Noah's political consultants had warned her to expect a query like this.

"In my lifetime, Heather, women have had to channel their masculine energy to succeed in a world that prioritizes unhealthy aspects of the male psyche. Focusing on love brings women into our greatest feminine power, allowing us to lead and to live from our emotional core while trusting our intuition, instead of imitating unhealthy alpha-male roles."

Heather, who was more of an alpha male than any man she'd met, smirked. "What do you say to critics who say love is a little shallow as a governing strategy?"

"I don't agree. Obviously."

Heather needed a better soundbite. "What about tough questions of governing and realpolitik, like war? I mean, how can one possibly lovingly conduct war?"

Julia closed her eyes and slipped back into a meditative state, seeking an answer to this question.

"I appreciate what Khalil Gibran had to say about love. Khalil wrote that love is both growth and pruning. I take this to mean that love isn't just a pleasant feeling or an act of mercy; love is also the hard choices we make to exist and act with integrity in our imperfect, sometimes violent world."

A rumble of discontent rose in the air.

"Sally Carlson, *USA Today*. Julia, can you explain what that means?"

"It means," said Julia, "that while reality dictates violence is sometimes necessary, leadership demands we act out of love in these moments, showing wisdom and compassion toward our adversaries, doing what is necessary to protect ourselves, but never confusing self-defense with revenge or retribution."

Jed Abernathy, who had slid back into the room, was salivating. Here he was in the most interesting out of the thousands of press conferences he'd attended—and Julia Conner had just fucked up.

"Julia," Jed shouted, "did you just quote a MUSLIM poet to answer a question about AMERICAN Security?"

"What? No." Julia raised her eyebrows in surprise. "Khalil Gibran was a Christian teacher. Have you never read his work?"

Jed, who smelled the blood and could already see this clip playing across ROX News, didn't let up. "A Christian with a Muslim name like Khalil? Ha!"

"I'm sorry, I didn't get your name?"

"Jed Abernathy, ROX News."

"Well, Jed, if you do some research, I'm confident you will find Khalil was a Lebanese Maronite. Next question?"

If there was anything anyone who knew him *knew*, it was that Jed Abernathy stood his ground. Julia reeked of opportunity and headlines, and he wasn't about to give up just because she thought she'd one-upped him about this so-called Lebanese Maronite with a Muslim name. And regardless, he had his assignment from Luke.

After the press conference ended, Jed introduced himself to Julia and asked if she was interested in being introduced to ROX News's God-fearing viewers. "I would love to sit down with you for a Barbara Walters-esque living room interview at your home in Tenino, Washington. What do you say?"

● ● ●

"Today during her first press conference, newly announced presidential candidate Julia Connor likely alienated many of her voters with a shocking statement," declared a breathless Heather Haliburton. "The so-called *love lady* of the election, who has been polling extremely favorably with women, said that all working women were channeling toxic masculinity—an insult that brings to mind the patriarchal ignorance we're used to seeing from Republican leaders and tribal peasants in places like Africa and the Amazon."

Heather had changed, by now, out of the rumbled skirt of her chic cashmere suit and into the no-nonsense pants-and-blazer look that screamed professionalism. God, what she wouldn't give for a picture of herself standing next to Julia Conner. Maybe *that* would wake people up to how shabby this grandma really was.

"And speaking of toxic masculinity, Jed Abernathy from ROX News once again proved how stunted his and his viewer's world views are when he thought Khalil Gibran, a famous Christian author, was a Muslim. How do you claim the religious high ground when you don't even know many early Christians were from the Middle East?"

Across the street at ROX News, Jed delivered equally important information to the American people. "In so-called presidential candidate Julia Connor's first press conference, she proved she is unfit for office after making reporters sit on the ground while stating that her foreign policy is inspired by a man named Khalil. Do you know who sits on the ground, America? Do you know who names their children Kahlil? Muslims. Muslims do these things. This did not go unnoticed or unremarked upon among political insiders—or anyone with half a brain. As one respected leader told me: 'I can't help wondering if Julia Connor is a secret Islamic agent.' Clearly, that member of Congress is not alone."

Melanie took to Beep-Beep, relieved the platform reached more eyeballs than both news networks combined.

Starting in the splits, she did the worm and then elevated into a handstand before landing on her feet facing the camera, with her "Mel P" graphic flashing on the screen in bold letters.

"Did you watch the news about our NEW PRESIDENTIAL CANDIDATE JULIA CONNOR?" she almost sang. "One network called Julia an Islamic secret agent; the other suggested Julia said all working women channeled toxic masculinity. Go watch the press conference—I put the CSPAN link in BeepFlow—and see what she said for yourself! This kind of coverage is what politicians and reporters call driving up the negatives. Ignore them. Listen to what Julia has to say. Judge her for yourself. These networks are all about the status quo. One supports O'Leary, the other supports Menendez. Neither supports hope, healing, or love! Do not fall prey to systems designed to operate in a world driven by fear."

Ten minutes later Melanie streamed another video.

"Friends," Jonathan said, staring into the screen, "for too long, active military and veterans such as myself have had to listen to politicians speak with nothing but bluster and bombast. Would it be such a bad thing to have a leader who understood the human cost of war? Who has helped thousands of veterans such as myself heal from the trauma of combat? Who prioritizes wisdom over ego and chooses the explosive, life-giving power of love over the explosive life-ending power of military might?"

After Jonathan finished videoing with Melanie, a military influencer best known for blowing up household items with military weapons, Alexi Pappasoutos, took his place across from the grizzled teddy bear of a man. "So, Jonathan. You ready to speak to my five million followers?"

CHAPTER 27

A FLOCK OF PATRIOTS

With one month to go before election day, Governor Jacqueline O'Leary's team barnstormed across the West.

"I," O'Leary promised, "will cut taxes for all Americans except the wealthiest Americans who don't have the sense to shelter their money offshore. I'll provide free school lunches, free college education, and solar panels for all! I will eliminate the risk of bedrock technology companies like Troojle or Orange outsourcing jobs to internationally owned AI conglomerates by passing the 'Data Rights Are Human Rights Act.'"

In the Southeast, Senator Menendez worked feverishly to prevent Evangelicals from abandoning the Republican party for Julia's message of God's universal love.

"America," he said over and over, "you may have thought we had done all we could do to eliminate the threat of men who think they're women and women who think they're men, but you're wrong. Some states haven't yet banned books using the word 'they,' I will right this wrong! You may think the border wall I will build will be enough, but it won't! By passing a law saying that only children born within our borders to parents with American citizenship will be awarded citizenship, I will eliminate illegal immigration. And finally, America, I will stop the scourge of beekeepers that is sweeping our nation by creating the Monsanto-funded United States Board of Beekeeping

Governance. No bees except bees genetically modified to survive Monsanto's pesticides and feed on Monsanto-modified flowers will live within our borders when I'm president."

Menendez's efforts fell far short of what Pastor Josiah McMillan would have liked to see. The pastor began preaching three sermons a day against Julia Connor on his Salvation Streaming Platform.

"My flock of patriots." He called upon the same theological spirit that Ronald Reagan had when he embraced Jerry Falwell and the Moral Majority in the eighties. "God was clear when he told us that HE is the way and the truth and the life. Life, he said. Life. Life only through him. Let us not be seduced by life-diminishing policies promising equality, or the heretical idea that there could be a love that is not of Jesus Christ. Let us not forget that God gave us dominion over the earth. Dominion! When candidates say we must prioritize the environment, they are trying to remove the life Jesus Christ promised us, the life Senator Menendez wants to see for all Americans of all colors and creeds and acceptable credit ratings!"

Campaigning with Melanie and Jonathan, Julia made only four stops a day, at each declaring that "in our America, in the America we are co-creating, the purpose of public policy will be to create conditions that prioritize human wellbeing and normalize emotional and spiritual awareness. In this new, better, fairer America, we'll remember our connection to the earth and to each other, making policy that honors the reality of humanity's interconnectedness."

At this point she would pause and wink at her audience. "Now my friends, you may ask how. How can we do this? Well, it's a good thing we can start modeling it now! So I want you all to go to Juliaforpresident.com and sign up to volunteer for a shift of door-to-door connecting. Will you be asking people to vote for me? No, you won't. What you'll be doing is asking your neighbors how you can help. Asking if you can listen to them tell you about their joys and their fears, their pain and their triumphs. Or if they need help with paying a bill or raking their leaves."

"Holy shit, she's a genius," one of Noah's consultants said to a media contact, working doubly hard to prove his importance since he knew Julia had yet to follow a single piece of his advice. "She's following our rule number one of campaigning: make a promise to the world with a slogan that means nothing. Obama had 'hope.' Trump had 'make great again.' Julia has 'love.' She's unstoppable with us guiding her campaign!"

Through the week, polling hardly moved. Julia remained tied for the lead and the news cycle began to froth about two upcoming events that "could be," "were almost certain to be," "would definitely most likely be" of make-or-break importance.

The first was the approaching presidential debate. Despite thousands of hours of research from harried opposition-research professionals, no one knew what to expect from a debate that featured a gentle geriatric who had written twenty books and the two major-party candidates. Would they both try to burn the love vote to the ground on live TV? Claim it as their own? Find a new way to attack Julia's character?

The second event was Julia's sit-down interview with Jed Abernathy. Rival networks screamed for equal time, but Julia diffused the controversy by simply noting, "He asked first."

After that response, the network honchos concluded the Love candidate deserved whatever hell Jed Abernathy rained down on her. It seemed to journalists on either side of the political aisle that the Abernathy interview was an act of extreme naivety as Jed had yet to find a hatchet he wasn't willing to bury in a convenient target's back.

Others disagreed. Bradley was one of them. "It must," he told O'Leary as he examined his chin in the reflective surface of his phone, trying to determine if he had another damn stress zit, "be Julia's consultants. They must have a plan for the Abernathy interview."

CHAPTER 28

AN AWFUL LOT OF BLACK PEOPLE

On Julia's farm, trees full of plump apples begged to be harvested. Leaves' lush summer greens were turning to faded reds. She would have loved to spend this beautiful day plucking veggies and gourds from the ground before she prepped her rows for their winter slumber.

Instead, she felt like a prisoner in her own home. ROX News vehicles clogged her driveway. A cameraman walked through her garden getting B-roll, doing his best to capture buzzing bees.

Inside Julia's house, she met with Noah's consultants. They had worked with Bush and Obama, according to Noah. "What should I expect?" she'd asked the consultant in the hat. She could never remember their names, or tell them apart, but she knew one of them wore a hat some days, so she focused on him.

"He's going to smile like a pussy cat and then hit you like a hurricane."

"I know that. But on what? How?"

"He'll come after you for abortion and black people. For love being a threat to national security. It's Abernathy, so he is probably going to revisit your 'Muslim Mistake.'"

"The Muslim Mistake? Really?" Melanie had told her the talking heads on ROX used that phrase. Were these consultants just repeating TV talking points?

"Exactly." The second consultant said. "You quoted a poet to answer a question about war. Khalil Gibran, remember? We'd advised that you say that you would 'trust your generals to do the right thing.'"

"But what I said was a true representation of what I believe."

"Julia! What you believe doesn't matter."

"Are you kidding me?"

"Of course it matters, but the point isn't *saying* what you believe to be true. The point is to say what you have to say to win. The hopes of the entire love vote are riding on your shoulders! You owe it to the people to keep your beliefs to yourself."

"I'll bear that in mind." Julia sighed.

From the front porch, Jed watched the set stylist move Julia's potted plants around her living room and adjust the loveseat. He got a call from Luke. It was final instructions time.

"Listen," said Luke, speaking into the speaker phone in his office, "do not pull a single punch. You know the playbook. It's worked for years. Julia is no different than any other communist, God-hating, left-wing loser."

"OK, you got it. I'll soften her up. But don't expect a kill shot."

"Exactly. Menendez wants that for the debate."

Jed ended the call. An assistant told him they were almost ready, but Julia was refusing to let them put make-up on her.

"But Julia," pled Abernathy's producer Nancy, who was wearing a giraffe sweater to maximize her likeability, "everyone wears makeup on TV. We even put makeup on the Pope. You'll look terrible without it, like a ghost. Hi-definition is the most unforgiving invention in history."

Julia gently rolled her eyes. "I haven't worn makeup in over twenty years. I'm not going to start kowtowing to this silly ritual now."

This was going to kill it on Beep-Beep, thought Melanie, who was filming the exchange. She filed it away to keep in reserve in case this ROX asshole's interview drew any blood.

Finally, Nancy worked out a solution. The lights on Jed would be as bright as normal, but the lights on Julia would be lower wattage. "It may look a bit odd," Nancy said. "But we can't risk scaring viewers with hi-def wrinkles."

"I'll pretend I didn't hear that," Julia said, touching her wrinkles, which she loved. "Are we ready?"

Nancy nodded and Julia cast a last longing look at her typewriter. She hadn't written a thing in months, and she didn't see that changing anytime soon. She walked into the living room to face the cameras.

When she extended a gentle hug to Jed, the beard on his Civil War–general-like face tickled her forehead. "Jed, I'm just so excited about this interview. I think getting to know you better will be fun!"

Jed's smile froze on his face. Was she trying to get inside his head? He couldn't tell, so he steeled himself against her disruptive kindness. "I know I'm looking forward to it too, Julia. And I know our viewers are as well." He winked into the camera, which was already rolling. "Is it OK if I call you Julia?"

"That is my name, Jed," Julia said, settling into her deep, blue thrift-shop loveseat, the "lower wattage" lights still feeling hot and sticky on her face.

"So Julia," Jed began as the cameras rolled, "you've caused quite the kerfuffle over the last several weeks. Some call you the president-in-waiting. Others call you a lunatic. I just want to help the American people get to know you."

"That's so kind of you, Jed." Julia leaned in toward the camera. "As long as we all remember that my candidacy is about the people of this country taking responsibility for themselves and for our democracy, I'd love the American people to better know me!"

"Then you won't mind if we jump right into the rapid-fire questions." Not waiting for a response—he hadn't asked a question, after all—he said, "What is love?"

"I don't think the English language has enough words to define love. There is love for a parent, for a best friend, for nature, for a pet, for a child, and even for an enemy." Julia caught herself. She was supposed to be giving concise, pithy answers. She got back on track. "To quote the great Reverend Martin Luther King Jr., 'Love is the supreme unifying principle of life.' To elaborate, love is the essence of human existence, of God's connection to each of us and to the world as a whole."

Jed glanced at his notes. He couldn't get off script; they'd planned this to the letter. "What is God?"

"God is love."

Jed smiled. Now they were getting to the meat of it. "Are you a Christian?"

Julia smiled brightly. "Of course I'm a Christian. I've been a follower of Jesus since I was a young woman."

"Yet you believe in a universal God whose love is available to all humans regardless of what religion they follow?"

"I do."

"You know that means you'll go to hell, right?"

"Excuse me?" Julia took a quick breath in and raised her eyebrows.

Jed grinned a bit too broadly. "If you don't believe salvation comes only through Jesus Christ, then you're a heretic and you will burn in hell. My pastor, the great Josiah McMillan, is very clear on this."

Julia regained a look of calm composure. She leaned forward. "Jed, I believe exclusionary approaches to God ignore what are literally thousands of years of human experience to the contrary. And it ignores my personal experience knowing God and worshipping with those who know God all across this world. Yes, I'm a Christian, and yes, I love Jesus, but I also believe seekers can know God through other traditions. God, after all, is love, and love exists everywhere."

"So Julia, you're basically saying that every Christian in America, and in the world, is wrong about God's word as revealed in his son Jesus Christ—that we'll be sharing heaven with people from other faiths?"

The camera zoomed in on Julia, catching her gentle, unwavering smile. "What I'm saying, Jed, is that many of us have allowed ourselves to be led astray by those who focus not on God's love and compassion but on religion's obsession with being right and maintaining authority."

"Julia, that's just ridiculous." Jed theatrically shook his head. "So faith and doctrine are bad things?"

"Please don't put words in my mouth. Faith is a wonderful thing. But it can be harnessed and manipulated in ways that foster division and hate, which is, in a very real sense, the opposite of love."

He switched gears. "So, abortion?"

"I support supporting life. In such a bountiful nation, women shouldn't be forced to choose between their child and poverty, or face the hard reality of raising a child without the father around. Yet we live in a world where men often fail to live up to their potential, putting women in impossible situations, and where our government and our communities don't support mothers' needs. So Jed, I absolutely support a woman's right to live as she chooses, to decide if she is ready to be a mother or not. The idea of a man like you deciding if a woman should be having a child is alarming, to say the very least."

"So you believe in killing babies and you're a socialist. Got it."

"Julia," Jed paused as an assistant carried over a stack of framed pictures, "we found several photos of you scattered around the house. Would you mind telling me about these?"

"Of course, I'd be happy to!" Julia's face brightened. She loved reminiscing about the wonderful people she'd met over the years. "I probably have hundreds of these around the house. I can't wait to see which ones you've chosen."

Jed handed her the photos. "Why don't you hold these up to the camera and tell us about them."

"Well," Julia began, looking at the photos and holding them up as she spoke, "this is me with Desmond Tutu and Nelson Mandela's wife, Winnie, in South Africa. This is President Obama back before he ever ran for office. This is me with Maya Angelou; we've known each other since we were young women. This—"

"I think that's enough, Julia. Our viewers get the point."

"The point?"

"Julia, that's an awful lot of black people. Why do you believe in dividing America based on our race and ethnicity?"

Julia glanced at Melanie, who, thank goodness, was filming on the side. She couldn't believe Jed's nerve!

"Well, Jed, I don't. I believe so many people's obsession with racial or ethnic identity is, ultimately, harmful to communities that define themselves in ways that separate us from each other. But we were born a slaving nation into a violent colonialist world, and we still have not fully acknowledged our past. We, as Americans, must not only repent for sinning against God, but we must do right by our black and brown brothers and sisters who often continue to exist as second-class citizens in this country and abroad. Until we make peace with our history and act with integrity in the present, we can hardly expect people victimized by white America to focus on togetherness. Frankly, I am amazed by the faith and grace I see in much of the African American community. Talk about turning the other cheek."

"Is that the sort of defeatist, white-victim-blaming logic you applied when you said, and here I'm quoting from your book *Decolonizing Spirituality*"— Jed studiously maintained his grim look as he opened to his bookmark—"that westerners should 'seek spiritual guidance from our indigenous brothers and sisters as we learn to be death doulas for modernity'?'"

"I don't think that is defeatist at all!" Julia was mad, madder than she'd been in ages, in years. Jed was saying all the things she most wanted to believe people no longer believed. "Acknowledging the past isn't victim blaming; it's part of being loving, responsible, caring humans. If we can't acknowledge our past, how can we ever be reasonable, informed, compassionate people in the present?"

Jed couldn't believe how well the interview was going! "Julia, you sound like a crazy libtard to me. Why are Democrats so mad at you?"

"Jed, that is not acceptable language! Oh my, just oh my." Julia, known for a smile so serene it made everyone wish she were their grandmother, set her face in a scowl. "I am not going to answer that question. I demand an apology or this interview is over!"

"For the word libtard?" Jed grinned, twisting the knife and enjoying Julia's elderly-person temper tantrum. God, she was cute when she got mad.

"Say it again and I will end this interview. Apologize or we are done here!"

Jed kept grinning, speaking like he was talking to a child. "I apologize for offending you, Julia. Will you forgive me?"

"It is an offensive word!" Julia boiled at his haughtiness, her heart racing despite her best efforts to stay calm. He was doing this intentionally, on live TV? The disrespect that had made her stop watching television felt far worse in person than she could have imagined. She hoped people watching at home could excuse her anger. "And you should know better than to talk to any person with as much disrespect as you're showing me right now. I, frankly, am flabbergasted at your behavior."

Jed smirked, still having the time of his life. "I will rephrase the question. You sound like a typical radical leftist. Why are Democrats so mad at you?"

"Jed," Julia countered, fighting for and finally finding calm, "I think *many* Democrats and Republicans don't see me as a threat. If you look at the polling, many from both parties support me. But Democratic political leaders? Well, they see me as a threat for the same reason Republican leaders do. I threaten a two-party system that depends on fear and hate to raise money and motivate voters as part of a political duopoly whose business model is threatened by alternative ideas and candidates." Julia slipped into her kindest voice. "Wouldn't that explain why you're sitting here trying to assassinate my character?"

"Julia, you old kook of a hippy grandma, I would never." Jed leaned across and condescendingly patted Julia on the shoulder. "But thanks so much for joining us and sharing your home."

"My pleasure."

Pausing, Jed looked into the camera and delivered his last line. "America, you heard it here. Julia Connor, in her own words, is a baby-murdering, race-baiting heretic. But tune into the debate next week to make up your own mind!"

• • •

The interview aired on TV and online. Point and counterpoint were made on Beep-Beep and Flitter and in reader comments on newspaper websites. ROX News and NATN cherrypicked highlights to discuss on their broadcasts. Both candidates responded with a commercial.

Staring into the screen, an American flag rippling in the hot southwestern wind behind him, Senator Menendez spoke in grave tones, his baritone voice pouring forth to convey the gravity of his words.

"America," he said in the closing seconds of his ad, "Julia Connor called Americans slavers. Slavery was abolished in this nation over one hundred and fifty years ago, yet Julia and dangerous liberals like Governor O'Leary continue to drag us through a painful past that we all would be best off pretending never happened. Don't get caught looking to the past—vote for the future and vote for Christian capitalism. Vote Menendez."

Smiling into the camera, Governor Jaqueline O'Leary tried to thread a minuscule and shrinking needle. Handcuffed by what Bradley and Alison called political paradox—needing to attack the love vote candidate, but not the love vote itself because it polled so well with her voters—she positioned herself as the experienced *true* liberal.

"Julia Connor has never cast a single vote in favor of Medicare. She has never stared down a Republican trying to take your human rights. She has never even won an election. In a year when every free human's human rights are on the ballot, can you trust someone with no political track record to be president? For the thinking person, the answer is no. Vote for a proven track record of success. Vote O'Leary."

Bradley groaned watching the commercial produced by the governor's former chief of staff's advertising firm. "We're between a pillow and a soft place getting smothered to death."

CHAPTER 29

DEBATE PREP

F riends." The word softly made its way through Christ Church Charlotte's reception hall, landing like a warm hug around Julia's neck. Surrounding her, lovely Episcopalians bowed their heads in prayer, filling the room with their friendship and their support. Julia was so happy to be praying among their ranks today.

The church's rector continued, "we are subject to systems and ways of knowing that separate us from ourselves. A world that has lost touch with the spiritual and emotional wisdom that guides people to and then through our pain and our wounds."

Julia felt the wisdom of which he spoke flood her heart. She was so grateful to be away from the supporters and demonstrators who swarmed outside the performing arts pavilion of UNC-Charlotte, where the presidential debate would take place. And away from the muckrakers hanging on every insult, slur, and threat being lobbed across unclear enemy lines.

"Julia," the minister continued, "has cast a vision of what life could look like if we all learned to love with as open a mind and heart as Jesus modeled in his life. Today, we pray for her and our success."

She had attended seminars and events at this church for thirty years, and when they'd invited Julia to be blessed, she had gratefully accepted, intuiting that several hours of prayer in the safe bosom of believers would do her more good than hours spent debate-prepping with Noah's consultants.

She felt the urgent, sincere energy of her fellow congregants: they knew what was at stake. Yes, this was a presidential election, but even more, it was a movement of the spirit. Spirit didn't only embrace love; it rejected cynicism. Such a movement couldn't be directed by poll-tested talking points, and it wouldn't succeed through traditional politicking.

Now a woman in a wavy maroon skirt and a light wool sweater stood up. "Julia, you have been part of communities doing this work for decades. Now the seeds we've planted are blooming. Today we're here to provide encouragement and support, to fill you with the gratitude we feel, so you can channel God's love in the debate tonight."

Others shared their stories—about beekeeping, about bonding at a silent retreat, about Julia's poetry. Julia relaxed into the safety of their presence, releasing tension ahead of the debate, her mind slowly humming in the background, strangely confident she could continue earning the trust of the nation while facing the bright lights and sky-high expectations of a country that expected battle royale.

• • •

Backstage, Luke approached Senator Menendez as makeup assistants hovered over his face, ensuring he would look as tan and powerful as possible under the debate's bright lights.

Menendez hated the makeup, but he knew he needed to look good. Look young. Look presidential. Trump, with his cartoon combover and Oompa-Loompa skin, had almost destroyed that expectation, but it still mattered to a significant swath of the electorate.

Tonight was the make-or-break moment of his career, so he sat with his eyes shut tight, visualizing what victory might look like. Governor O'Leary was shedding voters faster than chemo patients shed hair. What an image. He smiled, imagining the robust, curvy blonde as an emaciated political figure barely able to lift the phone for her concession call.

The problem was that he wasn't the one who had taken O'Leary out. No, that love purveyor Julia Connor had done the dirty work. She'd plunged the knife straight into O'Leary's back, not even pausing to admire her handiwork or wipe off the blood. Frankly, he admired what she'd done.

And what *was* it she'd done? She'd made his road to the Whitehouse infinitely easier. It was one thing to beat a candidate like O'Leary, who was guaranteed to win the popular vote of her bloated blue states and boasted the backing of the country's tech titans. That required seizing the middle in swing states with fear and guile, and then getting the base to turn out like their salvation depended on it.

But beating Julia Connor, a woman who barely had any campaign infrastructure and was taking fire from every side? Well, that wasn't going to be too hard. He knew the polls showed them tied, but he was confident that he'd feel the axe blade slide through her neck as he had with Bush IV and Glockenspiel in the primaries.

Luke watched Menendez's facial expressions rapidly change as the makeup team tended to his sixty-four-year-old face.

"Are you ready?" Luke said.

"I think so." The makeup artist grabbed a hand mirror. "Here, Senator. It may look a bit heavy, but on camera it's invisible."

The senator opened his eyes. "Jesus. If I don't win, you can cast me in a zombie flick." Then he saw Chief Strategist Micah Roberts hovering. "Any last words of advice?"

"We BREAK Julia for wanting to break the financial system," Micah replied. "Wall Street will love it."

"And," Luke added, "we call out her godless ways at every turn. Remember, she's attacked the faith."

"Right, right! Break the system, godless. Got it!" Menendez said.

He jumped to his feet and launched his large, athletic frame toward the stage. When he got to the wings, Jacqueline O'Leary was there flanked by Bradley and Alison. All three flashed weak smiles. "Good luck, Senator," O'Leary said.

"I won't need it, but thanks! Maybe you should keep it for yourself."

What an epic asshole, thought Bradley, who had a lot on his mind. Specifically, Governor O'Leary's inadequacies as a candidate. She'd always relied on a surprising sense of moral certitude to power her attacks on opposing candidates. Against Julia, Jacqueline just didn't have that fuel. It wasn't that she didn't want to win. She did, desperately. But he knew she felt neutered when attacking someone who looked and sounded so damn kind. It was like kicking a puppy or slapping a child. He'd tried to have her look at Julia and visualize Newt Gingrich or Ronald Reagan, but not even visualizing some mangled hybrid of the two seemed to work.

Now, thanks to Julia Connor, he was facing defeat at the hands of Menendez and that bastard Pastor McMillan.

He knew that to win, he would need to pull a rabbit out of the hat. He thought he'd found that rabbit hiding in Beijing, but in the meantime, his only goal for the debate was for the governor to seize the middle ground between Julia's love-vote kookiness and Menendez's vile conserva-fascist hate. If she could hold onto that middle ground, there was still a chance he could work his magic.

"Remember," he advised her now, "you agree with Julia whenever possible, and you attack Menendez at every turn."

· · ·

Pastor McMillan's Salvation Super PAC—irate so many Christians were supporting Julia Connor—ponied up for a wall-to-wall fifteen-million-dollar ad buy in swing states and red state major markets. A five-hour block, with the ninety-minute debate at the center, ensured American viewers heard the spot during every other commercial break.

"Jesus Christ did not die for your sins so that God's love would be available to all," the narrator intoned over a montage showing a cream-skinned Jesus being nailed to the cross by Julia Connor. "No, Jesus Christ died for our sins to make the path to God as narrow as possible, ensuring that only the deserving would drink from eternal waters. Choose to be among the chosen. Choose Jesus Christ. Vote Republican."

Noah's Sovereign Love Super PAC also purchased time. Their ad eschewed love for time-tested antiestablishment talking points.

"America," a pleasant-looking early-thirty-something white woman wearing yoga pants said from her seat at a pristinely clean marble-top counter, "Julia Connor is the only candidate in this race with the courage to say what we're all thinking. We've all known the major political parties have sold out to seek power, but Julia didn't mince words when it came to calling them out. The men and women who lead this nation serve the system instead of the people. Only by electing someone like Julia Connor, someone who has no ties to entrenched special interests, can we hope to build a new, better world. Vote for Julia Connor. Vote for the future. Vote for love."

CHAPTER 30

ONE GOD, ONE WORLDVIEW

The three candidates took the stage, pantomiming comfort and collegiality with handshakes and smiles beneath an enormous backdrop with bold red lettering declaring The Future Is Now: Presidential Debate 2028.

All took their places behind walnut podiums with gold-embossed bald eagle seals. Senator Daniel Menendez, looking resplendent in his replica Reagan suit. Governor Jacqueline O'Leary, noble in her cardinal-colored pant-and-jacket ensemble. And Julia Connor, for once eschewing her traditional faded navy-blue khakis for a blue dress. "You've got great arms!" the sartorial consultant Noah flew in from New York had crowed. "Let's show them off."

In Beijing, Premier Wei Zhao watched with interest. China's Premier and the leader of the Chinese Communist Party considered himself the most important man on earth, something his apparatchiks confirmed daily.

He watched events unfold in the American backwater town of Charlotte, which an aide informed him was the 16th largest city in the US but would only have been the 133rd largest city in China. The same aide, his chief Hegemon Strategist, had also brought him a proposal that an American tech magnate had funneled to him on behalf of Governor O'Leary's campaign.

Interesting, Premier Wei Zhao thought, wondering about working with a woman president. Women had been largely banished from government in

China as part of a return to life's natural order, but he'd successfully worked with foreign female heads of state. *We'll see how this goes.*

Thirty minutes into the debate, Governor O'Leary was pleased. She'd gotten a couple of great zingers in against Menendez, and she thought she'd been even more loving than Julia.

Menendez was antsy. The debate felt normal. He hated normal. He wanted a show, something to happen that would settle the election in his favor. Decisively!

"Julia," the debate moderator said, "Would you like to respond to the many American political experts who believe you bring no substance to your campaign and have no chance to fix our country?"

"Well," said Julia, flashing a bashful smile, "I don't agree that I am 'substance-less,' but I do agree that I can't fix our country alone. For that reason, I've created a three step 'Union Saving Policy Platform' that I believe is the simplest way to fix the incentives in our broken, often corrupt political system. With better incentives," Julia shrugged and raised her hands beseechingly, "perhaps all elected officials can become part of solving our problems."

"Hmrph." Menendez couldn't hold back his snort. "You have policy now?"

Julia ignored him.

"The first step is to create room for independent voices and new political parties, making it harder for billionaires and corporations to buy dominance of our system. To accomplish this, as president I will ask Congress to bring me a 'Proportional Representation and Term Limit' bill. If our elections aren't winner take all and our representatives can't stick around forever, there will be more space for all voices to be heard and to have influence."

"Second," Julia said, barely pausing to breathe, "We must get the corrupting force of unlimited anonymous money out of our political system. The fix, if we're willing to do what is best for the country, is simple. I will ask Congress to bring me a 'Clean Money in Politics' bill. If donations to Super PACs are limited and regulated the same way donations to candidates are, and if none of that money is allowed to be anonymous, it will be far harder for the corrupting tentacles of greed to poison our politics."

Menendez's face was locked in a mask of shock. His mind froze as he imagined dollar bills being herded out of his and his friends' bank accounts like Choctaws on the Trail of Tears.

O'Leary grimaced and grinned all at once, instincts to attack the plan and instincts to protect her donors and instincts to agree with Julia combining in a mighty collision of confusion.

"Finally, we have to think about the kids. I believe we need to be educating our children to prepare them for navigating the world as it exists." Julia squared her shoulders to the camera as she made her final point. "This means a rigorous education in science, math, creativity, the natural world, and critical thinking. It also means we give our children an emotional education, preparing them to grow, heal, and know themselves as adults, breaking our terrible national cycle of depression, anxiety, fear and trauma responses."

Still bewildered, Governor O'Leary stuck to the plan. "I agree."

"You agree?" Menendez said with disdain. "All you've done tonight is agree."

"Well, I do agree," replied the governor. "Right is right."

"Well, I sure as hell don't," he thundered, preparing to repeat one of Luke's talking points. "The only education our children in public schools need is an education in a biblical worldview!"

Julia's heart leapt triumphantly; she was ready for this moment. Summoning her sweetest voice, she asked, "Which biblical worldview is that, Senator?"

Immediately out of his theological depth, and without a preplanned rebuttal, Menendez did the best he could, holding up a single digit and yelling. "There is only one biblical worldview. One God, one worldview!"

Doubling down on the sweetness, Julia replied in a voice like music, "I ask, because there was the biblical worldview that supported apartheid in South Africa, the biblical worldview that supported slavery here in the US, and, thankfully, the biblical worldview that underpinned the abolitionist movement and eventually ended slavery. There's also a biblical worldview that takes Jesus at his word, requiring Christians to serve migrants and the poor, showing compassion and forgiveness to all. Which one do you support teaching our children?"

O'Leary, who remembered Bradley's instruction to attack Menendez, saw her chance. "Exactly right. Which worldview do you support teaching

American children, Senator MENENDEZ? And what about a real education in STEM and critical thinking?"

Backstage, Luke was panicking. Menendez was out of his league, and he knew that look in the senator's eyes.

Without a theological comeback, Menendez fell back on the trademark contempt that had worked so well for him in the past. "Ladies, if I can call you that, I already answered this. Children in public school need an education in a biblical worldview as defined by church leaders. Now, do children who can afford a private school receive a rigorous academic education? Of course, this is America. The market makes sure you get what you pay for!"

Menendez congratulated himself on saving the exchange. And, at that, slipping in a line his Wall Street donors would love!

"So the plan," Governor O'Leary sneered, "is to keep the mindless religious masses mired in mediocrity?"

"Mindless?" Menendez roared, thrilled O'Leary had fallen into the traditional elitist trap. "Typical Democratic disrespect for the Deity and for rural Americans."

Julia thought of all her small-town neighbors in Tenino, of her sadness that most Democrats seemed to associate "of the land" with "dumb," and of the reality that so many of her rural neighbors, most of whom disagreed with her political views, lived far more environmentally connected and balanced lives than did her crusading environmentalist friends in the city.

"The senator makes a good point, Jacqueline. Even if we disagree with their politics, we must not, as a people, lose respect for *any* of the community-minded citizens of this nation. When we define the enemy as each other, we lose sight of the common humanity that bonds us all as one people."

Bradley frantically pressed his buzzer from the spin room, but it did nothing to dissuade Governor O'Leary. She finally had a real reason to hate Julia Connor, who'd threatened the sense of educated, urban superiority that formed the backbone of her identity. "So now rural Republican racists are the value voters?"

Menendez charged like a bull. "Governor, that is out of line!"

"Is it? Or am I absolutely right?"

"You are wrong about everything, which is why voters need to keep you in Illinois!" Menendez locked eyes with O'Leary over Julia's head.

"No, you are wrong. Wrong. Wrong. And wrong! You're the reason why New Mexico has shown zero economic growth in the last six years!"

"That's a lie!"

"Stop it! Both of you!!" Julia threw up her hands. "I have spent the last twenty years watching this type of ego-driven immaturity pass as leadership and it stops now!!"

In the ensuing silence, stakeholders took stock.

Bradley glanced at the live donation trackers, pleased to see that the second O'Leary had delivered her "rural Republican racist" line, small dollar donations had started spiking like bitcoin circa 2021.

Luke seethed, more certain than ever that he and Pastor Josiah were going to have to win this election themselves.

Media members ate up the election chaos. Let the ratings bonanza begin!

The American people, at least those who weren't madly dashing off donations to their favored candidates, watched intently. This Julia Connor, some thought, was powerful. She'd just brought silence to politics, a gift they suspected they now couldn't live without.

On the dais, O'Leary still wore her pissed-off glare. Menendez stood frozen by confusion—had he just been yelled at by a woman—by *this* woman? In between them, Julia Connor was recovering from the shock of her outburst.

Still, she was the one who broke the silence. "Oh my, I haven't yelled that loudly since I caught a bear raiding my beehives."

The audience laughed. Then clapped.

"No, no," Julia held her hand up to quiet the audience. "These types of exchanges, whether they happen on a debate stage or a social media platform, are breaking this country. Can't we all see that?"

Mercifully given something to be against, Menendez and O'Leary sprang to action.

"Wrong again, Julia," Menendez said through a grin, certain—as he frequently was—he'd just won the presidency. "These types of exchanges are necessary to preserve the union. Nothing is more American or more democratic than a passionate exchange of divergent ideas. It's alarming you're so eager to prevent me and my Wall Street friends from attacking your and Governor O'Leary's godless, communist ways."

Governor O'Leary secured the last word. "Julia, the only way for America to heal is for good to defeat evil, for Democrats to defeat Republicans. You are dangerous and you are naive. I mean"—here she remembered Bradley's instruction to promote her signature legislative proposal, which also happened to be responsible for Big Tech's endless donations— "you haven't even submitted a plan of your own to ensure Data Freedom. Our economy could crash without Big Tech's access to every American's data, and not only would you do nothing about it, but you're proposing that we cut Big Tech's voice out of our political discourse while undercutting the Democratic Party's power?"

O'Leary pulled herself up to full height and made memeably direct eye contact with the camera. "Anyone voting for a nominee other than me," she proclaimed with complete sincerity, "will be responsible for ending the experiment we call the United States of America."

• • •

Independent or party-sponsored, the post-debate polls all said the same thing. Senator Menendez and Julia Connor had extended their lead on Governor O'Leary, though they remained tied with 34 percent each.

Lagging behind, Jacqueline O'Leary claimed only 24 percent support, a clear indication that the Democratic voter exodus toward Julia Connor was accelerating. Mystifyingly, as with every election, 8 percent of those polled insisted they were "undecided."

On NATN, Heather Haliburton's hot take wasn't all that hot. "In tonight's debate," she reported, "Julia Connor and Governor O'Leary both displayed the value of a love-first approach to governing. Julia Connor, however, surprised viewers by agreeing with Senator Menendez's support for racist rural Americans and by pitching the anti-democratic idea that America should have more than two political parties."

On ROX News, Jed Abernathy had a different take. "In tonight's debate, Julia Connor again mocked the inerrancy of God's word as interpreted by

Pastor Josiah McMillan while Governor O'Leary continued her predictable political implosion. Both O'Leary and Connor, in a further display of weakness, supported limiting the influence of America's most wealthy and patriotic citizens."

CHAPTER 31

XINJIANG PROVINCE

Having rediscovered the disdain she needed to campaign effectively, Governor O'Leary felt betrayed by Bradley's "just be nice" to Julia strategy. The fact that she had agreed to the strategy did nothing to quell her rage.

Stewing in her anger as she waited for the debate post-mortem meeting to start, O'Leary was unaware of the fine mahogany table or the floor-to-ceiling drapes that opened onto the gorgeous lawn of the antebellum-era estate. The house—rented just for the debate—had hosted a stream of political bigwigs, donors, and campaign staff over the preceding days. Now, they were having one last meeting before they boarded the campaign jet for Cleveland.

Bradley walked in and, in lieu of hello, said, "We're getting fucking smoked."

"It's a bloodbath," said Alison, trailing behind him. "Forty-nine percent of Julia's supporters left us for her. Only thirty percent of her supporters left Menendez."

Governor O'Leary bolted out of her chair and planted her hands on the table. "Well, knock me over with a feather! What do you expect—I basically surrendered over the last month. Your strategy of being nice to Julia to win back Democrats sure as hell hasn't worked!"

Bradley grimaced, thinking of the middle ground. "Listen, Governor, we have to play the long game."

"The long game! The long game!" Purple veins popped from O'Leary's neck. "There are seventeen days left until the election and we're ten points behind. Don't fucking talk to me about the long game. We need results now!"

Bradley put his hands on the table, leaned forward, and looked the governor straight in the eye. Time to remind her he was the best political operator in the country.

"That, Jacqui, is why I've hatched a little plan." He raised his voice: "Come on in, Ben."

On cue, Troojle CEO Ben Blankenship swept into the room. The picture of understated billionaire charm, he wore jeans, scuffed leather Gucci boots, and a distressed, embroidered cowboy shirt that looked cheap but cost thousands.

"Governor O'Leary," he began, "I've donated and bundled two hundred million dollars into your support network. So you could say I'm overleveraged. Or"—he smiled broadly—"you could say I'm about to save your campaign."

An outsider may have mistaken O'Leary's silence as her digesting Blankenship's bold claim. The outsider would be wrong. She was trying to decide who to explode at first: Ben for his modernized–Marlboro Man meets tech bro pseudo-heroism, Bradley for taking so damn long to have a decent idea, or Alison for standing there contributing nothing except bobblehead nods.

O'Leary closed her eyes and tried counting to ten. She reached six before realizing she had no time for a tantrum. Time was of the essence, and she needed every weapon available to her—now.

"OK, gentlemen. Tell me."

"Well, Jaque—" Bradley started.

He was going to tee Ben up to take the credit, but Blankenship, having made a career of proactively taking credit, interrupted. "Jacqueline, I was sitting on my yacht off Ensenada thinking about the few hundred million dollars of mine you were wasting. Now, the money doesn't bother me. What bothers me is losing to a gardener from the previous century who doesn't own a single device or some bloated oaf always accusing tech titans of stifling free speech. That is such bullshit. The marketplace of ideas must flourish."

Or you'll have nothing to monetize, O'Leary thought.

Ben paused and took a sip of his Perrier, then continued. "As I thought about this, I found myself admiring Julia Connor's brilliant use of social media. Building her entire campaign with Beep-Beep videos? What a strategy! And then—it's amazing how great minds think alike—Bradley called me and observed that Beep-Beep is a Chinese company."

Bradley hoped his grimace read as a smile. *How nice of Ben to throw me a bone for my idea.*

Ben plowed ahead. "And there's nothing China wants less than an American president who doesn't understand that preserving corporate and political stability is the primary goal of being president. I mean, a woman who believes people should heal themselves by finding the freedom of love? Who's had her picture taken with the Dalia Lama? It's the Chinese Communist Party's worst nightmare!"

Growing impatient with hearing the long version of something she hadn't been offered the short version, O'Leary said, "And we're supposed to do exactly what with this information?"

Ben rapped his knuckle on the table twice. "It's done. I reached out to Chinese Premier Wei Zhao through his cousin, who just so happens to be a board member of my PE firm."

Just so happens. O'Leary concentrated hard on not rolling her eyes. Had she not been so annoyed with the man's pompousness, she might have seen where he was going.

"And I suggested that Premier Wei Zhao, for the good of global stability and profitability, mandate that all political content be kicked off of Beep-Beep."

It took a second for this—the first piece of good news in what felt like a long time—to register with O'Leary. "And Wei Zhao said yes? That is so brilliant!"

Ben liked delivering good news. He paid other people to deliver the bad news. He took a long look at Bradley.

Bradley gritted his teeth. "Governor, Premier Wei Zhao did say yes … with conditions."

O'Leary felt the spontaneous smile on her face contract and her mouth dry up. *I cannot be fucked over*, she told herself. *I will not be fucked over.* In times like this, she had to remind herself that all that mattered was the American people getting a noble leader with the right values—and that was her. The only way to offer the USA her leadership was to win, and the only way to win was to accept politics for what it was: a series of choices between bad and worse.

"And the conditions are?"

"He wants your guarantee that if you become president, you promise to diplomatically support Chinese operations in Xinjiang Province."

O'Leary tilted her head sideways. "Xinjiang Province? Is that where the microchip factories are? Or part of Taiwan?"

"No," Bradley replied, "that's where they're putting the last of the Uighurs in 'reeducation' camps. Pretty much every single human rights group in the world says it is ethno-religious cleansing."

O'Leary's face visibly relaxed. "Oh, Bradley, that's not a problem. Jesus, America has been ignoring the Uighurs for years. I thought they'd say something about Taiwan."

"They did," Ben drawled. "But Bradley told me to tell them it was impossible at this stage."

"*At this stage?* You were leading them on about Taiwan? Are you insane?"

"It was necessary," Bradley said, "to start the conversation. But then I told them to think of something else. Having exhausted African natural resources, Premier Wei Zhao wants more access in the Middle East, so he needs Xinjiang to never become a problem."

O'Leary nodded, resolute. "Now obviously we never had this conversation, but yes, tell Premier Wei Zhao whatever you need to tell him. Just get Julia and that nose-ringed girl off Beep-Beep ASAP!"

"Governor, that's great. Really great!" Ben cheered. "I'll backchannel that I sold you on the plan and you said yes."

"And great work on your part." O'Leary beamed. "Bradley and Alison, get the ad agencies on the line. Set up meetings. We need some new ads. With some fucking venom in them!"

CHAPTER 32

SCHEDULE ONE NARCOTICS

Menendez and his team flew into Tallahassee, boarded their bus and headed west to the Florida Panhandle: a delicious strip of gulf-adjacent land boasting some of America's most committed Jim Crow-era voters.

At the FeednSeed outside of Marianna, Luke grimly stared through the window at throngs of sign-waving Menendez supporters.

A guy in a white, over-starched button-down short-sleeved shirt and high-waters waved a sign that read, Gun Rites R Human Rites. Behind him, a woman in a T-shirt that appeared to feature Jesus and Menendez riding a unicorn together—and surely didn't mean whatever the woman assumed it meant—hoisted a sign reading, Real Americans Immigrated Legally.

They cheered as Menendez spoke from the bus's open front door.

"Just like I said last night," Menendez crowed, "one God, one worldview!"

Luke's eyes almost rolled out the back of his head. That line played down here with the faithful, but these folks would vote for Menendez no matter what he said. Although it would play well on TV, the whole trip was wasted effort. This rally wouldn't reach the people who most needed to be reached.

According to Salvation Super PAC's polling, thirty percent of Julia Connor's supporters had left Menendez for her. Most of those folks were suburban churchgoers seduced by Julia's heresies. That exodus wasn't just a political threat, but as Pastor Josiah kept saying, it was a mortal threat to all he and Luke believed in, "a threat to God's truth and God's people."

Jessica Davenport, Menendez's press secretary, was glowing in the seat across the aisle. "You'd think we'd struggle to build a crowd on a ninety-five-degree day like today, yet here we are, five hundred people sweating in the sun at a FeednSeed!"

Luke scowled at Jessica's positivity. "The diehards aren't the problem, Jessica. Our message is getting blurred—"

"You're right about that!" One seat behind him, Chief Strategist Micah Roberts held up an enormous stack of papers. "I've been pouring over polling results for the last two days, and we need some major recalibration."

Knowing Micah and the senator primarily spoke in the language of gross analogies, Luke tried one of his own. "Micah, our balls are sitting squarely in Julia's wrinkly little meditating fingers, and all you can say is we need to recalibrate?"

The senator pulled back from his adoring fans to reenter the bus.

"You hear that, Senator?" Micah called to him. "Luke asked if you like the feel of Julia's hands on your balls."

Menendez paused and smiled. Like Micah, he wasn't freaking out about being tied with Julia. He knew they would find a winning strategy. So he allowed himself the luxury of imagining what it might feel like to have Julia's hands cupping his rotund balls. He could feel the sensation shooting up his body almost as if she were actually massaging his testicles. He felt how plump and juicy both big guys felt in her hands and his penis followed suit, fruitlessly trying to press through his slacks.

"Balls are made to be touched. If she wants to love my balls, who am I to complain?"

"Y'all don't get it!" Luke snapped, regretting he'd stooped to their level. "That woman is dangerous. And not just to our campaign. That woman is a threat to God's holy church!"

Micah and Menendez exchanged annoyed glances.

"Then do something about it, Luke," Menendez sneered. "Your job is to God-fuck my competitors. The fact that that's not happening is a you-issue, not a me-issue! And speaking of issues, Micah, any more numbers?"

"More weirdness, Senator. Among Julia's self-identified supporters, fifty-seven percent have been in therapy, worked with a life coach, or attend yoga regularly, and a full ninety-four percent have friends or family that have."

"I'm not surprised her supporters are mentally unstable," Luke said. "But how do you explain the veteran support?"

The senator and Micah looked at each other—then burst out laughing.

Luke joined in, momentarily released from his anger. Menendez bent over double, slapping his knee. Micah was sprawled over his printed spreadsheets, shaking with mirth.

"OK, OK. Dumb question," Luke said.

"But seriously," Menendez said, "that one does bother me. I'm the military candidate. Make sure y'all tell me how to fix the veteran problem. Those are my voters."

Micah paused, thinking about all the Beep-Beep videos his opposition research team had surfaced of that Julia-loving veteran named Jonathan. He was a nobody, yet he seemed to be leading Julia's charge to secure veteran support. And what he talked about—well, he had some very odd ideas.

Micah had never considered attacking veterans. It broke rule number one of supporting the military. But maybe...

"Have either of you watched the Beep-Beep videos that Julia's veterans put out?" Micah asked.

"No! I'm not watching their videos," Menendez said, "do I look like someone who has time for dancing teenagers?"

"Not those, the veteran videos. The ones about magic mushrooms?"

Luke's eyes narrowed. "The schedule-one narcotic?"

"Exactly. Julia is *really* into mushrooms. And so are her veterans, according to the videos. Now, they apparently work through a church, so it's legal because of religious freedom, but—"

"Legal or not," Luke grinned and narrowed his eyes. "What I hear you saying is that she's a drug pusher?"

"I'm saying," Micah responded, "that she's been pushing mushrooms and even MDMA for decades, and that according to our polling, voters don't know it."

"Wait, wait, wait." Menendez jumped in. "Pull up her picture on your laptop."

Micah obliged, Troojling Julia Connor and then clicking on the first image, a picture of Julia standing outside in her beekeeping suit, smiling at the camera as her gray hair sat sideways on her head, a literal picture of aged natural innocence.

For a while, the men just stared, as though waiting for the photo to reveal its hidden message.

"She's a beekeeping geriatric saint running on a platform of love," Menendez finally said, "and you want to run the druggy playbook against her and her veterans?"

"If we run the druggy playbook," Micah jumped in, "and combine it with the polling data that shows Evangelical voters switching to Julia because they're losing their fear of God's wrath, we might just have a path forward."

Luke raised his eyebrows and smiled. Now they were speaking his language. "I'll talk to Pastor Josiah."

CHAPTER 33

GOD'S GRACE

From each seat and every row, the sounds of the faithful echoed through the forty thousand seat Pastor Josiah McMillan Salvation Megachurch Arena. The arena had been designed by the same architects and artists responsible for the church's salvation-securing augmented reality experience in Las Vegas. The venue in Las Vegas could save thousands of souls at a time by exposing them to the visceral horror of Jesus' crucifixion, the glory of his resurrection, or the justice of the crusades. That state-of-the-art venue was responsible for ten figures of annual revenue, but it was just practice for this arena—the jewel in Pastor McMillan's crown, the seat of his power, the home for his congregation, and the earthly embodiment of his spiritual ascendance.

On stage, the seven-member praise and worship band rocked out. The lead guitarist, dressed in tight black jeans and a leather vest, long hair swooped across the face, shredded on his Les Paul. In front of him, Elizabeth McMillan, the pastor's wife, was resplendent in a simple white Dior dress and a pear-shaped cascading diamond necklace from Harry Winston. She couldn't help but admire how the spotlight reflecting off the diamonds and her dress's sheen broadcast purity to everyone watching.

Hands and voice raised, she stepped to the front of the stage, urging the faithful on. Beside her, a holographic Jesus dressed in a three-piece suit and a crown of thorns was on his knees, belting out the lines in unison with her and the band.

"Amazing Grace, how sweet the sound, that saved a wretch like me."

On the side of the stage, seated in his throne-like minister's chair and surrounded by holograms of Jesus' twelve disciples, Pastor Josiah McMillan nodded with approval as the joyous sounds of worship cascaded down upon him. He thought of love. It was the topic of this election year, after all.

He loved his wife, and he loved that she was such a fabulous, shining example of God's desire to change lives and build wealth. He loved leading his flock, guiding them in the never-ending battle to secure God's kingdom here in the modern chosen land. But most of all, he loved preaching.

He was hooked on the feeling of standing before his congregation, explicating God's word. The feeling of having thousands of individuals hanging on his every utterance, the knowledge that millions of others across the country would do the same through his Salvation Streaming Platform. It was the ultimate proof of God's Grace and his vision of ministry that, now, thanks to the size and strength of his empire, his holy words affected elections and inspired public policies in the most righteous—and powerful—nation on earth.

Today, then, was a special day. He would serve and save America by opening a new front in the war against Julia Connor.

His adrenaline soared, spurred on by his wife's marvelous voice. The hymn's last verse poured out like a prophetic blessing over his children, but he could barely wait for the final note to fade.

"Amazing Grace, how sweet the sound, that saved a wretch like me. I once was lost but now am found, was blind but now I see, was blind, but now I seeeee."

Beaming, Pastor Josiah made his way toward his pulpit, high fiving the worship band members as they exited the stage. Reaching his wife last, he paused to give her a kiss of appropriate length and sincerity, modeling Christ-centered masculinity for his congregation. Above them, flocks of holographic doves dropped holographic olive branches all around the stage.

Reaching the pulpit, he held his *New Roman Living River Signed Pastor Josiah McMillan Edition Holy Bible* in front of his chest, knowing the camera was zooming in on the cover, ensuring a sales boost for the church's publishing wing. He set the Bible down and forced the joy of another dollar made from his mind, getting back to the important task at hand.

He stood, as he did every Sunday, waiting for complete silence to descend upon the vast arena he'd named after himself.

The expectant flock held their collective breath, waiting for the word of God from the great Pastor Josiah McMillan.

A single drop among the sea of congregants, Luke could barely sit still in anticipation of today's sermon. If Julia Connor thought she could withstand the full force of God's people, she was sorely mistaken. Yes, she'd made it this far. But no, she had no idea what it would feel like when the full might of Pastor McMillan's brilliant oratory—amplified by the Salvation Megachurch Network, the Salvation Streaming Platform, and the Salvation Super PAC—crashed down upon her.

Pastor McMillan began.

"This, my friends in Christ, is not a morning for pleasantries, so I will skip my usual hello. This is a morning for hard, honest talk about the state of our great nation. Did you all hear the last verse from 'Amazing Grace'?"

The question was rhetorical, but many called out, "Yes!"

"Good!" Pastor Josiah thundered. "But for those that need to be reminded, the last verse we sang said, 'I once was blind, but now I see, was blind, but now I see.'"

With his last "but now I see," Pastor Josiah lowered his voice as if he was about to let his congregants in on a secret.

"Let me tell you, many of us have been blind to a great threat building in this nation. Blind to an evil hiding in plain sight." As he spoke, his voice began to rise, lifting his people out of the darkness of his secret, and into the light of his knowledge.

"Listen," he hissed to the tens of thousands in front of him, the thousands more watching at satellite campuses around the country, and the millions who would watch the livestream on his Salvation Streaming Platform, "and I will shine God's light on this evil!"

Pastor Josiah basked in the electric flow of energy, in the holographic angels swirling around his pulpit, in knowing the Lord was working through

HIM to change the course of history. He was authoritative. In charge. About to give these folks a show!

"Now, I mentioned God's light. But let me ask you—who and what *is* God?"

He paused on the edge of the question, then plummeted off the precipice and into the righteous indignation of a great man disrespected by a small woman, one who had never achieved anything close to building an arena-sized sanctuary.

"I'll tell you about God! There is but one God. A God of love, yes. But equally a God of destruction and vengeance. A God whose word is inerrant. A God who JEALOUSLY guards his flock from false prophets!" In a voice that sounded like a revving engine, he asked them all, "Is it worth eternity in hell to embrace a false prophet's love?!" He raised both arms, bringing his people to their feet in anticipation as hell's flames holographically burned on the stage beside him, a cowering group of small, holographic children trapped in the fire's midst. "Say it with me now. HELL NO!"

The congregation exploded, repeating his famous catchphrase, the line he used to denounce the world's worst excesses—environmentalism, high taxes, and sex out of wedlock. Their voices joined his own to shake the Josiah McMillan Salvation Arena to its core. Their voices echoed with the help of a clever sound engineer: "Hell nooooooo. Hell nooooo. Hell nooo."

Pastor Josiah McMillan again waited for complete silence.

"Julia Connor is a false prophet. She says she is about love, but she says that all love is God's love. She says that many paths lead to God."

The pastor paused only to gather steam: "What she says is heresy!" he thundered, the holographic flames beside him shooting higher and higher. "The type of belief that can permanently sever your tie to God, costing you the salvation Jesus Christ died on the cross to secure for you! For your children! For all of us!"

Pastor McMillan let this sink in, the threat of an eternity in hell, the threat of being separated from the certainty of righteousness and rightness during life here on earth. He watched the twisting faces of his congregants, he felt the cold overtake them, he felt their fear. He rejoiced, for God's word was working.

"But," he continued, "trying to separate you from God's love isn't all Julia

Connor is doing. What if I told you that Julia Connor has engaged in illegal activities for years?"

"She's a Jezebel!" a parishioner shouted, overcome by the spirit.

"She is no mere Jezebel. No, Julia Connor is a drug dealer. She uses psychedelic mushrooms to 'heal.' She says these mushrooms help people like you 'better' reach God."

He paused again, waiting for his children to digest this curveball.

"Now, think about it. Using drugs that change the mind God gave us, to somehow heal something in us, God's"—and here he screamed—"PERFECT CREATIONS?"

His anger blasted off every wall in the church, reverberating not just in the congregants' ears but their very bodies. The holographic hell flames burned ever higher, now almost reaching the arena-height ceiling. His face glared at the congregation from the three-story-tall LED screen behind him.

It was time to tie it all together, to bring everyone home, to ensure that every parishioner in his arena or watching on his streaming network was clear about what they had to do.

"My friends, I live in love as Jesus commanded. But sometimes, we are called to fight for God, to speak words that pain us to say but are unavoidable if we wish to live in God's truth. So I will tell you a hard truth: Julia Connor is more than evil. She is the WHORE OF BABYLON, as we were warned of in Revelations."

A holographic scarlet beast soared from the rafters, swooping through the arena like a marauding dragon. The last of Pastor McMillan's words continued to echo—"WHORE OF BABYLON. WHORE OF BABYLON."—and each of the beast's seven heads and ten horns snapped in different directions while a witchy looking, white-haired woman drenched in jewels and holding a goblet of splashing blood perched upon the beast, silently cackling.

From stage, the pastor watched the weight of his words sink into an audience that was already terrified of losing their salvation and was now facing a seven-headed Biblical instrument of demonic destruction.

He lowered his voice, inviting his congregation back into alignment with him and with God's way.

"Never forget the example of Emperor Constantine, the man who answered God's call to turn Christianity into a Roman political force, and who first understood that Jesus's love could be spread by the sword and state. He, like I, understood that we are God's vehicle of loving destruction on this earth, and right now, in this election, the mandate for those who love God is clear. Julia Connor, the Whore of Babylon, must be stopped at all costs."

• • •

A few minutes later, after the last songs had been sung, seven figures' worth of offerings collected, and hugs received, Pastor Josiah made his way to his office for his traditional Starbucks caramel iced coffee. His assistant, Florence, always had one waiting. When he was a younger, less morally grounded man, a girl like Florence might have helped him unwind in other ways. He was grateful that, for a man of the Lord such as himself, coffee, cream, and caramel provided all the gratification he needed.

Opening the door, he couldn't decide which sight brought more relief: that familiar cardboard cup or his favorite apostle. "How'd I do?" he asked.

"That," said Luke, "was inspired. Truly, God's love shone through you, Pastor Josiah."

Pastor McMillan nodded, satisfied. "The video should be streaming on Salvation Streaming Platform by three p.m. Eastern. It'll run on cable all week, and a full-court press of press releases and social media posts are starting now."

"Good," said Luke. "But are you sure we can pull it off? Menendez doesn't seem to understand that we're his only path to victory—or that losing to a heretic would be even worse than losing to a Democrat."

"The glory of it, Luke, is that we don't have to rely on the senator. Sure, he's the candidate and this is a democracy, but if we have to ..."

Luke looked on eagerly as Pastor Josiah's thoughts took shape.

"We can take care of things," he finished, "in our own way."

• • •

The Beep-Beep vid started with Melanie laughing, a laugh that started unhinged, a sound of frustrated disbelief, before calming into a serious sounding silence.

"We live in a country where the top one percent of the population controls over fifty percent of our nation's wealth. Where the top ten percent control over seventy-five percent of the nation's wealth. A country where being poor, like I was growing up, is normal. In this country, a pastor whose wife wears a Harry Winston diamond necklace while praising Jesus Christ—who declined worldly wealth in order to feed and serve the poor—tells us Julia Connor is something called the Whore of Babylon because she believes in a love available to all?"

Melanie started laughing again.

"Oh come on! Now my peeps, here's what I need you to do. Take this entire series of videos, all five of them, and share them with people who know, trust, and respect you. Share them with love. Don't judge, but ask them—who is living in love?"

Lillie Rift saw the video as she browsed her feed from a nest of pillows and blankets next to one of the fireplaces in her suite at The Mark. She was supposed to be reviewing her choreography in preparation for her show at Barclay's Center the following night, but instead she was engrossed by the national "Whore of Babylon" uproar that was tearing social media platforms and family dinner tables apart.

As she contemplated how to stand up for her values and her beliefs, she did what she so often now found herself doing, she shared Melanie's video with three hundred million of her closest friends.

CHAPTER 34

THE GREAT FAMINE, REVISITED

On a secured video conference that took place on the Chinese Communist Party's private transpacific fiber optic cable, Troojle CEO Ben Blankenship made his move.

"I'll keep this quick," Ben said to Premier Wei Zhao. "Your conditions have been agreed to. If you make Beep-Beep one hundred percent apolitical, and if you find every Beep-Beep user that has any meta-data connection to Julia Connor content in violation of your new terms, you will strike a powerful blow against forces conspiring to disrupt American political consistency. With the threat removed, all trade, technology, and security pacts will continue."

That was all Premier Wei Zhao needed. He gestured goodbye and the screen went blank.

The truth of the matter was that Julia Connor had caught Wei Zhao and his most senior Communist Party Apparatchiks completely off guard. They were used to planning for the possibility that America would become a 1930s-style authoritarian power or an amoral Swiss-inspired socialist puppy. They were ready for the United States's second civil war. They had long ago erected the Great Firewall to quash dangerous Yankee ideas about free speech, freedom of religion, and freedom from political persecution.

But the prospect of America embracing and then beginning to export disruptive spiritual truths had never been considered.

Indeed, his advisors had stammered that such a threat had never been imagined in thousands of game theory simulations. Yet here was an ancient woman named Julia being buoyed by device-obsessed youth who were lapping up her message of spiritual revival and emotional freedom. It was like an American Falun Gong, but worse!

He looked down at the policy summary from Chou Yang, the Foreign Ministry's Chief America Strategist:

> *Connor's charisma and moral doctrine, taken to the ultimate logical extremes, risk detonating an anti-materialist revolution in America which would likely have stunning—arguably crushing—implications for China's economy. By focusing on spiritual and emotional well-being, where love and empathy are consumed instead of—for example—electronic devices; clothing for domestic pets; all manner of household items with Christmas trees, cats, or sports team logos printed on them; and convenience products like beer koozies and salad spinners, the Chinese economy as we know it would collapse. Indeed, should Connor's values—which sync well with those of environmental activists—take hold with just a quarter of American consumers and result in the diminished consumption of low-, mid-, and high-end products and technologies, a cataclysmic economic collapse might ensue not seen since the Great Famine.*

Wei Zhao grimaced as he looked around his opulent conference room decorated with hand-knotted silk hanging rugs that depicted not historical figures from ancient times but himself, in all his power. He maintained that power because he acted with force whenever a new threat emerged. Now would be no different.

Of course, he had to be careful. The American people were content to allow foreign powers to control their technology and industry, but they only stood for it so long as the power wasn't flaunted. The trick was to silence Julia Connor without raising the ire of an American people who were not, it seemed, as asleep as he'd assumed.

CHAPTER 35

CULLING THE HERD

The stylist—a cute, dark-skinned blonde thing with piercings along her ears, through her nose cartilage and one eyebrow, and who knew where else—had outfitted Senator Menendez in a plaid shirt, blue jeans, and a deer rifle with a wood-grain stock.

"Is it loaded?" he flirted, weighing the Remington Model Seven Hundred in his hands.

"I doubt it, Senator. The last thing you need is an on-the-set death."

"Ha. *You're* a pistol." He pulled back on the rifle pump to check the chamber. Empty.

"I'm a pistol? Is that supposed to be a compliment?"

"See? You are! What's your name?"

"Fatima. And the answer is no."

"I didn't even ask anything!"

"I think they want you on the set."

Menendez shook his head and stood up. *Fucking America. You can't even make a pass at a girl anymore.*

He left the trailer and walked outside. A gorgeous southern lake shone in the late afternoon sun, a green pasture stretching all around them. Bugs swarmed above the water, a reminder of nature's propensity to create annoyances. Menendez strode toward Luke, still scowling about Fatima. Some people forgot how lucky they were to be in this country in the first place.

Noticing the scowl, Luke assumed the senator needed to be put at ease. "Don't worry, Senator," he said, "the magic mushroom strategy is going to work. And, if it helps you relax, we could even stay after the filming is done and hunt for an hour or two."

"Hunt?" said Menendez, running his hand down the Remington's cold barrel. "We're in the south. They don't hunt in the South. They shoot pets."

Micah perked up at another chance to contribute. "What do you mean? They love hunting in the South."

"Yeah," said Luke, "I've been hunting since I was a kid in Tallahassee."

"Pshh." Menendez's scowl deepened. "Then you've never hunted a day in your life."

Luke narrowed his eyes, his southern pride flaring despite the fact he knew better. "I've got two eight-point bucks on my wall that say otherwise."

"Shot in Florida?" Menendez was settling into combat mode.

"One in Florida and the other in Texas." *That would show him*, Luke thought. There was no quicker way to prove manhood than to mention Texas, that glorious land of secessionism and Big Oil.

"Jesus Christ!" A mountain-west elitist, Menendez had and would never forgive Southerners for their misplaced machismo. "Texas? Then you sure as hell haven't been hunting. In Texas, they feed their deer corn all year, then when hunting season rolls around, they climb up into their little climate-controlled treehouse 'deer stands' and shoot their white-tailed friends when they come to dine. That's barely a step up from going to Albertson's to buy a steak."

Always on the lookout for an opportunity to humiliate Luke, Micah jumped in. "I bagged a bison in Montana last year."

"On a 'ranch?'"

Micah caught Menendez's tone but wasn't sure what he'd said wrong. "Yeah, a huge ranch. We rode horses out to hunt!"

"Fucking yuppie. If someone takes you to a herd of tame animals on their ranch and you shoot one, it ain't hunting—that's just culling the herd. Hunting is when you hump it seven miles up a mountain to bag an elk before field dressing it and hauling it seven miles back to your truck."

Before Menendez could further humiliate the two men he was counting on to get him elected president, the video assistant yelled, "Spots, please!
We're shooting in thirty seconds."

CHAPTER 36

BEEP, BEEP, BOOM

Melanie woke that morning to a stream of texts and notifications. The East Coast Beep-Beepers had a three-hour head start, and had, she learned, been freaking out since 5:47 a.m. Eastern Standard Time.

At 3 a.m., which was 3 p.m. in Shanghai, Beep-Beep's CEO Xao Cheng received a shocking telephone call from the illustrious Premier Wei Zhao informing him that five members from the Chinese Communist Party Central Committee's International Digital Security Division were arriving at Beep-Beep's two-billion-dollar headquarters at this very moment.

These men, Premier Wei Zhao said, were going to oversee a new policy for Beep-Beep users in America to eliminate a global threat to international peace and security. All political commentary on the US presidential election was to be banned until further notice. "China is a friend to all countries," the Premier explained. "We and our corporations do not interfere with the politics of other sovereign nations."

Remembering full well the financial and corporate carnage that Wei Zhao's predecessor, Xi Jinping, had wrought upon technology companies when they had begun to amass too much power a decade before, Beep-Beep's CEO said, "Yes, sir. It is an honor to serve. Do you have any talking points for me to deliver to the investment community?"

"Remind them that Beep-Beep was created to promote community, friendship, and fun for teens. Not tear down society. You are just adhering to your mission statement as required by your board."

The five members of the International Digital Security Division were personally escorted by Xao Cheng into the office of his CTO, Yihan Wang, where the men presented a jump drive of updated Beep-Code code derived from the most recent update to the Great Firewall, a three-page update to site Terms and Conditions, and seventeen pages of implementation instructions, including user notification emails.

Ninety minutes later, a team of Yihan Wang's best engineers had uploaded the new code. Tested it. Implemented it. Tagged the 390,260,339 Beeps and Re-Beeps to be deleted from over twenty million user accounts. Identified 5,139 user accounts deemed "notably political" and therefore in violation of the new terms and conditions.

Seventeen minutes later, each discrete action had been hardcoded and queued, waiting for the final go-ahead from Beep-Beep CEO Xao Cheng. At 5:47 p.m. Shanghai time, the first notifications began to pop up on the phones of Beep-Beepers in the US, alerting them that their Beeping and re-Beeping privileges had been removed or, worse, that their accounts had been deleted.

The first to discover these messages were members of Melanie's content collective and the teenage supporters who were part of the Lillie Rift brigade. Cut off from the dopamine hit they relied upon to start their day, they began sending annoyed messages to one another that quickly turned to panic as it became clear they had all been targeted.

Each successive time zone awoke, and the frantic wave of fury grew, cresting when Melanie discovered that she, the dancing love queen of Beep-Beep and the beating digital heart of Julia Connor's campaign, had also been deplatformed.

• • •

"Nooooo. NOOOOOOOOOO. NOOOOoooooo." Melanie's screams turned to a whimper, and then to silence.

Breathe. Keep breathing. She looked at the message on her phone. Her hand was shaking. *Uncontrollably* shaking, like an addict trapped without her fix.

She tried to steady herself. *I'm a dancer! I'm all about control.* What was it that Julia taught? Observe yourself feeling the feeling, sit in the center of self and let the feeling happen, but know the feeling is not you.

She put her phone down and closed her eyes, observing the panic within. *Breathe, just breathe.* She felt her right hand steady.

OK. That's better. Now don't move. She counted to ten and then picked up the phone again.

It must be some mistake. A glitch! A hack. *I'm too big for this! Too big to fail, too popular to be silenced.*

She looked at the screen.

The email didn't seem to care about the size of her audience, the revenue she created for Beep-Beep. What the actual fuck...

> You are receiving this message because your Beep-Beep content has been found in violation of company terms and conditions.
>
> In keeping with Beep-Beep's guidelines respecting the political sovereignty of all governments, Beep-Beep has removed all political content creators.
>
> If you believe Beep-Beep is in error, you may appeal for reinstatement. You will be notified within three months of your appeal status.
>
> Thank you for understanding our commitment to apolitical entertainment.
>
> Sincerely,
> Beep-Beep Nation

"Thirty million followers, gone!" she shouted. "Thirty MILLION followers! Are you kidding me?"

She psycho-clicked her phone's Beep-Beep icon, but the same bright red "Access Denied" filled her screen each time. Her hand was shaking again.

Had she missed something? Did the tech sites know this was coming? *Apolitical!?* EVERYTHING—everything is political!

She had helped Beep-Beep grow, provided her labor, and now had been tossed out. She searched her name to see if people were talking about her.

Nothing. I'm blacklisted. Canceled.

She searched for Lillie Rift. There was no way Beep-Beep was going to silence Lillie. She had over three hundred million followers.

"Omyfuckinggod!"

Lillie Rift's fans had pages, sharing her music posts. But Lillie, the Goddess of Goodness, the Billboard Chart-topping dominatrix of schlub chic, who made the personal political with every song—Melanie's number-one Julia ally—was ghosted by Beep-Beep too! Her record label must be shitting themselves, lobbying Congress to bomb Beijing!

Melanie's phone was vibrating—calls, texts, emails, Flitters, Fastagrams, Lignal, Yellegram, Thatsapp. Everything except DMs from Beep-Beep. Her home screen was blanketed with nonstop notifications.

Julia! Remember Julia's lessons. She sank back into self, feeling her fury, trying to accept it, trying to move out of self and into the presence of whatever it is people like Julia called God. Slowly the pain became familiar, weaker. Melanie reached out, seeking succor in her emptiness.

Then it hit her!

The pain and the fury of being kicked off Beep-Beep was nothing new. This was how she'd always felt. Not good enough for Mom. Helpless in the face of corporate abuse. Unable to stop the climate catastrophe. A pawn in the insurmountable momentum of systemic colonization.

This, she knew, meant war. Before she met Julia she had launched guerilla attacks via Beep-Beep. Now it was time for a full-scale assault.

She had half a dozen other platforms to work her magic; she and Julia were WAY bigger than Beep-Beep. That was just one platform, an easy-to-use network. She would go out into the world and declare Beep-Beep evil and over. Fuck them.

She sent a short status update to Julia, Jonathan, and Noah.

Subject line: Deplatforming Response Strategy Session.

All:

Beep-Beep has banished all political content, per a change to its terms & conditions. I have been deplatformed. So have our other social advocates and influencers, including Lillie Rift. This has infuriating, seismic implications for our movement (not to mention my brand), but channeling Julia's positivity, we must turn this into a growth opportunity for our campaign. I've scheduled a meeting for our core group. It's on your calendars.

See you all soon.

Melanie

Everyone in Julia's suite clutched mugs of steaming chamomile tea. Everyone needed them.

"Thanks for seizing the moment. It's no secret I'm just a bit less internet inclined than the rest of you," Julia said, "so I need an explanation. Melanie, do we know how this happened?"

"I truly have no idea. I've been reading tech and political sites. Troojling and calling friends. No one seems to know."

"But who could have done this?" Jonathan asked, a frown etched into his beard.

"You mean, who forced Beep-Beep's hand and got them to shift their policy?" Melanie paused, dramatically shaking her head. "Again, no idea. Let's hope someone leaks. But right now their official stance is that they updated their terms and conditions to ensure they remain apolitical."

"Even though it is clearly interfering with the election by"—Julia searched her memory—"what's the word?"

"Deplatforming?" Melanie supplied.

"Yes, deplatforming the only movement that truly benefited from their platform."

"But why would Beep-Beep target us?"

"I mean, why wouldn't they target us?" Jonathan thought back to old missions. "Meddling in elections is an international sport. As to who made this happen, I guess it could have been anyone. Noah, any thoughts?"

"There are too many hypotheticals," Noah answered, glad they'd finally gotten around to asking the only guy who might actually be able to figure it out. Though of course, even he didn't know. "I'm doing all I can to find out, but it's impossible to answer that question right now."

Julia didn't look disappointed; only confused. "Your network doesn't have any insight?"

"Julia, there are major donors to both political parties on Beep-Beep's board. Meanwhile, you are a threat to every single industrial complex that thrives in America: Big Oil, Big Tech, Big Pharma, Telecoms, Coal, the Chamber of Commerce, the aviation industry, weapons manufacturing. Every lobby in the nation is scared shitless because they have no access and you have no track record. You turned down meetings with every single one of them and have proposed destroying the multibillion-dollar political access industrial complex. That fear could, logically, compel any deep-pocketed player with access to Beijing to set this in motion. We have no idea until whoever did it decides to brag about it."

This was why Julia had moved to her farm. Why she had buried herself in books and teaching. The world was too big, too corrupt, too sharp-elbowed for her. In her mind blossomed a vision of her garden, colorful with veggies, fruit, and flowers. The melodic pinging of keys on her typewriter.

"Well, that's disheartening," she sighed.

"Disheartening, but unavoidably true." Noah continued his onslaught, mad at Julia for putting them in this situation through her recalcitrance, but even madder at whoever it was fighting so dirty. "I mean, with the possible exception of the health and wellness sector and regenerative agronomy, you have a target on your back from every conceivable special interest in this nation."

"But I'm not trying to threaten them. I'm just trying to model alternatives."

"What can possibly be more threatening than an alternative political system that isn't reliant on their money, and isn't built to maintain the influence of the already powerful. Julia, we all hoped for the best, but this was inevitable, and it could get far worse." Noah paused, catching his breath, looking around the room expectantly, hoping Julia would be ready to fight. But she said nothing, seeming to be lost in thought, retreating to her inner place.

"The question now," Melanie said, taking up the baton and bringing a smile to Noah's face, "is who can we attack? How do we strike back? Who do we blame?"

"Mel," said Jonathan, "is it even appropriate to blame anyone? I mean, if we can't prove anything—"

"Oh, I already talked with the consultants, and I have some ideas," Melanie interrupted. "We need to invite Senator Menendez and Governor O'Leary to condemn this gross, un-American act of censorship and note that this control of political speech is an anti-democratic way of life in China."

"I like that." Noah smiled.

"Thanks. I'm just getting started. I booked myself on *Colbert* tonight and I'm doing news segments. We're going to repackage every piece of Beep-Beep content we've produced for other platforms. Jonathan, all your Vet Group content promoting Julia was erased from Beep-Beep too. We both need to be out there talking to the media twenty-four-seven. Noah needs to develop another ad. And we all need to be working the phones all day. Tomorrow we will have the stakeholder meeting of all stakeholder meetings to launch our re-platforming counterattack."

CHAPTER 37

MAGIC x MUSHROOMS x SELF

Melanie went on ROX News to denounce meddling Menendez.

She went on NATN to publicly ponder the likelihood that investor pressure was the source of Beep-Beep's ban.

She Flitted, she Fastagrammed, she spent eleven hours on the phone.

That night on *Colbert*, the host introduced her as the Woman Under the Influence, Beep-Beep Goddess Melanie Pedreira.

Wearing a hot-gold metallic jumpsuit, she strutted out to thumping house beat, clapped her hands over her head, then leapt into a one-handed cartwheel, popped up high, landed in a split, jammed into an old school breakdance backspin; then she locked on all fours and started twerking to the breakbeats.

Now she was up and doing variations of the pony, making her way to the host table. And at the exact moment the music stopped, she locked again, her finger pointing directly at her butt, which was thrust out to the camera.

"I call that kiss my Beep-Beep from Julia."

The audience hooted and whistled in approval.

"My producer calls that a 'Viewer Complaint to the FCC,'" quipped the host.

The audience applauded.

"Sorry!"

Colbert turned serious. "Melanie, can you talk about what it means for a social media platform to change its rules overnight and ban thousands of users and censor millions of posts, likes, and comments because they are deemed political."

"I call it bull-bleep! I call it censorship. I call it anti-American. But what it is—obviously—is an attempt to stop Julia Connor's momentum. Nobody cared what I posted until Julia started climbing the polls. This is an attempt to stop a serious, committed independent candidate who knows, and whose supporters know, the current system is not working because our leaders are beholden to power and money, not love, compassion and justice."

"What's Julia's response?" Colbert asked, commenting without commenting on the obvious: Melanie was making the media rounds without Julia.

Melanie missed the subtext. She didn't see anything unusual about her crusade to save the campaign, and she didn't wonder why it was that Julia had turned down all interview requests citing a need for some time "to listen to God and her intuition."

"Nothing surprises Julia about cynical corporate behavior. But we are calling for users to delete their Beep-Beep accounts and follow us and the Love Vote on Flitter, Fastgram, WeTube, and every other platform imaginable. Americans will not be silenced! This is total bull-bleep!"

Soaking up the applause, Melanie busted a new move, rising from her seat to do a forward flip, she landed, slid into a split, popped up, and clasped her hands in prayer and bowed to the audience, as the host cut to a commercial.

The commercial began with the words "An important message from Senator Menendez" superimposed on a dark screen.

Slow, sinister piano notes accompanied a dark screen, which gave rise to a scary, mottled, crudely pixelated face of Julia Connor. "Julia Connor is the most dangerous woman in America," declared a solemn voiceover. "She takes illegal, psychedelic, mind-altering drugs—and she advises our military heroes to do the same."

The scene shifted to a quintessential small-town parade where happy military veterans marched with children in their arms. "Julia Connor," the narrator continued, "says our military members need to be healed. But I ask you, healed from what?"

Now a helicopter shot zoomed in on Senator Menendez standing in a beautiful, green pasture next to a lake. He was dressed in a tucked-in flannel shirt and holding a rifle. "Our heroes don't need to be healed," he said, sincerity etched onto his weathered face, "they need to be protected. That's why, when I'm your president, I will form the Bureau of Cultic Deviance and Plant Medicine Elimination to make sure untrustworthy women like Julia Connor stop poisoning our veterans and the rest of America with illegal drugs and demonic ideas."

Watching back in Austin, Noah's jaw dropped. The veins in his wrists throbbed. He made sweaty handprints on the cushy, organic linen arms of the couch where he sat. Menendez was attacking psilocybin?! The substance that could free anyone from the shackles of their past? The substance gifted from the earth that had changed his life?

Noah thought of the millions he'd invested in psilocybin startups, of his best-selling retreat, MAGICxMUSHROOMSxSELF. That course brought in a million dollars a year! What if Menendez won and continued this war on psilocybin, on healing? A Bureau of Cultic Deviance and Plant Medicine Elimination? That sort of bureaucratic black hole could kill all that was beautiful in the world.

Noah felt the stakes of the election rise. Julia winning wasn't just about better politics or saving America from itself; the election had become a battle for his very way of life. For his values. For his business. He picked up his phone and started making late night calls.

Tomorrow, at the meeting, he'd make everyone understand what was becoming more and more clear to him: losing was not an option.

CHAPTER 38

CANCELED

Sitting in the hotel's conference room, far from the feel of dirt between her fingers or grass between her toes, Julia felt an unfamiliar weight of responsibility on her shoulders.

As a writer and teacher, she never felt she owed anyone anything beyond sharing insight drawn from the depths of her open-hearted soul. She inspired, she served, and then others acted on her teaching. In the past, "others" had been people just like her. Individuals who sought to build a new world on the manageable scale of their lives and their families. But now the meaning of "others" had changed. National leaders and masses of voters looked to her. Their hopes rested on her, and in turn, her chances of winning rested on them.

Yearning to feel the breeze upon her skin, Julia instead looked around the room, marveling at the faces she saw. She recognized the executive directors of the Pachamama PAC, Therapists for a Better Tomorrow, the Indigenous People's Perspectives PAC, and Veterans for Love and Healing (VFLH).

There were a lot of new faces in the room too. Melanie and Noah had done an amazing job activating new supporters: the American Medical Association, League of Immigrant Rights, Human Liberties Union, Prison Reform Coalition, Entertainment Association of America, etc., etc., etc.

The new faces were a surprise—and a joy! If some of the biggest human rights and business groups were joining the movement, her vision was coming together. One America, united by love. From the darkness comes the light!

Julia braced herself to speak in the most serious, presidential manner she could muster, hoping she used all acronyms correctly in the opening statement she had prepared.

"Thank you all for coming on such short notice. Our movement received a blow yesterday. A cynical hit designed to impede our progress and limit our reach. The campaign issued a statement requesting the Republican and Democratic nominees align with us in calling for the Department of Justice, the FCC, and the SEC to investigate election meddling and free speech abuses by Beep-Beep. I know both candidates have paid lip service to protecting American citizens' rights to free speech, so I hope they will join me in this important action. We cannot allow our movement to be silenced. Thankfully Melanie Pedreira, just off the red-eye from New York—I'm sure you all saw her on *Colbert* last night"—Julia paused for the anticipated applause—"will lead us through a plan to ensure we are heard."

"Give it up for Mel!" someone shouted.

"Thank you, everyone. And thank you, Julia," Melanie said, beaming from the front of the room, standing in front of the powerful people, remembering the touch of destiny she had felt after Julia became a candidate. She'd come a long way from just being a Beeper, and, she knew, this was still just the beginning.

"What. A. Moment." She looked into as many glittering, upturned eyes as she could, soaking in the moment. "One that will live in infamy. I panicked when I woke up yesterday, when I saw that Lillie Rift and I had lost over three hundred million combined followers.

"But now I've accepted it." She took a deep breath, then sighed. "I've been deplatformed. That hurts. But it is not the end of the world. In addition to demanding investigations, Julia and I have asked the public to boycott Beep-Beep and follow us onto new platforms. That is what I am here to discuss with you. We will go from deplatforming to replatforming. You saw me on *Colbert* last night—it can work! There are so many other touchpoints to tell our story. And showcase Julia and the Love movement."

At Melanie's command, a screen descended bearing the message in fifty-point font: *SHARE THE LOVE.* "We are asking everyone to share our love message anywhere and everywhere."

Julia smiled at Melanie, so proud of her. "What do you think, my friends? Should we share our love?!"

The Pachamama PAC's executive director began a chant. "Julia, Julia!"

Melanie allowed the chant to continue for several beats, applauding and whooping herself, before she took back the reins: "So here's the plan. Starting tonight for the next seven days, we are going to issue videos, policy papers, meme swarms—"

"Actually," Angela Rodriguez, the executive director of the Human Liberties Union, said, "while we will encourage O'Leary and Menendez to join your call for an investigation, we will not be 'sharing the love,' or whatever else it is you want us to do."

Melanie froze, perplexed. "So then—"

"That goes double for my organization." Peter Weinberg, executive director of the Entertainment Association of America cut in. He had one of those voices that sounded like it should be giving the chef advice at a Michelin starred restaurant. "Your, Jonathan's, and Julia's appearances today and tomorrow on *Kimmel*, *GMA*, NPR, Armed Services Network, the Outdoor Channel, *KOX News*, NATN, Fixer Upper Network, plus the other fifty or so appearances we know of—they're canceled. All of them."

Jaws dropped and eyes narrowed. Olivia Lillard from the Therapists for a Better Tomorrow PAC started madly doodling a thundercloud on her notepad. Jonathan fell into a contemplative silence. He stroked his beard and observed the wild swing of emotions happening behind his stoic facade.

Noah fumed as he fingered the Amazonian jaguar tooth necklace master craftsmen from Peru's Shipibo tribe had made him. He'd personally invited Peter! "What?" he boomed. "Where is this coming from? There was no mention of this when we spoke yesterday. America needs to know the truth, especially now that Menendez is attacking psilocybin!"

"What America needs is stability." Peter smirked, looking straight at Julia and ignoring Noah. "You refused donations from my organization and many others you invited here. You didn't even meet with us. But now something goes wrong and you come begging for help?"

"Peter," Julia said, surprised to discover she had subconsciously prepared for something just like this. "I hear your point. But please understand, we started as a small group intent on creating political alternatives. Maybe we didn't have the conversations we should have when we started. That is my mistake and my fault. But if we're to create new, better political and social systems, we have to work together."

"We don't want new systems," Angela Rodriguez replied, unsurprised at how naïve Julia was proving to be. "We want to lead the systems we already have. Supporting you gets us nowhere."

Julia cocked her head, surprised and intrigued to be experiencing yet another confusing form of loyalty. "So, why'd you come to this meeting?"

"If you understood how politics works," Peter purred, completely at home in the combat of the moment, "the answer to that question would be obvious."

"Exactly," Angela continued. "Every group in this room is going to raise millions of dollars from our donors by blasting Chinese excess. Both of the other campaigns will do the same. And to raise our money, we have to say that we're working closely with all three campaigns to stand up for American rights and human rights. But do not be confused. We're going to raise our money and blast censorship, but we will in no way be supporting you."

Melanie felt herself starting to shake. Her plans to replatform, the love she felt from her followers and Colbert's viewers—all gone? Taken from her again?! Her chest beat to the drum of fury.

"I think you all should leave," Melanie burst out, glaring, "so the rest of us can get back to running the campaign that is kicking all your asses!"

Peter Weinberg turned to Angela Martinez. They were both openly laughing. "Jesus, could she be more petulant?"

And then the entire contingent of new faces—the groups Julia thought signaled growth and unity—filed out of the room under a barrage of glares from the love vote leaders.

Julia wanted to calm the anger, to center the now half-empty room, but Melanie didn't give her the chance.

With a thousand vengeful ideas running through her mind, Melanie said, "We got kicked off of Beep-Beep on the same day Menendez makes a play to bring some law-and-order Republican types back into the fold by attacking magic mushies, and now all of the quote-unquote 'rights protecting' organizations have walked out on us. Did I miss anything?"

"No," Noah said grimly, twisting his necklace into a helix, wild thoughts racing faster than his pulse.

"But it's wrong," Jonathan said. "People will see the truth through all the attacks. The polls say we're still doing great. Julia's psilocybin use is protected religious freedom through the church. And we don't need all those groups that just left. We were doing great without them."

"Exactly," said Julia, "people will—"

"Jonathan, Julia, come on!" Noah interrupted. "People line up to be told what to think and do. I know you're trying to wake people up so they can build a better world. But we are getting hammered!"

"Yeah!" Melanie continued. "This campaign happened because Beepers loved my content about Julia and her message, but also because they needed to be given direction. People don't just want to escape the reality of their own lives—they want new lives. *I*"—her first session with Julia, back when she was still fighting this journey, flashed through her mind— "want a new life!"

Noah nodded. "Agreed. Protecting those people, and protecting the reputation of psilocybin, is why we have to strike back."

"We don't need to strike back," Julia said quietly. "We need to continue showing an alternative to the way things are, modeling a different way of living our values and our ideals."

"You are right." Noah clasped his hands together briefly in Anjali mudra, the Namaste position, and made a slight bow to Julia. "Of course, those are our core beliefs. But we're at war now. Millions of people are counting on us. We need to attack—we need to protect our momentum and respond by launching truth and love bombs."

Julia hated the contradiction she felt in Noah's calculated manner. He was feinting peace and preaching war. She felt him becoming all the things she hated about politics.

"Thank you, Noah. I agree we should respond, but I don't like the aggressive assault language. I have made my career by sharing what I believe but also by listening to others, trying to understand why they believe what they believe. One of the things we have to do better as a people is listen."

There was a slight pause as Julia gathered her breath for what was coming next.

"When I first heard about the Beep-Beep deplatforming—and please, Melanie, don't take this the wrong way, because you have been and are always a shining light to me—but I thought, 'Is this so bad? Do I need Beep-Beep? Does love need Beep-Beep? People are addicted to Beep-Beep and their devices, it's destroying society even though it's helped our campaign. I think this might be a blessing in disg—"

"I JUST LOST THIRTY MILLION FOLLOWERS," Melanie gasped, tears coming to her eyes. She felt like a kid again. Out of control. Anger bubbled inside of her. Helplessness masqueraded as strength. She felt her spine stiffen. "And you're calling this a blessing?!"

"With all due respect, Julia," Noah asserted, "Melanie and everyone who has had a post deleted should take it the wrong way. Thousands of us—no, millions of us—have put our lives on hold to change this country. We've put our reputations, our livelihoods, on the line to WIN."

"What is it the Bible says, an eye for an eye, tooth for a tooth?" Melanie spoke through a glass-cutting glare, her eyes laser focused on Julia. "They've already come for our healing psilocybin and our Beepers, we don't know what might be next, we have to reply in kind."

"No. Absolutely not!" Julia's hands were on her head, her eyes wide, shocked, and sad. "Have the two of you lost all sense of perspective? We are building an alternative, not falling into the trap every political leader in this country has succumbed to for the entirety of my lifetime!"

Julia looked around the room for support, did everyone feel this way? "Jonathan? Am I wrong here? You've been in wars. Real ones."

"I share Melanie's fury and Noah's horror that Menendez is trying to rob the world of a true gift. One hundred percent!! But," Jonathan said sadly, "war inevitably causes collateral damage." The veteran looked out into the room, searching for consensus. Abe Jenkins, executive director of the Pachamama PAC, gave Jonathan an encouraging nod; so did Mallory Diaz of the Montessori Teachers Union.

"We're with you, Julia. We think we have to respond, but it can't be with rash anger. We've built this movement with humility, compassion, and grace. And that can't stop now."

●　●　●

Melanie's anger had spiked to an all-time high.

Madder than when her mother decided to move from Seattle to Tacoma in the middle of her junior year.

Madder than when her freshman crush, Omar Kennedy, slept with her then told her to come back when she'd lost fifteen pounds.

Madder, even, than when a Democratic governor had appointed the former general counsel of American Petroleum to supposedly liberal New York's supreme court.

They had treated her like a kid in the room. And Julia like an inconvenience. Embarrassed and angry with herself for doing so, she dwelled on the thought of revenge but had no idea how to get it.

Then came the text from Noah.

"I have a plan. Meet in my room?"

When he opened the door, the scent of sage wafted over Melanie. She no longer recoiled from Noah's oddities. If he thought smoke and spirit acted as one, so be it.

"A war plan that isn't a war plan?" she asked hopefully.

"That's one way to put it. And you actually gave me the idea. Do you remember when you threw oil on that CEO?"

Melanie unconsciously touched the still lingering bump on the side of her head, smiling despite herself. "The security guy's fist was rock hard."

"And why did you do it?"

"I did it because I had to do something! Just letting that prick get away with earth murder was too much."

"Exactly. I always thought your tactics were a bit too abrasive, but not anymore. We need to do something every bit as radical as what you used to do, but . . . secretly."

After listening to the details, Melanie shook her head, wide-eyed. "Thats nuts!"

"I know."

"Could it work?"

"There's no guarantee. But if it does work, we would change the course of history."

"But why Menendez? Those groups from yesterday hate him."

"True, but Menendez and the pastor are the ones attacking psilocybin. They're the natural target."

Melanie took a deep breath. The risk was enormous, but what was it that political and business leaders always said— "never waste a crisis?" She made up her mind.

"I'm in. How do we bait the trap?"

Noah smiled. "All we need to do is post one little message on 6Lee and wait for action."

"What's 6Lee?"

"After 4chan got shut down," Noah replied as he opened his laptop, "6Lee replaced it."

"Chan? Lee? What?"

"Turns out conspiracy-hyped incels love kung fu."

Noah opened a virtual private network on his laptop and navigated to an Estonian piracy site. From there he launched an onion router, used it to create a new account on 6Lee, and typed out a message from the user Midwesternjesusguy12. He read aloud as he typed: "I'm a pastor with a secret that will bring down Julia Connor. How do I get in touch with someone in Menendez's campaign?"

"That's all?"

Noah smiled and nodded. "I think that'll do it. The hard part will be pulling this off, but for now we just have to wait."

"We can't wait long." Melanie felt heat rising in her face and a sweat breaking out on her brow. "We've got two weeks till the election."

CHAPTER 39

SWEET TEA

Luke sat across from Pastor McMillan in his jet, the Soaring Salvation.

This, Luke thought, was their chance to end it. To finally put Julia Connor in her place, back gardening on that insufferable farm of hers so the real Christian leaders could guide the United States on its inevitable path to greatness.

Manifest destiny? It wasn't dead; it wasn't even slumbering. Not even with all the sky-is-falling environmentalist drama queens sounding false alarms, slamming the brakes on human progress. People had been predicting the end of civilization for thousands of years. It wasn't going to happen. With God's help and Pastor McMillan's leadership, America's superiority would power a new golden age of religious revival and sinlessness.

Luke smiled grimly to himself. Yes, he could see the future, but that future only existed if they won. The fact he was on this jet with Pastor McMillan was a clear sign that all was not going well.

He'd left Menendez in Micah's capable hands to complete three campaign stops and a fundraising dinner in greater Des Moines. "Well shit, Luke," Menendez had said, "you know I don't trust ministers, mullahs, rabbis, or any other man of the cloth, but if this small town ass-hat of a Bible church pastor can help me, then of course you should go meet him. Just don't let that pastor of yours pull any tricks."

They'd thought Julia Connor would fade, that her quaint little ideas would fall apart under the sustained attacks of party leaders and media mouthpieces reiterating the one indomitable political truth: fear of change.

They'd all been wrong.

Julia Connor seemed impervious to attacks. Attacking her on national security hadn't worked. Same with her being inexperienced and feckless. Ditto abortion and race. And all the normal theological attacks? Seemingly useless. The polls hadn't even moved after Pastor McMillan identified her as the Whore of Babylon!

Every accusation was met with a calm, kind rebuttal that was disseminated with exponential efficiency by her relentless army of PACs, influencers, and supporters.

"Julia's a different breed," Pastor McMillan said, sloshing around the ice and coke left in his cup. "We see the work of the devil everyday through the efforts of our political foes, but Julia is different. She doesn't just oppose us—she actively seeks Christian destruction through her claims of universal love. That is why she is the Whore of Babylon."

Luke nodded feverishly. "And that's why we must do everything in our power to defeat her."

The plane touched down on the airstrip outside of Windsor, Missouri. Luke jumped behind the steering wheel of a waiting rental car, and they made their way to Midwesternjesusguy12's church.

• • •

The defunct Methodist church, listed on Airbnb for $250 a night, was perfect. Noah had draped a 20-foot banner reading Windsor Bible Church across the front of the building, and he'd had a website hastily built that was populated with fraudulent metadata. It wasn't an in-depth con job, but it was enough to make an overeager observer believe Windsor Bible Church had been in business since 2024.

That morning Noah had lovingly minced eight grams of magic mushrooms in the church's kitchen. He had then placed those small pieces of life-transforming plant medicine in a boiling pot of Lipton Tea sweetened with five cups of sugar. Now the tea was cooling in the fridge, preparing for its icy introduction to the guests.

He and Melanie were in an old Sunday school classroom putting the finishing touches on their costumes. Noah, normally a muscular, tank-top-wearing icon of conscious masculinity, was now a bespectacled, portly minister dressed in jeans and a frayed blue dress shirt.

Adjusting his fake paunch to rest more comfortably on his hips, Noah looked in the mirror and hated what he saw staring back at him. He looked just like his dad. It was disgusting.

"Wow," he said, "our shadows are with us every step of our lives."

Melanie, whose face was caked with pale white makeup and whose dark hair was covered with a white wig, looked up at Noah. "What was that?"

"Oh, nothing. Are you ready?!"

• • •

Luke parked the rental car in Windsor Bible Church's empty parking lot and looked around approvingly. Just like he had requested, the lot was empty. No prying eyes allowed.

Pastor McMillan viewed the same empty lot from a different perspective.

He didn't like sneaking around, looking for daggers hidden in the heartland. He was a man of the stage. A man who thrived in front of screaming, adoring parishioners, or at the head of a table full of CEOs preparing to write checks to the Salvation Super PAC. Sure, his preaching was important, but the way to win elections was with money. Cold hard cash bought the airtime, the data, the consultants, and the get-out-the-vote operation necessary to drive home an electoral win.

That's why he worked as hard to raise money for Salvation Super PAC as he did for Salvation Megachurch.

Yet he was here, in an empty parking lot beneath a single tree, preparing to meet a pastor Luke's opposition researchers had found on a message board.

Midwesternjesusguy12? What kind of name was that?

"Ready?"

Pastor McMillan turned to face the church with what Luke could only describe as righteous swagger. "Let's do this."

A short hike up the cement steps deposited them beneath a cheap church banner. Luke took a deep breath before pulling open the large wooden church doors. A partially balding man stood in the foyer. He wore cheap jeans and a fraying shirt that obscured his well-fed belly.

The man lit up when he saw them and spun with surprising grace, extending his hand.

"Hello, hello! I'm Minister Billy. You must be Luke, the bigwig from the campaign. And you, well, I know you, Pastor Josiah. God bless you for blessing me with your presence!"

"Thank you, brother." Pastor McMillan shook his hand firmly. He was known for his firm handshakes; it was one of the thousand ways in which he conveyed to anyone who met him that he was chosen by God to be a leader.

Minister Billy beamed. "Welcome friends, welcome, and God bless you both. I promise your journey will be worth your time."

Luke looked around, feeling at home in the humble church. "I'm always happy to visit God's people, Minister. Thank you for having us."

A hunched woman with her gray hair in a bun shuffled in holding a platter with a jug of iced tea and two empty glasses. Noah glanced at her, then turned his attention back to Luke and Pastor McMillan.

"Can I offer you both a glass of iced tea? It's sweet, and made from scratch by our dear secretary Becky."

Pastor McMillan licked his lips. "Nothing says church like a glass of sweet tea on a warm fall afternoon."

Secretary Becky set the tray down on a small side table. "Please let me pour you each a glass. We're so honored you're here."

Carefully gripping the condensation-soaked pitcher of sweet tea, she filled the two glasses, leaving the pitcher two-thirds full.

She handed the glasses to Luke and Pastor McMillan and walked to a small chair, where she sat down out of the way, just like a good church secretary should.

Noah gestured toward the sanctuary as he lifted the pitcher. "If you'll both follow me, I've set up a few chairs and a table in the sanctuary. I'll bring Ms. Becky's refreshments along too."

As soon as the sanctuary's solid oak doors swung shut behind the three men, "Secretary Becky" straightened out of her hunch and slid a large metal rod covered in foam insulation through the wrought iron door handles.

Luke took in the aged but still beautiful sanctuary, the aroma of old carpet and over-mature wood saturating his senses. He followed Minister Billy down the center aisle toward the pulpit. Behind the pulpit rose an elevated row of seats for the choir and, beyond that, an old-school organ sat upon the wall, its majestic, symmetrical phalanx of copper-and-steel-colored pipes stretching to the ceiling, a symbolic representation of prayers rising to the heavens.

Luke's soul stirred as he imagined the organ's tone reverberating through the sanctuary, reminding parishioners who, surely, would be staring at the gorgeous stained-glass windows, of their sinfulness and their salvation.

He felt a sense of kinship with Minister Billy, who shuffled ahead of them. Small churches were a vital part of ministry, the foundation for outreach to the lost and downtrodden. He wondered if Pastor McMillan felt a similar glory.

The answer, if he'd asked, was no. Pastor McMillan found small churches to be depressing. He hated their scent, he despised that they reminded him of where he'd come from; he couldn't stand the thought that each of these churches, in their own little way, competed with his church, network, and platform.

Having reached the small table near the pulpit, Pastor McMillan and Luke sat facing Noah, who labored into his seat as, he imagined, an overweight pastor likely would.

Noah took in Luke and Pastor McMillan's mismatched faces. His job was to stall for thirty minutes so the mushrooms could kick in. He needed to deliver an Oscar-worthy performance, kicking the conversation off with a bang so they'd be hooked but also subtly preparing them for the journey they were about to undertake.

"I assume you both know why you're here?"

"Of course we know why we're here," Pastor McMillan purred. "We're here to put an end to the ungodliness that has swept this nation."

"Exactly," Luke followed up. "I trust God has brought us to you so we can, together, expose Julia Connor as the Whore of Babylon."

Minister Billy smiled, his chubby face momentarily appearing almost handsome. *What is this guy's deal?* Luke thought. *There's no shortage of zealot Bible pastors in this nation. How did this guy come to have the exact information we need?*

"You're exactly right, Luke. Julia is the Whore of Babylon, and I can help you prove it. I have video and I have pictures. But we'll get to that." Noah leaned over to refill both glasses. "First, I want to make sure you understand the full scale of the evil she brought down upon members of my flock."

"That is unnecessary," Pastor McMillan said after two more gulps of the sweet tea. "If you'll just show us the video, we can do the rest."

"You'll have the evidence, don't you worry. In fact, we'll watch it soon. But first," Noah droned, "I want to explain how what she did affected God's children here in Windsor."

Noah launched into preacher overdrive, recounting the "healing event" in excruciating detail, naming every attendee, their job, their family history, their spiritual challenges.

"So," Noah finished up, "Johnny's grandpa was Bob and John's father's uncle. In this sense, this really was a family gathering, so you can see why we took Julia's betrayal so personally."

Why, Pastor McMillan wondered, were people always trying to impress him with long stories? He was a busy man! He valued men who didn't waste words.

"Thank you for that story, Minister Billy. Can we watch the video now?"

"Absolutely!" said Noah. "But first, I want to talk about how these men were affected. Now you know their backgrounds, you can appreciate their pain."

Pastor McMillan's heart sank. More talk? His right hand twitched desperately toward the cell phone in his pocket, but he controlled the temptation for bad manners by pouring himself and Luke the last of the iced tea.

Luke took the refilled glass of tea and leaned forward. "Please tell us about their pain. We need to know everything."

"OK then! So after Julia lured me and all these men into the room by promising us healing. That's when she got to work with the magic mushrooms. Do y'all know much about the default mode network?"

Luke's eyebrows shot up. This could be even wilder than he'd known! "The hacker collective?!"

"I, well, I don't know what a hacker collective is," Minister Billy stammered, "so no. She started going on about the default mode network being part of the brain. Are you familiar, Pastor Josiah, with this concept?"

Pastor McMillan shook his head no, wondering why the minister was talking about the brain when everyone knew they were discussing the soul.

Noah realized he was on shaky ground. He was trying to thread the needle. To make sure Luke and Pastor McMillan would be receptive, not defensive, when the medicine hit. But doing that without alarming them was a tough task.

"Julia started telling us about Matthew Strike, a Christian neuro-theologist at Baylor University, and the important work he was doing. According to Strike, the default mode network is part of what separates our conscious mind, the five percent of our mind we use, from our subconscious mind. In other words, we don't have access to ninety-five percent of our brain in normal states of consciousness. So this default mode network is where our egos, our sense of individuality, exist. And it's the part of the brain that helps us make useful assumptions to simplify everyday living. Strike says the psilocybin in magic mushrooms quiets the default mode network, helping us connect to the most powerful part of our mind, our subconscious, the part of self that is attuned to feeling and emotions, the language of God's good news."

"Wow. That's actually kind of interesting." Luke found himself unexpectedly transfixed.

"Interesting?" A scowl cut into Pastor McMillan's brow. "God separates us from our subconscious mind for a reason. When we're in our subconscious, Satan can have power over us. It's dangerous, right Minister Billy?"

Noah's mind locked up. He had to say it was dangerous to stay in character, but he needed both men to know it wasn't dangerous if they were to have a good trip. He glanced at the empty pitcher. The first dose had been in their system for thirty minutes already. It was almost time.

"Well, that's the thing, Pastor Josiah. I made the exact same point. But this expert neuro-theologian, Strike, found it's *not* dangerous. Our conscious mind, and our ego, often separate us from our true selves—and therefore from God. There is actually nothing safer and nothing more powerful than sinking into the subconscious center of ourselves, opening to God and to the universe. When our ego and all the assumptions we have about what life *should be* are stripped away, we can sit with ourselves, beginning the work of knowing who and what we are, of knowing God's exact plan for our lives and feeling God's unconditional love."

"What are you saying?" Pastor McMillan blustered. "I don't have time for more of your talk. We need to know what Julia did to these men, and we need to know now. Show us the video!"

Noah's heart sank. He'd wanted the men to understand the beauty of psilocybin and the positive power of subconscious exploration, but he sensed only suspicion.

He glanced around the room, noting the soft pillows on a pew and the folded blankets beside them. He'd tried to set them up for success, but he couldn't control every aspect of the journey. *That was the, uhm, flaw*, he thought, *in secretly dosing people.*

"I don't think what I'm trying to communicate is coming through," Noah said, "Maybe it's time for us to watch the video?"

"That would be GREAT!" Pastor McMillan fought the urge to shout and calmed a bit. Who cared what Minister Billy said so long as the video showed Julia serving demonic, brain-addling drugs to veterans?

Noah stood up, summoning his Minister Billy act one last time.

"I'll be right back with the video. I forgot my laptop in the office. In the interim, will you both pray together? I ask that you seek peace, calm your mind, and ask God that today is a success."

Something in Pastor McMillan bucked at the idea of being nudged to pray by another pastor. He suppressed it. "We'll happily pray, Minister Billy. See you in a moment."

Shuffling through the only side door, Noah tried to hide his elation. It was time! As soon as he'd locked the door behind him, the die would be cast, the results would be in the universe's hands.

Pastor McMillan turned to Luke as the door closed behind Minister Billy.

"That tea was delicious, almost as good as Salvation Bible sweet tea! And the conversation, well, that Minister Billy is an odd duck, but if he comes through for us, he'll have struck a mighty blow for God's kingdom here on earth."

"He threw me off with that brain talk," Luke said, rubbing his calves. "That tea must have a ton of caffeine. My legs are tingling."

Pastor McMillan laughed. "Tingle tinkle calves. That's funny."

Before Luke could even wonder why the stately Pastor Josiah McMillan had said something as out of character as "tingle tinkle," he was silenced by dimming lights and the whirl of a screen lowering from the ceiling, obscuring the organ.

Luke blinked in wonder at a light beam that pierced the air. *Was this a visitation?* Then he realized it was Minister Billy's video projecting from the back of the sanctuary.

The broad, clean-shaven face of a large man filled the screen. Below his face, the text: *A Veteran Speaks about Julia Connor.*

Luke beamed, feeling a bit lightheaded but otherwise more at peace than he'd felt in years. The moment of deliverance! Julia Connor's downfall had arrived.

"Before I met Julia Connor," the man in the video said, "I was lost and broken. I served in Iraq and Afghanistan. I killed for my country, and that killing nearly killed me. From boot camp to Baghdad to the Battle of Kamdesh, I endured years of incoming fire, IED explosions, near-death experiences for me, and death for some of my friends. These blasts and our missions seemed hard, but nothing prepared me for how hard it would be to leave the service and become a civilian."

Luke listened with a soft smile. *Poor guy*, he thought. *Get to the point, soldier*, Pastor McMillan thought beside him.

"When I came home," the vet continued, "politicians pretended we weren't at war, civilians ignored me, and I became a prisoner of PTSD. It got bad. Real bad, but all my doctors wanted to give me was Zoloft."

Zoloft. Pastor McMillan thought of how amazing it was that God, through the gift of modern medicine, had found cures for people's anxiety. Watching through the double-sided glass behind the baptismal, Melanie—no longer

Secretary Becky—thought of all those years her mother had thrown pills at her as a way of washing her hands of Melanie's "issues."

"Then I was introduced to Julia. She told me the medication numbed me. That to heal, I had to confront my pain and face my trauma while loving myself and the divine glory that exists within me. She introduced me to a group—a new band of brothers—who had come through hell with the help of myce-lium, the mushrooms whose psilocybin helped forge new connections in the brain and the soul. With Julia's support, these veterans healed, they reversed the damage of actual and emotional violence by focusing on and opening up to love. I know that sounds funny from grunts who lived on MRE's, vodka, and a survival of the ill-est philosophy, but it's true."

"What is this?" Pastor McMillan cried out. "Minister Billy, either you have the wrong video or you have been overcome by the devil's power." No response. "In the name of Jesus Christ, I command you to leave us, Lucifer!"

Luke looked around the sanctuary, wondering why the light coming through the stained glass was *so* beautiful. He could feel the feeling of the holy spirit swimming through his veins. What was Pastor McMillan yelling about? Didn't he sense the presence of God edging into the room?

"Luke!"

Luke shook his head, trying to focus on Pastor McMillan, who kept yell-ing, but unable to focus on much of anything in a room that was suddenly swimming in an array of rippling purples, greens and blues.

"This is a scam! That Minister Billy is no pastor. I bet this isn't even a church!" Pastor McMillan was up now, marching to the back of the sanc-tuary. "Hey, *Minister Billy*, this is Satan's propaganda! In the name of God, turn the thing off!"

He tried the handle on the massive wooden doors. They didn't budge. He pounded on the door until his knuckles throbbed. But the soundtrack of the veteran was louder.

"Julia made me feel safe and helped me recognize I not only needed to love myself—I needed to love other people as well. Julia taught me that all love is God's love, and that the peace that comes with love is accessible to us all. With her help, I healed. Now instead of killing, I serve."

Pastor McMillan kicked the door, but the iron bar on the other side held. "What in the name of our loving God is this heretical bullshit! Minister Billy, where are you?!"

"Pastor Josiah," Luke said, overwhelmed with compassion for the man on the screen, "this is a beautiful video. I'm trying to listen. Please keep it down."

Dazzling close-ups of cushy, cream-colored mushrooms. A graceful infinity of striates—the under ridges of a mushroom cap—fanning out. Luke sat mesmerized by the visual feast that had replaced the veteran on screen.

He almost didn't notice a new voice was narrating. A warm, inviting, beguiling voice that was oddly familiar. Like someone he knew.

"You," came Melanie's soft voiceover, reading Noah's script, "are about to go on a profound journey to the center of yourself. The mushroom tea you drank is powerful. It will be quite the trip." Her melodic tone softened the news. "But remember, the psilocybin won't show you anything that's not already inside of you. And because you're made in God's image, you're safe in the hands of a God that desperately wants to know you and wants us to know ourselves. Now, take comfort in love, embrace life, and open yourself to spirit."

"Mushroom tea?!" Luke sprung to his feet. "Did you hear that pastor Josiah—he drugged us!" Then, despite himself, Luke giggled. *This* was being drugged? The light streaming through the stained-glass Jesus's eyes shone like the sun. It was glorious.

Pastor McMillan continued kicking the door. His toes stung. His mind was frenzied. Mushrooms? Hard drugs? Hallucinations?

Hallucinations—they were the gateway to hell. The onramp to homosexuality! Ground zero for AIDS and—*oh God!*—*herpes!*

How many times had he taken communion, wondering if transubstantiation could be real? Now—*Lord save me!*—he would experience its opposite, demons delivered through tea.

He stuck a finger down his throat.

He retched. But nothing came up. Tried again. Nothing. Falling to his knees, he prayed for vomit. He rubbed his face on the short-shag maroon carpet before he knew what he was doing. The fiber caressed his face—like a woman's soft, lotioned hand. *Amazing.*

"Pastor?" said Luke gently, watching him rub his face on the ground. "I think we have to accept this and seek Jesus through the experience."

The absurd statement brought Pastor McMillan back to his senses and his feet. "Are you fucking kidding me?"

Pastor McMillan jumped to his feet and lost his mind. He slammed his fists against the locked doors, growing more furious each time they rattled but didn't budge. The bruise on his hand was welting. Purpling. His knuckles began to bleed. He didn't care.

"Help, help! Let us out! We are trapped with the Devil. Becky! Secretary Becky, fight evil. I know you have it in you. HELP!"

He turned, looking for a projectile. The hymnals! He raced to a pew and grabbed a book that he launched at the stained glass. The hymnal clattered off harmlessly.

The folding chairs! He ran to the front of the church shrieking profanities. "You rat bastard cracked out pastor! I will ruin you. Ruin you!" He grabbed one of the chairs with both hands and flung it. It grazed the window, but the damn things were too high. He needed something small and dense. A rock to be his redeemer! But there was no rock.

Exhausted, Pastor McMillan finally sat next to Luke, who'd arranged the pillows and blankets for them in front of the pulpit.

"Son," he said, catching his breath and licking the blood off his left hand, "you are about to face demons, the devil. Stay strong and remember that all I've said is true!!!"

Melanie and Noah watched the mad-hatter panic, wincing at every Pastor McMillan door punch, hoping he'd calm down.

"This isn't best practice, is it, Noah?"

"It's the worst, but what can we do? We had an entire script intended to make them feel safe, but that pastor didn't let me get through it."

Melanie was still fluffing out her hair after changing out of Secretary Becky's makeup and wig. "They're terrified. Do you think they'll be OK?"

"I don't know. Set and setting matter so much with psilocybin. I've never dosed someone against their will, and I've never seen anyone panic like this *before* the trip starts. But, at this point, it's beyond our control."

CHAPTER 40

THE OAKS OF LEBANON

Slowly, in a twist of cosmic fate that strained the bounds of belief but not the laws of quantum physics, Luke and Pastor McMillan sank into a shared journey, their brains and their energetic signatures fusing into a single hallucination.

Luke expected bright psychedelic colors or visions of marauding demonic hordes, but as the psilocybin flicked the switch in his serotonin receptors, he felt nothing but tingling sensations. Odd.

Then the stained glass began to melt.

A lamb beneath an Oak of Lebanon began to slide down the wall. Luke watched transfixed as the tree followed, its broad branches and green leaves melting like butter in a pan before puddling in the center aisle. From the stained-glass puddle, the tree and the lamb reconstituted themselves.

He smiled in disbelief as the tree grew anew in the sanctuary's center, its green leaves brushing the walls, the whole tree glowing as if a softly setting sun was directly behind it, deep space surrounding it on every side. And now, now the colors! Morphing patterns of light and energy traced through blackness; the tree stood as a glowing green ember in an energized nothingness.

This, Luke thought, *is amazing. I love this. Oh my goodness. Oh my goodness. I've never seen anything cooler. This is the best!*

He looked over at Pastor McMillan who, with eyes wide open, was whispering to himself, "The tree is not real. The lamb is a demon. The tree is not real. The lamb is a demon."

Then the lamb began to frolic, running, spinning, and jumping with joy. First around the tree, before approaching Luke and Pastor McMillan, speaking to them in an angelic voice. "You are loved. Know the peace of God. Feel the love, let God's peace settle into you and through you."

Pastor McMillan bolted upright, swiping at the lamb, which playfully avoided his arms, "baaahing" a gentle reproach.

Luke giggled. Talking lambs. What a trip!

Stained-glass Jesus began to melt, rolling down the wall like multi-hued magma before traversing the floor and settling in front of the tree. From the shining puddle of liquified Jesus a figure began to form.

Pastor McMillan's mind howled with outrage and fear! The attack was intensifying. A devilish lamb was bad enough, but was Jesus himself now taking demonic form? He wanted to run, to scream, to hide, but he felt glued to the ground, unable to avoid the blasphemy.

Jesus stood, his face an open expression of unadulterated love, and began walking towards both men.

Luke smiled. Pastor McMillan snarled. A warm ball of light began to form in Jesus's hands.

Luke saw Jesus release the ball, watching it float slowly toward him as the psychedelic son of God, the lamb and the tree all watched in the background. When it had almost reached him, the ball split into two, one settling above his face, the other above Pastor McMillan's.

Luke felt the ball of light. He felt its warmth, and basked in a sense of unconditional love he had never before felt. His insides were mush, joy manifest. A gurgling stream of bliss, a raging torrent of belonging threatened to burst out his chest. He could almost see the eruption, the lava flow of love spouting above him, carrying him into heaven.

And then, Jesus spoke. "My children. I come to you in love. Pure, melodious, joyful love."

Luke remained mesmerized, the words vibrating in every cell of his body, a childlike smile frozen in ecstasy on his face.

"Do you remember the Pharisees? These men followed religious rules but lacked a heart of love and mercy. Do you not remember it was they, not the prostitutes or the adulterers, who I cast out of the temple?"

Every part of Pastor McMillan screamed in rage. He felt the ball of loving light as searing pain. He fought back with every ounce of his being, hating the floating light's glorious glow, despising Jesus's words.

"So I speak of the heart, and to your heart. Let go of rules, even if you believe them to be my rules. Hold only to love and mercy, compassion and gratitude, the forces which will guide you to me."

Luke called out to God, overcome by feelings of loving acceptance that he could feel rewiring a mind that had only sought righteousness, purity, and victory. His face froze in a smile, tears glistening as they ran down both cheeks. Bathed in this glory, surrendered to love, he lost all awareness of Pastor McMillan.

Suddenly released from the bonds that had held him on the floor, Pastor McMillan shot to his feet with Jesus's last damning words echoing in his mind.

"Let go of the rules…"

Let go of the rules? Impossible! The rules were what separated the righteous from the sinner. The rules demarcated right from wrong, truth from lies. Live in love and mercy? Of course one must live in love and mercy, but such high-minded principles had no value without judgment!

His eyes aflame and the scent of sulfur in his nose, he looked around the room, completely unable to ascertain how, in the midst of what looked like deep space, he came to be in a place where a glowing tree stood amidst bright, flowing cosmic energy, sheltering a blaspheming Jesus under its branches.

His mind shattered, breaking into a million pulsating pieces of fear and fury.

He sprinted straight ahead, intending to disappear into the blackness but instead running full speed into the first row of pews. His left leg first made contact, shattering his femur. The impact spun him and the momentum carried him forward, slamming his right shoulder into the seatback, before he flipped over the pew and came to rest on the carpet, his twisted and broken leg splayed across the bench, his face bleeding on the same carpet that had softly caressed his cheek a few moments before.

CHAPTER 41

IMMEASURABLE BLACKNESS

Jed Abernathy swept his arm behind him, indicating the ambulances, fire trucks, and police cars that were scattered across the church's parking lot. He locked into his cameraface, a perfect steely gaze that projected importance and concern.

"EMT workers who rushed to the scene of this defunct church in sleepy Windsor, Missouri, were stunned to find two of America's leading conservative figures—Senator Menendez's campaign manager, Luke Lockwood, and the renowned Pastor Josiah McMillan—in extreme distress. Authorities are working to discover what the men were doing here and why they were, apparently, locked in the church. ROX has obtained footage that reveals Pastor McMillan was extremely disoriented. In the clip you're about to see, Pastor McMillan describes a battle with agents of Satan, suggesting they were working at the behest of Love Party candidate Julia Connor. Viewer discretion is advised."

ROX cut to a close-up of Pastor McMillian: gaunt, agitated, and spewing spittle from an EMT gurney. "The Whore of Babylon—JULIA—was there! She stripped me naked, and a horde of demons attacked me with whips and chains, chanting vile things about love and America. I fought them, twisting and kicking, I think I nailed the lamb, but one can never be sure. It was a cage match with the devil and the whore was the referee. It was the drugs. She drugged me, Julia and Secretary Becky!"

Abernathy returned to the screen: "That footage was captured by a passerby as Pastor McMillan was rolled out on a stretcher. He is now under observation at Liberty Hospital, where I'm told he will undergo a battery of tests. Despite McMillan's charges, Julia Connor—according to thousands of eyewitnesses—was in Seattle, over a thousand miles away. We've reached out to the Menendez campaign for comment, though they have not yet responded. For now, details of these bizarre doings, far from the campaign trail, remain scarce."

"That was perfect, Jed," said Nancy, who was wearing a safari-themed t-shirt. "You nailed it."

"Thanks, Nance. Some stories just tell themselves."

Actually, this story was going to need a lot of telling. It was going to require creativity—and sources.

He'd gotten a call from a hyperventilating local newsman in Kansas City telling him Menendez's staff had been involved in a Holy War. He immediately thought a terrorist attack had occurred and ordered Nancy to commandeer a private plane so they could make it to Windsor in record time. But this was no guns-and-Allah skirmish.

He'd arrived in front of the church in time to find a raving Pastor McMillan tied to a gurney, spouting about swooping demons, talking sheep and cosmic bolts of energy that had broken his legs amid "immeasurable blackness."

Jed was relieved when Nancy found a teenager who was on the scene filming with his cell phone. He had caught the pastor ranting about Julia Connor. *That* was the story—at least until they could gather more details.

Then he realized something. "Nancy, where the fuck is Luke?"

"I don't know. But I got a clip of him too. From the same kid. I don't think we should use it."

"*What?* Show me the video!"

She held up her phone screen. A silver bracelet featuring a procession of elephants jangled on her wrist.

A shaky camera followed Luke wandering across the parking lot, a small flower in his hand. He seemed completely lost, his red, puffy eyes standing out on his normally calm and collected face, the part in his hair mussed for the first time in Jed's memory.

The teen filming yelled out, "Sir, are you OK?"

When Luke looked up, a piece of grass fell off his hair. "I've never had a more beautiful experience. I met God, I felt love, my heart burst open with compassion. I died, I was born, they felt like the same thing. I, I—" Tears streamed down his face. "I'll never be the same."

"Jesus. I agree—we can't show that. In fact," Jed said, "let's just delete it."

• • •

The digital screamers and political experts did their thing, extrapolating nothingness into the certainty of somethingness. Like a flock of chattering sparrows, media outlets repeated speculation, elevating rumor to possibility until they'd formed the perfect shitstorm. The suggestion of drugs, the bizarre behavior, the political connections, and a mysterious duo—Father Billy and Secretary Becky —were the only facts on the ground. But they could be stewed into the perfect shit storm. Everyone was compromised.

Everyone but O'Leary.

That was Bradley's initial take after watching ROX. And that was the story he needed Heather Haliburton to tell on NATN. It was obvious, he almost shouted into his earbuds, his arms flailing as he finished explaining his opus to Heather: Menendez's campaign manager had gone to rural Missouri looking for dirt, and the result had been a certified psychological breakdown by the most famous pastor in the country. The whole thing was downright Nixonian. Or Clintonian. Or Trumpian, for that matter.

If that was how the story broke, it would be enough to kneecap Menendez. And probably Julia Connor, given that the whole thing smacked of psychedelic drugs and stunt engineering by her fanatical supporters. It was pretty high-stakes stuff, considering it could put Julia's true believers in jail for ten years. Each.

What a lesson for the nation, Bradley thought—leaders had to show the wisdom to not get caught. Both of O'Leary's opponents had just proven they were incapable of that.

Heather sighed and lamely poked at the pumpkin and roasted leek "fall delight" salad she was eating in her NATN studios dressing room. She was going on air in an hour and while everything Bradley said felt right, it was all just a feeling. "There's one problem with your take."

"What am I missing?"

"Nobody is talking."

"When has that ever stopped you?"

"Jesus, Bradley." Her scowl cut through the phone line. "I'm a journalist. If it happened, and if my viewers need me to interpret it, I will serve them the version of the truth they need to hear. But I am not some hack in the business of just making shit up. Believe me, Menendez's loons and Julia's freaks will find a way to sink themselves without me having to make it up."

"But…"

"Everything you said is likely true, but no crime was committed without a complaint or complainant. We can dig up all the circumstantial evidence and interview EMT workers about what they saw, but we know Julia wasn't there. The only unusual activity locals noticed was a chubby bald man and what they assumed was his mother puttering around the church." Heather looked at her closet, she still couldn't decide what to wear tonight. "And, I mean, did you see Menendez's quote?"

"What, no! Did he just release it?"

She curled her legs underneath her body and picked up her laptop to read the news article. "The devil, demons, and Satan himself have no power over my staff or Pastor McMillian. This appears to be a Cuba-esque sonic attack on my most trusted advisers, deploying drugs, holograms, and the deepest of fakes. To proceed with caution and preserve American hegemony in the Caribbean, I've asked my colleagues in the Senate to immediately sanction an exploratory land invasion of Cuba."

"He's trying to spin this into a jingoistic campaign against communists?!"

"More than one president has used war fever to win an election." Heather nibbled at the salad and made a face as the squash and maple-mustard dressing clashed. She was so over the age of designer salads.

"That's fucking insane. You can't just bury a story like this, Heather!"

"We're not trying to bury it, but no one seems interested in telling it!"

"I know! But this is a gift."

"We're digging, but so far it's a gift that may never be opened."

Bradley sank back into his chair, dejected. "Fuck me."

"Look at the polls, Bradley," Heather threw her salad in the trash and grabbed a sleek forest-green pantsuit off its hanger. "They have. And they are."

CHAPTER 42

LOVING KINDNESS

Sunrise filtered through the front windows, casting leafy shadows on the back wall, giving Julia's living room an otherworldly feel of peace and possibility. This was supposed to be a day of rest, a day off from the campaign, but instead, the peace held her pain and her overwhelming sense of betrayal.

She squinted through the morning rays, touching the wrinkles on her face, feeling the effects of time. People were out of balance with the earth and with themselves, and so was she. Off balance. Off kilter. Crushed. She sought her balance, a reprieve from the screaming headlines in the morning paper, the inky sadness that sought to fill every corner of her soul.

She felt her breath. The rhythm of life. She felt the sun. The giver of life. She felt for God within. The kernel of the divine that illuminated all.

She didn't know how she knew, but she knew. The movement, the campaign, had been betrayed. A movement that had felt so pure, and a campaign that had become something else.

She wept soft, hot tears of betrayal, the inky blackness of her pain dripping down her face, turning her wrinkles into rivulets. Her mind kept moving.

Drugging people against their will? How could they?!

Julia felt her coursing anger, the bubbling resentment spilling onto her living room floor in a mix of spit and snot and tears that soaked the rug beneath her now prostrate body.

But wasn't she also to blame? She had felt their rage and ignored it. She had failed to lead with empathy. She'd dismissed Melanie's pain, forgetting that for Mel, the digital was real, as real as Julia's bees were to her. She'd left Noah's concerns unanswered, assuming he would fall into line and do as she wished.

She had been surprised by the scale of the attacks against her, and in the silence that followed, she had left them with a sense that to act, they had to act alone. So they went behind her back, compromising the campaign by adopting the energy, the values and the tactics of the very system they'd vowed to change.

I am not to blame, she decided, though I am not faultless. And there is nothing to forgive, for we are all people and beings of darkness and light, fear and love, capable of anything.

She kept sitting, waiting for the door knock, still not knowing exactly what to do.

· · ·

Noah's fast eyes caught everything as he sat on a cushion in the middle of Julia's sitting room. He'd seen the room on her ROX News interview, but now that he was here in person, he could sense how perfectly it reflected Julia's inner reality. Potted plants seemed to explode from every available space, enormous windows looking out on a messy garden, a small orchard, and a few fir trees. Floors and walls were practically invisible behind Tibetan Dragon rugs, West African statues, masks from Asia, Africa and Central America, and paintings of Hindu gods and Buddhas.

He crossed his legs and looked from Julia, tired and wounded, to Melanie, shattered but relieved to see her mentor.

But what was there to feel bad about? Menendez and his team, Noah thought, had attacked the very heart of the change Julia sought. What were they supposed to do—just let it happen? What was Melanie supposed to do after getting kicked off Beep-Beep? Surrender? No, they did what was necessary. They took a chance to change the hearts and minds of Menendez's top advisors. Politics had always been about winning, not playing nice or playing by the rules. That was true now more than ever.

Melanie watched Julia shuffle around the room lighting candles and wondered if Julia regarded candles as her Catholic grandmother did—a necessity to help prayers along. How many thousands of candles would she need to light to achieve penance for drugging two people against their will? In her mind's eye clips played of Pastor McMillan wheeled out on a stretcher, his leg broken, ranting about a horde of demons, whips, and chains. She'd given her life to a cause; she'd launched this wonderful woman—and now she'd ruined it.

Her only solace was that Pastor McMillan and ROX News's decision to call the whole thing a demon attack orchestrated by Julia had so confused the nation that no one was invested in the little sleuthing it would have taken to reveal that Melanie and Noah were absent from the campaign and had both flown into Kansas City several days before.

Taking her seat on a cushion across from them, Julia lowered her puffy eyes. "Noah, what were you thinking?"

"With all due respect, Julia, I don't think that's the right question. I've searched my conscience, and I know my truth. I meditated for hours before and after. What I did had to be done. There is no remorse within me because my actions were pure."

Julia smiled gently, thinking about the power found in spiritual practice, but also the danger inherent in disconnecting practice from the full body of teaching from which it stems.

"You were practicing mindfulness, I assume?"

Noah smiled, the conversation now in his sweet spot. He'd been practicing and teaching mindfulness for fifteen years. Mindfulness was how he'd built his empire, advancing from a run-of-the-mill coach with a few clients to a public figure, investor, and CEO whisperer.

"Of course I was practicing mindfulness." Noah spoke clearly and slowly, looking into the would-be president's eyes. "Mindfulness is power. It calms the soul and focuses the mind. It brings peace to any individual willing to learn the practice. Not practicing mindfulness would be irresponsible and would go against everything you and I both believe."

Julia held his gaze, feeling the sun warm the right side of her face. "Do you ever practice loving kindness meditation, Noah?"

"I don't. I never found it helpful when I was building my business or coaching my clients. Yes, love is all important, but confidence in self is what unlocks the power within. That is what my clients demand, and it's what I crave."

"What about you, Melanie?"

Melanie shook her head. "This is embarrassing. I've really never meditated at all, Julia. I am—or was—all about being active. Beep-Beep meditation is probably a thing, but it wasn't *my* thing. Enlightenment has always seemed out of reach."

Julia let out an enormous breath. "Well then. Will you both join me in a loving kindness meditation? Remember, meditation is not enlightenment. Meditation is observation. Simply be with your thoughts. Notice them. By noticing, you sit in your center, watching and feeling each story, belief or emotion that is part of your experience."

Noah nodded, albeit with a certain air of humoring their hostess. Melanie smiled. She would have walked on hot coals if Julia asked.

"First, we'll breathe together for a few moments, focusing on our breath, grounding this experience in the body. To start, take a deep breath and count to six, before releasing your breath to a six count. We'll breathe for two minutes like this."

They started breathing and Julia continued talking.

"Now keep breathing. But focus on your feet, clenching your toes, and then relaxing them, feeling the softness as the tension recedes." They continued like this, moving from toes to legs to torsos and arms to, eventually, faces, relaxing further and further into self.

When Julia sensed Melanie and Noah were in the same settled place, she said, "I want you to picture someone you not only love but find it *easy* to love. Maybe it's your niece or your grandpa, a friend or your lover. Focus on this person, open your heart, and slowly send them these messages, repeating each three times: May you be held in love, in kindness, and in compassion. May you be secure, safe, and happy. May you be healthy, emotionally and physically. May your heart know love and peace."

Melanie pictured her aunt Kendra. Aunt Kendra was the opposite of Melanie's ranting, angry mother. She had always loved Melanie for the creative, bizarre child she was. When her mom yelled at her for failing science, Aunt Kendra told her that even if she failed every class, her love for Melanie would not waver. In an insecure childhood, Aunt Kendra had been her safest place. As Melanie sent love to Aunt Kendra, she felt a wave of love engulf her. Anxiety turned to open-hearted bliss.

Noah chose to picture himself. He'd hated who he was as a young man. He was spineless. Weak. Unable to impact the world. But he'd learned to love himself, and in doing so, he'd found freedom and enormous power. He sat in a bliss that equaled Melanie's.

Julia continued in the same calm voice. "Now, I want you to picture someone you feel neutral about. An acquaintance or a colleague, perhaps. See their face and focus on their well-being, repeating the same lines of loving kindness. May you be held in love, in kindness, and in compassion." Repeated in her melodic voice, the remaining *may you*s took on the sound of a spoken hymn.

Noah pictured a young man his staff had hired to run his "Viking Masculinity Ascendance Community Coaching" program. Noah knew nothing of the man, which made him perfect for this silly exercise of Julia's. As he sat in the calm certitude of the love he felt for himself, his bubble of energy widened, enveloping the new employee in warmth. To his surprise, he found himself wondering about the man's life, which he realized he knew nothing about. He didn't even know the man's name. As he sent acceptance and compassion toward the man, Noah made a note—almost despite himself—to take him out for an adaptogenic superfood smoothie as soon as he was back in Austin.

Melanie chose to focus on a girl she'd known in college. A girl she'd never spoken to but had often recognized at parties. She felt the depths of her love for Aunt Kendra encircle the nameless young woman, which transitioned into the vibrant feeling of her arms enveloping the woman, their unknowing transitioning into love. The namelessness of this love, which matched the intimacy of Aunt Kendra's acceptance, left Melanie with an internal glow.

Julia sat in silence, observing her motionless friends, hoping new vistas of awareness were opening inside them.

"Finally, focus on someone you don't like at all. Someone who inspires animosity or hate. Someone whose very existence sets your heart ablaze in disgust or anger. Sitting in the same place of love you find yourself in now, picture this person's face and again repeat the lines. May you be held in love, in kindness and in compassion. May you be secure, safe and happy. May you be healthy emotionally and physically. May your heart know love and peace."

Melanie pictured Pastor Josiah McMillan. She heard the echo of his words in her mind: "WHORE OF BABYLON. WHORE OF BABYLON. WHORE OF BABYLONNNN." Her fury rose like bile. *What kind of man sentences people to hell for the culture they were born into, or for how they experience God or love other people? What kind of man would call Julia Connor a whore?!* Her antipathy slammed into the love and compassion that had encircled her heart. She shuddered under the immense conflict she felt, a tear slowly forming in her right eye and tracing its way down her cheek as love's endless capacity dissolved her hate for Pastor McMillan.

If Noah hadn't forgotten himself at this point, he would have been shocked at the cast of characters that sprung to mind.

He saw his mom, who had called him "a spineless woo woo equivalency machine" after he suggested that calling Republicans "Reagan-loving, women-hating, trickle-down idiots" wasn't the best way to inspire compassion toward the poor.

He pictured the stranger who had called him a "pussy bitch" when, at a party, he'd suggested that invading Iraq wasn't just bad policy but was likely to karmically set the universe against the United States, leading to a recession. God, that man's emotional blindness had pissed him off!

Then both Senator Menendez and Governor O'Leary came to his mind's eye. He felt his rage at their obsession with petty party politics, and he felt his indignation rise as he considered the enormous body of spiritual, scientific, and psychological information they and the entire country ignored. Knowledge that could set people free but that was widely mocked by most of society. Finally, a single image settled. He too saw Pastor McMillan. He felt his disgust at the pastor's close-minded obsession with a God that judged, not loved ... and he remembered the petty joy he'd felt when he heard the Pastor had broken his leg after coming face to face with Jesus.

The bubble of peace and love the meditation had built inside Noah suddenly, inexplicably, did its work. He started to sob.

Oh my God, oh my God, every feeling of rage and anger I identified in others also exists in me. I sought to win at any cost. I demonized the other in the name of love. And in doing that, I failed to live in integrity with my most heartfelt values.

Noah ripped his shirt at the neck, small pieces of white linen scattering on the ground, his despair and guilt overwhelming him. Then he sank back into a place of compassion for each of those he'd hated, including himself.

Behind her shut eyes, Julia saw only Noah. She felt her revulsion at his breed of spirituality. A man with so much power, who so often chose to use it for his ends. A man with great influence, who used it to build up those who could pay but paid only lip service to those without means. And then she felt her love.

She saw Noah as a child, remembering what she knew about his past. The hurt he'd endured, feeling like an outcast in high school and, later, within his own family. The enormous victory that was his spiritual awakening, leading him to reject his family's atheism while earning their scorn. She saw that his career had turned him into a force for good, imperfect though he may be, and that her own distrust of him was born of not only his faults but also her envy, her sense of having failed for decades to gain the influence and popularity he enjoyed.

She heard Noah's tears and scooted toward him, placing her head on his neck, crying alongside him. Hearing their movement, Melanie opened her eyes and joined the hug, wrapping her arms around both their necks and placing her forehead on Julia's head, amid her shock of gray curls.

They sat like this for minutes—bonding, crying, sitting in the cleansing pain of repentance and the beauty of forgiveness.

Finally, Noah gently pushed them both away and sucked in a deep breath, clearly seeing Julia for the first time. This woman wasn't a tool to use to advance his agenda and right social wrongs; this woman was just a woman striving to do right. That such a person ever could have risen to a place of political prominence was a miracle. A miracle! And he had compromised it all because he'd been blind to his hate.

He had long believed that people had to first love for themselves, and while he hadn't dropped that belief, he now clearly saw how self-love unbalanced by compassion and generosity could foster ego-driven pride.

"Julia," Noah asked, "is this why my CEOs love working with me? By focusing only on mindfulness, emotional freedom, and personal power ... by disconnecting the practice of self-love from the practice of generosity ... I accentuate their skills while absolving them of responsibility for all that happens in the rest of the world?"

"I don't know. Is that what you think?"

Noah shrugged and was again lost in thought.

Melanie, who felt anxiety beginning to again bubble up, asked Julia, "What now?"

"I have some ideas," Julia said, "but I want to hear yours too. What do you think is appropriate?"

CHAPTER 43

THEY WEREN'T MEN, THEY WERE DEMONS!

That afternoon Sovereign Love Super PAC dropped a press release. It read: "Executive Director Noah Glasnapp is stepping down. Despite his absence, SLSPAC will continue to focus on bringing love and compassion into the political and public policy mainstream."

Sitting next to Noah on the back of a Frontier Airlines flight bound for Washington, DC, Melanie ventured, "Your stepping down is basically an admission of guilt, right?"

"If anyone is paying attention, yeah. But it's nothing like what we're about to do."

"Still no word on where Luke's at?" Melanie swirled her sparkling water. She used to order ginger ale, but Julia and Noah had convinced her to get off sugar.

"Nope. No one seems to have heard a thing from him since the dosing. The Evangelicals for Love PAC claim to have heard rumors that he's been working the phones like mad, but they don't know what he's up to or where he's at."

"So it's just the pastor, then?"

"Yep," Noah said. "Just him."

• • •

His leg in a cast and his arm in a sling, a raw cut across his forehead, Pastor McMillan watched Senator Menendez lean over the conference table in his Senate Office, his unbelieving eyes locked on the pastor's own.

"So they lured you to the church and conned you into drinking a sixty-four-ounce pitcher of magic mushroom iced tea. Who were these men?"

"Men? Have you listened to a word I've said?! They weren't men—they were demons!"

Menendez rolled his eyes. "How do we press charges against a demon? Julia's guy Noah all but admitted it was him when he resigned. All you have to do is identify him and the whole campaign is toast. Wasn't that the point of the trip?"

Pastor McMillan sucked his broad cheeks into his face. "I will not be pressing charges, Senator Menendez, because this is not a matter for men to decide. Only spiritual warfare can cleanse this nation."

"And here I was thinking the goal was to win." Menendez snorted like a bull elk during rutting season. "Well, Pastor Josiah, you can take care of it as you see fit. But if a holy war doesn't involve Israel finally taking out those pesky Persians, I don't think it'll help me win this election. So I'm done with you and your little incident. I have to stay focused on keeping Wall Street happy, especially now that Luke disappeared."

Pastor McMillan's eyes narrowed. "What do you mean Luke disappeared? I thought he's been with you since I got put into the hospital."

"I haven't seen him since the two of you traipsed off to Missouri."

• • •

"It's like nothing has changed and everything has changed. I'm so discombobulated." She spoke the words out loud, but no one heard. There were ten days to go and the sprint to election day held everyone in its vice grip.

Julia looked around the hotel conference room doubling as their San Francisco office-for-the-day.

Jonathan sat across from her, working his phone. Alexi Pappasoutos, who'd stepped in to replace Melanie, was giving instructions to other members of the content collective. Another staffer managed appearances and statements from the droves of Hollywood types who had followed Lillie Rift to Team Julia. The video team ensured campaign appearances were livestreamed on WeTube and her campaign website while disseminating clips of her appearances to Alexi, who then made them available to the army of influencers who had traded Beep-Beep for other more friendly platforms.

With Noah away from the campaign, there was no longer anyone walking around yelling "Triangles!" at random moments, but his consultants still did their best to give unsolicited advice and take credit. The staff they'd hired in all fifty states were still doing their jobs. *I guess this is why people are so into staff,* Julia thought. *Redundancy is a good thing when people drop the ball.*

"Jonathan?"

He looked up from his phone with lifted brows.

"Can we run through the next several days?"

"Want me to get the team?"

She shook her head. "I've just been feeling the autopilot effect of the schedule. I want to make sure I'm not being lulled to sleep."

Jonathan hefted the leaf-green binder in front of him. "Well, we're obviously in San Francisco today. Tomorrow we're in LA for several appearances and then Phoenix, followed by Durango, Colorado. From there it's Denver, Pueblo, Santa Fe, Albuquerque."

"Should we be in New Mexico?"

"I know it's Menendez's home turf, but the numbers say we have a real shot. That state is crawling with retreat centers, monasteries, and ashrams."

"If you say so, OK."

"At this point, I'm just trusting the numbers. There is so much happening that trying to track more than just what we're doing is overwhelming. I mean"—he glanced at the papers in his hand—"just today, our supporters hosted two thousand different 'Love In' events across the country. The plan of noncampaign campaigning you sketched out is working like a charm."

Julia smiled tiredly. "Alternatives, Jonathan. We're building alternatives."

"Exactly. Then, of course, the biggest event of all is on Saturday. We're going back to the start of the campaign, back to the state you're unexpectedly winning, back to your favorite body of water in America. We'll arrive in Austin

Friday morning, driving the bus down after you wrap up in Oklahoma City on Thursday evening. Lillie is already in Austin working with local staff, getting the permits and logistics in place. From what I hear, the crowd will be enormous for our 'Love In March to the Capitol.'"

"Thanks, Jonathan," Julia said with warmth, feeling her strength return after the shock of betrayal. "Any word from Noah or Melanie?"

"Not yet, but they should be having the conversation this afternoon."

"And we're ready for the fallout?"

"I'm not sure ready is the word, but the content collective is prepped for a full-frontal wave of taking responsibility once Pastor McMillan goes public."

CHAPTER 44

HAVE SOME GRACE

ove, Fire, and Brimstone: A Guide to Controlling Your Congregation had been
written for pastors around the world, serving to encourage and empower
Evangelical ministers from Uganda to Cambodia. And this copy, which the
pastor had open on his desk as he worked on sermon notes, was extra special.
The note from the author was signed,

"To Josiah, with love in Christ, your Dad."

There was a knock on the door.

"Enter," he called, hoping to see Luke's scowling face.

Instead, his ginger-haired youth pastor, Josh Emerson, entered wearing an
oversized white T-shirt, acid-washed jeans, and a gold chain. "Do you have
a second, Pastor?"

Pastor McMillian liked Josh. Many of the younger staff emitted golden
retriever energy, but Josh had true charisma—an easy smile, eyes that focused
on whomever he was talking to, an aura of sincerity. Today, though, the ever-
present warmth seemed in short supply. Josh looked grim.

"Hello, son. How's my favorite youth minister?"

"Pastor Josiah, I may not be your favorite for long." He pursed his lips.

"I find that difficult to believe, Josh. You've been a wonderful example of
Christian virtue since you started working with us."

"Yes, Pastor. I've loved my time here." Josh paused, awkwardly fingering the standard issue Salvation Megachurch Youth Minister gold chain around his neck. "However, I feel a stronger calling now. I'm joining a coalition of pastors supporting Julia Connor that Luke is organizing."

Slowly Pastor Josiah shut his copy of *Love, Fire, and Brimstone*, and held it with both hands, his face darkening like a storm. "Luke's doing what?"

"I thought you knew. He's been talking with pastors around the county organizing this new coalition." Josh shrugged. "Pastor, what can I say, I've been praying with my brothers and sisters from seminary. We all agree: Julia Connor loves God and she has a beautiful vision for America. It's like Harry Styles and Lillie Rift sang in their duet, 'The difference between doing something and not doing something is doing something.' I'm choosing to answer God's call to love all my neighbors."

At the mention of "God's call," Pastor McMillan let out a guttural scream, the rawness of his violated soul escaping with the sound. He flung *Love, Fire, and Brimstone* directly at Josh, the spine of the book drilling his fleshy cheek.

Josh froze and Pastor McMillan squinted at the young man's face. On his cheek—the result of raised type on Pastor McMillan Senior's book—was a clear mark that read "LOVE."

Josh rubbed his face and looked at his hand, checking for blood. Then he bent down, picked up the book, and placed it on the pastor's desk. "I thought you'd be mad, but I hoped you might have grace."

"Grace? Grace?! What this moment has confirmed is that grace can come only through God's righteous anger. Look in that mirror, son, do you see your face?!"

Josh looked in the mirror, squinting to read the welt backward. "It says 'love,' Pastor."

Pastor McMillan leaned forward, his voice softening as he smiled. "Love. Love. I acted in violence and God said 'Love.' I've never received a clearer sign in my life. To defeat the Whore of Babylon, to send the demons that attacked me back to the hell they've escaped, we must act in love gilded with the glimmering gold of righteous rage. You dare to walk into my holy office to tell me you are following the Whore of Babylon? Then you will burn with her when the Lord's Angels Raptor Strike Force strikes!"

"You wouldn't!"

"I must."

Josh gasped as he turned to leave. "You say love, but I hear only hate in your voice. I will not be the last to walk out these doors."

Pastor McMillan sat breathing deeply as the sound of Josh's footsteps faded. He had lost his temper, which grieved him. Emotions were untrustworthy; the devil was working to separate him from God's love. But God had granted him clarity in his moment of weakness. He'd even sent a sign. Jesus's love—that mark on Josh's face told him clearly—could not be spread by normal tactics. No, if the Whore of Babylon was to be stopped, more than prayer and traditional spiritual warfare were needed.

Glancing to the heavens, Pastor McMillan thanked God he had the foresight to build a private army of his own ten years before.

Writing on his notepad, he started experimenting with a new idea:

> *In these dark times when a woman masquerading as God's messenger is misleading the faithful, we, God's chosen people, have only one choice. We must respond with force. We must do so to protect our salvation, our power, and our clear calling to be God's vehicle for earthly transformation.*

Reading back over these words, the God-ordained path forward was clear: It was time for violence.

• • •

A red-haired man dressed like a teenager almost knocked Melanie and Noah over as they entered the Salvation Megachurch tower. Recognition flickered in his teary eyes as he paused to look at them before continuing to the parking lot. It happened so quickly they barely registered the red welt on his face.

"That guy looked as anxious as I feel," Melanie said, aware her heart was sitting squarely in her throat.

"'Accepting consequences,'" Noah said, "sounded good when we talked with Julia."

"And now it feels like a death sentence?" Melanie didn't even have to glance at Noah to know he was nodding.

They made their way through the marble lobby into the gold-plated Salvation Express elevator, and exited on the lavish sixteenth floor, too stressed to admire the Italian tile or the stunning view of the Potomac from the floor-to-ceiling windows.

"Please take a seat," Pastor McMillan's secretary said. "The pastor just had an emotional meeting, but he'll be ready for you in a moment."

Before they could sit, Pastor McMillan's voice boomed through the door. "Just send them in. God granted me clarity in this darkness. I'm ready to hear from the Whore of Babylon's emissaries."

Noah glanced at Melanie. They both glanced at the secretary, the buxom auburn-haired woman who brought the pastor his beloved caramel iced coffees. As committed to his cause as she was, as accustomed as she'd grown to the mercurial spirit incumbent on a leader so attuned to the greater good, lately even she couldn't help but feel she was out of her depth. Pointing them toward the door, she said in a hushed voice, "He's been in quite the mood since the demon attack."

Pastor McMillan was sitting behind his enormous mahogany desk, a blown-up movie style poster depicting him on the cross next to Jesus on the wall behind him. He was calm, leaning back in his chair with his hands behind his head, his broken leg resting on a stool.

"I expected you to be wearing scarlet and purple, as Revelations foretold." Pastor McMillan stood up and placed his crutches under his arms. He dragged his leg behind him so he could better look Noah up and down. "You're here to join me then, you wish to be a Judas? She will meet her earthly end on Saturday, so your timing couldn't be any better."

"Uhm, what? We're not here to join you."

"Then why are you here? Does she wish to surrender?"

"Well—" Melanie took a deep breath and paused, unable to will herself onward.

"We're here to apologize." Noah rushed the words, sure this exchange would end Julia's campaign and his not-in-jail status. "We're the ones who dosed you with the mushrooms in the church. It was wrong of us, and it was disrespectful of the power and the beauty found in plant medicines like mushrooms. It was—"

"It was just so out of step with what Julia is trying to accomplish," Melanie added. "We feel terrible for what we did. And we realize that by coming here we're probably going to end up in jail and Julia's going to be roasted by the media, but it's the right thing to do, so here we are."

Pastor McMillan's eyes narrowed beneath his fearsome brows.

"Last time something too good to be true happened, I ended up in Missouri being attacked by demons flitting and flying among the rafters of that God-forsaken church." Stumbling even closer on his crutches, he planted his nose on Noah's neck, then in Melanie's hair. "Neither of you smell like sulfur. I smelled sulfur in that church."

"But Pastor," Noah said, "what we're trying to tell you is that that wasn't a demonic attack. We did it, we—"

"Do not question me! I have spent untold hours in prayer since that attack. I've asked God for guidance, and I've been given signs. A sign of love, in fact." Pastor McMillan raised his hands to the heavens. "Love. I was shown the true meaning of love."

"Soo . . ." Melanie dared to hope, momentarily, that he'd accepted *some* facet of Julia's message.

"Both you disgusting heathens should leave and stop wasting my time! You will see Jesus's love in action soon enough, and then you will know the true power of God!"

• • •

Noah and Melanie walked out the doors of Salvation Megachurch and entered the parking lot.

Melanie's heart was still racing, her mind confused. She thought they were about to put a nail in the love movement's coffin, but instead, they'd been granted a stay. Or so it seemed. She didn't understand the conversation at all.

"Pssst! Pssst! Over here!"

Melanie looked at Noah. He'd heard it too. They looked around them. A scattering of vehicles were in the parking lot, but no one was in sight.

"Pssst!" The sound came from a souped-up Mazda. "Don't look at me! Just stand there."

Noah and Melanie paused, pretending to look at the sky.

The person slouching in the driver's seat continued. "Meet me at Elite Coffee in Arlington. It's a fifteen-minute drive. We have to talk."

"Why?" Noah looked from the sky to the Mazda, confused by the wounded face and bright red hair staring back at him.

"Not here!" There was panic in Josh's eyes.

"But why there?" Melanie rolled her eyes. Men were so melodramatic.

"Because," Josh hissed, his eyes beseeching Melanie to listen, "Julia's life is in danger and Luke Lockwood wants to join Julia's campaign. I have to explain somewhere private, somewhere safe."

CHAPTER 45

IT'S JUST A PLOY

The campaign bus barreled through Western Colorado, eating up the miles between Durango and Denver. Out the windows, the autumn colors of the Rocky Mountains flashed by. In a normal year, Julia would have loved nothing more than to be sitting among the Aspens on a leafy carpet of yellow and orange, watching gently swirling leaves drop from above.

But this wasn't a normal year. Instead of bathing in the forest's fall foliage, she was sitting next to Jonathan to take an "insanely, life threateningly, world shakingly urgent" call from Melanie and Noah.

"He didn't believe you?!"

"No!" Melanie's exasperation was evident. "He smelled us and said he didn't smell any sulfur so we couldn't possibly be the demons that attacked him."

"And it's not just that he didn't believe us," Noah said, sharing earbuds with Melanie from a bench outside of Elite Coffee. Next to them, Josh Emerson observed the call. "We have worse news. Jonathan, are you familiar with the Lord's Angel's Raptor Strike Force?"

"I wouldn't say I'm familiar, but I've heard rumors. They're a private militia?"

"More than a private militia," Melanie glanced at Josh Emerson as she talked, hoping they were right to trust him, "Noah and I were just told they are Pastor McMillan's private army. A private army with orders to eliminate the Whore of Babylon at her love march on Saturday."

"Are you kidding me!" Julia's exclamation was the high-pitched warble of a songbird in distress. "The pastor didn't believe you and he's sending an army to eliminate me? That's insane!"

"I think," Jonathan's bemused, rumbling voice calmed everyone on the call, "that we left the bounds of traditional sanity quite some time ago."

"Sane or not, my political consultants would tell us Pastor McMillan just gifted us an enormous opportunity," Noah said, a bead of sweat sliding unnoticed down his bald head, "but they'd be wrong. Just because he didn't believe us doesn't mean we're absolved of responsibility for dosing him."

"You're right," Jonathan replied, involuntarily flexing his biceps, feeling the power that still coursed through his muscles, "and we can't make accusations of war against the Pastor. If his legion of goons are going to strike, we have to be ready to defend ourselves."

Julia had lapsed into silence, surfing the waves of self, hoping for clarity in the madness. She refocused on Jonathan, the twinkle back in her eyes. "I don't think our next move is complicated at all. What better curveball to throw America than a heaping spoonful of the truth?"

One hour and twenty minutes later she watched one of the consultants hit send on a new press release.

For Immediate Release *** CONNOR 2028

Julia Connor Issues Apology for Unethical Campaign Behavior

Presidential Candidate Seeks to Model New Behavior of Political Accountability; Explains "Honesty, Love, Compassion are the only ways forward."

November 1, 2028- Love Movement presidential candidate announced today she has extended heartfelt apologies to Pastor Josiah McMillian and Luke Lockwood, senior campaign advisor to Senator Menendez, whom she says were secretly given large doses of psilocybin mushrooms by two of her most trusted supporters.

Candidate Connor said advisors, who were incited to act after misleading campaign ads by Menendez villainized the undeniable therapeutic benefits of psilocybin, have apologized to McMillian and seek to apologize to Lockwood.

"The advisors came to me and admitted their actions and are eager to make amends," Connor said. "They realize a desire to protect the greater good—in this case, by showing influential leaders the positive power of psilocybin—cannot excuse their ethical and moral lapses. Because they seek to atone, I have forgiven them.

"In keeping with my campaign's policy of love, empathy, transparency, and responsibility, I choose to share this news with the nation, rather than sweep it under the rug. This kind of honesty and accountability is essential to a loving, transparent, efficient federal government whose priority is working on behalf of people, not systems. The buck stops with all of us, but especially our leaders."

• • •

Heather was leading an emergency meeting of NATN's executive editorial team. Around the room serious eyes stared at her, trying to make sense of Julia Connor's most recent ploy.

"The only thing we know," Heather said, in answer to the question that none of them had to ask, "is that Julia is up to something."

"Clearly!" Jamal Johnston interjected while scratching his head. "But for the life of me, I can't figure out what it is."

"Precisely," a feverishly nodding executive with classy, greying temples replied. "The press release said she was taking full responsibility for their unethical and ill-advised actions and was asking the American people for forgiveness. I've heard that line a million times, and I know one thing—anytime a politician claims to take responsibility, they're lying."

"Exactly! But what is it she's trying to hide?" Heather furiously looked around the room. "Ideas, anyone? We can't take her at her word, but I have no idea what that statement truly means. We have to get to the bottom of this!"

• • •

Menendez had no idea what to do. Luke was missing in action. Micah had advised him to demand Julia quit, calling it "the only reasonable move." But he couldn't do that! That's clearly what Julia wanted—enough reason, right there, to refuse it. But what in the ever-loving name of that saint Ayn Rand was going on? Wanting to either drown his frustration in Johnny Walker Black or hurl an ax at a wall, Menendez instead called Jed.

"Damnit Jed, none of this makes any sense. She was in the clear after Luke disappeared and the pastor kept insisting the demons were real. But now she's just proactively sticking the knife in her own back? And she claims she's doing it to show the American people some type of alternative leadership model? That's piss down your own pant leg crazy!"

"She's a crafty one," Jed said to Senator Menendez. "I'm certain this is a strategy to win over more of O'Leary's voters, but I can't figure out how either."

"Maybe a plant spirit told her to do this?" Menendez rumbled. "Or maybe she's trying to trap us just like she trapped Luke in Missouri?"

"Senator, I just don't know. No one here knows. ROX News executives' consensus was to ignore her. Since we can't figure out her angle, we're planning to just stay silent."

"You can't stay silent—we have to bury her!"

"But you just said we can't play into her hands."

"I know! But I'm tied with her. The election is in just six days. We need an attack that puts us over the top!"

CHAPTER 46

LISA MOODY FROM EAU CLAIRE, WISCONSIN

Bradley studied the spreadsheets, reading through the polling crosstabs. They all revealed the same damn thing. Julia's support was steady. His China strategy had failed. The attacks weren't working. O'Leary had no chance of making a comeback.

If the governor had just taken his advice and offered Julia her VP spot a month ago, none of this would have happened. But *no*. Jacqui, positive "love" was a passing fad, had been unwilling to work with or spend resources attacking a political novice. By ignoring Julia, by choosing to neither coopt her nor destroy her, Governor O'Leary had turned Julia into a monster. And now that monster was coming for him.

Bradley felt his future slipping away. The consulting gigs, annual six- and seven-figure retainers from Saudi Princes, Zambian Presidents, corporations and self-important heirs that funneled their millions into self-gratifying political passion projects... all disappearing, gone like a puff of smoke.

He thought of all the kids that *All Types and Colors* served. Those poor kids had been rejected by their parents, ignored by society, and attacked by self-serving conservatives. If he could just win, if he could just ascend to a place of power in society, he could do so much good! He was destined to do good! To become a wealthy titan of the political industry holding court in the highest echelons of America's power structure.

Ohh! The board seats and the dollars, the prestige and ability to fight for justice on his terms. It was all in jeopardy.

Now was the time, he realized, for drastic action. He had to signal his priorities to the real powers that be. Maybe they could save the campaign. And if not, at least they would treat him like royalty after the last votes were counted.

• • •

"It's remarkable," a visibly distraught Heather Haliburton told America liberals, "that voters believe electing a beekeeper as president can fix our broken political system. Here to discuss is Governor O'Leary's campaign manager, Bradley Bishkoff."

The camera turned to a stone-browed Bradley sitting with his hands folded on the studio table. The LCD screen behind him scrolled headlines of the day's greatest tragedies and celebrity headlines. "Thanks for having me, Heather."

"Bradley, with less than one week to go before election day, woman-hating, drug-advocating candidate Julia Connor is tied with Senator Menendez for the lead, and your candidate, Governor O'Leary, has fallen ten points behind in polling. What's the mood in your campaign?

"Heather," Bradley said, "we are more worried about America than about our campaign. Our concern is voters will see a repeat of 2000, when third-party dreamer Ralph Nader cost Al Gore the presidency, ultimately causing the ruinous wars in Iraq and Afghanistan and depriving the world of Al Gore's climate change leadership."

"I just want to remind viewers," Heather explained while trying to disguise the panic she worried might be showing in her eyes, "Bradley is talking about a consensus of post-election analysts who concluded Nader's campaign cost Gore a victory in Florida, handing George W. Bush the presidency. Can you talk a little bit more about the cost of Julia Connor's independent candidacy?"

Bradley nodded studiously. "I think any reasonable person would admit that Ralph Nader, because of his selfish campaign, started two ruinous, catastrophically expensive wars and is responsible for our climate change crisis. I fear Julia Connor will be just as dangerous. Polling numbers indicate that if Connor abandoned the race, Governor O'Leary would scoop up enough of her supporters to obliterate Menendez on Election Tuesday."

"Bradley, who are these people putting their selfish desire for some pie in the sky notion of a 'new' political system ahead of the good of the country?"

"Sixty three percent of her supporters are, or were, Democratic voters. But of course, there are others. Thirty percent of her supporters are Evangelical Christians. Ninety-seven percent of Americans that identify themselves as healers, shamans, light angels, yogis, starseeds, and gurus are also supporting her."

"Those are truly shocking numbers. Where do you go from here?"

"We're planning an enormous Love and Good Governance countermarch against Julia's march in Austin on Saturday to remind voters all over this country that the Democratic Party—not *love*—is the answer to our problems."

"Thanks for sharing, Bradley. I know I'll be there, America. If you can travel," Heather addressed the nation, "I want to encourage you to join the campaign in Austin on Saturday to make a statement supporting O'Leary, the rightful next president of the United States. We'll now take a few questions from our viewers. Our first is Lisa Moody from Eau Claire, Wisconsin. Hi Lisa!"

"Bradley and Heather," Lisa Moody began in a high-pitched but not at all screechy voice—the voice of a person holding onto her composure for dear life. "You're both ignoring the obvious! Stop pretending everything is OK and tell me—should I be praying for an O'Leary miracle or should I throw my support behind Julia Connor? Because I'll tell you one thing, the only result I truly cannot handle is a Menendez win."

Bradley stared gravely into the camera. "Lisa, it's more than just this election we have to worry about. The business and the reality of American politics rely on having just two parties whose focus is to win. If Julia upends the balance, chaos could ensue."

"Chaos such as?" Heather bobbed her head encouragingly.

Bradley took a deep breath. Was he really such a shill?

"Heather, let's be real. Our political system is built to raise money and satisfy big business. Believe me, we do not want to upset that Big Money apple cart by prioritizing people's whims over a system that works." Bradley's face screwed into a look of fear and disgust. "Can you imagine the damage the captains of commerce and power brokers of Wall Street might cause if they lost their ability to influence our government and society to an elderly, God-fearing gardener? Their hissy fit could destroy our entire economy. We can't afford that risk as a nation!"

• • •

Brittany Hollister, the most powerful woman in America, watched Bradley's interview from her office in Atlanta.

For centuries, she and her predecessors had successfully maintained their anonymity, operating the levers of political and economic power from the background. Yet now, with the system they had controlled since the 1700s again at risk, she had to flex her muscles.

This wouldn't be as brutal as her predecessor's failed actions 150 years before. Unlike the slave industry, which could only be controlled or defeated by brute force, she had more subtle weapons to yield.

She punched a number into her phone.

"This is Bradley."

"Bradley, an email just arrived in your inbox. We're going to need you to meet us in Atlanta the day after Julia Connor's Austin rally. Bring Jacqueline. And before you ask—yes, you have to bring her."

The line went silent while Bradley checked his email. His eyes widened.

"This is really you?"

"Of course it's really me."

"Why would we meet with you? I don't think our interests are what I'd call sympatico."

"In this case, Bradley, they are. My interests are to see Julia Connor lose and to reward those who help make that happen. I wouldn't tell you I had a solution if I didn't. Just be there."

She didn't wait to hear Bradley's answer. After watching his interview, she knew he was smiling.

Having failed to reach Luke Lockwood on five different occasions, Brittany dialed a new number and waited for Senator Daniel Menendez to answer. He, she knew, wouldn't have to be convinced.

CHAPTER 47

GOD IS LOVE

Enjoying the dappled shade of an oak tree in a central Austin backyard where she rested ahead of tomorrow's march, Julia smiled at the man walking toward her—he was thin to start, and made thinner by a baggy polo shirt tucked into loose tan slacks.

As he didn't look particularly huggable, she offered a handshake. "Welcome," she said with a genuine smile. "I'm so glad to meet you, Luke."

He grasped her hand. "And I, you, Julia."

Julia paused, a thousand questions running through her mind. "I'd love to spend the time to hear your story and understand your heart, but I'm not sure either of us have time for that right now."

"That's probably for the best." Luke smiled shyly. "You might find my story horrifying."

"Or I might find that your story closely resembles my own."

"Resembles your own?" Luke looked deep into her eyes. "Julia, I hated you. That Whore of Babylon thing? Connecting you to the Biblical instrument of demonic destruction? That was my idea."

"I once poured blood on a politician who supported the Vietnam War." Julia shrugged, holding Luke's eyes with her gentlest gaze. "Many of us act without wisdom when the stakes seem highest. I'd imagine that our desire to do what is right is the same, even if our backgrounds are different."

Luke took a deep breath, wondering if she were so forgiving, wishing he had hours and days to spend with her.

"Julia, I, I don't really understand what happened."

"What did happen, Luke?"

"In the church, after I drank that tea, I saw Jesus, I felt his actual, literal, unconditional love, and I was told that love and God are available to all."

Julia's grin split her face, memories of academic texts experimentally applied flooding her senses. "There's a strong case to be made that what you experienced was the original Eucharist. But, we'll have time for that conversation later. The question for this moment is, what do you want to do now?"

• • •

"So, you're ready to make your first video?"

Luke paused and looked around the rental he was sharing with Josh Emerson. Orange juice sat out on the kitchen table. An oil painting of a longhorn graced one wall. A grinning woman he'd recently considered a consort of the devil stood in front of him.

"I guess," he said to Melanie, "I'm as ready as I'll ever be."

"Ok, but before we start, I have to apologize to you." She looked up at him imploringly, her eyes open and remorseful. "You know that it was me that dosed you, right? I was Secretary Becky."

"Melanie, that was the most amazing day of my life! I learned that loving Jesus didn't mean attacking those that know God differently, I was reminded that loving my neighbors meant loving *all* my neighbors, not just those who behaved exactly how I thought they should. This may sound obvious, but it was news to me."

"It's not obvious at all! Before Julia, I was just like you, but fighting for the other side."

"Amen!" Luke grinned, still surprised to find himself here, standing with *the enemy*, choosing a new path. "I always thought that to serve people and to serve Jesus, I had to be at war. But now, well–"

"That's the story to tell!" Melanie got out her phone and set it up on a small tripod.

Staring into the camera, Luke began to livestream.

"Hi, I'm Luke Lockwood, Senator Menendez's former campaign manager and Pastor Josiah McMillan's protégé. What's always been clear to me is that I love Jesus more than anything else in the world. I love that Jesus spent his life serving the poor, befriending social outcasts and sinners. I love that Jesus stood up to the Roman Empire's despotic authority, acting with the confidence and the freedom of one who intimately knew God's love."

Across the country, thousands tuned in, alerted by the links Melanie's content collective and Luke's coalition of pastors were posting to the world.

"All my life, I've tried to follow Jesus's example. As a child, I was taught that if I was to receive the ultimate blessing, salvation in the name of Jesus Christ, it would come only if I believed certain things and followed certain rules. I was taught that to ensure my salvation and to righteously serve Jesus, I had to fight against evildoers and those whose theology differed from my own. These people, I was told, were homosexuals, feminists, socialists, mainline protestants, Muslims and sinners of all stripes."

Luke paused, gathering his thoughts and running his hand through his hair. The perfect part was a thing of the past. Otherwise, he didn't fidget or stall. He was winging his words, but he spoke with the absolute confidence of someone speaking from the most love-touched part of themselves.

"Since I knew that my salvation, and my sense of value, rested on me being 'right,' and because I was trained to fight sinners, who were 'wrong,' I've spent my life opposing what I thought were the forces of evil in this nation."

He leaned forward, intently staring at the phone, a smile breaking out on his face as he remembered the electrifying warmth of God's unconditional love.

"But then, just a week ago, I met Jesus in a new way. I was shown that, far from being a single verse in the book of John describing an attribute of God, 'God is Love' is the entirety of Jesus's message, the reality of God revealed to humanity. I was reminded that in his lifetime, Jesus spent his time loving the hurt, wounded souls that came across his path—not fighting to diminish their standing in society."

Melanie had to admit to herself, the guy was a natural. A born teacher. A brilliant leader who communicated without the melodrama she depended upon to make her points.

"And what about those who warped God's message of love? Jesus saved his just rage for a single source—the Pharisees, those who were more concerned with religious rules and self-righteous acts than with showing God's love to their neighbors."

"To follow Jesus, I realized that my job was not to demonize sinners and gain power, but simply to love. I don't understand all the theology, and I'm certain there is more I don't know than what I do, but at this moment, I'm sure that Jesus would want me to support a woman who has selflessly committed her life to channeling God's love."

Comments poured in from every corner of the globe.

"OO MM GG!!!!!!" Julia's fangirls flooded the stream with emojis and exclamations. "When the final accounting takes place," a Baptist parishioner in Eastern Oregon commented, "Luke Lockwood's Judas turn will not be forgotten."

"Bastard!" "Praise source!" "Luke is drunk on the blood of the martyrs!" "Is a new America being born?" "Modern America is the new Noah's Ark. Let's get on board!" "Don't you mean the modern Epic of Gilgamesh?"

"When this election is over," Luke finished, "I'm going to go back to doing my favorite thing in the world. I'm going to study scripture, read the mystics and seek to embody love by serving downtrodden and oppressed people who desperately need Jesus's love in all its forms. But right now, I'm going to be marching in Julia Connor's 'Love In' tomorrow with other evangelical leaders who believe that God, in the core of his being, is LOVE."

CHAPTER 48

CALM BEFORE THE STORM

The Love-In March to the Capitol and Bradley's counter-march occurred on a crisp, clear, blue skyed Austin day and Bradley was in awe.

Of himself. Fifty thousand O'Leary supporters had assembled on the University of Texas campus.

Since campaign staffers, ultimately, were unable to control election outcomes, their entire purpose became to control optics, ensuring that even in failure, it at least LOOKED like they'd done their job. He wasn't at all convinced this countermarch would do anything to help the governor win, but he was confident the visual optics from the rally would be top fucking notch.

Spread across the lawn in front of him were groups representing the core of the Democratic party.

Unions had come out in force, bringing busloads of teachers, hospital workers, trade workers, wall builders and government employees. Operatives in Texas's blue cities—Houston, Dallas, and Austin—activated black church groups, gay groups, Birkenstock-clad environmentalists, and women's rights activists. This last group was key. Tens of thousands of women stood in small groups admiring each other's signs, lamenting the fact that their daughters and granddaughters were across town to march with Julia and Lillie Rift.

The one surprise—and Bradley would take full credit for this—were the tech workers. He'd asked Troojle CEO Ben Blankenship to organize, and he'd delivered. Twenty thousand masters of monetizing the world's information had come from as far as Seattle to hold signs supporting O'Leary's 'Data Rights Are Human Rights Act'.

"Good American Democrats!" Bradley roared, holding his microphone to his lips. "We are here today to turn the momentum back in our favor. And we are going to do what Democrats have always done best. Who are we here for?"

"O'LEARY!"

"And why are we here today?!"

The crowd roared back, "TO PROTEST!!"

"That's right! For generations we have fought to keep religion's insidious obsession with God out of public life, but now we are being told the path forward is to heal with God's love. We all wish that were true, but we know better! Keep God in church and the home, not in Washington!"

Pausing while the crowd roared its approval, Bradley kept rolling. "There is no way forward except to peacefully and politically demolish our opponents. Does that mean standing in the way of a political force that is sapping support from Democrats and big tech's battle for the soul of America? Damn right it does!!"

The crowd began to chant as one. "LOVE IS NOT THE ANSWER! LOVE IS NOT THE ANSWER!"

• • •

Near the intersection of South Lamar Avenue and Slaughter Lane, the Lord's Angels Raptor Strike Force gathered in the parking lot of the South Austin Salvation Bible Campus, one of Pastor McMillan's highest grossing satellite churches.

In front of the not-quite-arena-sized church, a well-watered lawn that stayed lush even in Texas' scorching summers stretched to the street. The lawn was graced by a larger-than-life nativity scene. It was only November, but the Salvation Christian Commerce Platform was ready for holiday sales, which meant each of the in-network churches had to be ready too.

Arrayed in an enormous circle behind the church, obscured from the street by the sanctuary, twenty-two roided out machines of war glistened in the morning sun, their black and red paint obscured only by Ford's 'Raptor' logo. A few of the vehicles were newer, their logo included not just the 'Raptor,' but also the updated branding, 'Assault.'

Like a general overseeing his troops, Pastor McMillan stood on the cargo bed of the lead vehicle, unable to contain his smile. He had been raised on stories of history's greatest spiritual battles— from the Crusades to the United States's never-ending fight against communism and collectivism. And there had been literary battles—unputdownable epics like *This Present Darkness* and *The Left Behind Series*.

Now he too would lead a real battle for God's glory.

The Strike Force, originally conceived as a last resort against government overreach and the end-of-America tide of immigrant-loving liberals, had been useful for much more than protection. He'd once used the Strike Force to eliminate an extortionary contractor holding up Salvation Tower's construction. He'd twice employed it to surreptitiously sabotage pastors competing with his Salvation Megachurch Network. And members of the Strike Force had been deployed countless times to scare husbands with a wandering eye back into the grace of God.

But all those operations were covert. This was prime time. In fact, if he wasn't mistaken, this was the End Times, praise Jesus! He, like Constantine before him, was unleashing the Lord's Angels Raptor Strike Force on the demonic hosts who opposed his God-ordained right to create the world in his image.

He turned to the enormous, hyper-muscled man standing beside him in a black, tight-fitting tactical T-shirt.

"Brandon," Pastor Josiah asked his general, "is this all of them?" Both men knew "all of them" referred to the biblically glorified number of seven days of creation multiplied by twelve, the number of Jesus's disciples, and the tribes of Israel.

Brandon nodded gravely, his eyes intense and every sense alive to the gravity of the mission at hand. "Yes sir, this is all of them. Just as you instructed, eighty-four men, all combat veterans, all pledged to kill for God."

"And they all are briefed on the mission?"

Brandon nodded again. "We will find and destroy the Whore of Babylon, and we will then melt into the crowds, disappearing without a trace, leaving our California registered trucks—owned by an untraceable LLC funded by Moscow—to confuse the mainstream media morons."

"Good, we're ready then." He picked up a bullhorn and handed it to Brandon. "General, will you say a word?"

Brandon took a deep breath and then bellowed into the bullhorn, "Men, are we ready??!!"

The Raptor Strike Force Responded as one. "Ahhhh!!!"

"Men," Brandon repeated, "I said, are we ready to serve the Lord God our Savior?!"

"AAAAHHHHHHHHH!!!!!!"

Pastor McMillan took the bullhorn from Brandon, the energy of the men's scream and God's righteousness coursing through his veins, making the cast on his leg vibrate with the energy of salvation. He wished he were going with the men, though he knew his role was to direct and to inspire, not to fight.

"Men," he began, hoping with all his soul to impart the fervor, the fear, and the righteous hatred he felt, "demons wrapped in the garb of love have infested our nation. I met these demons—I met them deep within my soul. And I can tell you, they seek to destroy the theology of the chosen!"

"AAAAHHHHHHHHH!!!!!!"

The screams further filled his heart, igniting his soul. He witnessed a sparrow flit across the parking lot before landing in a shrub. The morning sun hovered behind him and the smell of wet grass filled every man's nostrils as he raised his right hand to consecrate his children.

"Dear Jesus, bless these men as they wield your sword of love. In the scripture, you tell us that we are fallen AND that we are created in your image, redeemed by your grace."

Taking a deep breath, he let the truth of redemption seek in, all the better to assure the men their eternal souls were safe in God's hands.

"Lord God, today, there are demons loose among us. These demons have declared war on your word in the bastardized name of a love available even to those who don't profess belief in your narrow path to eternal salvation. But these men in front of me—these men walk your path, they are the chosen! Protect them as they fight for you, and help us to redeem your word by defeating the Whore of Babylon. Now men, let me hear you!!"

As one, eighty-four men began banging their AR-15s and their Barret MRAD sniper rifles on the asphalt, channeling their pastor's commission into the courage they'd need to attack in enemy territory. "Ahhhhh!! Ahhhhhahhhhahhhhaahhhh!!! Ahhhhh!! Ahhhhhahhhhahhhhaahhhh!!!"

The asphalt, had it not been so well manufactured, would have split from the noise and the passion and the desire to selflessly sacrifice to protect God's righteous word.

• • •

Safe on the grass behind the high walls of Austin School for the Deaf, Jonathan looked around, stroking his beard and squinting through the bright morning light. "This is not what I expected when we said we'd gather 'all available' protective resources."

Noah shrugged. He'd secured access to the private school, which sat on a vast campus, just a few blocks from the march's route. "I didn't know what to expect either, but I think this land and those vehicles fit the plan, right?"

Jonathan gave a small grin. "Fits like a glove."

A cavalry of armored personnel carriers were in formation, ready for action. Next to them, a neatly stacked pile of rocket launchers awaited a shoulder to perch upon. One of the men from Jonathan's healing circle, who had spent his past life dealing weapons in Latin America, had volunteered ten M113s and MK-153s from an inventory sitting around gathering dust.

Jonathan expected the unnerving, militaristic scene playing out on the school lawn; what he didn't expect was the bevy of Teslas and Robinson R22 commuter helicopters.

"How did you pull this miracle off?" he asked Noah, nodding in the chopper's direction.

Noah's face lit up. "Told you I had wealthy clients. They may not be into loving kindness yet, but the millionaire and billionaire love-and-light folk will go to great lengths for a government that'll do something to address the global environmental carnage. Donating a helicopter is a small ask."

Jonathan nodded. "We'll need to retrofit the M113s with the Tesla's auto-navigation systems."

"Already done," Noah replied.

Jonathan spotted a group of women who were dancing and chanting around one of the M113s, blowing smoke as they shimmied. "Who and what are those women? They weren't part of the plan, were they?"

"Don't worry, they're not going into battle with us. They're just purifying the vehicle's evil energy. That one must have seen a lot of combat." Noah grinned. Then, just as quickly, his brows pinched together in confusion as his eyes scanned another patch of the campus. "Who are those thirty-year-old men dressed as teenagers?"

"You know them!" Jonathan laughed. "That's Luke, Josh Emerson, and their collection of youth pastors. They're here to advise us on Evangelical psychology if the battle takes a grim turn. Speaking of unusual turns, how is our star doing?"

"I just finished giving Lillie the final briefing."

"And she got the required lesson?"

"She is literally Wonder Woman now."

"And her fans know the deal?"

"She says they're on board."

"Perfect. And the drones?"

"They're flying already, simulcasting to all our devices."

"Amazing."

"So, we're ready?"

"As much as we can be." Jonathan replied, his mind on bloody battles of the past, his heart desperately hoping that such bloodshed could be avoided today.

Noah called for everyone to gather and handed a bullhorn to Jonathan.

"Over two hundred thousand people will be marching for love alongside Julia Connor today. One hundred thousand of those people are young women led by Lillie Rift. The other one hundred thousand are love and compassion-seeking people just like us. As you all know, there have been rumors of violence. As Julia's security force, we'll be on hand to provide protection."

Noah took the bullhorn. "By now, you know the plan in detail. Any last questions?"

A former Army ranger sporting a full blonde beard and worn fatigues bearing the nametag "Mickelson" raised his hand. "Just so we're all crystal clear. If worst comes to worst, we wait until these Lord's Angels clowns are about to fire and then we launch the rockets? What if we wait too long and Julia or the teen girls pay the ultimate price?"

Jonathan took a deep breath. "Look, the attackers are just like us, only they haven't yet started down their healing path. We've gamed this out."

Noah nodded encouragingly beside him. "An overwhelming show of force is the only way to protect Julia and all her supporters. But we need the timing to be perfect for maximum impact and minimal carnage. We all agree that it's worth the risk."

"Besides," Jonathan said, "half those yahoos probably have daughters marching with us. They might think we're the enemy, but we have to trust they will do the right thing when the stakes are highest."

CHAPTER 49

LOVE, COMPASSION, HEALING AND JUSTICE

Jonathan's hand drawn map of central Austin:

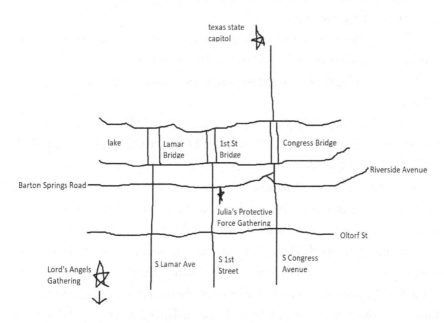

irds chirped. Cheering families lined the street. The mid-morning sun reflected off Julia's iconic white hair as she marched at the head of an endless crowd. Amateur and professional photographers recorded the moment for posterity, the moment when, perhaps, the world changed.

Looking all around her, smiling uncontrollably, resisting the urge to stop and hug every person she made eye contact with, Julia felt like she was floating.

With Lillie Rift raising her left hand and Melanie her right, her spirit soared and her heart burst with gratitude.

Ahead of them, South Congress Avenue stretched empty toward the bridge and downtown Austin. Behind her, the mass of marchers stretched out, chanting, singing, and laughing. "Is this what a quarter of a million people looks like?" she asked Lillie, who knew all about audiences larger than the human mind could comprehend.

"Give or take a few!" Lillie was dressed to thrill in platform combat boots and a next-century Gautier getup—leather, lace, corset with a black turtleneck that spread out to white sleeves with hot-pink racing strips, and a futuristic rectangular backpack. She grabbed a phone from a skintight pocket on her hip and then pushed away the mouthpiece on her headset. "Look at this, Jonathan sent me the drone view."

Julia was astounded. A throbbing, slowly moving, multicolored mass of human optimism stretched as far as the drone could see.

And a singsong chant echoed so loudly Julia could imagine it being heard miles away.

"LOVE, COMPASSION, HEALING, AND JUSTICE! LOVE, COMPASSION, HEALING, AND JUSTICE! LOVE, COMPASSION, HEALING, AND JUSTICE!"

Julia thought back to Vietnam War marches, or seminars with Ram Dass. Nothing compared to this. Never, she was certain, had she seen God's love or human energy or whatever one wished to call it move on this scale.

For a moment she thought of the threats, the possible attack. Should they have begged for Secret Service protection? Would Jonathan's security plan be enough if the worst happened? She brushed the concerns from her mind. She knew the power, the yang of love had to be balanced by yin, by darkness. It was inevitable, so why worry? What would come would come. For now, all she could do was be present in this moment.

Melanie tightened her grip on her hand. "We've got company. O'Leary marchers." South Congress Bridge was filling with counter-marchers, blocking their route to downtown Austin.

"I wonder what they're chanting." Julia strained to hear. "Our crowd is deafening."

Lillie Rift waved her hands in the air to draw attention, pointed to her ear and then raised and lowered her hand, bringing their supporter's volume down. The rival marchers' chant became clear: "LOVE IS NOT THE ANSWER! LOVE IS NOT THE ANSWER! LOVE IS NOT THE ANSWER!"

Lillie turned her palms up and raised them, encouraging the volume once more. "Come on!" she yelled, pumping her fists to underscore each word. Two hundred thousand marchers roared in unison: "LOVE, COMPASSION, HEALING, AND JUSTICE! LOVE, COMPASSION, HEALING, AND JUSTICE! LOVE, COMPASSION, HEALING, AND JUSTICE!"

The dueling marchers faced each other, growing closer by the step.

As they chanted, their voices grew, each group seeking an upper hand. On one side: "LOVE, COMPASSION, HEALING, AND JUSTICE!" On the other: "LOVE IS NOT THE ANSWER!"

• • •

Jonathan checked the drone views one last time, then turned to Noah. "They're on the way. It's go time, brother. Wish us love and luck!"

Noah nodded grimly, terrified. He'd never been in war. He wasn't even in this war, technically. He was just coordinating. But he felt like he was about to die. The possibility of death, or of being responsible for someone else's death. How could anyone stand this pressure? "All the love, my friend," he said to Jonathan, placing his shaking hand on his heart.

Jonathan placed his steady hand over Noah's. "War was—and is—my business. Everything will be fine."

He walked outside, circled his arms above his head, climbed into the lead Robinson R22 chopper, engaged the whisper-mode technology, and silently lifted off, watching seven other helicopters rise into the air, each containing a combat veteran armed with an MK-153 rocket launcher.

• • •

Jonathan's voice crackled into Lillie and Melanie's headset. "Check the drone array. It's going down."

Lillie pulled up the view, Melanie looking over her shoulder.

Jonathan continued. "The Raptors are barreling down South Lamar Avenue. Our spotter chopper said they're running red lights, wreaking havoc. We think they'll turn onto Barton Springs Road, then intercept the march at the intersection with South Congress Avenue."

"Soooo?"

"Gives us five minutes."

Melanie gave Lillie an enormous hug, locking eyes and smiling. "Be safe."

"Be safe? I'm about to turn the concept of cannon fodder inside out!"

Jonathan's voice crackled back on the headset. "Mel and Lil, if you're ready, initiate Operation Preserve Love!"

Melanie cued the traveling DJs, Sophie and Tukker, rolling beside them on a mobile DJ booth. The familiar, infectious house groove of "Lovetopia," Lillie's global anthem, boomed out.

Lillie's voice—which one critic had called "a sonic flower, with more layers than an artichoke: beguiling, serious, sensuous, rasping, soothing, childish, wise"—filled the air. Ecstatic cowbells and ethereal electric cellos layered over a hypnotic, feel-it-in-your-heart 4/4 beat boomed over the crowd from a wireless sound system that lined the parade route.

Lillie breathed deeply, one last second of guaranteed survival before she pressed the go button. She looked down at her costume. The outfit wasn't just space-dominatrix chic—it housed a lightweight turbo jetpack.

With the press of a button and a WOOSH, the jetpack vibrated into action and lifted her until she was levitating one hundred feet into the air. Crossing her legs, floating like a leather-clad, marionette Buddha, she took out her phone, opened the Fans of Lillie Rift app—and pushed the enormous, red "SAVE JULIA" button.

Throughout the crowd, one hundred thousand phones vibrated and pinged with urgency, the screens flashing, "Follow Lillie! Save Julia! Follow Lillie! Save Julia!"

Lillie's fans looked up to see her hovering in the air, gesticulating for them to all follow her. They'd been briefed; they knew what was required of them.

The teens and twenty-somethings surged, cheering, an ocean of humans flowing like a river, following Lillie's elevated form straight toward Barton Springs Road.

Lillie scanned ahead of her, Jonathan's voice in her ear. "Lillie, can you see the intersection?"

"Yes sir," Lillie said, wind flying in her face, people stretched out as far as she could see.

"Lead the way to the intersection, then put the women in place. The Raptors should be there in four minutes."

"Hey, Jonathan?"

"Yeah, Lillie?"

"Were you scared when you went into battle?"

"I was always scared before, but once it starts, it's all adrenaline and focus. Honestly, it's addicting."

"Whew! Just making sure I'm not a freak, because this is amazing!"

• • •

When Lillie floated away, Julia, like everyone else, watched spellbound. Even though they had told her this might happen—Jonathan had walked her through the Operation Preserve Love plan on his iPad, talking about various scenarios— she could not believe it was happening. A battle, here? At her Love-In March?

"Julia, excuse me." It was Eli Rappaport, Jonathan's longtime friend and their healing-circle collaborator, now in a tight-fitting black performance shirt. "I'm sorry it has to be like this, but I'm supposed to protect you."

"Oh yes." Julia was pleased to see Eli even though she hated he had to be here. "I guess we'll be sharing this remarkable moment?"

He was carrying what looked to her like a machine gun and a heavy black jacket. Julia noticed a group of similarly outfitted men behind him.

"Yes, exactly." Eli was all business. Not even a smile for his old friend. "I need you to wear this Kevlar vest and stay close to me."

She put the jacket on. "This is so heavy!"

"Yes ma'am, it's designed to stop bullets. We hope that won't be necessary, but just in case, we need you to kneel."

Julia complied and was immediately surrounded by twelve leanly muscled men in two concentric protective circles. Four men kneeled and the rest stood, their guns leveled out toward the crowd. It was just like a diagram on Jonathan's iPad. Except it was real.

Eli addressed the crowd. "Keep calm, everyone! This is just a precaution! We hope to be moving shortly!"

A calm descended. Lillie Rift's song swamped all auditory senses. The marchers that hadn't followed Lillie stood around, confused, not knowing what was happening.

Julia's heart, which had been so filled with love and hope, sank into her chest. She knelt among the armed men, feeling the smallest she had ever felt in the midst of what might become her worst nightmare.

CHAPTER 50

TARGET ACCESS PROBLEMS

The Lord's Angels Raptor Strike Force turned right off South Lamar Avenue onto Barton Springs Road, tearing through the stoplights and past barbeque joints, scattering onlookers like a snowplow through fresh powder.

Jonathan watched their progress from his helicopter and uttered the words he'd been dreading for days. "Operation Preserve Love is a Go. GO GO GO!!" He shouted into the digital ether. "M113 personnel carriers, deploy! Choppers, move into battle position. Lillie, hold the road! Do not forget, this is a war of love!"

Then everything seemed to happen at once.

All eight helicopters jetted into position, tracing the progress of the Lord's Angels Raptor Strike Force, each with a man at the open door, MK-153 multipurpose assault weapons perched upon their shoulders.

The auto-navigated M113 armored personnel carriers rumbled toward the projected confrontation point, their payloads ready to go. Hidden back at headquarters, the engineers who'd jerry-rigged the Tesla Nav systems onto the M113s manned the manual controls; if the plan of attack went wrong, they were the ones who'd step in.

From her jetpack perch a hundred feet up, Lillie hovered above the middle of Barton Springs Road, one hundred thousand young women fanning out in an impenetrable ring of angsty optimism. Together, they all took a knee and began singing.

• • •

Speeding down Barton Springs Road in the lead Raptor, Pastor McMillan's Strike Force general, Brandon, felt a long-lost surge in his groin. The battle bulge! How was it he had almost forgotten? Combat and coitus. Nothing like it. It had been more than ten years since his last raid on those ISIS sand-eaters. Man, did he love that gig, gunning and funning on those half-baked holy warriors who hated Jesus and America, and therefore, hated him. He took it personally.

To Brandon, Julia Connor and her followers were the other side of the Jihadi coin. As Pastor McMillan had pointed out, "they hate our way of life." Well, to-hell-with them and their march. His ears captured every sound around him. His eyes zoomed in on the people diving out of the way, and he smiled.

They were going to do it. They were going to take the march by surprise.

As soon as they barreled into the intersection of Barton Springs and South Congress Avenue, the bleeding heart of the march, the men would disperse to hunt Julia. From there, they would shed their guns and equipment—every man was wearing an "I Heart Julia" T-shirt under his fatigues—and disappear into the pandemonium.

He steered his truck left around the last corner, running through his last-second preparations for battle. He loosed the cross he wore under his black T-shirt, kissed it and then briefly held it skyward. He white-knuckled the wheel. He devoted one final thought to the awesome power of his disciplined rigidity. It was time.

Then he saw it.

"What in Jesus's name!" He was already grabbing his walkie-talkie as he stomped the brake. "Lord's Angels, we have a problem!"

As far as he could see, ahead and to the left and to the right, thousands of kneeling teenage girls blocked his path. The intersection was a sea of pro-Julia T-shirts, artfully ripped jeans, ponytails, braids, and eyeshadow. What *was* this?

He rolled down his window to get a better look. They were singing, all of them, and smiling sweetly.

A song being sung in plaintive, hopeful voices filled the air. He listened, incredulous.

Jesus loves the little children
All the children of the world
Red and yellow, black and white
They are precious in His sight
Jesus loves the little children of the world
Jesus died for all the children
All the children of the world
Red and yellow, black and white
They are precious in His sight
Jesus died for all the children of the world

In the passenger seat, his deputy Jedidiah, who had been peering into the sight of his AR-15 as they drove, lowered his weapon. Stunned, he asked, "What the hell is this, Brandon? I didn't know the demons would be teenage girls!"

"Me neither!" Brandon yelled. The battle bulge was gone. His adrenaline was surging with nowhere to go. "I'm not sure, but I don't think these girls are demons. Pastor Josiah's intelligence must have been bad!"

"Bad intelligence?! He says his word is the word of God and his orders were clear."

"Look at those young ladies, Jedidiah! They sound like demons to you?"

"I don't care what they look or sound like, you heard the pastor. Our obligation to God is to fight!"

"I'm no theologian, but we cannot fire on these teenage freakin girls. They ain't ISIS!"

Brandon picked up his walkie-talkie and looked out the truck window, trying not to make eye contact with any of the singing teens.

"Lord's Angels, Commander B in Raptor One. We are experiencing unforeseen target access problems. Over."

"Commander B, Mammoth Raptor Twenty-One. No shit! Over."

"Copy. Mammoth Raptor Twenty-One. Confirming there's a human barrier of at least fifty thousand teenage girls blocking our access. Over."

"Lord's Angels, Dragonslayer Raptor Three. There is not one damned visible demon. Over."

"Dragonslayer Raptor Three, HAWGman Raptor Eleven. I believe demons may be what English teachers call a metaphor. Over."

"That's right!" Jedidiah said to Brandon, nodding like a five-year-old who'd drunk too much Coca-Cola. "I remember learning that in high school. That's why they say the devil's in the details!"

Brandon shook his head. "That's not a metaphor, Jed. That means what it says."

"Lord's Angels, Mammoth Raptor Twenty-One. Reporting multiple choppers above us. They appear to be outfitted with ManPads. Repeat, hostile forces appear to be targeting us with Man-Portable rocket launchers. Over."

"HAWGman Raptor Eleven, this is Commander B. Please verify Raptor 21's observations. Awaiting confirmation. Over."

Every single member of the Strike Force, now fenced in by oceans of young women, looked up at the sky in unison, including Brandon, who stuck his head out the driver's side window and yelled, "Holy shit!"

Two hundred feet up, Jonathan said the same thing as he watched eighty-odd men gawking at the various choppers.

He spoke into his headset: "Team Love, the Lord's Angels have clearly identified us and our positions. Remember, initiate armed response ONLY if they open fire!"

CHAPTER 51

A MILLION
SPARKLING SUNS

Lord's Angels, this is Commander B. EVERYBODY SHUT THE FUCK UP!"

Brandon was rewarded by the hum of static. "Thank you! I apologize for my language. We came here with a plan and mission. But at this point, we are sitting ducks. Meanwhile, there are about one hundred thousand other sitting ducks—teenage girls as old as our own kids—surrounding us. It's almost as if they knew we were coming, which makes me wonder if there was a security leak."

"What the hell do we do?" Jedidiah yelled into his headset, a subconscious fear of eternal damnation overriding any sense of self-preservation or mercy, "We need orders! Doing nothing is not an option!"

"That was Jedidiah in Raptor 1 ignoring protocol," Brandon said.

"Screw protocol. We need to take action!"

"Lord's Angels, I'm a Christian first, warrior second. I know my values and I trust my eyes. We're surrounded. There is an army of angelically singing teen girls between us and Julia. We must surrender. Lay down your weapons."

"The hell I'll surrender," Jedidiah screamed. "Revelations says the Whore of Babylon will be drunk on the blood of the Martyrs of Jesus. That's gonna be us! We've been gifted this opportunity to become biblical!"

Jedidiah snarled, jumped out of the truck, and screamed into his headset. "Pastor Josiah was clear—his and God's word is inerrant. I can't risk losing salvation!" He raised his AR-15 toward the nearest helicopter.

Hovering two hundred feet above, Jonathan saw a man dart out of the lead Raptor and raise his weapon. His military training took over. He aimed his MK-153 shoulder-launched multipurpose assault weapon.

"Fire!"

A custom-designed and manufactured 83mm-caliber rocket barreled toward Jedidiah, who seemed to fall over before Jonathan had released the trigger.

Seven other rockets, concurrently fired, raked the sky like asteroids entering earth's atmosphere.

Seven high, horrible squeals.

The teens slamming their hands over their ears as one.

The Raptor Strike Force frozen in their trucks.

Time slowing.

Stopping.

Jonathan braced for impact.

Forty feet above the ground, the rockets detonated simultaneously, blasting a cloud of rainbow-colored Unicorn Dust™ brand biodegradable glitter into the sky. The thunderous bursts rattled and dazzled the crowd, showering the march with sun-catching purples! Blues! Golds! Greens! Pinks! Above the Love In, a technicolor jewel-toned cotton-candy sky.

Not pausing to admire the shimmering glitter rainbow unfurling above the march, Jonathan barked his last command: "Commence the second deployment!"

"Roger that. Tech team ignition complete!"

The M113s armored personnel carriers had been slowly rumbling through the crowd and now surrounded the Raptors. Two barrel-sized silver canisters on the back of each M113 began spewing a fog into the sky.

"Holy shit, it's working!" Jonathan crowed into his headset as the wave of glitter washed over his helicopter.

"Jonathan! I don't know where you got the idea to 3D print the rockets using compressed Unicorn Dust™, but you are a certified genius!" Noah screamed back, unable to believe it may all actually go as planned. He hoped his video crews were getting it all on tape. The mushroom plan had backfired, but this? This was the greatest mass performance in history. A protest, a party, a war, and art wrapped into one. This was Fluxus—a flood of art and movement—saving lives and launching a revolution!

Like synchronous ballet, the fog lofted high into the sky, mixed with the glitter and drifted down to engulf the Lord's Angels, Lillie Rift, and one hundred thousand marchers, protesters, and observers.

This fog wasn't condensed water vapor. No, it was a fog of nitrous oxide. The facilitator of culinary cream. A completely harmless substance sold by most online retailers. Laughing gas!

As planned and on queue, reality shifted. The fogs of war gave way to a sparkly panoply of glitter and giggles as the nitrous oxide flooded everyone's lungs, turning chants of "Love" and the attacker's scowls into wide-eyed expressions of wonder and astonishment.

CHAPTER 52

DANCE DANCE REVOLUTION

When Jedidiah stepped out of the Raptor, hell bent on war, Brandon thought about pulling his 9mm Glock and shooting his friend. He quickly realized the collateral damage if he missed might be a dead teen girl, which would be extremely counterproductive, as would future murder charges if he hit his intended target. That was no way to end a friendship.

So he did the next best thing: He grabbed his *Thank Jesus for Coffee* thermos on his dashboard, opened his door, stood on the Raptor's running board, and winged the thermos as hard as he could at the mutinying numbskull. The thermos was fully loaded with Starbucks decaf, which Brandon had been too nervous to drink. When it connected with the back of Jedidiah's head, he went down in a heap just as rockets exploded above.

When Jedidiah came to, he was lying on the ground, surrounded by giggling glitter-covered girls, every single one of them wearing an I Heart Julia T-shirt. He pulled himself into a sitting position, and huffed, "Where's my gun?"

"This is a love march," said a tall girl with a backward hat. "We can't have guns here!"

"What if they love guns!" screamed a redhead with braces.

"Ohmygod! Love gun!" The giggles morphed into full-blown cackles. "That's a different kind of love march!"

Jedidiah scrambled, pawing the ground around him for his gun. They were on a mission! Why the hell was he grinning at these girls?

"You alive, Jed? I thought you were a goner." It was Brandon, standing over him with an enormous smile. "You look good with all that sparkle on your face." His wide eyes took in every shimmering flash of glitter light and his heart was near bursting as the joy of avoiding a teenage bloodbath sank in.

A woman with long blonde hair dressed in what seemed like an S&M space suit dropped from the sky and popped up in front of him.

Lillie Rift didn't know Brandon's name, but with his battle fatigues, body armor, and helmet adorned with a haloed figure holding a cross, she assumed he was the leader of the Lord's Angels Raptor Strike Force. He was grinning like an idiot through his beard, his face a picture of awe-inspired joy. He looked nothing like what she expected the Evangelical assassin to be.

Brandon eyed Lillie through the scintillating, foggy haze, trying to suppress his giggles. "We were going to shoot you and Julia just a moment ago."

Lillie laughed, then smiled at Brandon and raised her eyebrows. "And I was going to let you shoot me!"

"I think I'm glad I didn't."

"Me too!"

"So what's next?"

"Just a second." Lillie knew the last part of the plan started now. She took out her phone to message Sophie and Tukker.

"DJs, hit it!"

The sound system roared back to life, playing music that was house before house, a hypnotic keyboard beat pulsing with fifty years of dance floor joy.

A familiar, distinctly feminine moan united the grooves with an enticing "OOOohhhhh" that gained volume as Sophie and Tukker amped up the sound.

Lillie knew the song. Looking at Brandon through the glitter and laughing fog, she knew he did too.

Donna Summer cooed, penetrating every confused, amazed, joyful soul – "Ooh I feel love, I feel love. I feel love, I feel love. I feel love."

Lillie locked eyes with Brandon and pointed to her ear. "You hear that? There's only one thing we can do!"

Brandon looked confused. So Lillie took his enormous, meaty hand in her own small, fingers. "Come on, soldier! Dance like a man!"

Before the Lord's Angels Raptor Strike Force could come to terms with the fact the helicopters had reigned glitter instead of a burning death down upon them, and as they attempted to see in a world that had, suddenly, turned into a multi-colored madhouse shifting like psychedelic Sahara sands, they were dancing.

Strike Force assassins and teen girls, tech executives and breathwork bros, meditating moms and curiosity seeking bystanders. EVERYONE was dancing.

• • •

Julia stood with Melanie, surrounded by Eli Rappaport and his security brigade. They were buzzing; bouncing in place; watching the throbbing, glitter-covered outdoor disco.

"Look," Melanie said. "The Lord's Angels are dancing. Oh my God! They've got Lillie on their shoulders."

"Is she going to be safe?"

"This is a love-in, Julia. Everyone is safe."

"And everyone is giddy when they should be terrified. This is heaven!"

Melanie pulled out her phone and pointed it at her boss. "Say that again!"

"I'm giddy when I should be terrified! But that's the power of love!"

CHAPTER 53

WHO THE HELL KNOWS WHAT HAPPENED

Normally red faced ROX News anchorman Jerry Sparks spoke directly into the camera. He was all-outrage, all the time. But that evening his crimson face looked a little rosier than usual.

"This morning in Austin, Texas, the race for president hit an all-time low as a so-called political rally for so-called independent candidate—hippie, drug-pushing, heretical Julia Connor—erupted into an all-out war as a mob of brainwashed teenage girls led by pop icon Lillie Rift and an unstable group of Julia Connor's veteran supporters attacked a group of peaceful Christian activists by detonating a glitter bomb. Jed, out to you."

Jed Abernathy stood on South Congress Bridge, glitter bits fluttering around him, trying not to gloat. Had anyone ever had such a hot streak of campaign chaos? Not since Dan Rather covered the Kennedy assassination. At least, that's what his producer Nancy had said.

"Yes, Jerry, exactly right." he intoned. "Today, Julia Connor's seemingly peaceful supporters showed the true colors of women everywhere, luring military veterans into firing glitter rockets on peaceful, armed protesters. Not only that, but we are hearing there was widespread drug use, which is no surprise given Connor's drug-dealing history."

"Wow, Jed, just wow," Jerry said from the studio. "The level that Julia

Connor's unhinged supporters will stoop to continues to amaze us all. Will charges be filed?"

"Jerry, no. This whole fiasco was live-streamed on a variety of different social platforms, meaning everyone in America saw several of the peaceful men in the Ford Raptors point their AR-15s at the helicopters. In Texas, that means those men no longer had any legal right to live."

"One of those men reportedly died from glitter asphyxiation. Does that mean he was killed legally?"

"Correct, Jerry. Correct," Jed responded while vigorously nodding his head. "Texas legal experts tell me that the only recourse the dead man's family has would be to sue in civil court, claiming that the rocket-firing men were obligated to kill all of the AR-15-toting men in the Ford Raptors, and that by not killing them all, they had inflicted undue harm on the family of the single man that died."

"Jed, that makes absolutely no sense."

"You're right Jerry. Though one legislator did tell me he was hoping language from one of Texas's many anti-trans laws could be used to prosecute the veterans for the public use of glitter, but it will take some time for lawyers to either find or appoint a judge who will interpret the law in such a manner."

"Well, thank you, Jed. Despite these scenes of terror, Julia Connor maintains her small lead over Senator Menendez."

· · ·

Not far from the ROX news crew, Heather Haliburton's partially unbuttoned blouse allowed glitter to gather along liberal America's favorite left breast. Facing the camera, she spoke with the NATN studio in New York. "Jamal, contrary to reports from the Connor campaign that today's glitter war was an expert de-escalation of an assassination attempt on Julia Connor, sources tell me that the attack was an effort by radical love activists to stem the momentum that Governor Jacqueline O'Leary has gained in the last week."

Behind her, a teen girl with lavender extensions cartwheeled, laughing, through the frame, her joy a stark contrast to Heather's ominous message.

"I'm hearing this has caused hand-wringing among some establishment backers who were playing footsie with the Connor Campaign. If these love despots are willing to resort to weapons of war like glitter bombs, the establishment types should be rethinking their support."

"Thank you, Heather," Jamal replied. "A snap poll conducted by Marist University shows little movement in the presidential race following today's embarrassing display by Julia Connor, but both Connor's rivals said they were confident these shocking events will mark a critical downturn for the surprise candidate."

• • •

The American people, who hadn't known what to think in decades, knew less of what to think than ever before.

Aliens landing and declaring the Redwood Trees emperor of the earth would have been less unexpected than hearing the news that, depending whom one chose to listen to, a deadly glitter war for control of the nation had taken place in Austin, TX, or that Julia Connor had almost been assassinated by a group of crazed veterans or that she had been saved by a different group of veterans or that, well, hell, who knew what had happened.

All America knew, as every pollster was quick to mention on news shows and podcasts, was that they were fed up with the status quo, they didn't trust anyone—especially not each other—and if finding a way to break the two-party monopoly on power meant electing a beekeeping glitter mongerer, then so be it.

CHAPTER 54

THE BEGINNING
OF THE ENDGAME

Julia," one of Noah's consultants said, a sugar free donut clutched in his left hand, a cooling mug of coffee in his right, "I can't believe I'm saying this, but we think you're going to win."

"Win the election?" She realized, in a moment of panic, that she'd never really considered winning a possibility. Her as president. What?!

"Exactly!" Noah's other consultant said, three different newspapers clutched in his hands, his butt firmly planted on the lawn chair sitting across from what Julia had taken to calling her campaign blanket. "California and New York are both in the bag. That puts you twenty percent of the way there. O'Leary will definitely carry Wisconsin, Illinois, Michigan, and Minnesota. Menendez has the entire southeast plus Wyoming, Utah, Idaho, and Arizona on lockdown. So, if you can pick up the right combination of Texas, Colorado, Montana, North Carolina, and the New England states..."

Jonathan, sitting on the blanket next to Julia, was the one to say it as he made gleeful eye contact with Mel: "Then you'll be president of the United States of America!"

Noah gave Luke a friendly punch on the arm. "Thank goodness we have folks on the team with some real bureaucratic know-how. We've got to start thinking about how to run government in a way that makes decisions based on people's best interests. Should we launch a Department of Compassion?!"

"We will do no such thing," said Julia, surprised at the certainty she felt. "The surest way to kill a movement of the spirit is to centralize and bureaucratize it. Government will be government. We will bring different values to the table, we will try to use systems in more just, more humane ways. We will eliminate some systems and create new ones, but we will not try to turn the laws of the heart and the soul into the laws of man."

. . .

Brittany Hollister stood at one end of a spotless glass table built for twelve, her cascading, cornsilk blonde hair glinting in the overhead light. Her deputy, Jared Gates—who was always so stone-faced that people didn't tend to notice he was the very epitome of tall, dark, and handsome—sat at the table's other end. On the wall between them, a pure gold sculpture of sugarcane was mounted on the wall. Next to it, a polished emerald sign read, American Sugar Association.

When Governor Jacqueline O'Leary entered, she nearly allowed the heavy door to hit Bradley Bishkoff in the face. A moment later, Senator Menendez entered by himself. After Pastor McMillan had attempted to start a Holy War and Luke deserted, Menendez had decided to advise himself for the last few days of the campaign.

"I'll cut to the chase," Brittany Hollister started before the three of them had finished sitting, "Your efforts to defeat Julia Connor have been a pathetic joke."

"A joke?" Bradley said. "We've been attacking like starved rottweilers, but she's made of Teflon! We played the no more Medicare and Medicaid card, we called her naïve and presumptuous, we attacked her as anti-woman at every turn, we had the NAACP run a national set of ads saying her values didn't align with Black America. Again, none of it worked!"

"No," Jared replied, "you've been getting played at every encounter. By rank fucking amateurs."

"Now listen here," said Menendez, "I couldn't agree more with your assessment of Jacqueline and Bradley's incompetence, but I'm still tied with Julia.

Can we at least agree I've run one hell of a campaign? My campaign called her a Muslim and a communist sympathizer, said she was weak on crime, and accused her of hating white people. We played the national security and especially the Evangelical card. We even wrote a draft bill to ban all spiritual texts that weren't Christian. If it weren't for our efforts, we'd probably be polling as poorly as Jacqueline is!"

"A *great campaign?*" Brittany's glare x-rayed him. "Your campaign manager went to work for our opponent after having a "spiritual awakening." Your highest-profile Evangelical supporter went on an unhinged rant about demons on national TV before attempting to assassinate Julia Connor. And you've allowed twenty percent of your Evangelical support to flip into Julia Connor's camp. Do you realize this year is the first time Evangelical Christians have, in a statistically significant way, planned to support anyone other than the Republican candidate since the '80s?"

Jared piled on: "Senator, it's not all that surprising that the bleeding hearts on the left would bail on the governor's icy bureaucratic speak for Julia's campaign of love, but to lose the Evangelicals? That's a level of incompetence we've never before seen."

"I thought," O'Leary snarled, "we were here to get a last big check before the election. Why are you insulting us? I don't care who you are—I will not let a lobbyist who's not handing me a check talk to me this way."

She got up to leave, but Brittany's words stopped her in her tracks. "Oh, we'll do better than a check. We're here to hand you the election if you'll just hang on."

"Senator, Governor, we're not here to insult you," Jared said as O'Leary sat back down. "Really, you're both just the victim of poor timing."

"Something happened this year that we all feared would someday happen, but we never imagined would happen quite this way." Brittany paused to adjust her blouse. "The American people, to put it simply, finally have had enough. Both major parties have effectively had the country in an inescapable equilibrium since WWII, but that equilibrium has run its course."

Jared nodded grimly. "The balance that existed has failed. A critical mass has finally been alienated. The important thing now is that we create room in both the parties for ideas like Julia Connor's, ideas about human value and emotional awareness, without actually allowing anything to change."

"Exactly right," Brittany continued, "and that's why we're here." She pulled a stack of stapled papers out of her bag and handed them around the table. The title on each packet read *ASA SOS: The Plan to Save America*.

"We've known this plan could work for seventy years," Brittany continued as she tapped on the papers in her hands, "but we've never had to use this information before now." With that, she took them through it.

A few minutes later, Bradley interrupted. "You're saying that we just follow your plan, and the American people will magically fall in line?"

"Every focus group, every statistical model we've run, says it's infallible. Don't forget, sugar is the most powerful force in this world—that's why the associations and unions for health care, insurance, fertilizers, pesticides, entertainment, computer games, dieting, supplements, higher education, k-thru-twelve education, snacks, and on and on all donate to us. Turns out every industry depends on the sugar-obsessed to power commerce. This means the American Sugar Association is the most influential force in this country. Do what we say and, yes, the dominoes will fall."

• • •

After they left the meeting, Bradley made a call.

"Heather," he said, "we may finally know how to finish Julia. I'm going to send you an email. Follow the instructions."

When he hung up, he made dozens of similar phone calls—all off the record— to journalists, podcasters, and bloggers across the country.

Sitting in his Bombardier 7500 on the runway outside of Atlanta at Dekalb Peachtree Airport, Menendez instructed Micah, his last advisor standing, to make his own calls.

This was it. Time to save the nation.

CHAPTER 55

THE GOLD OF
THE PLAINS

"Julia, just remember," Melanie said, "now is the time for caution." By *now* she meant "two days before an election we're currently winning."

"Exactly right," Jonathan said. "Answer their questions but volunteer no new information. Go out there and talk about bees. Talk about the earth. Talk about love and change. The rest will take care of itself."

Julia nodded and steeled herself for another press conference. She was no longer scared of the press, but she still found the bright lights and aggressive questions off-putting. Today—the first press conference since Austin—would be especially chaotic. At least today she was on a farm, safe in the friendly confines of North Carolina land owned by one of her biggest supporters, the chair of the Regenerative Farmers Association.

After this press conference, she had seven more campaign stops before the day was done. She channeled her exhaustion, using it to focus her senses the same way one used hunger when fasting.

She walked through the renovated barn, Melanie and Jonathan escorting her past the reporters. She carefully used a step ladder to stand on an apple barrel and the reporters started yelling questions.

"Was the glitter war loving?"

"Have you sent condolences to the man who died from glitterphyxiation?"

"Can you confirm the attack was an assassination attempt on your life launched by Salvation Megachurch?"

"China has declared compassion illegal. Do you think the US will follow?"

Julia slowly raised her hands until silence descended. "Friends, let's slow down. Obviously, now more than ever, we need peace. Will you join me in centering prayer? Today, I'm going to meditate on the word forgiveness."

"We didn't come here to pray!"

"Guys!" Heather Haliburton yelled, "let Julia have her moment. These have been a tough few days for her. It's been a tough few days for us all. Maybe we need to breathe."

Julia looked at Heather with surprise. Was her toughest critic finally coming around? *Ah*, Julia thought, *the power of love.*

"I'm going to close my eyes. I invite you all to join me, observing how you react to the word you've chosen today."

Minutes later Julia opened her eyes and smiled at the reporters before focusing on Heather. "Heather, thank you for the support. I'll let you go first."

"Thank you, Julia," Heather began. "A quick question to help us get back to important issues affecting Americans. Will you talk about the role of sugar in the American diet?"

"Well, that's a surprising question, Heather," Julia laughed. "I was expecting nothing but glitter-war questions, thank you. I do think we have more pressing challenges—solving the environmental crisis and transforming our society into one in which all are not just created equal, but are treated equally—but as you all probably know, processed sugar, like processed grains, fats, and oils, is one of the many destructive addictions that leave the American people at the mercy of their bad habits, companies that put profit ahead of people's health, and a government that refuses to protect us from predatory packaged food manufacturers."

"Will you elaborate?"

Julia still smiled warmly. She still thought she was answering a run-of-the-mill if unanticipated press question. "Have you ever tried to eat food or buy drinks without any sugar in it? Once you start reading ingredient lists, you realize that our bread, our broth, our sauces, our cereal, already insanely sweet fruit pies, and just about anything else that comes in plastic or contains preservatives, is filled with sugar. There's also high fructose corn syrup, which is more refined liquid sugar made from mono-culture corn. All this sugar, it's killing us in a thousand different ways. And if you've ever tried to quit sugar … well, goodness, the cravings are just unbelievable. As president, I will work to right this wrong. I don't think it's a stretch to say the sugar industry will someday face the same reckoning big tobacco did in the nineties."

Watching the press conference live at their office next to Coca-Cola's headquarters in Atlanta, Jared offered Brittany a fist bump.

"Soundbite jackpot?" he asked.

Brittany smiled. "Time to remind America that our favorite food also happens to be a force more powerful than love."

• • •

It took less than fifteen minutes for Julia's comment to enter the news cycle amplification process. C-SPAN and the major networks all livestreamed the press conference. The seventy reporters on hand started spinning as soon as her press conference ended. Flitter, Fastagram, and Beep-Beep exploded with hot takes from influencers, activists, and academics.

Holding the apple crate Julia had just finished speaking from, Heather Haliburton stared into the camera as grimly as if she were reporting on a genocide.

"Just moments ago, while standing on this apple crate"—she shook it for all to see—"Julia Connor, the woman many Americans have put their faith in, revealed herself to be a charlatan. Calling America the land of the weak, helpless sugar addict, she specifically singled out America's racial minorities, America's mothers, America's senior citizens, America's millions of citizens struggling with health issues, and America's regulators at the FDA, calling all of them corporate tools unable to decide what is best for their children or for themselves. Political pundits I've talked to are in a state of shock over Connor's contempt-filled tirade. They all say that a woman like this, a woman who despises us for our most basic human right to enjoy the pleasure of a sweet treat, cannot be president!"

On ROX News, Jed Abernathy was more long-winded but just as vicious. "Do you feed your children Honey Nut Cheerios or Pop-Tarts? Do you drink Coke or put sugar in your coffee?"

Jed angrily held up a box of cereal as he spoke, before pivoting to pick up a bottle of Aunt Jemima's.

"Do you enjoy the eighty-seven percent of American manufactured goods that contain the gold of the plains, high fructose corn syrup? If the answer is yes, then Julia Connor has a message for you."

Here Jed paused, curled his lip into an I-just-drank-sour-milk face, before declaring:

"Julia Connor wants you to know that you are an addict, just like those heroin junkies mucking up the streets in San Francisco. Julia Connor wants you to know that you are a brainless corporate shill, bowing at the feet of 'evil' American staples like Nestle and Hershey. Julia Connor wants you to know that you are not as good as her and her 'enlightened' kind, people who eat only "natural" foods, people who eat leafy greens and exercise."

He let his words hang in the air. Silence set in.

Then he boomed, "America! Julia Connor is an elitist who makes Hillary Clinton look like a woman of the people. Can we afford her self-righteousness in the Whitehouse? I THINK NOT!!"

• • •

By the time, Julia rolled into her last stop of the day outside of Asheville, North Carolina, the right-wing and left-wing hate-o-sphere of multiple cable news outlets, podcasting thugs who monetized hotheaded hot takes into cool cash, and the incendiary *NY Post* and *Daily Mail*, had been going apeshit for ten hours, fed by a constant stream of talking points from Jared and Brittany; talking head bloviators and lobbyists working for Kraft Heinz, Procter & Gamble, Nestle, Mars, Kellogg, General Mills; every Valentine's Day, Easter, Halloween, and Christmas candy-hawking drugstore chain; and the $175 billion weight-loss industrial complex.

"IS CONNOR CALLING MOMS STUPID?" blared a New York tabloid.

"Sourpuss presidential wannabee calls white Americans that eat white bread pathetic sugar addicts!" moaned Breitbart.

"Connor's Cavity: Love Candidate Ripped for Tone-Deaf Sugar Comments," intoned Politico.

"Julia Connor attacks packaged foods with high sugar content in racist attack against black Americans," reported NPR.

"Mexican Americans revolt after Julia Connor threatens their churro supply," reported the *San Antonio Express News*.

"Julia Connor, the Whore of Babylon: Christian Consumers Doomed to Hell," condemned the Salvation Megachurch publishing platform.

Other media outlets took a slightly nobler road. They launched podcasts and ran articles and news segments that reported Julia's remarks and then reported on the reaction from Julia's campaign rivals, food lobbyists, body image activists, and doctors whose research was funded by the American Sugar Association. Sticking to their corporate-approved "both siderism" editorial policy, these articles also contained quotes from nutrition experts, health coaches, ayurvedic practitioners, holistic doctors, and independent scientists—all of whom supported Julia's primary contention: that sugar is a huge problem in America. "It is arguably the number one killer in America," Dr. Dwight Smith of the Cleveland Clinic told the *New York Times* in the article's nineteenth paragraph. "It's a leading cause of heart disease, acne, an imbalanced gut-biome, obesity and diabetes, which means it kills more people than tobacco. No question."

The Connor campaign witnessed the backlash—and whiplash—in real time.

Talk show favorite Daphne Marks, whose tagline was "Every Mother's BFF," announced a week-long series on "Julia Connor's secret war against food freedom."

Mauritania Roberts, the bestselling lifestyle author and Democratic Party donor tweeted, "I have never felt such betrayal from an inspiring figure. For all her empathy, Julia turns out to be another skinny, white privileged b***h."

Julia flinched with each take, aghast her words were so willfully twisted out of context.

"But I never said any of those things. Fat people, skinny people, they all deserve just as much love! Body type is actually a terrible way of judging 'health' anyways!"

"Doesn't matter," Melanie said. "They've finally found a weakness. Once people smell blood, facts are useless."

The campaign bus pulled into the event. Asheville was prime Julia territory. The previous week's polls had her carrying the local precincts in a landslide. Yet when Melanie exited the bus to prep the crowd, it was as if she'd walked into a storm.

"Love, Compassion, Healing, and Justice!" chanted five thousand Julia supporters.

"Kiss Our Sugar Sweet Ass!" chanted a horde of seven thousand well trained protesters waiving signs for Menendez and O'Leary.

Melanie shook her head at a giant banner hanging from a tree: "Sugar Is Not the Problem—You Are!"

"Love, Compassion, Healing, and Justice!"

"Don't tell me how to feed my child!"

"Love Compassion, Healing, and Justice!"

"Skinny! White! Bitch! Skinny! White! Bitch!"

Melanie stopped next to the stage—an elevated flatbed truck outfitted with a giant PA—to work out the stiffness by touching her toes. When she straightened, she was greeted by an earnest-looking young man with tortoise shell glasses, an argyle sweater, and a clipboard.

"I'm the local field organizer, Joe Moritz. I'm thrilled to meet you, Melanie. But I'm sorry to say we've got a situation here," he said.

"No problem." Mel P's eyes glittered. "I was made for these types of problems. Did you get the music file I sent you?"

"Yes. On my phone."

"Let's silence this crowd." Melanie pumped her arms and started to limber up. "Put on the sound system and we'll get this party—"

"Actually, don't." Julia stood behind Melanie and Joe, smiling sadly. "I'm going to go out there, alone."

"Are you sure? They're pretty riled up."

"I'm sure."

Julia walked away from them and slowly climbed the steps onto the flat-bed. As she walked to the microphone, the chants picked up. Her supporters were so loyal, she thought. But the protestors were *so mad*.

The instinct welled up inside her to fight back. To call them idiots. It was a heavy feeling, dark and welcoming. *Stop!* She told herself. *This is exactly how this country got here in the first place. And you knew—you always knew this was coming.* The yin to the yang, the darkness to the light. It was inevitable.

She went to the microphone and held up her hands, waiting for silence.

It never came. The protesters got louder. "My children, my food choice! My children, my food choice!"

She went from waiting for silence to praying for it. Trying to calm the crowd like she calmed her bees.

"Friends, I'm afraid that I, that you all, have—"

"Don't tell me how to feed my child!"

Julia's eyes flashed. She felt a strength surge inside her.

"This isn't about how you feed your child! Or what your body looks like. It's about our physical and emotional health. About how we've let ourselves become subject to systems that take advantage of us. Too much sugar is a terrible thing—it literally kills us, but whether we eat sugar in every meal or not, we're still all deserving of love. Deserving of compassion. Deserving of the unwavering knowledge that our creator loves us unconditionally!"

Julia felt something strike her face. It was small and dense. Something else hit the podium. She looked up and saw a group throwing things at her. They were silver, red, and dark brown.

What the hell? Jonathan rushed out from the wings as the barrage continued and pulled Julia off-stage.

As they rushed to safety, he heard more boos and a tiny missile hit his leg and bounced to the ground. He picked it up.

It said, "Snickers."

CHAPTER 56

THE NEW SIXTY-SEVEN-POINT PLAN

Twenty hours after Heather Haliburton posed her query to Julia, the pollsters had their hot takes. Overnight polls of all stripes reported unanimous declines. Julia's support, they were all certain, was dissolving faster than a cup of sugar in boiling water.

On NATN, Heather Haliburton barely contained her glee. "Political neophyte Julia Connor will soon be little but a bad, distant memory if the post Sugar Gate polling numbers hold. According to the latest nightly tracking poll by the esteemed Quinnipiac University, Connor lost forty percent of her support. The numbers indicate Connor's shockingly racist attack on the eating choices of every group of Americans except vegans has turned—as I predicted—into a deadly self-inflicted wound.

"The same poll reveals Governor O'Leary has stormed back, gaining eighteen percentage points on Senator Menendez, putting her within the poll's margin of error. With their eye on the finish line, Governor O'Leary's team is working hard to appeal to voters who mistakenly believed Julia Connor's Love platform included them. Today she unveiled her new sixty-seven-point Environmental Rescue Plan, designed to save the environment in just sixty-seven years." Heather paused and briefly posed, letting the good side of her face linger on the camera, before finishing her thought. "Let's take a look at her ad."

"I know the future when I see it …" said the governor, standing in a lush grassland in front of a gleaming white windmill.

The shot was replaced with the candidate in front of a black, smoke-spewing power plant. " …and I know a threat when I smell one."

The view shifted to a high alpine lake superimposed over a swelling American Flag. "Senator Menendez," Governor O'Leary continued in a voiceover, "has no plan for the climate and is happy to see places like this fade from existence."

Now O'Leary sat with a group of children and their mothers. "That's why I'm releasing my sixty-seven-point Environmental Rescue Plan to begin cutting emissions and reversing the climate crisis in just sixty-seven years. My plan not only will solve the climate crisis by 2094—it will do so in a way that means the American people and our precious children won't have to change their lifestyle a single bit. If that's not love and compassion in action, I don't know what is!"

A graphic flashed across the screen as she finished speaking. *Vote O'Leary— the Loving Choice for America.*

• • •

As Jacqueline O'Leary's last salvo flashed across digital time and space, Senator Menendez's final commercial did the same.

Senator Menendez shook hands with Pastor Josiah McMillan beside the giant golden crucifix in Salvation Mega Church's sculpture garden. "I'm Pastor Josiah McMillian and I believe the 2028 presidential election has always been about God's love."

Instantly Senator Menendez, now standing in front of a row of seven Abrams tanks, responded. "That's right. The election has been about God's plan to keep his chosen ones safe."

Service members and their families flocked from behind the tanks to join Menendez. "And the election has been about God's demand that we protect his children from the ravages of homosexuality, high taxes, and unhinged Americans who think they need to heal."

The shot returned to Salvation Mega Church, where Menendez was again standing with Pastor Josiah. "God never asked us to love everyone."

Senator Menendez picked up the thought. "God told us to follow our elders."

Pastor McMillan took it home, "Which is why I'm telling you, America, to vote Senator Menendez for president."

• • •

With election day looming, Governor Jacqueline O'Leary and Senator Daniel Menendez were neck and neck, racing to the finish line like the political thoroughbreds they were.

Now survival of the system was secured for at least another four years, the National Sugar Association had decided to flex its muscles one final time before election day.

Brittany stared at O'Leary and Menendez from the head of the table.

"We all understand what happened here, correct?"

Deeply anxious about the election result, but even more relieved to have avoided the ignominy of losing to a third-party candidate, O'Leary nodded. "What happened is that we're back to the status quo. I don't know about you, but I smell a popular vote victory coming my way!"

Menendez chuckled. "Sure, but I'll still be president."

"I doubt it, Senator," Bradley quipped. "Those Julia voters are fleeing straight to our camp. I think we'll finally have a she-president."

Pastor Josiah McMillan was shaking his head, still coming to terms with what would turn out to be the most important lesson of his career. "I can't believe Americans care more about sugar than salvation."

"Ah!" Brittany got everyone's attention. "That, Pastor, is exactly what happened. We learned that the American voter, for now, still values sugar over love, compassion, the church, and even political party loyalty. But we also learned that every other belief system of control we've used for the last four decades no longer works. Julia almost won! Make no mistake, that's the lesson here. So regardless of which of you win, all of us in this room have just four years to integrate Julia's ideas into both parties' policy platforms before the forces of spiritual, emotional, and physical health can again threaten us."

"I'm guessing you have some ideas about how we can do that?" O'Leary asked.

"We do, but it's not rocket science," Jared said. "Any decent political mind can see how to corral the forces of love into the party politics paddock. The real challenge will be dealing with those who have found *emotional freedom*." Jared paused to let it sink in, aware that neither he nor anyone else in the room knew what that felt like, but certain it existed because of the focus groups he had been feverishly conducting across the country. "We probably can't outlaw therapy, prayer, and meditation, but we have to turn back the psychedelic tide that has helped so many people take control of their lives."

"But what about the veterans?" Menendez grimaced. "I've never seen so many angry patriots as I did after proposing the Bureau of Cultic Deviance and Plant Medicine Elimination. They really believe those substances lead to healing. I can't risk alienating them."

"Really?" Brittany asked, "it's like you've never seen us run one of these operations before. It's simple. We'll outlaw any naturally grown psychedelics and create legal loopholes for patentable industrially grown or lab-created substances served by certified clinical healthcare providers. That'll keep the pharma firms, Monsanto, and the insurance companies happy while making it almost impossible for dangerous types like Julia to bring healing harm to American citizens at scale."

• • •

"So," Troojle's CEO Ben Blankenship said as he leaned on his yacht's starboard railing, the sun setting in the distance, "we did it."

Bradley nodded to himself as he watched O'Leary strut across the stage at the University of Denver gymnasium. He put a finger in his ear to drown out the crowd's cheers.

"Ben, it was real touch and go, but we got it done."

"Bradley, I just want you to know that whether you and Governor O'Leary win or lose today, we'll take care of you." He paused to sip his margarita. Fresh limes had been choppered in that afternoon, and the fresh citrus tingle brought him unending joy. "That China Beep-Beep gambit was a stroke of genius. And, well, whether you and O'Leary ever get to implement your agenda or not, the fact you've spent so much time talking about the Data Rights are Human Rights Act means it'll eventually get passed. I mean, there's even a chance Menendez will do it if he wins—we donated almost as much money to him as to you."

Bradley narrowed his eyes. "There's no way you donated as much to Menendez as to us."

"Fair point. But fifty million should get us somewhere in his administration."

"Not nearly as far as you'd get with us." Bradley glanced back at the stage. A troupe of Girl Scouts were singing God Bless America.

"And that's why I'm calling. If Governor O'Leary doesn't win, if you're not the president's chief of staff next year, I'd like you to come work for me. With you at the reins of Troojle's Public Policy Team, I'm confident we'll get the Data Rights are Human Rights Act passed no matter who is president."

Bradley thought of the meetings he had scheduled tomorrow, the day after the election. There was a Russian oligarch, an Azerbaijani oil executive, and the Brazilian heir of an Amazonian lumber empire. Yes, no matter what happened with the election, he'd get his payout, and he'd be able to continue supporting the causes he cared about at a scale far greater than he'd ever imagined as a young teenage activist.

"Ben, that's kind of you. I'm going to stay focused on this election right now, but let's connect. Would Thursday work for a call?"

After Ben hung up, Bradley walked backstage to avoid the noise and called the Executive Director of All Types and Colors. "Hi Shirley, this is Bradley, how are you?"

He listened for a moment then continued. "This is a little premature on my part, but I just wanted to let you know that whether O'Leary wins or not, I'm committing to either raising or giving twenty million dollars for All Types and Colors next year."

He listened again, then replied. "That's very kind of you Shirley, but I'm no genius. I had to do a lot of things I didn't want to do to get to this place. The compromises, to be honest, were gut-wrenching, but I'm confident that I'll now be able to support you at the level I've always wanted."

CHAPTER 57

BACK TO THE BEES

At a retreat center on the Oregon Coast, Jonathan walked into the lodge and shook the winter wetness off his boots. He carried a load of firewood in his arms and sadness on his face.

Sitting in front of a roaring fire in the wood stove, Melanie sat on a sheepskin surrounded by kilim pillows, her eyes closed. Sage burned in a bronze prayer bowl beside her.

Luke walked into the room, his part perfect, a wool sweater enveloping his lanky frame and prayer beads around his neck.

They've never been here, Luke thought. The campaign crash hits even if you win—but for those who'd grabbed the ring and felt the power only to then see it slip away? There might be no lower low.

"Guys, buck up!" his happy eyes flashed around the room. "Julia won twenty percent of the vote. No, she's not president, but we inspired the world to think differently. You did the impossible—you saved me, and you almost saved the country. You realize that, right? Nobody has created a third wave since the Whigs, and they, well, honestly, no one even knows who they are."

Jonathan grunted. Melanie opened her eyes, smiled, and then closed them again, beginning to hum.

"I'm serious, guys! I've been there. I have worked blown elections. Every operative has. But you two—nobody has just come from nowhere like you and turned the country upside down!"

"Maybe it's for the best," Jonathan said. "I don't think Julia wanted to be president anyways."

"No, she didn't," Melanie replied, her eyes still closed, "but she did want to embody love, peace, and compassion. She did want to remind America that the power to create new worlds exists within each of us. I think she did that to the very end."

"You're right," Jonathan agreed. "It's kind of like working with medicine. Psilocybin helps one do the work needed to heal and to embody love, but the psilocybin isn't the point—the work happening inside us is the point."

"That's what I'm talking about!" Luke said. "We didn't win, but you succeeded. Now we just need to decide what's next."

Melanie opened her eyes. "I think what's next is that we keep doing what we're doing. Of course there will be healing ceremonies across the country, new PACs designed to eliminate all the other PACs, and more campaigns, but for now, we need to grow and listen to self and God. I, for one, am going to spend the next weeks tuning out everything but my Dharma."

"If you could only hear yourself," Jonathan chuckled. "You're a new woman after just a year doing the work."

"I know! So come sit next to me? Let's drop in."

"Sounds good," Jonathan said. He turned and looked up the stairs to the loft. "Noah, come join us for some group time?"

"Sure thing," Noah yelled, his face peeking over the banister, "but give me just a moment. I'm about to push send on an email to my new Compassion in Action Service Corp. The triangles, guys, the triangles always produce!"

Luke and Jonathan made their way to Melanie, sitting on either side of her, feeling the warmth of the wood stove on their faces. Noah ran down the stairs and slid onto a cushion, joining them.

They locked hands and began to breathe, noticing the thoughts in their minds and the feelings in their hearts.

• • •

Julia Connor sat in her garden. The sun shone brightly as it rose above the trees, birds chirping in the background. She traced a single bee across the sky before it landed on a flowering bud. It was spring, and her rows of vegetables were just starting to sprout. She stopped, turned her face towards the sun, and smiled, aware that she could feel the force of life in the earth, the sky, and every living thing around her. One of her favorite mantra's came to mind, verse from a man named Thich Nhat Hanh that had once been her friend and teacher.

Breathing in, I calm my body.
Breathing out, I smile.
Dwelling in the present moment.
I know this is a wonderful moment.

THE END

ACKNOWLEDGEMENTS

I n 2019 I thought I had life pretty figured out. I was making good money and had equity in a tech startup that was doing well. I had amazing friends in Austin and around the world who I travelled regularly to see. I was in good health and I was, generally, happy.

But, beneath that outward reality dissatisfaction lurked. I knew what it felt like when I was at my best professionally, and I knew I rarely hit that mark. I was unable to maintain committed romantic relationships, and I often found myself falling short of the standards I set for myself in how I communicated with women. I'd always had a vision for the type of man I would become in my 30s, and it was clear to me that I was not evolving into that person.

So I very hesitantly, and with an enormous amount of trepidation, began to look for a therapist or coach. After several attempts that weren't a great match, I found the right man. What followed were twelve months of "work" that turned me from a "shit together" kind of guy who always projected success into someone that was viscerally aware of just how wildly out of whack I was. In the emotional chaos of that year, I also learned that when I changed a belief or healed parts of my past, my present reality dramatically shifted. Like so many who discover the alchemical, energetic reality of self as it relates to both our conscious and unconscious existence, I was hooked.

The therapy-like work surfaced deep, hidden, still festering wounds left over from fully embracing, and then fleeing, the Evangelical faith of my youth, so I began to again seek God. That process led me back into the daily habit of listening for "the silent voice within" and it introduced me to plant medicine communities filled with kind, open hearted people who were masters at facilitating internal transformation. Through these processes, I not only rediscovered my capacity to love, but I experienced version after version of what it meant to live in the full, visceral, breathtaking, body shaking reality of the Divine's unconditional love.

Somewhere in that process I was reminded that I'd spent my life "trying to be" without ever stopping to ask "who am I." Asking that question led me to

Dharma and my pursuit of Dharma, somehow, inexplicably, led me to writing this book. In the process I became fairly unemployable, relatively anti-social and deeply invested in a life that I increasingly lived from a place of service and surrender.

On this path, so many have supported me.

First among these is the love of my life, my soon(ish) to be wife, Audrey. She has been my greatest cheerleader, a routine reader, and when she feels like it, the book's creative director :)

My family supported me from day one, humoring my early assertions that I was going to write a book, always having the grace not to question my drive when so many "responsible" or "normal" pieces of my life were dropped. A special thanks to Brett, who was one of my earliest readers, and Wade, who steadfastly maintained the "book" read like a "book" long before that was the case.

I have been blessed by many lifetime's worth of friends, all of whom, in their own ways, provided the safety, support and encouragement I needed to repeatedly plunge into the lonely black hole of writing one's first novel.

Looking to my past, I wouldn't be who I was today if Tom and Chris Sine hadn't taken it upon themselves to show me a world where Jesus had more to do with social justice than Republican politics. I'm forever grateful to Kelly Riechers, Jeremy Snyder, Bethany Bylsma, Ty Olson, Brittany Quinn, Clint Baldwin, Mark McCleod and so many others who were my spiritual companions and teachers in university. Gillian Bergeron answered the phone when I Skyped an Obama campaign office in January 2008, encouraging me to "just show up" and start volunteering. I left Guatemala for South Carolina the next day.

More recently, friends and teachers who may or may not be aware of their influence on my journey include Melanie Weinberger, Lauren Walsh, Stephen Cope, Emily Collins and Ivan Chocron.

I've been blessed with four balding Jewish men who have had profound impacts on my life. Gabriel Lifton-Zoline is a former boss that became a best friend and writing thought partner. Anthony Garrett was a mentor and father figure during my years in DC, he opened door after door I didn't know he was opening until I'd left and he was no longer there to open them for me. Barry Blesser, the man who introduced me to my inner child, was the third. I am forever grateful to each of these men, but when it comes to this book, it is the fourth Jewish man I must thank the most.

Seth Kaufman is a brilliant editor, writer and writing coach who found my Upwork listing and immediately understood what I was trying to accomplish with this novel. Seth started working with me when I was just a couple drafts deep, and while I'm certain I would have "finished" the book if I had not met Seth, the book would have been a shadow of what it has become. We spent hours together on zoom. He edited five drafts of the novel, contributing ideas, words and concepts that shaped the book from beginning to end. He also served as an endless well of cynical optimism from which I was able to draw encouragement and practical advice.

A final word of thanks goes out to Hannah Eason, who edited the final draft and did beautiful work spit-shining my prose.

To help publish this book I ran a Kickstarter, and my friends showed up! The following individuals are the **Patrons of the Loving Arts** who made this book possible: Nate Kayhoe, Andrew Thompson, Ruth Austin, Ty Olson, Patrick Framel, Roger Low, Brett Mackey, Kathryn Solow, Jeremy Snyder, Heather Hargreaves, Gabriel Lifton-Zoline, Vikram Jindal, Spencer Kaye, Margrette Thompson, Josh Holmes, Stephanie Sparks, Andrew Oseran, Brenna Houlihan, Rajdeep Kanwar, Zachariah Hamstra, Paul Selker, Timothy Andrew Bainum, and Sam Laine.

Last of all, thank you, my readers, for sticking with the story, for getting this far, and for, I hope, tagging @scottmackeywriter on social media and asking all your friends to read this too.

Thank you!

—Scott

SCOTTMACKEY.ME

Made in the USA
Middletown, DE
30 August 2024

60044658R00189